Praise for Melissa Cutler

"A hilarious, sexy, and entertaining read filled with light-hearted banter and exuberant and distinctive characters. The passionate and heated chemistry between them will have readers instantly falling in love."
—*RT Book Reviews* (Top Pick, 4½ stars) on *One Hot Summer*

"Melissa Cutler is a bright new voice in contemporary romance." —*New York Times* bestselling author Lori Wilde

"Sizzling." —*Publishers Weekly* on *One Hot Summer*

"A fun contemporary Western romance. Cutler brings Texas ambiance and color to this delightful and sexy tale."
—*Booklist* on *One Hot Summer*

"A red hot romance with a sexy cowboy and a great story!"
—*Fresh Fiction* on *The Mistletoe Effect*

D1048294

Also by Melissa Cutler

One Hot Summer

ONE MORE TASTE

Melissa Cutler

St. Martin's Paperbacks

This is a work of fiction. All of the characters, organizations, and events portrayed in this novel are either products of the author's imagination or are used fictitiously.

ONE MORE TASTE

Copyright © 2016 by Melissa Cutler.
Excerpt from *One Wild Night* Copyright © 2017 by Melissa Cutler.

All rights reserved.

For information address St. Martin's Press, 175 Fifth Avenue, New York, NY 10010.

ISBN: 978-1-250-07187-3

Printed in the United States of America

St. Martin's Paperbacks edition / October 2016

St. Martin's Paperbacks are published by St. Martin's Press, 175 Fifth Avenue, New York, NY 10010.

10   9   8   7   6   5   4   3   2   1

I dedicate this book to my fourteen-year-old self, and to all the many women and girls who have had to discover that we are all braver and more resilient than we ever dreamed possible. Sisters, together we rise.

Acknowledgments

This book could not have been possible without the wisdom and patience of my editor, Holly Ingraham. Thank you for guiding me towards the light with Knox and Emily's story. May this be only one of many collaborations in a long and fruitful partnership. I also extend my thanks to David Morgan for freely sharing his extensive business knowledge, and to Natalie Morgan for being the very best cook I know and whose devotion to her culinary art was a huge inspiration for this book.

Chapter One

Not everyone was lucky enough to drive a haunted truck. Then again, *lucky* wasn't a word Knox Briscoe would use to describe his current predicament. On a prayer, he turned the key in the ignition, but the Chevy offered him nothing but a dull click in response.

"I don't believe in ghosts," he said, although if anyone had actually heard his declaration, it'd have to be ghosts, or perhaps some unseen wildlife. Because there was nothing or nobody in this stretch of backcountry other than him and his truck, a roadside sign proclaiming Briscoe Ranch Resort straight ahead in three miles, and a wide, calm lake nestled in the Texas hills.

He tried the key again. Nothing but that maddening click.

He tapped a finger on the steering wheel, denying himself any more grandiose a reaction because Knox was nothing if not a man in command of his emotions.

He popped the truck door open to the crisp October day. His freshly buffed black dress shoes hit the gravel with a crunch. Given the statement he'd planned to make on this, his first day as part-owner of Briscoe Ranch, it wouldn't do to soil his suit with engine grease. He shrugged out of his sports coat, hung it on a hanger he kept in the back seat for just such a purpose, tucked the ends of his blue silk tie into his shirt, and rolled his shirtsleeves to the elbows before pulling the truck's hood up.

He'd never considered himself much of a car guy until he'd inherited this one through his dad's will three years earlier. It'd taken a lot of YouTube videos and conversations with his mechanic for him to get up to speed on maintaining the thirty-year-old truck, but it'd been worth every hour and dollar spent. None of that new knowledge was going to help him today, though. Nothing obvious was broken or out of place, and the engine had plenty of oil and other fluids.

Knox patted the truck's side. "Okay, Dad. Message received. You don't want your truck on Briscoe Ranch property. I get it. But don't you want to be there to see poetic justice done, even if it's just in spirit, with your truck?"

God, he felt like a moron, talking to his dead father, but what other explanation was there for the '85 Chevy Half-Ton's mystifying quirks or the neck-prickling sensation that he wasn't alone every time Knox got into the cab? Even in death, it seemed, his dad had decided to stubbornly hold his ground against the father and brother—Knox's grandfather, Tyson, and his uncle Ty—who'd excommunicated him from the family before Knox's birth. Even in death, his dad refused to let his prized truck lay one spec of rubber down on Briscoe Ranch property. Which sucked, to be honest. It would've been icing on the cake to have his dad's spirit there, watching Knox take control of the very business his dad had been robbed of.

Behind the wheel again, he gripped the key in the ignition and closed his eyes. *Please work. Please.*

Click. Click. Click.

"Okay. But this sucks. I didn't want to show up for the meeting in a Town Car with a driver like a mobster goon who's there to shake everybody down. Would you at least let me get to the entrance of the resort before stalling the truck again?"

Wow. Bargaining with a ghost. Knox's freak flag was really flying this morning. "Never mind. I don't believe in ghosts."

After another futile turn of the key, Knox grabbed his messenger bag and stepped out of the truck, then rummaged around the copies of the Briscoe Ranch shareholder contract his lawyers had prepared until he found his cell phone.

As the phone rang with his office in Dallas, he spotted a *for sale* sign ahead of him, demarcating a gated driveway a few yards from the lake. He walked along the road to it, the phone to his ear. Was there a house at the end of that twisty, tree-lined driveway? Did the property border the resort? Looked like it might. Perhaps he'd buy it and expand the resort even more than he'd originally planned.

Shayla, his younger sister, who also worked as Briscoe Equity Group's office manager, picked up on the fourth ring. "Don't tell me Ty Briscoe's giving you shit already. I told you that you should've brought Yamaguchi and Crawford with you."

Maybe another boss would've bristled at such insubordination, even by a blood relative, but Knox had developed a deep mistrust of kiss-asses over his years as an entrepreneur, which was why he valued Shayla's loyalty and honesty so much. And, in this case, she was absolutely correct. Linda Yamaguchi and Diane Crawford were his firm's lawyers, who Knox should have brought along today as he usually did for business acquisitions. But Knox wanted to close this deal on his own, eye-to-eye with the uncle he'd never met before they'd started this negotiation—the uncle whom Knox was going to ruin, just as Ty had ruined Knox's family.

"You can tell me 'I told you so' later, but that's not why I called. My truck broke down three miles from Briscoe Ranch. I need a driver, and I need him to get here in—" He lifted the flap of a clear plastic box affixed to the *for sale* sign and pulled out a flier.

The photograph gracing the center of the flier drew his eye. A grand, modern house sitting on a hill overlooking the lake. It was exactly the kind of dwelling Knox was hoping to move into somewhere in the vicinity of Briscoe Ranch since he couldn't very well run the show from his home base of Dallas, five hours away.

"Hello? Are you still there?" Shayla asked.

"Sorry. Something caught my eye. If you could have the driver here in less than an hour, that would be great. Can you find me someone?" His meeting with Ty Briscoe wasn't for another two hours, but he wanted to take one last walk around the resort without any of the employees knowing who he was or why he was there.

"I can't imagine that being a problem." He heard the fast click-clack of keyboard typing. "And . . . let's see . . . Nope, no problem. Your car will be there within the half hour."

"Thanks, Shay."

"You bet. And Knox? I'm proud of you. Dad would be proud, too. You know that right?"

Knox eyed his broken-down truck. He had to believe Dad would be proud of him for taking ownership of the family business, despite this hiccup. Otherwise, what would be the point of Knox putting himself through all this? "Thanks, Shay. I'll talk to you soon."

As the call ended, the crackle of tires on gravel snagged Knox's attention. He pivoted around, expecting to see a

Good Samaritan pulling to the shoulder to see if Knox needed help, but his truck was the only vehicle in sight—and it was rolling backwards, straight toward the lake.

Dropping the flier, his messenger bag, and his phone, he took off at a sprint. "No! No, no, no. Shit!"

This couldn't be happening. He'd engaged the emergency brakes—hadn't he?

The truck was picking up speed as it backed towards the lake. Knox lunged toward the door handle. He was dragged along a few feet before finding his footing again. He dug his heels into the ground and yanked. The door swung open. He staggered and hit his back against the side of the hood, but managed to rebound in time to throw himself in the cab.

He stomped on the parking brake. It activated with a groan, but the truck wouldn't stop. He pumped the manual brake. Nothing happened. The truck bounced over rocks hard enough to make Knox's teeth rattle. He turned the key. Again, nothing. Nothing except a splash as the back of the truck hit the water.

"Jesus, Dad! Help me out, here!" he shouted.

The truck slammed violently to a stop, pitching Knox forward. He bit his tongue hard. The burst of pain and taste of blood was nothing compared to his relief that the truck, with him in it, hadn't submerged any deeper in the water. His pulse pounded in his ears, even as his labored breathing turned from panicked to annoyed. "I don't get it. What are you trying to tell me? I thought this was what you wanted."

With a hard swallow, he thumped a fist against the steering wheel, jolting himself back into composure. All this talking to ghosts was getting out of hand. Today, of all days, he could not afford to be off his A-game. He fixed his Stetson more firmly on his head and gave himself a stern mental lecture to get a grip.

All business again, he assessed the situation. Not knowing what had caused the truck to stop or if any sudden movements would jostle it back into motion, he rolled the driver-side window down and peered over the edge to stare at the brown-green water, thick with silt and mud that roiled through the liquid like thunderstorm clouds. The water lapped at the bottom of the door, not too deep, but the back tire and back bumper were fully submerged. If the truck had rolled only a few more feet into the lake, Knox would've been in real trouble.

As things stood now, though, Knox's main problem was that there was no way for him to avoid getting wet on his walk back to shore. Carefully, so as not to jar the truck back into motion, he unlatched his belt then opened the zipper of his pants. Shoes off, socks off, then pants. If he got to his first day at Briscoe Ranch on time, in one piece, and dry, it would be a miracle.

Clutching his pants, socks, and shoes to his chest, and dressed in only his shirt, a pair of boxers, and his black hat, he opened the door and stepped into the water, sinking knee deep. Silt and muck oozed between his toes. The cold ripped up his bare legs, making his leg hairs stand on end and his balls tighten painfully. Grunting through the discomfort, he shuffled away from the door until he could close it.

A series of exuberant splashes sounded from farther in the lake. It sounded like two fish were having a wrestling match right up on the water's surface. He turned, but only saw ripples. Setting his mind back on the task at hand, he pulled his foot off the lake bottom, muscles working to overcome the suction, and took a carefully placed step toward shore.

From seemingly out of nowhere, something blunt and slimy smashed into his calf. The surprise of the hit knocked

Knox off balance. With a yelp totally unbefitting a thirty-three-year-old Texan and former rodeo star, he danced sideways, fighting for his footing and clutching the clothes in his arms even tighter.

He desperately scanned the water around him, but the swirling silt had reduced the visibility to almost nothing. He held still another moment, listening, watching.

"Holy shit, are you okay?"

The man's voice startled Knox. He looked up and saw a young guy of maybe twenty-two standing on the bank of the lake, dressed in a suit and with a panicked expression on his face. Behind him, a black sedan idled on the shoulder of the road.

"I'm fine. I think. Are you my driver?"

"Yeah, Ralph with the Cab'd driving service app. Shayla at Briscoe Equity Group ordered a premium lift for Knox Briscoe. I'm guessing that's you since your truck's underwater."

And observant, too. "Yep. You see a cell phone and messenger bag somewhere up there, Ralph?"

"Hold up. Is that an '85 Chevy Silverado? That's a hell of a truck."

"It is." Except when said truck was haunted and decided all on its own to take a swim despite its owner's better judgment.

"You're lucky the tire got snagged on that rock."

Knox took a look at the front of the truck. Sure enough, the passenger side tire was stopped by a boulder, though he wasn't entirely sure luck had anything to do with it. "About that cell phone and messenger bag, Ralph. Would you mind?"

"Oh. Yeah. On it."

With Ralph in search of Knox's stuff, Knox chanced another step toward shore, keeping his head on a swivel, looking for whatever the hell it was that had slammed into him. An attack beaver? Did hill country even have beavers?

Despite his vigilance, he still startled at the sight of a massive, charcoal gray-green fish swishing through the water, coming straight at him. It had to be longer than his arm. It turned on a dime and surged at him. Knox's curse echoed off the hills surrounding the lake.

Time to scram.

He made it two more steps before his foot snagged on a rock and pitched him forward. Desperate for balance, he reached out to grab on to his truck, but the fish had other ideas and head-butted his leg again. Knox splashed down, nearly dunking all the way underwater.

The bite of cold stole his breath all over again. He exploded back out of the water and onto his feet, spluttering and gasping.

"Fuck!" he shouted, loud enough that even if his father were in Heaven and not haunting the truck, he would've heard him just fine. He held himself back from adding, *Thanks for nothing, Dad.*

Sloughing water from his face and breathing hard through flared nostrils, Knox shifted his attention to the water in search of the piranha on steroids that had put his ability to keep a cool head to the test. The fish was long gone. Though his pants floated around his knees like dark seaweed swishing in waves, and his shoes bobbed like little black boats only a few feet away, his hat had drifted into deeper water. Terrific. Just terrific.

He was sopping wet from head to toe and standing next to his equally waterlogged truck on the most important day of his life.

"What was that thing?" Ralph asked.

"I was hoping you'd gotten a clear view of it."

"Naw, but I did find your cell phone and bag."

That was something, at least. Knox fished his soggy pants from the water, removed his wallet and set it on the roof of the truck, then tossed the pants in the truck bed. Next, he grabbed his shoes and tossed them onto the shore. Maybe they wouldn't squish too loudly when he walked.

With that taken care of, it was time to get the inevitable over with. He loosened his tie, then unbuttoned his shirt and peeled it off.

"Uh, sir? Are you stripping? I mean, uh, why don't you get out of the water first?"

"Going after my hat." It wasn't until he'd spoken that he realized his teeth were chattering. The sooner he was out of the frigid water, the better. He added his shirt and tie to his pants in the truck bed, then drew a fortifying breath and pushed into the water for a freestyle swim across the lake.

Technically, the hat was replaceable, but this particular one had been the first he'd bought with his own money, back when he was fifteen and working his first real job outside of the local junior rodeo circuit. Over the years, it'd become a habit to wear it to new jobs or when he needed a little extra boost for a negotiation. He believed in good luck charms like he believed in ghosts—which meant surreptitiously and despite his better judgment—but there was no denying the slight edge that the black Stetson with the cattleman's crease and the rodeo brim provided him.

He was a solid fifty yards into the water when he reached the hat. Grabbing on to it tightly, he ignored the fact that his legs were going numb and made short work of returning to shore. He shook the water off the hat and placed it firmly on his head again, then took his phone from Ralph and dialed his office again.

Shayla answered on the first ring this time. "Hey, Knox. If you're calling about a tow truck, one's already on its way. I forgot to mention that before."

Ladies and gentlemen, Shayla Briscoe, World's Best Office Manager. "Thanks. You're awesome, sis."

"Figured you'd need one for that awful truck. It always was unreliable, even when it was brand new."

Knox glanced again at the Chevy. It might be a pain in the ass, but some of the best memories of his life involved that truck. "It has its moments."

"Is the Cab'd driver there yet?" Shayla said. "Should be, any minute."

"He's here. One more thing. I need you to email me with some information on a property." He rattled off the address of the lakefront home from memory and thanked her again. When the call ended, Knox turned to Ralph and sized him up. The two of them were roughly the same height and build. "You're, what, six-one? One-eighty?"

Ralph gave him the side-eye, apparently on to Knox's plan. "Six even and one-ninety," he said hesitantly.

Close enough. Knox took out three, soggy one hundred dollar bills from his wallet. "Ralph, I'm going to need to buy your suit."

It wasn't the first time Emily Ford had spied on a VIP guest at Briscoe Ranch Resort. In fact, she considered it a mandatory part of her research as the resort's Executive Special Event Chef. Wowing elite guests with personalized, gastronomic marvels was her specialty. As long as the guests never checked her internet search history or spotted her peering at them through binoculars, she was golden.

She didn't usually involve her best friend for life, Carina Decker, in her covert ops, but today was an exception. Because today's resort VIP was Knox Briscoe—a cousin of Carina's whom Emily had never met, and Carina had only seen a handful of times, though they'd grown up a couple hundred miles from each other. He was about to sign on with Carina's dad as the heir apparent of the resort, making him Carina's future landlord and Emily's newest boss.

Since Carina was eight months along in a pregnancy that had supersized her whole body from her ankles to her face, stealthiness in this covert ops mission was not easily achieved. So, once Emily had gotten the call from the security guard manning the resort's cameras that Knox had arrived, Emily and Carina had settled for spying on him from a window in the bridal gown shop Carina operated in the resort's lobby.

A shiny, black sedan matching the description the security guard had given Emily came into view on the long road through the property leading to the circular driveway in front of the resort's main building.

Carina nudged Emily in the ribs. "This is exciting. I'm glad he's here, and I'm proud of my dad for putting the rift behind him. Whatever my dad, Uncle Clint, and Grandpa Tyson fought over that made Uncle Clint leave, it's been more than thirty years. That's ancient history."

Ancient history that was still shrouded in silence and speculation, Emily added silently. To the best of her knowledge, no one but Tyson, Ty, and Clint knew the reason for the fight—and Clint and Tyson had already taken that secret to their graves.

Carina wrapped an arm around her belly. "With a new generation of Briscoes coming along soon, it's time for the family to forgive and move on. And I think Knox represents a new era of greatness for our family and for our business."

Carina was right. Probably. Knox's private equity firm's investment in Briscoe Ranch might just be the monetary boost the resort needed to propel it to the next level in luxury destinations. Including the building of the dream restaurant that Emily had been working toward at the resort for a decade. Only weeks earlier, Ty had finally, *finally,* agreed to give Emily the space to build her restaurant at the resort. All they needed now were investors. Knox's timing couldn't be more perfect—unless it wasn't.

"You don't think this all feels too good to be true?" Emily said. "I mean, I get that Knox is family, but the man's amassed a net worth of millions by buying and flipping failing businesses. How can we trust him not to sell us all out?"

"I was skeptical when my dad first told me his plan, but I trust my dad. And I trust his lawyers. They're too business savvy to make it possible for anyone to sell the resort away from the family."

When the car rounded the driveway and came to a stop, Carina and Emily crowded together, ducking their heads low in case either Knox or his driver looked their way.

Emily already knew what he looked like from photographs accompanying write-ups and interviews in business magazines, as well as the occasional photograph of him attending a charity ball or museum opening, posted online on Texas society blogs. From what she'd seen, Knox was loaded with money, charm, and ambition. An impeccable business reputation. A scandal-free personal life. By every account, he'd made his fortune the most ruthless way possible—fair and square.

None of that research, however, had prepared her for the sight of him.

Knox Briscoe stepped out of the back seat of the sedan one long leg at a time. He buttoned his black suit jacket and surveyed his surroundings, looking far more intimidating in person than the confident, intellectual spirit that his photographs conveyed. He was younger. Larger. His features were darker and more brooding. His leather shoes were as shiny black as the paint job on the limo, as slick as his black cowboy hat and suit.

"Oh, wow," Carina said on a breath. "I forgot how much he looks like my dad."

Emily had been too wrapped up in ogling him to notice, but now that Carina mentioned it, he did look a lot like a young Ty Briscoe back before he'd gone bald. "The Briscoe genes are strong, there's no doubt."

"What are you feeding him and my dad at their meeting?" Carina asked.

Emily flushed with a sudden, rare case of insecurity as she considered the lunch menu she'd created for the meeting. How could she possibly feed Knox Briscoe pheasant? He looked like he dined on nothing but porterhouse steaks and the tears of his enemies. "Brine-roasted pheasant with an heirloom sweet potato puree and a wild mushroom reduction."

"Sounds tasty."

"Everything looks tasty to you these days. You're an eating machine, but look at Knox. I can't pair him with that menu."

Carina snickered. "He's not a wine."

Definitely not as decadent and sweet as wine. He had the muscular grace of one of those hard-core Crossfit athletes who bench-pressed semi-truck tires in his spare time and had a single-digit BMI rating. He probably didn't even drink wine. He definitely didn't eat sweet potato purees or mushroom reductions. Though he should. It would probably do him a world of good to indulge his senses like that.

Just like that, inspiration struck. "That man needs peaches."

Specifically, the late season peaches she'd gotten that morning from her orchard supplier in Fredericksburg.

"Come again?" Carina said.

"Sugar. Butter. Fat." Inspiration jolted Emily like a zap of electricity. She slid down the wall to the floor, closing her eyes to visualize her new masterpiece. "Charred peaches with a balsamic vinegar reduc—no, not vinegar— a pinch of cayenne lacing a brown sugar brûlée crust. Oh my God, that'll piss him off." She rubbed her hands together like the evil genius she was. "All that butter and sugar. He'll hate that. Right up until he takes a bite. Then he'll understand."

Carina poked her with her shoe. "You're doing that weird fantasy food rambling thing again."

Emily barely heard Carina's teasing; she was too busy perfecting the recipe in her mind. "Huh?"

"I love you. But you're crazy."

Carina was right; Emily was crazy. All great chefs were. She stood, hung the binoculars around her neck, and smoothed out her chef's jacket. "I've got to go. I have a lot of work to do."

"I thought the meal was ready."

"Not anymore. I'm going to share my peaches with Knox Briscoe."

Carina poked her tongue against her cheek as her forehead crinkled with delight. "Someday, one of my lessons about double entendres is going to sink in."

Emily wasn't daft or naive. She knew a double entendre when she heard one—or, more accurately, inadvertently said one—but it wasn't her fault that the vast majority of people didn't understand that sex and food were incomparable. The perfect meal trumped sex every time, and anyone who claimed otherwise had obviously never experienced Emily's cooking. Knox Briscoe didn't know it yet, but his tongue was about to have the ride of its life.

With food, of course.

Two hours later, Emily pushed a loaded food cart behind the resort's main reception desk, then through the maze of cubicles and offices tucked away from the guests' view. She nodded to Ty Briscoe's secretary, then let herself into his corner office.

Knox's fierce intensity beat like waves of power through the air in the room. Emily froze near the door, stunned to find herself suddenly, uncharacteristically, intimidated.

From where they were deep in discussion at his conference table, Ty afforded Emily a brief glance, but Knox's focus remained unrelentingly on Ty and the business at hand.

"That idea has merit," Knox was saying to Ty in a deep, firm voice. "But my equity firm's vision extends beyond a cosmetic update. This resort has the potential to become a self-contained city, a beacon for travelers from all over the world. But we have to be willing to take risks."

Even from the door, Emily could see beads of sweat on Ty's bald head. His thick, bulldog neck had turned red, something that only happened when he was keeping his anger in check. Emily wasn't sure she'd ever seen the larger-than-life man, her father figure for all intents and purposes for the past decade, cowed by another man before. But he was definitely not the alpha in the room today. "Yes, I know, but not—" Ty said.

Knox plowed ahead. "Yes, but nothing, Ty. You came to my equity firm earlier this year looking for investors and a new vision for your company. You came to me because I'm the best at what I do."

Emily shook herself out of her eavesdropping trance

and busied herself creating place settings on the table in front of each man. She could have brought along an assistant to do such menial labor, but she'd wanted to make a strong first impression.

"I came to you because you're a Briscoe and I'm not getting any younger. It was time to pass this business to the next generation of my family. Our family."

Knox's jaw tightened. He glanced at Emily, as though her presence required him to censor himself. She retreated to the food cart, willing herself invisible so the two men would keep talking without paying her any more mind.

"Let's not pretend that warm, fuzzy family feelings made you pick up the phone to schedule that initial meeting with me," Knox said. "You needed equity. But it was my ability to see the untapped potential in this place that allowed me to put together a team of investors so quickly. The trick is, there's no such thing as free money, Ty."

"You don't think I know that, boy?"

Knox's eyes gleamed, but rather than address Ty's question, he continued. "You and I are now beholden to Briscoe Equity Group's investors, as the majority shareholders, and they expect us to make their money back plus at least a twenty percent profit in record time. We all stand to make a lot of money, you included, but we're not going to do that by giving the resort a simple facelift."

Ty dabbed at his forehead with the cloth napkin from his place setting. "I hear what you're saying, but we already have a world-class stable of horses, and hill country's premier golf course. And we're a world-renowned destination wedding location. Other than adding another wing of rooms, what more do you plan to do?" Ty said.

Emily set servings of chilled peach soup in front of Knox, then Ty. She'd labored for nearly two hours on the soup, which was in the running for her best culinary creation ever, if she did say so herself.

Knox picked up his spoon and poked at the crisp brown sugar brûlée. "We'll add a wing of timeshare condos, for starters. From there, we'll add enough rooms to double the guest occupancy, add a bar or two, expand the number of upscale shops in the lobby, and install a five-star destination restaurant, featuring a top-tier chef."

On his next breath, Knox frowned down at the soup, then pushed it ever so slightly away.

Emily gave a quiet gasp. *The nerve . . .*

"Agreed," Ty said. "And we just so happen to have plans for a new restaurant in the works. It's one of the reasons I asked our special event catering chef, Emily Ford, to showcase her skills by preparing us lunch today." He gestured to Emily, who was still gaping at Knox's untouched soup. It wasn't until Knox's eyes roved over her in a dispassionate study that she realized she was wringing the bottom of her chef's jacket in her hands.

Ty continued, "She's been working with me to develop a dynamic proposal for a world-class restaurant here at the resort. All we've been waiting for is the right investor, and here you are."

Knox's mouth gave an almost imperceptible frown. "No offense to Ms. Ford, but my investors have shelled out millions of their own dollars to transform Briscoe Ranch into a world-class luxury resort, so we need to aim higher."

Aim higher? And here she'd thought Knox's whole claim to fame in the business world was *not* being a jackass. Her loyalty to the Briscoes meant nothing to this man. And very little to Ty, either, obviously, who was allowing his family's business to be yanked away from them. No, not *yanked*. Knox Briscoe had too much poise to do anything so passionate as yanking. Rather, this was chess. Or, perhaps, Monopoly. A slow, deliberate erosion of his opponent down to nothing.

Standing tableside, she touched the edge of the plate on which Knox's soup bowl sat. Oh, how satisfying it would be to flip it over onto his perfectly pressed slacks. Her masterpiece deserved a better fate, but the temptation rippled through her with wicked glee.

Knox's body tensed. He knew what she'd been contemplating, too. His hand twitched as though in preparation to grab her wrist and stop her before she could soil his clothing.

"Emily," Ty warned.

Was she so obvious? So predictably reckless that both Ty and Knox could read her thoughts so plainly?

Screw them. Sure, they held her career in their hands, but neither deserved to eat her cooking today. With outrage pounding through her veins, she pulled out the seat at the head of the table between the two men and dropped into it. She slid Knox's bowl in front of her, grabbed his spoon, and—as both men gaped at her—cracked through the brûlée and dipped into the sunset-orange soup.

The soup exploded in her mouth in a burst of complicated, unexpected flavor. Perfection. Better than sex. Better than just about anything else this heartless, cynical planet could offer.

She flattened her palm over the bound stack of papers in front of Knox. His grand plans for her home, her career, and the livelihoods of so many of her friends and colleagues. He was going to ruin everything, and there was nothing she could do to stop it; not if Ty was just going to roll over and let Knox walk all over him.

She pulled the dossier in front of her. Ty and Knox sat, stunned, watching her flip open the contract. Neither had yet to say a word about her brazen intrusion. How the hell was she getting away with this?

Her anger was too blinding for her to focus on the words or make heads-or-tails of the legal jargon. But she'd heard all she needed to know. Knox and his investors were going to turn the resort into yet another cookie cutter chain hotel. "Ty, this is a bad deal. He's going to sell out. He's a business flipper. That's what he does. He doesn't care about the Briscoes at all."

"I am a Briscoe," Knox said in a dull, even tone.

Emily was too pissed off to look him in the eye. She took another bite of soup to keep herself from telling him that he wasn't a Briscoe in any way but his name. Instead, to Ty, she said, "If you do this, you're going to lose everything your parents built, everything you've worked your whole life for."

"That's enough, Emily," Ty said, but there was no mistaking the tinge of regret in his eyes.

Knox rose slowly, buttoning his suit jacket as he loomed over Emily. "Are you asking to be fired, Ms. Ford? Because I was hoping the chef I hire for the new restaurant would see the value in keeping on some of the resort's restaurant workers as line cooks."

Oh, this man. Emily visualized the way his perfect suit would look covered in mushroom reduction, sweet potato puree, and bits of roasted pheasant. In the end, she decided against the childish act, more out of respect for Ty than any sense of dignity or self-preservation.

Ty jabbed his spoon in the air at Knox. "You watch your tone with her. Emily's too valuable an asset at this resort to work as a line cook."

Spoken like the father figure he was to her. Emily's heart warmed for the man who'd taken a huge risk in hiring her right out of chef school, homeless and without a penny to her name. Of course, she didn't reveal any of that. She carefully schooled her features, refusing to splay open her chest and give Knox Briscoe one single glimpse of her heart. His careless response to her peaches was proof enough of his lack of a soul.

The gleam in Knox's eyes turned cool and calculating as he turned his focus to Ty. "I wouldn't have expected that from you, Ty. Sleeping with the special event chef. Interesting. And against my business policy."

Emily's self-control snapped. She pushed up from her chair, ready to get in Knox Briscoe's face and give him a piece of her mind. She slammed her hands onto the table for emphasis, but instead of hitting the table, her right hand caught the rim of the soup bowl. As though in slow motion, the bowl launched itself at Knox. Emily lunged for it, but she was too late. Bright orange soup splashed all over the front of his suit.

Mortified, she stood over him and watched glops of peach and brûlée topping ooze like lava into the creases of his waistband and belt.

For his part, Knox didn't rise or curse at her—as Ty was doing, she noticed out of the corner of her eye—nor did he attempt to clean himself off. He kept his cucumber-cool gaze locked on hers, a slight smirk curved on his lips. "Did I hit too close to home on that observation, Ms. Ford?"

Holy shit. She'd spilled soup all over her new boss. There was no way she was getting the restaurant now. She'd be lucky to keep her job. What she refused to give up was the last shreds of her dignity. Nobody insulted her by insinuating that she'd slept her way to the top and got away with it, not even the intimidating Knox Briscoe.

She rose to her full height. "I may not know what your father did to get disowned by the Briscoes, but it's no wonder you're trying to deflect some of that shame you inherited from him onto the people of this resort. Even after all these years, it still stings, doesn't it? Whatever he did to get shunned? The shame of it all?"

A shadow crossed Knox's face. Good. She'd meant for that to hurt.

A hand closed around Emily's arm and tugged her away. Ty pushed between her and Knox, scolding her, apologizing to Knox. When did the giant she'd long revered as a force of nature turn into a spineless, apologetic noodle? She would've never expected her idol to fall from grace in the blink of an eye.

Emily glared past Ty, to Knox. "It makes sense, now, this whole alpha power vibe you've got going on. You know what they say about men who seem like they're overcompensating for something."

The shadow vanished from Knox's eyes and the shark-like calculation returned. "That they have big feet? Or am I mixing my old wives' tales?"

"Emily, please. Leave us," Ty said. "You're embarrassing yourself and insulting me."

That pulled her up short. She was way beyond damage control when it came to her own embarrassment, but she did care about insulting Ty. She might not trust Ty to know what he was doing, not after this crippling deal with the devil himself, but she still respected Ty enough to honor his plea. With a nod, she walked with stiff, proud steps to the door.

"Ms. Ford, the suspense is killing me. What do they say about men who seem like they're overcompensating?" Knox said, sounding amused.

Gritting her teeth, she paused with one foot out the door and tossed a look over her shoulder, startling all over again at Knox's aura of cool perfection. The cut of his jaw, the fullness of his lips, eyes that were as cruel as they were wise. How had she ever thought she could win over a man like that with peaches and pheasant? Whatever family shame Knox was overcompensating for, it wasn't going to save Emily or her beloved resort. Knox Briscoe was beyond redemption, her career was over before it had even gotten off the ground, and life was never going to be the same again.

"Haven't you heard?" she said. "The thing about men who seem like they're overcompensating for something, is that they always are."

Chapter Two

Four weeks later . . .

Four miles into his inaugural trail run, Knox emerged from the tree-lined path and into a clearing at the top of the hill above his new house—the one he'd put an offer on the very same day his truck had backed into the lake and nearly drowned them both. He ground to a stop, hands on his hips, sweating like a beast.

Trail running in hill country was no joke. If only he could blame his breathlessness on the beauty of the view of the brilliant sunrise reflecting off the lake and the lush, green, rolling hills as far as the eye could see. The landscape was interrupted only by Briscoe Ranch Resort, which sat along the same kidney bean-shaped lake, separated from Knox's house by a hill that cut into the lake from the right.

He brought his phone out and dialed Shayla's number. "Yo, bro."

"I figured out the equation," he said between labored breaths. "Every mile of trail running is the equivalent of two miles of city running. No, make that three."

Shayla snorted derisively. "As long as you don't use

that as an excuse to slack off on your miles. Don't leave me high and dry for the Dallas Marathon this spring."

He grinned at the reminder. Racing with Shayla was one of his main motivational tools for working out. If she were to beat him too badly, he'd never hear the end of it. "You know me better than that."

"Hey, shouldn't you be getting ready for your first day at the resort right now?"

"Just about done with this run, but I had to take a break to admire the view. You'd love it."

As the early morning fog burned off, the details of the resort shone in the sun in stark detail. The resort's golf course began at the edge of the lake and extended out in rolling hills of manicured green grass. The resort itself looked like a wood and river rock Wild West castle. Beyond the main building on a hill to the north sat a chapel, looking the part of a lighthouse beckoning believers to its doors. On the west side of the golf course was the new, massive equestrian center that Ty Briscoe had reportedly agreed to finance as a gift to his son-in-law, the husband of his oldest daughter, Carina, in order to entice them to remain living at the resort. That was how important it was to Ty to keep the Briscoe family together.

Knox snorted through his nose at the thought. What a pile of crap. Ty Briscoe had spent thirty-five years shunning his only brother and his brother's family. And that equestrian center he'd so generously footed the bill for had been yet another nail in his company's financial coffin. Some family man he was.

"Eh," Shayla said. "I prefer the city. Though I do wish I were in Dulcet with you so I could watch you stick it to Uncle Ty." She infused the words *Uncle Ty* with venom that caught Knox off guard. Shayla was one of the most optimistic people he knew. She was born with the unique gift of being secure in her bones. The strife in their house hadn't affected her like it had Knox and Wade. She'd risen above it all. Or so Knox had thought.

"I wish you were here, too, Shay. And for the record, the only things that are going to happen to our dear Uncle Ty will all be of his own doing." All Knox was planning to do was give the elaborate house of cards that Ty and Grandpa Tyson had built a gentle flick that had been a long time coming. "And the best part is, when I've done what I came here to do, everyone involved will walk away with richer bank accounts—even our dear Uncle Ty, even if his pride and reputation are ruined for good."

Shayla made a grumbling sound of protest at allowing Ty any sort of profit, but Knox's attention was snagged by a splash and a silvery form disappearing into the rippling water. "Oh, shit, I think that was it. Either I just saw the fish that knocked me over, or there's a hell of a lot of freakishly large fish in this lake."

"Guess you'd better learn how to use a rod and reel," Shayla said.

"I plan to." Just like he planned to eat every last bite of the rabid piranha that had attacked him for dinner.

"I still can't believe you own a lake," Shayla said.

"I don't *own* it. It's county property."

"But you're the only private residence bordering the lake, and Briscoe Ranch comprises the rest of the lakefront real estate, so close enough. Good luck today."

"Thanks, sis."

As the call ended, he gave the resort another long look. Today was his first day as the on-site second-in-command to Ty. It was a role he'd fulfilled enough times before with other companies he'd bought, so this was nothing new and only slightly challenging. Besides, his measly ten percent stake in the company—compared to his equity firm's forty-one percent and Ty's forty-nine percent—was only temporary. Patience was the name of the game right now.

The only wildcard in his day was whether his truck would allow him to drive all the way to the resort's employee parking lot without stalling out. More than likely, there was a perfectly good explanation—one that didn't involve ghosts—for why he had yet to successfully drive the Chevy onto Briscoe Ranch property. The employees' entrance, the main gate, day, night—it didn't matter what tricks Knox had tried, his truck stalled out every time, sometimes feet from the gate, other times, miles.

Knox gave his new empire one last look, then pushed off into a jog once more.

Two hours later, Knox stood in the employee court-yard behind the office suites and dabbed at his perspiring forehead with his pocket square. His walk from the employee entrance gate where his Chevy had died to his office had to be nearly a mile. A mile wasn't usually a distance that made him break a sweat, but the sunny morning combined with the exertion of lugging his box of office supplies and personal effects and his messenger bag had made for an unexpectedly arduous trek. At least he'd managed to roll the truck onto the shoulder of the road before embarking on the trek over the resort grounds.

Once he'd eliminated all traces of exertion, he put on his game face and opened the office door. The time was still early, so the office was mostly empty, but it didn't take long for the smattering of workers to notice him. Some stared, while others returned his nods of greeting. An empty secretary desk sat like an abandoned guard post in front of his office door. As was the case every time he took on a new project far from the equity firm's headquarters in Dallas, he chose a new secretary, hiring from within, someone to fill him in on the nuts and bolts—and the gossip—of the company. That would be task number one today, as soon as he'd set his office up to spec.

The office he'd been given shared a wall with Ty's, which meant it boasted the same expansive view of the resort grounds and golf course from wall-to-wall windows. His eyes were on those windows as he entered, which was why he started at the sight of Ty leaning back in Knox's chair, his boots resting on the desk top.

"You're late," Ty said by way of a greeting.

It was only eight o'clock. Not exactly late, but not as early as Knox had hoped. "You're in my chair."

With an amused crackle of laughter, Ty rose. "Catch!" A ring of keys jangled as they arced through the air.

Knox scrambled to catch the flying keys one-handed while balancing his office supply box in the other hand. "Keys to the resort?"

"You got it. We'll swing by HR on our tour today, and they'll get you fixed up with a universal keycard, but those will work for now."

Tour? Knox slid his box onto the nearest horizontal surface, a small table holding a coffee caddy and an unopened bottle of scotch. He pocketed the keys, then tipped the bottle back, reading the label. Expensive scotch. Nice.

He jumped at the slap of Ty's hand on Knox's shoulder. "From me to you. Welcome to the family."

Ty's overeagerness to be buddy-buddy with him came across as borderline desperate. Disgusting, really. Welcoming Knox to the family as though the two of them being related was a new concept. It took some effort for Knox to stop himself from shoving the scotch into Ty's hands with a pointed, *I already have a family, and I don't need yours.*

"Thanks. We'll have to crack it open sometime soon," he said instead.

Ty folded his arms over his chest, drill sergeant style. "You're gonna earn a stiff drink by the end of the day. I've got a lot to teach you."

For the time being, Knox would play along, soaking up all the information about Ty, his weaknesses, and the resort that he could before Knox made his next move. He'd let Ty act the role of the wise mentor, with Knox as the eager student. "All right. Sounds good. When do you want to start?"

The slightly off-key music of a horn honking out the opening strains of *La Cucaracha* filtered in from the office hallway, drawing both men's attention. Ty rolled his eyes and cursed under his breath.

The next moment, the office door flung open wide and a hot pink motorized scooter pushed inside carrying an itty-bitty wrinkled ball of energy wrapped up in a shiny turquoise jogging suit. Knox recognized her immediately as his grandmother, June, though he'd only met her a few times, and never once when she was in as good of spirits as she appeared today.

Crowding around her scooter was the rest of Ty's branch of the Briscoe family—his daughters, Haylie and a very pregnant Carina, along with their husbands, Wendell Halcott and James Decker, respectively. So much for a low-key first morning.

Knox extended a hand in greeting. "Grandmother, I—"

He could say no more as she launched herself from the scooter and threw her arms around Knox. "You came! Blessed be."

It only took a moment for Knox to warm up to the idea of hugging her back. It didn't hurt that he could tell how peeved Ty was that his mother and the rest of the family had arrived on the scene. The truth was, it was a relief to see his grandmother so full of life, since the last time Knox had seen her, a little over a year ago, it had been to visit her in the hospital after she'd been injured in a fire at the resort's chapel. And the time he'd seen her before that, it had only been a glimpse of her slipping into the back of the church during Knox's father's funeral. He recalled with perfect clarity how her body had been bent and trembling with grief. She'd stayed until Knox's mother had noticed her and had ordered her escorted from the building. It had been a request in his father's will that neither his parents nor anyone from Ty's branch of the Briscoes attend his funeral.

"Yes. I came," Knox said.

Grandmother cradled his cheek in her hand. "You've got the Briscoe blood running thick in your veins, my boy. You're the spitting image of my Tyson. Bless his soul." She produced a purple rhinestone encrusted smartphone from the pocket of her jogging suit. In no time flat, she had it mounted onto a long stick that Knox had originally mistaken for a cane. "We'd better snap a picture to mark the day."

The flash went off before Knox had a chance to process her request. He blinked spots away from his vision.

"Granny June, you should let me take the picture for you," Haylie said, tossing a full head of heavily highlighted, wavy, brownish-blonde hair. She wiggled her French-tipped fingernails in the universal sign for *hand it over* and let a pout form on her glossy lips. Knox recognized her brand of high-maintenance, spoiled princess look so common in Dallas's social circles, the kind of look that many of his firm's older investors preferred as their arm candy.

Grandmother swung the selfie stick in a wide arc, forcing Haylie and the rest of the family to duck so as to avoid getting smacked upside the head. "Oh, hush. You know I've got these selfies down. Try again, Knox, honey, and this time, put your chin up to keep them neck wrinkles away. And bend your knees more to help this poor old lady look tall. Now smile."

Knox did as he was told, crouching down to put his cheek near hers and forcing a smile to his lips just as the flash went off. When he'd recovered his wits, he got on with the obligatory handshakes to his cousins' husbands and questions to Carina about her pregnancy.

"I didn't expect such a greeting this morning, but here you all are," Knox said, scanning the crowd of people.

"The whole Briscoe clan except for Shayla and Wade," Grandmother said.

Knox had to swallow back bitterness. He wasn't sure how much more he could take of their complete erasure of his dad and mom from their conversation and memory, much less the way they jubilantly ignored thirty years of shunning silence.

"Mom's not here, either," Carina said.

Grandmother's wrinkled face drooped into a frown and her eyes turned hard. "Aw shucks, you're right," she said with tepid regret.

Everyone shifted uncomfortably. Carina and Decker exchanged a look. Ty swallowed hard.

Interesting. Carina had struck a nerve with that one. The hallowed Briscoe clan could pretend all they wanted that they were one big happy family, but their dysfunction was simmering right below the surface of every smile and warm embrace. But whatever the story was with Eloise and the rest of the family, Knox couldn't care less.

"Speaking of mothers, how's Linda?" his grandmother asked, perhaps realizing her error of omission.

"My mom's doing great. Busy at church, as always."

Grandmother gave his arm a pat. "That's good to hear. We have room for her in the family compound, here on the resort grounds, if she'd enjoy being near you."

It was a kind offer, and one he'd extend to Carina, Haylie, and their grandmother once the resort belonged to him. He would be the bigger person, if only to prove how small and spiteful they'd been in comparison.

"That's sweet of you, but there'd be no convincing her to change churches." Guess the members of Ty's branch of the Briscoe clan weren't the only ones skilled at pretense because that lie rolled right off Knox's tongue. There was no way his mom would set foot on Briscoe Ranch Resort. She was still spitting mad at Knox for buying in as an owner. He'd never seen her get so worked up as when she'd tried to persuade him against going into business with Ty, even knowing the partnership would only be temporary and for the express purpose of reclaiming the legacy that should have been his dad's. He'd assumed she would support him, but clearly she didn't share Knox's and his dad's need for eye-for-an-eye retribution.

"We'll have to invite Wade and Shayla up soon. I'd love to reconnect with them," Carina said.

Reconnect? That implied they'd connected a first time. "Shayla runs my office in Dallas, but I'm sure she'll be around soon for you to meet. And Wade's a SEAL in the navy, operating out of Germany. We rarely know where in the world he is."

Carina pulled her face at that news. "He's a soldier? I had no idea."

"He enlisted when he was eighteen. It suits him." While Shayla had a heart of gold, Wade had been born with a chip on his shoulder the size of Texas, and since he'd come of age, he'd perfected the art of staying gone.

His grandmother's attention drifted to the window. "I pray for you and your siblings every night, and I always say a special prayer for Wade, knowing he's in harm's way."

"Thank you, Grandmother."

She shifted her attention back to Knox, her eyes sad.

"Granny June is what everyone calls me 'round here. I'd love it if you would, too."

She'd been *Grandmother* in Knox's household growing up. As in, *Grandmother sent you a birthday card. Take the money, son. You're owed that and so much more from my thieving brother and father.* And, as said by Knox's mother in hushed whispers when Knox said his nightly prayers, *Don't forget to pray for your grandmother. She aligned herself with that devil of a husband, but that's something we have to forgive her for, as Christians.*

The room descended into an awkward silence that Knox was in no mood to endure. "Ty and I have a lot to do today, he tells me. But the first item on my personal 'to do' list is to hire a secretary, preferably someone who's already an employee of the resort, someone who's a go-getter and can show me the ropes. So I'd love any suggestions y'all might have."

Ty smacked Knox's back again. "I'll help you hire a secretary, but there's no need for one who can show you the ropes. That's my job, so don't worry."

"What about me?" Haylie said.

From Knox's years of studying Ty's family from afar, Haylie was the *other sister*—the foil for the competent and successful Carina. She didn't seem either very secretary-like or motivated to work hard. Sure enough, behind Haylie's back, Ty cringed and gave a vehement shake of his head.

That was nearly endorsement enough for Knox. Haylie might not seem ambitious, but she'd certainly be able to provide him with an insider's perspective on the resort. "What are you doing now for work?" he asked her.

Haylie shifted, transforming instantly from a spoiled beauty to a self-conscious young woman before his eyes. "I'm working part-time in the children's activity program right now, but it's so boring. Like, I don't even want kids anymore. I'd kill for a new position. I mean, if you think I'd be any good at it."

"I think you'd do a great job as Knox's secretary," Carina said quietly.

"Carina, don't go filling her head with notions. Haylie, honey, I love you, but I don't think you're up for such a demanding job," Ty said. "You've never worked an honest day in your life."

"Dad, could you stay out of it? I mean, seriously. I'm a grown woman."

"You can't type," Ty countered.

"I can so. I text people all the time."

"I meant the proper way, like a secretary needs to be able to do."

Her face flushed. "Last week I saw a 'learn to type' app. I can download that tonight. And I'm an expert at talking on the phone."

Yikes.

To Knox, Ty said, "See what I mean? Let's leave Haylie out of this. My secretary can handle both of us until I can find you a qualified candidate for the job. Let me take care of everything around here while you're getting yourself settled in."

With a snicker, Wendell hooked his arm around Haylie's shoulders. "No one cares about her typing skills, Ty. Just put on one of those smart little secretary get-ups like on *Mad Men*, maybe pop a couple extra buttons open, give the guys in the office a little motivation to work . . . that's what really counts. Am I right, Knox?"

What a dick.

Everyone shifted uncomfortably, including Ty. Haylie cast her eyes down, blushing furiously.

Knox squared a look at Wendell. "No, actually."

A knock sounded at the open door. Everyone turned,

relieved at the distraction. A woman Knox would recognize anywhere filled the doorway, a folder clutched in her arms and a hard-set look of determination on her face. Chef Emily Ford. The first and only woman to ever overturn a bowl of soup onto him in anger—even if it had been an accident. The occasion also marked the first and only time he'd managed to ruin two perfectly good suits in one day.

On the night of the soup incident, as he'd lain sleepless in his hotel room, he'd given the matter some thought. Emily had had good reason to attack him with food. He'd insulted her by implying she was sexually involved with Ty. It'd been a reasonable conclusion, given their obvious closeness, but still. It was rude and sexist. An apology was owed. He'd already added the task to his calendar. For the coming Friday, if memory served. But it seemed she'd messed with his careful plans—again.

Today, she wore another crisp white chef's jacket unbuttoned over black leggings and a thin, charcoal gray T-shirt. Her curly hair had been tamed with a headband, a ponytail, and innumerable bobby pins.

She took in the crowd in Knox's office with a gulp. After a nod and a nervous smile at Carina, she settled her determined gaze on Knox. "I couldn't help but overhear, and, for what it's worth, I agree with Carina that Haylie would be a terrific secretary."

Ty and Haylie both raised their eyebrows.

"You do?" Haylie said.

"She does," Carina said. "I do, too."

Knox wasn't sure why he trusted Emily's opinion over Ty's or the others, but he did. Emily had proven, when she'd pulled up a chair during his meeting with Ty that she didn't pander. As opposed to the Briscoe clan, pretense wasn't in her vocabulary.

Knox thrust out his hand to Haylie. "Then it's settled.

Haylie, you're hired. Unless you need more time to consider my offer."

"No!" Haylie said with enough gusto that she covered her mouth and seemed to take a moment to settle herself. "I mean, I accept."

She sealed the deal with a limp handshake that had Knox fighting a cringe. That seemed to be happening a lot now that he was working at the resort.

Grandmother, er, Granny June—damn, he was going to have to give that some practice—wormed her way through the crowd to Emily. She hooked an arm around Emily's waist and dragged her into the room with the strength of someone decades younger. Kind of made Knox wonder what she was doing with a motorized scooter in the first place. "Knox, I want you to meet a young lady near and dear to my heart, an honorary member of our family. Emily, I want you to meet my grandson, Knox."

"They've met," Carina said.

Knox glanced at his cousin and found her eyes dancing with mischief. She'd clearly been informed about the soup incident.

Emily's cheeks pinked. For the first time, he noticed a light sprinkling of freckles on her skin. "I'm not here to apologize," she blurted.

Well, that settled that. Her proclamation was the perfect opportunity for him to counter with, *I'm the one who owes the apology.* But all he could do was study the shifting color of her skin and watch her shoulders stiffen with pride.

"Emily, now's not the best time," Ty said.

Knox experienced an unexpected jolt of panic at the idea of her leaving. Probably because her arrival might spare him from any more agonizingly awkward small talk with Ty's family. That had to be it because he was struck with a sudden, acute need to clear the room of everyone but Emily so he could find out what was on her mind.

Emily tucked an errant lock of hair back into her plum-colored headband. "I can see that. I'll come back later."

"No," Knox said, perhaps a bit too forcefully. He realized too late that he'd stepped between Emily and the door. Clearing his throat, he added, "Sorry, everyone. If you'll kindly take your leave. I need a private audience with Ms. Ford."

So formal, but he couldn't help it. Sometimes when he felt himself slipping out of control, correcting his language was the most efficient way to get himself back in line again, even if he came off sounding like an eighteenth century butler.

"Not a problem. We'll let you two kids talk," Granny June said, plopping down on the faux leopard fur seat of her scooter and firing it up.

Knox took his chair behind the desk as the family filed out.

Ty was the last through the door. "I'll be in my office. Get me when you're done. We've got a lot to do today." He wagged a finger at Emily. "Behave yourself."

A part of Knox hoped she would while the other part very much wished she wouldn't.

Emily closed the door behind Ty, then wrapped her arm back around the folder she'd brought in and clutched it with even more vigor. Clearly, she was winding up to say something serious. *A speech face,* Shayla called it. He'd bet money the folder held the restaurant proposal she'd worked up for Ty, and that she was about to try to persuade Knox to green light. Not a chance. With an eight-figure budget on the line and a team of investors to answer to, Knox didn't have the luxury of taking a chance on a no-name chef, even if he admired her gumption.

He gestured toward the empty chair in front of his desk. "You didn't bring any dishes of food to throw at me, which is surprising. I expected a cream pie to the face the next time I saw you."

She perched on the edge of the seat, curling the corners of the papers in the folder with the pad of her thumb. He kept silent, feigning patience while she gathered her thoughts.

"You haven't fired me," she said finally.

Neither had Ty, though Knox wasn't surprised at that now, given how close Emily was with the Briscoes. As for Knox, he probably should have considered it, or at least consider writing her up with human resources to start a paper trail that would justify an eventual firing, should it come to that. But he wouldn't. For the same reason he'd taken her advice about hiring Haylie. An honest employee was a rare gift. "True."

"Are you waiting to lay me off along with the rest of the restaurant staff? If I were you, that's how I'd play it. All of us at once." She said it matter-of-factly, and as though she'd given it a lot of thought in the weeks since their first meeting and had worked up to a healthy emotional detachment from the prospect.

"Are you trying to convince me to fire you?" Knox asked.

"No. I'm trying to figure you out, but you're resisting." She tipped her ear toward her shoulder and narrowed her eyes at him, as though gazing at him sideways might help her see him more clearly.

"I'm the one resisting? I'm your boss. You don't need to figure me out. That's not a job requirement."

"It is for me," she said. "You should have eaten the peach soup."

What was she thinking, dredging that back to the surface when she should have been buttering him up to hear her restaurant proposal? He didn't owe her an answer. What he ate was not her concern, but he found himself answering anyway. "Food is nothing to me, nothing but fuel and an inconvenient necessity."

"I figured," she said on a sigh. It was a wonder she didn't reach out to pat his hand and tell him she was praying for his soul.

Maybe he should have eaten the damn soup, after all. "You came to my office to see me. Why? I can't believe it's to rehash the soup incident."

On her next exhalation, she splayed her hands over the folder in her lap. "I'm more than qualified to open a five-star, destination restaurant at Briscoe Ranch. And I'm here this morning to ask you to let me prove that to you."

Having anticipated the reason for her visit, he was ready with his reply. "That sort of qualification is proven with credentials, of which you have none. Show me a James Beard award. Show me an apprenticeship at a Michelin starred restaurant. Show me the names of the award-winning chefs you've trained under."

She was silent, her expression remaining regal. She curved her fingers over the edge of the folder and gripped it tight. Her nails were short, her fingers stubby. The backs of her hands were splashed with freckles in the same hue as those on her cheeks. Her stalwart pride was too much to bear. His thoughts drifted to her no-nonsense fashion sense and her passion for her cooking.

He looked into those proud green eyes and something cracked inside Knox. Screw his policy to never over explain his choices to a subordinate. If it hadn't been so early in the morning, he would have cracked open the scotch and poured them each a finger.

"Emily, listen. It's not personal, I assure you. My job is to transform Briscoe Ranch into a luxury resort. Not only for weddings, but for a complete five-star experience, from the rooms to the spa, from hospitality staff and the golf course to the dining experiences offered here. What I'm setting out to accomplish here is bigger than you and your dream."

He cringed inwardly at that last sentiment. It was the truth but brutally worded. Even if she hated him for it, he hoped she could appreciate his forthrightness the way he appreciated hers.

She didn't reel in defeat. If anything, the fierceness in her eyes shone even brighter. "You buy under-performing businesses and transform them so they'll reach their true potential. Every article I've read about you goes on and on about your sixth sense for detecting diamonds in the rough."

"That's true. I do." God, he sounded like a pompous ass. That wasn't usually his style, but Emily's unconventional ways were throwing him off his game. She'd gotten in his head and scrambled his composure like few people could. He stood and buttoned his jacket, prepared to usher Emily out of his office. Time to end this slow bleed of his dignity. "Let me show you out. I have a busy day ahead."

Emily took his cue and stood, though she didn't budge from her place before his desk. "I am like this hotel, Mr. Briscoe. Knox. I am an under-performing business that hasn't reached its true potential. But you won't give me the chance to prove that to you. I bet that sixth sense of yours is telling you to give me a shot at this. I also bet you're ignoring it. Why, when you've built a fortune listening to your gut?"

He stopped short. How could it be that this woman, this stranger, had such insight into him? She was right; his sixth sense was on high alert. Could it be that he'd found yet another diamond in the rough in the hills of Texas?

He shook the crazy notion away because the facts

remained. "Ty told me about you. You've worked at this resort since right out of culinary school a decade ago. No internships, no stints as a sous chef at a celebrated restaurant, nothing remarkable, not even a chef competition show on TV. Your whole career, you've been here at Briscoe Ranch, laboring in obscurity. If you're so talented, then why have you been holding yourself back?"

He watched the shift of her weight from one foot to the other, the extra squeeze she gave the folder in her hand. He'd hit a nerve. Good. Turnabout was fair play.

"I'm not holding myself back. All the years I've worked here, *laboring in obscurity*"—she said with a scoff—"I've had the freedom to cook what I want, every dish completely original instead of imitations of more prominent chefs or attempts to pander to critics' fickle tastes. Over the last decade, I've risen from a graveyard-shift line cook in the room service kitchen to the executive catering chef, one of the principal roles at the resort." She spun the folder onto his desk and speared a finger on it. "A few months ago, Ty agreed to my proposal to open a high-concept, signature restaurant at the resort. Subterranean, I'm going to call it. We were in the process of securing funding when you showed up and ruined everything."

He took a step nearer to her, then another, stopping just short of arm's length. This close, those freckles on her cheeks came into focus again, as did a faint, hairline scar along her jaw that curved to her chin. He refocused on her furious green eyes. "I did not take this opportunity away from you. Ty did. He was the one who contacted me, looking for investors. My presence here to execute my vision for the resort, as well as the timing of it, was at his invitation. If he let you believe your restaurant would be possible under this new vision, then he was stringing you along. He's your enemy, not me."

Emily blanched, but only for a split second before

recovering her wits. "He wasn't stringing me along. I'm sure he was grooming me for your takeover, knowing you'd want to step up the caliber of the resort's dining options. He's not my enemy. He's the employer who gave me a chance. All I need is an open door and a budget and I will give you the restaurant of your vision."

She'd been dead on about his sixth sense and the rush he got with each thrill of discovery. He felt that familiar rush right now while sparring with her. He couldn't wait for her to leave so he could read her proposal. He should have eaten the damn soup. Now he'd never know what he'd missed. "You and I aren't so different in our ambition, you know."

She sniffed at that, feigning a nonchalance he saw right through. "You couldn't be more wrong. I possess a patience that you clearly lack."

Oh, this woman. She wouldn't stop pushing his buttons. He felt heat rising on his neck. He had to stuff his hand in his pockets so he wouldn't give in to the discomfort and tug his tie loose. Emily had no idea how much patience it had taken to wait for the right time to make his move against Ty Briscoe. Years of planning and strategy, years of positioning himself in the right business, with the right connections, silently closing in on his prey, waiting to pounce until the time was right—until the prey thought it was his idea and came to him, on the verge of bankruptcy and begging for a bailout.

"Prove it," he heard himself say, not knowing exactly what he meant by the dare.

Her gaze was unflinching. "How?"

He had to think fast. "I'll give you four weeks. If you can prove to me in that time that you're as gifted a chef as you claim, then I'll hand you the reins of the restaurant along with whatever budget you require for this . . . Subterranean."

She was not nearly as grateful as he'd expected, throwing him off yet again. "By taking over at the Chop House? Is that what you mean? Fine. As long as I have your approval to change the menu. Javier will be pissed to be booted from his job, but it's just a month. He'll understand."

He hadn't thought the challenge through to its details, but it only took a moment to decide what he really wanted from her. "Not taking over the restaurant. Guests have an expectation of the steakhouse that we have to uphold. You'll cook dinner for me. As my personal chef for the month."

The laughter she burst into caught him off guard yet again. "As in, cook for the man who thinks that food is nothing but fuel? A man who wouldn't taste my locally harvested, lovingly created, perfect peach soup? Because I'm not going to agree to this if you expect me to be your personal protein smoothie artist."

Knox's blood pounded through his body, saturated with adrenaline. When was the last time anyone tested him like this? When had he last felt so alive? "My food philosophy makes me the perfect candidate for this challenge. Change my mind. If you're as good as you claim, then that shouldn't be a problem."

Her fierce countenance fell away, and he could plainly see the wheels turning in her mind. "Luckily, October is a light wedding month. The menus are done and the food ordered, for the most part. I can supervise during the day, and then my assistant, Nori, can run the kitchen during the events since I'll be busy in the evenings devoting all my energy to . . . to . . ."

"To pleasing me." Holy shit, that'd come out wrong.

Emily didn't blink an eye. "No. To bringing you to your knees. In four weeks, you'll be begging me to run your restaurant."

Another rush coursed through him. He gritted his teeth against a smile. Emily Ford was stubborn, arrogant, and driven. Just like him. If she really was as extraordinary a chef as she claimed, then maybe he had discovered a diamond in the rough, one that might prove to be a lucrative investment, indeed.

"You're going to need more than dinners. Breakfast and lunch, too. I can serve them here at your office."

"I don't eat breakfast."

She didn't seem to hear him. "I'm going to need keys to your home and 24-hour access."

Right. She was going to be in his home, every night. Another part of the challenge he hadn't thought through. The realization had his control tilting off balance again. He dashed off his address on the back of a business card, then extricated the house key from his personal key ring. "Of course. As I said, I don't eat breakfast and I take most of my meals here, so the keys to my house will rarely be necessary."

She curled her fingers around the key, clearly taking his words as a further challenge. "And yet, that's where I'm going to feed you tonight. At your house. I'll see you at seven."

"Make it eight. And plan on dining with me. What good is a fine meal when eaten alone?"

He wasn't sure what made him tack on that last requirement of the challenge, but his blood heated at the thought. What better incentive for pulling himself away from the office earlier than sharing nightly meals with the beguiling Emily Ford?

The pink returned to her cheeks. "That's not necessary."

"Oh, I think it's very necessary. Consider it an extended interview."

"Fine. Then I'll see you tonight at eight."

Anticipation coursed through him with intoxicating purpose as he watched her stride from the room. No matter how this little experiment turned out, the daily battle of wills with Emily Ford was bound to keep him on his toes. He couldn't wait.

Chapter Three

Emily stood on the wooden dock attached to Knox's boat-house and watched the final rays of sun dance on ripples in the lake. Her mind drifted over the menu she'd built for her and Knox's first dinner together.

Damn it. She sucked a breath in through her teeth, royally peeved at herself. She had to stop doing that, turning even the most benign thoughts into something pseudo-sexual—especially when it came to the man who held her future in his hands—no matter how achingly handsome he happened to be. She'd long considered herself immune to desire, ever since her epiphany after a bad date two years earlier when she'd realized how much more satisfying food was than sex or men or any sort of lust-fueled bullshit. Like a nun, she had a higher calling than succumbing to a mere mortal's baser needs.

She forced her attention back to the lake, where tendrils of fog were settling in for the night. More than any other season, she loved the way autumn felt. The chill in the air and the low, early retiring sun made people hungry for the types of foods she most loved to cook: hearty, soul-nourishing foods that connected people to the earth and the soil. The kind of food Knox Briscoe should be eating, if only he would abandon his ridiculous 'food as fuel' naivety.

Nearby, a fish jumped from the water with a tremendous splash that sent droplets raining down on the wood and her feet. She wasn't the greatest when it came to identifying species of fish unless they were on ice at her favorite fishmonger's storefront, but she was pretty sure it was a carp. Or maybe a bass. Either way, it looked like a protein she'd love to design a meal around, if only she knew how to fish.

It was a tough sell to tear herself away from the peace of the water, but she wanted to make one more pass through Knox's house and search for future menu inspiration before he arrived to dine on a meal that included seared foie gras with vadouvan-spiced bread and huckleberry compote. It was a great menu with a flavor profile sure to wow anyone, but she was still having trouble figuring out exactly what made Knox tick, and therefore, the ideal emotions to elicit in him with her food.

She walked up the well-worn dirt path from the lake to the stairs that led onto the deck, then let herself in through the kitchen door. Her produce was drying on a towel near the sink and the huckleberries cooled in a pan on the stove, but she barely gave the room a look before pushing through the swinging door to the house's great room.

What Emily considered her greatest skill and the secret to her culinary success was that she was part fortune teller. She read people, their past and their future and their emotional temperature. She could spend a little time with a couple and understand what was missing in their lives, what they needed, what food could provide for them beyond their own limited understanding of taste and nourishment. She'd been perfecting the art for years, but as she'd told Knox that morning in his office, she couldn't get a clear read on him, try as she might.

She'd spent the afternoon trying to read him through his home and the land he'd chosen, but something was missing from her analysis. She had no inspiration at all. Clearly, he craved beauty and solitude, as evidenced by the view. The house itself was modern and cavernous. Though she suspected it had come fully furnished, she bet the cold, minimalist aesthetic appealed to Knox's need for control. Beauty, solitude, and control did not a satisfying meal make, especially for Knox, especially after stepping into the warm, inviting aura of his study.

In the study, on a table against the wall, she'd found a record player attached to a high-end sound system. Next to it, a collection of classic rock. Near to that were photographs of Knox's family sitting on the lowered tailgate of a truck, his parents crouched behind the three kids. Knox sat in the middle, looking to be seven or eight years old, and had his arms around his brother's and sister's shoulders. Emily had never seen a photograph of Knox's father, Clint, before. The family resemblance to Knox and Ty and Tyson Briscoe was strong. The same nose, the same angular jaw and high cheekbones, the same looks of intensity in their dark eyes. Clint, on the other hand, drew his looks from Granny June's side of the family, as Carina did. Emily recognized Carina's smile on Clint, as well as the shape of her head and the shading around her eyes.

There was only one room Emily had yet to explore. After a quick check of the driveway and the garage to make sure Knox wasn't home yet, she stole upstairs through the waning light. She counted five bedrooms on the second floor and as many bathrooms, but the master suite at the end of the hall was the only one with any semblance of personal touches to it.

The moment she stepped through the threshold, she

expected to be overcome with warnings from her conscience that she was trespassing, but her drive to slay the
challenge Knox had set up for her superseded any ethical
or moral concerns about invading his private space. How
could she mind overstepping some boundaries when her
future was at stake?

The room smelled clean, fresh. Several sets of cufflinks sat in a dish on a darkly stained wood vanity near
the entrance to the ensuite bathroom. One window in the
long row of them had been cracked open. Beyond the glass,
the bedroom boasted an expansive view of the lake. Behind the hill on the opposite shore, she spied the rooftops
of Briscoe Ranch and the chapel.

She flicked on a light switch near the door, and a row
of tasteful, recessed lights came to life above a large,
masculine-looking bed. After another glance down the
hall and a quick listen to make sure she was still alone,
she walked into the room, heading straight for the bed.
She smoothed her palm over the gold, black, and red
duvet, in a style that reminded her of the Far East, covering his king-sized bed. An embroidered image of a black
rose adorned one corner, the petals tumbling away from
the stem like shaved slices of black truffle over a golden
sauce.

Her spine snapped straight and she gasped aloud,
rocked by a sudden explosion of inspiration. She'd been
right about the peach soup. About foie gras and vadou-
van, butter and cayenne. Knox's whole world revolved
around the yin and yang of old and new. His pricey, stylish
suits worn with old-fashioned gold cufflinks; a minimalist, modern home contrasting starkly with the well-used
record player in the study. And especially the line of
work he'd chosen, taking old businesses and giving them
a new shine. Even beyond that, the act of buying a huge
stake in Briscoe Ranch was the biggest yin and yang of

them all—a new opportunity, colliding with an old family name and an old family rift.

"Of course. That's perfect," she muttered, collapsing back on the duvet. She closed her eyes and spread her arms over the fabric, feeling the textiles with not only her hands but the skin of her whole arms.

She knew how to feed Knox so that the food would seep into his skin, through his layers of comportment. She had a plan—an irresistible plan that would turn him to putty in her hands—but his room was barely the tip of the iceberg. She needed so much more information. What had he been like as a child? What dishes had his mother made him? She needed his stories and history and—

"I feel like one of the three bears right now. Goldilocks, is that you sleeping in my bed?"

Emily practically levitated to her feet.

A distinctly male figure appeared in the twilight shadows beyond the bedroom door. "Knox," she breathed, mortified.

He stepped just inside the room, into the light far enough for her to make note of his amused grin and playful, if onyx eyes. He leaned against the door jam, his thumbs hooked in his pants pockets. He looked intimidating. Confident. And undeniably, gorgeously male.

Awareness pricked through her body like needles of fire. "I would never sleep in your bed," she announced.

His lips quirked, then he pushed off the door frame and strode toward the vanity. "Whatever, Goldilocks."

Raising his wrist, he unfastened his watch, then set it into the jewelry dish.

He might have caught her off guard, but she had herself under control again. "Did you mistake me for someone who likes to joke around?"

He had the grace to wipe the grin from his lips, but

only just. His eyes still glinted with amusement. "Absolutely not."

Damn right. "My hair's not even blonde like Goldilocks'. All I was doing was looking for inspiration on what to feed you."

He shifted his attention to his sleeves, methodically removing each cufflink. "In my bed?" he asked, glancing up from beneath thick lashes.

Her skin turned impossibly hot. Did he have to keep saying *bed* as though it were the most erotic word in the English language?

"Among other places," she snapped.

She should leave the room. She should dash back to her kitchen at the resort and load up the black truffles she was going to need for dinner tomorrow. Except Knox was blocking the door and she wasn't sure he'd let her pass before he had a definitive explanation about why she'd been in his bedroom. At least he hadn't caught her rifling through his medicine cabinet.

Her skin flushed even hotter.

"Did you find it?" he asked.

"Find what?" Was something missing?

He tossed the cufflinks into the bowl on the vanity. "Inspiration."

Ah. "Maybe."

He looked around, as if the inspiration was something visible. Then his eyes settled back on her.

She swallowed. "How was your day?"

She'd meant for him to find that question humorous in an ironic way, but it seemed to plunge him into deep thought. He walked towards her, then past her, to the bed, shrugging out of his suit jacket as he moved.

"Long. Good." He tossed the jacket on the duvet, then hooked a finger behind his tie and tugged it loose. So intimate a move, undressing at home after a long day. What the hell was she still doing in his bedroom? She side-stepped towards the door, cutting him a wide berth.

"Haylie had a bit of a rough start today as my secretary," he added, tossing the tie on top of the discarded jacket. "She was really nervous, which surprised me."

Shifting his weight to one leg, he slipped out of his shoe, then repeated the move on the other. Until that very moment, Emily had never thought of socks as intimately personal before, but *oh my God*. Knox's stockinged feet, the outline of his toes against the thin weave of the beige fabric, made her feel like he'd shown her a sliver of his most intimate self. She swallowed hard. "I'm sure she'll do better tomorrow."

As would Emily. No more covert missions to Knox's bedroom.

Knox sat back on the bed and pressed his knuckles into the mattress, looking at her with honest, if troubled eyes, and his face completely devoid of pretense. "Are you sure I'm not making a mistake with Haylie? Ty thinks I am."

What was Emily, his advisor? Her focus slipped to his stockinged feet again. "No. Not a mistake. She's going to rise to the occasion. I'm sure of it."

For reasons that turned Emily's stomach if she thought on them too hard, Haylie needed the job perhaps even more than Emily needed the new restaurant.

Knox studied her, perhaps weighing her sincerity. "Why? Tell me about her. Why was hiring her the right move? And why didn't her dad think so?"

What could Emily say without betraying Carina's confidence? Her friend had needed someone to share the burden of the secret Haylie had entrusted her sister with. "The thing about Haylie is that, for her whole life, her parents coddled her and gave her everything she wanted without demanding anything from her. The problem with that kind of princess treatment is that it doesn't build up a person's confidence. It only breaks it down."

"They didn't coddle Carina?"

The idea brought a smile to her face, it was so preposterous. "No. She was the victim of oldest child syndrome. Until recently, she was kind of the family doormat."

"What changed?

Emily wished there was a different answer to that question. She wished Carina could've found her own voice and her own power without Decker's help. She wished Carina could have internalized what Emily had been telling her for years, that she needed to follow her heart and stand up to her family, but it took a man sweeping onto the scene and telling her the exact same thing for the words to sink in. But such was life. "She married James Decker. And he helped her find herself."

Knox popped the top two buttons of his shirt open. If his belt came off next, Emily was out of there, post-haste. But he only laid back on the bed and threaded his hands together behind his head. Her gaze slipped of its own volition to the flatness of his abs, the way his shirt strained and stretched across his chest, then lower, to the curve of fabric outlining his groin. Oblivious to her perusal and lost in thought, he moved a hand down to rest on his stomach. What a hand. Big, strong, a thick wrist and long fingers.

Knox Briscoe was stunning. Way too goddamn stunning for his own good. Disgust arrived with the next wave of lust that rippled through her. How dare she be attracted to this . . . this . . . interloper? This invader who'd swept in and assumed power over her and the people she cared about. It had to stop immediately.

"Just because Haylie was dealt a tough hand doesn't mean she's qualified for the job," he said. "As I told you,

I'm not here to run a charity program for the Briscoes and their friends."

Ouch. "Haylie's life with Wendell, the guy she married, is not . . ." Emily was dancing perilously close to the truth, but if it helped Haylie hang on to her first good chance to change and grow, then Emily had to try. "She's not happy. And I don't believe she thinks highly enough of herself to change that. She doesn't need your charity, but she could use a lucky break, a chance to rise." *Like me.*

Except not like her because Emily knew her worth, and she'd known it for a long, long time. "Did you agree to this challenge so you could pump me for information on the Briscoes? Because my loyalty is to them, in case you hadn't noticed."

"I noticed." He sat up and pinned her with an inscrutable gaze. "And no, I didn't hire you with the hopes that you'd share Briscoe family secrets with me."

Another thought occurred to her. "But that's why you offered Haylie her job, isn't it?"

His eyebrows flickered.

She was shocked that he was being so honest with her. Then again, he'd been honest all along, hadn't he? Brutally so. He behaved like a creature at the top of the food chain, with no fear of getting eaten. Which, she supposed, was the truth. "You don't expect anyone to surprise you. What a boring way to go through life."

Only a slight downturn of his lips betrayed his displeasure at her assessment. "Look at you, knowing so much about me."

The tension in the room was rising again. Emily shifted, unnerved anew by the intimacy of it all, battling him in his bedroom while he undressed. Why did every encounter with this man turn uncomfortably intense? Would they ever have a normal conversation instead of a chess match? "If you'll excuse me, I have ingredients to fetch."

She'd taken two steps into the hall when he called to her. "Emily?"

She allowed herself a dramatic wince, then turned.

Knox was standing again, bedside, his legs hip-width apart, his hands in his pockets. "I don't want to forget to tell you that my sister will be joining us for dinner tomorrow and staying overnight. But she doesn't eat breakfast either, so don't get any ideas."

His sister. Excellent. With any luck, she would provide yet another window into Knox's soul.

"One last thing." He paused as though selecting the perfect words. "I'm looking forward to the meal tonight."

Emily was, too. A little too much for her own good.

Chapter Four

A second day as a Briscoe Ranch owner, a second day spent under Ty's watchful, enthusiastic tutorship. The patience and acting required of Knox to allow Ty to believe he was still top dog at the resort was draining, though Knox had passed the hours in eager anticipation of the visit from his sister and another meal from Emily. The first night, she'd hit it out of the park with a foie gras dish unlike any he'd ever sampled. The fact that he couldn't stop thinking about the meal, or the wild boar hash she'd tried to ply him with that morning, or tonight's meal, for that matter, suggested that perhaps his sixth sense had been right about her. As far as diamonds in the rough went, Emily was a remarkably polished one.

After dark, an hour before Shayla was set to arrive, he set out from his office in a golf cart across the resort grounds. Happy guests strolled about, taking in the resort's gardens, splashing in the pool, and enjoying cocktails at the candlelit pavilion as an acoustic guitarist plucked out a jazzy tune. For all Ty's faults, he'd built one hell of a resort. Knox could hardly wait to make it even better, bigger, and more luxurious. He'd transform the magic of the resort into profit in a way that Ty had never accomplished.

Smiling at the thought, he parked it at the end of the paved road, then walked up and over the hill where his truck was parked just beyond the resort's eastern border along a fire road. It was a hike, for sure, but that had been as close to the property as his dad's truck would get that morning. One of these days, Knox would have to make a trip to San Antonio and purchase a second car. It wasn't as though he couldn't afford one, but his stubborn streak demanded that he give his dad's ghost a little more time to get used to the idea of his truck parking at the resort.

Beyond the fence demarcating the edge of the property, he spied the truck. The twinge of relief he felt was undeniably silly, but a part of him was grateful the truck hadn't decided on its own to randomly lose braking ability and roll away.

He looked the truck in its headlights, as though they were eyes. "What do you think, Dad? How am I doing so far?"

It wasn't until he was even with the front bumper that he noticed someone sitting on the lowered tailgate. His anger was swift and unreasonable. He stormed in her direction. In response, she smiled and lounged back, propping her hands on the truck bed behind her.

"Whatever you were going to say, don't," he said. A hell of an opening line. What was it about Emily that made him fly off the handle like that?

"So this really is your truck. Hmph."

He attempted a calming breath. "How did you know I'd parked here?"

"I saw you walking from this direction this morning and I came to investigate."

"This is none of your business."

Her smile fell. "That's true." She hopped off the tail-gate. "Were you talking to your dad just now?"

He closed the tailgate. "Nope."

"Right."

She smoothed a hand along the side of the truck bed. "Why park here? Is it that you don't want your employ-ees to see you driving this old truck?"

He bristled at the accusation of vanity, but if she were trying to bait him into baring his soul, she was going to be sorely disappointed. Oversharing with his personal chef wasn't on his agenda for the day.

He brushed past her and unlocked the driver's door. "Think what you will."

She strolled his way, feigning casualness, though her eyes gleamed with her usual sharp intensity.

His heart rate took on an erratic urgency. *Here it comes, the wrath of Emily.* At least she wasn't holding a bowl of soup.

She stopped before him, nose-to-nose, and narrowed her eyes. "What are you smiling about, all of a sudden?"

Smiling? Him? Preposterous. "Why are you here? Don't you have a dinner to prepare? My sister's coming, in case you'd forgotten."

But Emily wouldn't be swayed off course. "You won't let anyone see you in this truck. Your first day, the day you and Ty finalized your deal, you arrived in a fancy car with a driver who pulled right up in front of the main entrance for everybody to see. All I could think about when I was watching you was how cocky and full of power you were. It was quite a show. But this truck . . . It's old and the paint's deteriorating and it doesn't have any bells or whistles. It's the opposite of powerful and showy."

She'd been watching him that day? "If you're accus-ing me of parking here out of vanity, then—"

"That's just it. On the surface, it looks so vain, except that I know how sentimental you are. This truck means everything to you. It's either the exact same truck I saw in old family photos at your house, or it's the same make and model. And yet you park it out of sight. I don't get it."

How did she *do* that?

She smoothed her hand over a dent above the front wheel. "How'd you get this dent? It seems fairly new because the paint's scraped."

What was she getting at? First, she rifled through his bedroom and probably every other room in his house, and now she was brazen enough to interrogate him about his truck? Why? He was just curious enough to humor her question. "The day Ty and I finalized the contract, on my way to the resort, the truck broke down and hit a boulder."

"You hit a boulder? Okay, that's random."

"I wasn't in command of the truck at the time." He glanced at his steering wheel, debating. He was under no obligation to explain himself to this woman. None at all. Except, what was the harm in confessing to her? He had nothing to be ashamed of.

Except that you believe in ghosts.

There was that. "The official diagnosis was a brake fluid leak."

"But what really happened?"

"You'll think I'm insane," he said.

"Try me."

She said it like a challenge—and he was never one to shy away from one. "All right. I know my dad's looking down on me from on High. And I'm pretty sure he doesn't want me to drive his truck onto the resort property. Even as a ghost or a guardian angel or whatever, he's still hold-ing a grudge against this place. So, the truck breaks down whenever it gets near the resort." He allowed him-self a rueful smile. "Doesn't matter which road in to the resort I try to take. As soon as I get to the gate, it dies. Every time. Sometimes it doesn't even let me get that far." It was the first time he'd ever voiced his belief to another person, and it sounded even more insane out loud. "Crazy talk, I know."

"No. Not at all." Her gaze shifted to the truck as though studying it with fresh eyes.

"You don't think I'm crazy, believing my dad's spirit is tampering with his truck?" He refused to use the word *haunting*.

"I don't." She rubbed her chin, a speculative frown curving her lips. "You're working at the resort where he wasn't welcome. Do you think he doesn't want you here?" She leaned in close to the side mirror as though it were the truck's ear and whispered, "Is that what you're trying to tell Knox? That he should give up this crazy idea and leave the resort managing to Ty's branch of the family?"

A surge of protectiveness had him reaching out his arm and tugging her away from the mirror. As crazy as believing in ghosts was, he harbored the even crazier feeling of not wanting anyone else talking to his dad, in-vading such sacred territory. "You're patronizing me."

"I'm not. I'm really not, and I'm sorry if it came across that way."

He paced to the crest of the hill and stared down at the blaze of light and activity on the resort. "I understand that you want me to leave so your life can go back to normal, but even if I did leave, you can't go back to the way it was. The resort was bleeding money. If I hadn't bought into it with my private equity firm, then the resort would've either been sold to someone else or closed down."

Her hand touched his shoulder, turning him to look at her. Her face was pale, her eyes huge. "Are you serious?"

Damn, he'd miscalculated. She hadn't known that the resort had been on the verge of bankruptcy. Given how close she and the Briscoes were, that surprised him. "Did you mistake me for someone who likes to joke around?" He was gambling that tossing her own words from the previous night back at her might distract her from his inadvertent oversharing, but no dice.

"What happened? The resort's always booked solid. Every year we seem to get more and more crowded. I don't understand how we could be in financial ruin."

The proof was clearly laid out in the accounting records, but he knew Emily wasn't looking for him to spout cold data as an answer. "The *what* and *why* hardly matter now because I did buy into it. And I know how to transform a failing business into a profitable one. I'll have Briscoe Ranch turned around in no time."

On a sigh, she gave a slight full body tremor as though shaking away the unpleasant truth. Straightening to her full, proud height, she turned back toward the truck. "Right now. Let's do it. Let's drive your truck onto the resort."

The hasty change of topic had his mind racing to catch up. "It's not going to work."

"If we can push it over the top of the hill, it'll roll downhill on its own. Even your ghost daddy can't defy physics."

Knox was pretty sure Dad could, but more importantly, "Could you not call him Ghost Daddy—ever?"

"Fine." She extended her open palm. "Where are your keys?"

My God, she was serious. "Don't you recall a little story I told about the brakes malfunctioning? The truck rolled into Lake Bandit and was barely salvageable. We can't take the chance of the brakes failing again and the truck crashing. Or worse, hitting a resort guest."

To his great frustration, she crouched again with her mouth near the side mirror. "Tell you what, Clint. I know you don't want Knox here. I don't either, but he is here. And he's right that it's probably the best for the resort. So instead of being an asshole, why don't you support your son? Hmm?"

"I'm sure he's not interested in your opinion."

"Guess we'll find out. Unless you're chicken."

Maybe seeing would be believing for her. Knox climbed into the driver's seat, started the truck, then reached across the bench seat and unlocked the passenger door. "Get in."

"Ready?" he asked once she was settled with her seatbelt on.

"Let's do it."

Imprudent hope took hold of him. Emily was so committed and passionate about everything she did that it was easy to get swept away by her confidence. He disengaged the parking brake, put the truck in gear, and eased the gas pedal down.

Lo and behold, the truck rolled forward toward the property line.

"Come on, Clint," Emily whispered.

At only a few yards away from the edge of the resort, Knox's imprudent hope turned into full-fledged faith. This was going to work. Emily was the key, somehow. She—

As the front bumper crossed the cattle guard, the engine died. No warning, no gradual slow down. Just dead. So much for that wild flare of faith.

A hard bark of laughter escaped his chest. "See? Told you."

Emily's mouth had fallen open. "That's . . . I don't know what to say. I mean, I believed you. I really did, but I still thought maybe this time he'd cut you a break."

"Nope."

She puffed her cheeks with a sigh. "He's really not happy you're working at the resort, is he?"

"I can see how you'd think that, but it doesn't make sense. I have to believe he's proud, and that he knows I'm restoring balance and righting a wrong. He has to know I'm doing all this for him." There he went again, over-sharing with Emily. How did she manage to disarm him so completely? Here she was, pulling from him some intimate truths he'd never shared with anyone, Shayla included, while he knew barely anything about her save for the sparse details from her personnel file, which he'd opened and skimmed today.

"Did you grow up in Texas?" he asked.

Her face went blank. She stared straight ahead, though he wasn't sure she registered anything but the darkness. He sat in silence, waiting her out, hoping she'd cave and start talking.

"Houston." Her clipped tone held a warning not to question her further, but she'd done more than her fair share of probing him, so it was only reasonable.

"Are your parents still there? Any brothers and sisters?"

"I'm an only child." She sat in silence for a moment more. Then, in a flash of movement, she unclipped her seatbelt and opened her door. "So I'm just gonna go . . ." She hitched her thumb toward the resort's main building. "I've got ingredients to pick up in the catering kitchen. Dinner's in two hours. I'll see you at your house."

"Emily!" he called out his open window, but she didn't acknowledge his call.

She stalked over the cattle grate and onto the resort grounds, then down the hill and out of sight.

Knox's sister, Shayla, was a tightly wound ball of positive energy, with an ultra-fit body to match. She probably rolled out of bed in the morning and straight onto a work-out mat to perform rear leg lifts and crunches. She didn't look like she carried an extra ounce of fat, which probably meant, like Knox, she thought of food as fuel and nothing more. Such a pity.

Knox pulled Emily out of the kitchen to meet his sister in the living room while the biscuits were cooking. Emily kept one eye on the oven, while also trying to make small talk with Shayla—not an easy feat for an introverted chef with a well-rooted disdain for wasting time with conversations that went nowhere with people she'd probably never meet again.

Maybe it was a mistake to have set the kitchen table for dinner, where they'd have a front row seat to watch Emily's every move. On occasion, she pulled that move at the resort, serving VIP clients at a chef's table in the kitchen, but the stakes had never been this high. It had been one thing to share a meal alone with Knox the night before. As nervous as he made her, they'd had no shortage of topics to banter about. But with Shayla there, as well as Emily's surprise guest—who was on the verge of being late—the feeling of being on stage had her surprisingly anxious.

"It's great to meet you," Shayla said, shaking Emily's hand. "When Knox told me he was auditioning a chef for a restaurant he's opening at the resort by using her as a personal chef for a month, I thought that was a genius idea. I had to come check you out for myself."

"Yeah, check me out." Ugh. So awkward.

"I don't see any place settings at the dining room table," Knox said. "Are we eating on the deck?"

"In the kitchen," Emily said, gesturing for them to follow her.

Shayla seemed delighted by the news. "How kitschy!"

Shayla's joke landed with such a thud that Emily's step

faltered. Knox groaned good-naturedly. "You did not just go there."

"Damn right, I did. You know me, the most awkward girl in the room."

Looked like Shayla and Emily would have to compete for that title. "And here I thought that was my cross to bear," Emily said.

"We can share the crown."

If this meal were designed to wow Shayla instead of Knox, there'd be no way Emily would seat them in the kitchen. No, instead she would have indeed seated them on the deck. She would have tapped into Shayla's amusement at the world with fresh air and quirky gastronomic marvels. Sparse plates and exotic flavor bursts.

But this challenge was about Knox, and he didn't need quirky. Their confrontation-turned-conversation at his truck convinced her all the more of his need for nostalgia with a modern twist. Hence, why she'd led them to a table in the kitchen next to the brick fireplace that looked to have been used by the previous owners for baking bread and pizza and any other matter of wood-fired food.

Earlier that day, Emily had dragged the kitchen table in front of it and loaded the fireplace with wood. She'd then gathered Knox's framed family photos from the study and arranged them on the thick wood mantle above the oven. A little touch of hominess and warmth, the perfect setting for Emily's take on comfort food.

She'd just gotten Knox and Shayla seated when the doorbell rang. Knox made to rise. "Sorry. I have no idea who that could be."

"I'll get it," Emily said, waving off his offer.

Granny June stood at the front door, her espresso-stained wood cane with purple carvings loaded with three thick, leather-bound photo albums tucked under her arm.

Emily took the albums and whispered, "You're right on time. Thanks for doing this."

Granny June steadied her cane against the floor and stepped into the foyer. "Oh, thank heavens. I just knew I was gonna be late. Paco was my Cab'd driver again. You know how he gets because he has the sweets for me. It's why he drives so slowly. He likes to keep me all to himself, that rascal."

Granny June had agreed to give up her driver's license the same year she'd bought her first smartphone—after the fifth time she'd mowed down a mailbox while texting. Ever since, she'd had to rely on the kindness of friends and families to drive her around, along with the occasional taxi ride, though they were scarce in the backcountry of Ravel County. Then, she'd discovered driver service apps like Uber and Cab'd, and she took to them like a kid to candy. Emily shuddered to think of the bill Granny June probably racked up every month.

"How old is this Paco the Cab'd driver? Are you flirting with younger men again?" Emily teased.

Granny June had been the first member of the Briscoe family to take Emily under her wing and treat her like family, filling the roles of the mother and grandmother previously missing in Emily's life, though just as often, the two were co-conspirators as much as kin. Whatever crazy plan either of them dreamt up, the other one was sure to jump on board. Like tonight.

"Oh, pish! You know my Tyson is the only man for me, God bless his soul." Granny June got a kick out of imagining herself an irresistible siren to men, even if she'd never as much as gone on a single date after her husband's death more than twenty years ago.

"Poor Paco. Yet another broken heart you've left in your dust."

Granny June fluffed her hair. "It's a burden I have to bear. But enough about that." Her gaze shifted past Emily, skimming Knox's house. "I haven't been inside this house in ages. Not since the Madisons sold it. I barely recognize it now, it's so modern. The million-dollar view's still here, though."

"That it is."

Granny June nodded to the empty dining room, just visible off the foyer. "I thought you said I wasn't late."

"No, you're fine. They're in the kitchen. I'd only just gotten them seated when you arrived."

"Let's get on with it, then. I've lost enough time away from Clint's children. It's time for me to get to know my grandkids."

Emily led Granny through the foyer toward the kitchen, but stopped short of the swinging door and faced her guest. "Just remember to act surprised that you're crashing their dinner, and don't let on that this was my idea."

For Emily to launch her full-scale assault on Knox's senses in such a short timeframe, she needed to use every weapon in her arsenal, including a heavy-handed dose of nostalgia courtesy of Knox's grandmother.

"I've been an expert at subterfuge since before you were born, honey. Let Granny June show you how it's done." With that, she brushed past Emily and used her cane to push the kitchen door open.

Knox shot to his feet. "Grandmother."

"Granny June, m'boy."

He allowed Granny June to envelop him in a tight hug. "Right. Sorry."

His apology fell on deaf ears, though, because Granny June's full attention was on Shayla. She looked like she wanted to reach out to Shayla, but wrung her hands instead as her eyes welled with unshed tears. "Shayla," she croaked. "That has to be you, doesn't it? I haven't seen you in . . . since . . ."

Unlike Knox, Shayla stayed rooted to her chair and extended her hand. "I don't believe we've met," she said coldly. The storm clouds behind her eyes crowded out her brightness.

Emily wanted to shake some sense into her, to tell her how snitty it was to be so cold to her own kin. Except that Emily could see both sides of the coin. If today her father's mother miraculously reappeared from beyond the grave, Emily wouldn't rush to embrace her either—kin or not.

Granny June was undeterred. She took the seat Knox had pulled out for her between the two siblings, her focus remaining on Shayla. "I used to sneak into the back of the auditorium at your school and watch you in all those plays. I used to watch your dance recitals the same way. I was at your high school and your college graduations. All those times, I wanted to meet you, but I could only look on you from afar. I don't blame your folks. I know they did the best they could, but I sure did miss being a part of your life. I'm hoping we can change that now."

Granny June's words seemed to disarm Shayla, who reached for her cheddar biscuit and took a nibble. "I didn't know you were there."

Granny June swiped at a tear in the corner of her eye and drew herself up proud, then gestured to the stack of albums Emily had set on the hearth near Knox. "Maybe after dinner, we can have a look in that pink album, there. That's my scrapbook about you that I've been updating all these years, hoping someday to share it with you."

Knox settled back in his chair, studying his grandma with warm, searching eyes.

Emily allowed herself a brief feeling of triumph, then slipped quietly back from the family scene. Assuming the role of the near-invisible household help, she set a place setting for Granny June, then ladled stew into three bowls and delivered them to the table. "Tonight you'll be dining on stew made with locally raised beef, as well as truffled cheddar biscuits."

"This is our only course? No first course?" Shayla said.

Emily returned tableside with a fresh black truffle and a shaver. "I wouldn't want to waste your appetite on an appetizer."

Shayla glanced between Knox and Emily. "I'm sorry. I guess I just thought this was an audition for a restaurant and assumed . . ."

Shayla went quiet as Emily shaved thick truffle slices over Granny June's stew, then hers.

"I think what Shayla's trying to say is that most restaurants have courses," Knox said. "Especially five-star restaurants. And so it's no wonder she figured you'd want to showcase as many dishes every night as possible." He plucked a truffle slice from on top of his stew as Emily shaved slices over his bowl. He used the slice to gesture to his sister. "Understandable, but Emily's restaurant would take a different track." Then he popped the whole truffle into his mouth.

So, then, he had read the restaurant proposal she'd left on his desk. Her esteem for him rose even higher, despite that she tamped down her gratitude in favor of professionalism. "I decided that in order to be truly revolutionary, a high-concept dining experience shouldn't follow such standard dining patter."

Shayla raised her eyebrows. "Revolutionary? That's ambitious."

"Ambitious is just the word I use to describe my Emily," Granny June said.

Emily poured Granny June her signature drink of

bourbon on ice, then cracked open a can of beer and poured it into a chilled pint glass for Shayla. "I'm pairing the meal tonight with a craft Belgian-style ale from one of my favorite breweries in Austin."

"A can of beer? Interesting," Knox said. "You keep surprising us."

Damn right, she kept surprising them. That was the whole idea.

Shayla smiled. "That you do, so I hope you won't take it personally if I don't partake of the beer. I love beer, but I'm training for a marathon and can't indulge in empty calories and carbs."

If Emily were personalizing the meal for Shayla, she would have never served beer, but Italian soda with freshly-rendered blackberry thyme syrup, with only the slightest drizzle of cream. Just enough to swirl among the ice like storm clouds—reminiscent of the hint of storminess that complicated Shayla's bright, joyful eyes.

"Careful, sis," Knox said. "If you offend the chef, you might end up with a plate of food in your lap."

Shayla snickered good-naturedly, in a way that told Emily that Knox hadn't informed his sister about the soup incident. "Should I be worried?" she asked Emily.

"It was a bowl, not a plate. And, of course, you shouldn't be worried," Emily said.

Knox made a clicking sound, a subtle *I beg to differ* protest.

Granny June did a little shoulder shimmy. "I'm guessing there's a juicy story there."

Emily winked at her. "Tell ya later."

Once her diners were eating heartily and reminiscing, oblivious to Emily's presence, she stoked the fire once more, then grabbed a mug of stew she'd ladled for herself and crept outside to take her meal on the deck. It wasn't until she was in the darkness of the deck that she allowed a broad smile onto her lips. This was what she lived for, nourishing people. And if it won her the job of a lifetime, then all the better.

Chapter Five

When Knox had accepted Ty's invitation to buy into the company, both with his own personal money and with his equity firm's, he'd anticipated a welling of emotions long forgotten. He'd braced for it, not wanting to be taken by surprise. But the emotions he'd expected were grief and resentment. He'd expected to resent the Briscoes for the lack of a supportive extended family and wealth they'd deprived his parents of, and for the legacy that he and his siblings had been denied. He'd expected a fresh wave of grief for the father he lost too soon. He hadn't expected, in his wildest dreams, to feel this elemental connection to strangers who weren't really strangers at all. His grandmother, his cousins. Even, perhaps, his uncle.

On his first bite of Emily's stew, the flavor assaulted him. That was the only word for it. The beef was of the finest quality, as all her ingredients were, but even beyond that, he took one bite and, in an instant, he was at his mother's table, the plastic protective covering over the tablecloth. His father was there, leading the prayer. They ate canned biscuits with stew made with beef bought at a discount that had to be simmered for hours until it was tender enough to chew. And yet, Emily's stew was so much more than that one memory. There was a heartiness that touched on the kind of decadence he'd only known since becoming wealthy. And a depth of complex flavors that still left him hungry for more. It was the past, the present, and the future.

How could a mere stew do *that?*

He lifted the truffle cheddar biscuit and took a bite. Too many sensations to name. Another burst of memory. This is what family tasted like. Sharp cheddar, complicated and rich; black truffles, earthy and whole. Even the beer took him back to his high school days, to the smell of his father on Sunday afternoons while watching football. It was as though the whole world had been condensed into this meal and the company he shared it with, along with the stacked albums of family memories on the hearth— tangible proof that their grandmother had loved them their whole lives. That thought alone felt like a blanket of calm he never knew had been missing from his life.

When he'd scraped the last morsels from his bowl, he turned, seeking Emily out to praise her for her creation, but she wasn't in the kitchen. He hadn't even noticed her leaving; he'd been so wrapped up in his grandmother's stories and his meal. He supposed that's what extraordinary food did—it commanded one's full attention. Still, she needn't have left. Dining with him was part of their agreement, though he'd hazard a guess that she'd wanted to give him time alone with his family. He would have done the same had their roles been reversed.

As Granny June launched into another story about their father when he was a boy and the trouble he used to get into while running wild over the countryside, Knox slipped his feet out of his shoes and stretched his toes. The fire in the fireplace had warmed the women's cheeks, turning them pink, probably Knox's, too. When he'd bought the house, he'd thought this fireplace was a waste of valuable kitchen space. Leave it up to Emily to see the value in it and put it to use, turning a simple dinner into something so much more—a hearth for him and his family to gather around and swap stories of days past and fill their bellies with hearty food meticulously crafted with great care.

When his sister emptied her glass of beer, which she'd almost absentmindedly started drinking as she'd sunk deeper into Granny June's stories, Knox excused himself from the table and found another couple of cans for them both in the refrigerator.

On the way back to the table, looking at his dinner companions, a sense of belonging—vast and profound—hit him, hard. He was in Dulcet with his grandmother, with his sister. On property that looked out on the very land his father had been exiled from. No matter what, he was a part of the Briscoe Ranch legacy now. His sister, too. This business venture had become so much more complicated than he'd anticipated. He'd assumed his resentment toward the Briscoes would shield him from becoming attached. How naïve.

Why had he thought this was going to be easy? What had made him think he could handle all this . . . this *feeling*. Feelings he didn't want. Yearnings for family and love and connection that he had no use for. *This is business. Ty's family doesn't love you, and you don't love them. Remember that . . .*

At the table, Granny June and Shayla were flipping through a scrapbook that Granny June had compiled of newspaper clippings and online announcements and so forth of Shayla's, Knox's, and Wade's accomplishments through the years, including finishing times of various marathons and races that Shayla and Knox had completed.

"Our grandma is a stalker," Shayla said with an almost sad smile. All vestiges of the cold distance she'd lobbed at Granny June before dinner were gone. Now, her eyes were glassy and she seemed to be falling into melancholy.

Knox set a hand on Granny June's arm. "A very thorough stalker."

Granny June patted Knox's hand. "Family is everything to me."

"Then how?" Shayla's voice cracked with the question. "How did you justify shutting my dad out like that? He was your son. I can tell that you loved him."

Pain shone in Granny June's face. From the purse she'd set on the floor, she pulled a stack of envelopes and handed them to Shayla. Their dad's handwriting was instantly recognizable in the angry scrawl across the envelopes with a red marker: DEAD—RETURN TO SENDER.

"These are from you to my dad," Shayla said in an awed whisper.

Granny June touched the date stamped on the top letter. She'd sent it a month before their dad's death. "Yes. I never stopped hoping he would forgive me."

It was in that moment that Knox realized how devastated his grandmother was about her estrangement from his dad, her son. Despite Knox's memory of her sneaking into his dad's memorial service, frail and trembling, he'd never thought about the rift from her point of view, not really.

"But . . . you sent birthday cards to us, and Dad let us have them. Why would he reject these letters?" Shayla said.

Knox knew why. Dad had made sure all three kids understood the reason they got to keep the cards. "The birthday cards had money. That's why he let us keep them. He thought . . . well, it doesn't matter what he thought."

Knox refused to hurt Granny June any more with details of his dad's bitterness.

"Yes, that was my thought, too, when all the other letters I sent to your father and to you two and Wade were returned, everything except the cards with money." Granny June didn't sound resentful, but full of regret. "I should have put money in them all, I suppose."

Other letters? Knox slipped his shoes on, pushed away from the table, and paced to the window. *Damn it, Dad. You never mentioned that to us. You told us she didn't care about us. Why did you lie?*

"I knew that was what your dad was doing, but I wasn't mad," Granny June continued. "I was grateful that you three knew I was thinking about you on your birthdays. The truth was, I was thinking about you all the time. Every day. You were always in my heart."

Through the window, only darkness was visible where Knox knew the lake to be. Above the silhouette of the hill on the opposite bank, the lights of Briscoe Ranch glowed like a golden beacon in the wilderness, rather than the hell his father had painted it to be.

What other secrets did you keep from me, Dad?

As soon as Knox thought that last question, guilt dropped like a stone in his gut. He expunged the words from his mind. No, he refused to entertain such a disloyal accusation. This family dinner was getting under his skin. His grandmother with her photo albums and old stories, his sister's melancholy, Emily's stew.

That was it. That's was had started this whole mess tonight. For all he knew, it was Emily who'd tipped off Granny June that Shayla was having dinner with him. For all he knew, she'd masterminded this dredging up of ancient pain as a way to weaken him, to throw him off his game.

Movement of light on the deck caught Knox's eye. It

was the faint blue glow of a cell phone. Emily. Coherent thought was impossible as Knox flung the door open and stormed outside. His hands curled into fists. He planted his shoes on the decking and stared her down, ready to call her on her manipulation.

Emily shot to her feet. Even in the dim light from the window, he could see a look of innocent concern on her face. "Is something wrong?"

Hell, yes, there's something wrong.

He opened his mouth. Then it hit him how out of control he was acting. More than his treasonous thoughts about his father keeping secrets, Knox was allowing his emotions to run roughshod over his self-control—and that was just as disloyal to his father's memory. Was Knox really so weak-willed that a tasty bowl of stew and the ramblings of an old woman would make him crumble?

On his next breath, he looked into Emily's searching eyes. His fight wasn't with her or his grandmother or even his father. The only person he was fighting was Ty Briscoe. One more breath, and he'd found the strength to wrestle his anger back into its box and lock it closed.

"The stew was exceptional," he said.

The stiffness in her shoulders drained away. "I know."

Her reply diffused the last of his misplaced anger, it was so *Emily*.

He nodded to the empty bowl on the bench where she'd been sitting. "You and I have a deal. Tomorrow night, you'll dine with me, and every night after that until the challenge is done."

Her attention drifted to the view beyond the deck railing. "Why?"

It was a question he refused to investigate too deeply. "Because it suits me."

The door to the kitchen creaked as it opened. Shayla stood in the doorway. "Hey, Knox, I was going to wait until you came back inside, but I'm tired. I'm headed to bed. I've got a long drive back to Dallas in the morning."

It was only nine o'clock, but Knox knew his sister well enough to know she was as emotionally drained from the meal and Granny June's stories as he was. But rather than deal with discomfort and painful memories of their past, Shayla was checking out. She'd been that way their whole lives. Perhaps that was the reason she'd avoided the anger issues that plagued Wade or the overdeveloped sense of responsibility that Knox had cultivated.

"Understood. It's been a long day."

Shayla offered Emily a little wave. "Dinner was great. Thank you." And then she was gone.

"I'd better head back in, check on Granny June," Knox said.

With a nod, Emily stood and gathered her dinner dishes, then followed him to the kitchen.

Granny June was up from the table and shrugging her coat on. "Emily, my dear, you outdid yourself with that meal."

Emily helped her smooth down her coat collar. "I'm glad you enjoyed it."

"Ready to leave? I don't know how you got here, but I'm happy to take you home," Knox said. Of course, he'd have to borrow Shayla's car, since Granny June lived in the Briscoe family compound in the northwest corner of the resort grounds and Knox wasn't about to take a chance that his truck would agree to get her all the way home.

Granny June took her cane in hand. "I'll certainly take you up on that offer, but first, I'm curious. Is the old boathouse still standing?"

"It is. You know a thing or two about this house," Knox said.

"The Madisons, the couple who lived in this place for ages, were good friends of Tyson and mine. They had a boy, Jacob, who was your daddy's best friend. Those two were inseparable right up until Clint left."

Knox sifted through his memories but came up blank. Then again, his father rarely spoke of his childhood, and he especially never reflected on happy memories. The sellers hadn't been the Madisons, but the Rozcowskis, and his dad had never mentioned a friend named Jacob. Had his dad been forced to give up his best friend when he was banished from the family? "What happened to the Madisons?"

"After Jacob and his sisters graduated and moved on with their lives, Agnes and Chuck decided it was time to move on, too. We're friends on Facebook. They're in Florida, doing well." She took Knox's hand in hers and her eyes twinkled with fondness. "I don't think it was an accident that you ended up buying this house. I think God brought you back to us and set you down here in this very house for a reason. If that boathouse is still here, then it has a secret I'd like to show you, something about your daddy that I think you'll appreciate, if you'll walk with me down there."

Knox was suddenly envious of Shayla's graceful escape. He wasn't sure he could handle any more memories or revealed secrets that night. "Of course. Let me get my coat."

"Emily, you come with us, too," Granny June said. "I think I'm going to need both of you to help this old lady find her footing on the path."

After Knox had located a flashlight, the three of them picked their way down the stone and dirt path to the lake.

"As soon as Clint and Jacob were old enough to run a boat on their own, they took up fishing. And, oh boy, did they ever fish. They were obsessed. Every so often, we'd catch Clint sneaking off in a skiff from the resort across the lake in the middle of the night to meet up with Jacob, who'd snuck out, too, to do some night fishing or camping out in sleeping bags on the lakeshore. They were wild boys like that. Never minded the dark or the wilderness. After a while, we stopped minding Clint sneaking away because we always knew where to find him. Right here."

Knox's dad had always professed to hate fishing. Swore he didn't have the patience for it. Yet another facet of his father that he'd never known.

The boathouse was little more than a glorified shack situated at the water's edge. It was large enough to fit a couple of kayaks, along with boating and fishing supplies, but little else. Truth be told, Knox had been considering tearing it down and rebuilding a new one with modern amenities and more weatherproof building materials.

By the light of her cell phone's flashlight app, Granny June led the way around to the back of the boathouse, though their progress was halted by the thick brush surrounding the building. "Move those branches, there," she said, pointing with her cane.

Knox handed his flashlight to Emily and moved to do Granny June's bidding. When he saw what the secret was, his ribs squeezed tight and his breath caught, the discovery was so exhilarating.

On an old, weathered board, beneath the crudely fashioned, burned letters reading *Clubhouse* were the names *Jacob* and *Clint*.

There was no doubt in Knox's mind that his dad's ghost had led him to this property, to this lake, so Knox would find these clues about his dad's childhood. This wasn't about secrets, but about discovery. It was about growing even closer to the father he'd lost too soon.

This time, the emotion fuzzing up his head was love and peace, a renewed closeness to his dad, and an appreciation for his childhood at Briscoe Ranch. His dad hadn't always been so bitter. He'd been a young man, full of energy and a bounding joy for life. Knox would give anything—*anything*—to have an hour with his dad again, to ask him about growing up in Dulcet, about fishing on this very lake, but having his spirit guide him here, to this place in this moment with Granny June and her treasure trove of stories, was the next best thing.

With his finger, he traced the burnt letters of his father's name. As soon as he could, he'd hire landscapers to clear away the brush from around the boathouse, and he'd hire a contractor to renovate the structure, rather than tearing it down. Knox had never put much value in old buildings and sentimental treasures—his job of renovating businesses practically demanded that he didn't—but this discovery changed everything. If Knox had had any doubt about his mission in returning to Briscoe Ranch and restoring his father's legacy, he sure didn't now.

What other treasures about his dad's past did the resort hold? Where else had his dad left his mark for Knox to find?

By the time Knox roused from his thoughts, he realized that Granny June and Emily had relocated to the dock. They stood arm-in-arm in the moonlight, chatting.

"How's the fishing been for you?" Granny June asked when he'd joined them.

Knox cleared his throat. "I never fished much. Or at all. It's on my 'to do' list, though. As soon as I have the chance to give it a whirl."

If either Granny June or Emily thought it odd that his dad hadn't taught him to fish, then they kept it to themselves. "I'm sure Ty would be happy to teach you," Granny June said.

Knox bristled. Ty was the reason Clint had given up fishing, his friends, his life. Knox would no more seek out Ty for advice than he'd ask the Devil. "I think I'll be fine teaching myself."

"Well, when you catch one, I'll cook it up," Emily said. "Deal."

Granny June tucked her cane on her elbow and rubbed her hands together, her eyes twinkling again. "Have you ever seen the view of Briscoe Ranch from the water at night?"

"No," Knox said. "It's good?"

She gestured to the rowboat moored to the dock, the one the previous owners had left behind. "Tonight seems as good a night as any."

As drained as he was, he found it impossible to turn Granny June down. "If that's what you'd like. I haven't been out on the water yet, but I rowed crew in college, so I'm sure we'll manage. As long as the boat doesn't spring a leak," he added with a wink.

Emily took a step back. She gave a little wave. "See you two tomorrow. I've got to get on with the dishes and then get out of here. It's a long drive home."

She'd been quiet and unobtrusive during this walk, as she had throughout the day. He'd thought he'd overshared with her about himself and his dad while in his truck that afternoon, but now that he was considering it, she probably knew more about his family history than he did. She'd been that same quiet observer to the Briscoe family's goings-on for more than a decade.

Her calm presence, and the fact that she wasn't a Briscoe, with that same loaded history, was comforting. He was glad Granny June had insisted she join them on their stroll, but there was no logical reason that his personal chef should take a boat ride with him and his grandmother. The trouble was, he found himself very much wishing she would, and yet he had no earthly idea how to ask her to stay without making it weird.

"Wait just a second, there," Granny June said, looping her arm with Emily's. "I insist you come along. Besides, you're my ride home. Make an old woman happy and take a rowboat ride with us."

"I thought Knox was going to drive you home." Emily blinked, then a thought dawned on her and she looked at Knox. "Oh. Your truck. I forgot, you can't. Yeah, I'll have to be the one to drive her."

Knox could have corrected her—he *should* have corrected her—and told her about him borrowing Shayla's car to get Granny June home. But he didn't.

Emily looked at him pointedly and nodded at the rowboat, as though checking in with him for permission to join them. He faked a nonchalant nod and shrug, as though to say, *Why not. There's no harm in it.*

"All right, then. A boat ride it is," Emily said.

But if there was truly no harm in Emily joining them, then why did it feel dangerous for her to take his hand and step onto the boat with him. Why did it feel as though they were crossing over into uncharted territory?

After helping Emily get seated, he reached a hand back to aid Granny June, but headlights distracted him. A red, compact car bounded up Knox's driveway.

"Whoops," Granny June said. "That's Paco. I've got to go."

What? "I thought Emily was taking you home."

Granny June tapped her temple. "This daffy old mind. I can't keep anything straight these days."

"But . . ." Emily spluttered.

Knox couldn't decide if he should call bullshit or agree with Granny June because her mind did seem to tip onto the daffy side. Before he could speak, Granny June had crouched down with a litheness that belied her age and untied the boat from the dock.

"You two go on ahead and have fun. Don't forget to take pictures of the resort from the lake. They'd look great on my Facebook page. Speaking of which—" She brought forth a smart phone and before either Emily or Knox could do more than open their mouths in protest, she snapped a shot, blinding them with the flash.

Knox was blinking away the bright spots from his vision when the boat rocked. Granny June had shoved them off.

"I'd better not keep Paco waiting. You kids have fun, now."

"But . . ." Emily said again.

But Granny June was already walking at a brisk clip toward the sedan. It might have been Knox's imagination, but she seemed to have a bit of a skip in her step.

Chapter Six

No. No. *No.* Granny June was *not* trying to play match-maker for Emily. And especially not with Knox, of all the men in the world. Granny June knew Emily didn't date. She knew how critical this month was for Emily's career. What the heck was she thinking?

Over the years, Emily had been a gleeful spectator of Granny June's matchmaking antics around the resort and the town of Dulcet. The woman had practically strong-armed Carina and Decker into falling in love, as well as a lot of other Briscoe Ranch employees. Emily had even played assistant matchmaker on occasion, delivering co-vert gifts and acting as wingman for Granny June's plots, but Granny June had never tried to set Emily up with a man before, so Emily had figured she was in the clear.

And yet, here Emily was, duped into a boat ride with her hunky boss. In the moonlight.

Granny June really was a master of subterfuge.

"You don't see it coming when it happens to you," she muttered.

"What?"

Emily shook her head. "Nothing. Never mind." Boy,

would Granny June be in for a disappointment with this misguided attempt. It was totally going to ruin her match-making success rate.

An awkward silence settled over the boat, with both Knox and Emily sitting, frozen as though stunned, as the boat drifted farther from shore.

"We don't have to . . ." Knox's voice trailed off.

"No, definitely not."

With stiff, robot-like movement, Knox took up the oars. Fog swirled over the water and reflected the moon-light, shining bright silver over the fathomless onyx depths of the lake.

Nearby, a fish jumped, landing with a tremendous splash and rocking the boat. Knox seemed to come to life again. His eyes glittered as he scanned the water. "I think that was it."

"A fish?"

He scooted to the edge and looked directly down into the water, frowning. "Not *a* fish. *The* fish."

"A friend of yours?"

"More like a mortal enemy. The son of a bitch that knocked me over when my truck rolled into the lake. It's like some crazy, huge attack fish. And now it's taunting me, jumping out of the water every time I'm near it."

She grinned. That might have been the most prepos-terous thing she'd ever heard, except that she had also seen a huge fish performing acrobatic feats out of the water that week. "An attack fish?"

"Laugh if you want, but it's no joke. That thing was insane. It definitely wanted a piece of me."

Emily felt the muscles in her back relax. She enjoyed Knox's company, especially this side of him that believed in ghosts and sentient fish. Just because they were out on a boat together didn't mean it had to be romantic. Noth-ing wrong with having a bit of platonic fun. "I think your fish enemy needs a name. Hot tip, though. Moby Dick's already taken."

"How 'bout just Dick?"

"Since you're already being haunted by the ghost of your dad, and now you're being shadowed by a fish, how 'bout we call this guy Phantom?"

Knox gave a slow nod. "I like it. Phantom."

"Tell you what. If you catch Phantom someday, I'll cook him for you. Even if it's after the challenge is done and I'm busy with my new restaurant."

He offered her a keen smile, as though they were co-conspirators in a diabolical plot. "Deal." Then his expression turned contemplative. His eyes seemed to take in their surroundings again. They'd drifted far out toward the center of the lake. What a beautiful, peaceful night. There was a nip in the air every time the breeze picked up, but Emily's chef jacket was thick enough to stave off a chill.

As though in preparation to row the boat back to shore, Knox rolled up his sleeves to his elbows, revealing the perfect musculature of his forearms beneath a dusting of dark hair and the same designer watch he'd worn every day so far. Her pulse quickening, Emily thought back to their run-in in his bedroom, to the way he unwound from the day by stripping off the artifice of his business attire. He was halfway there tonight. No tie, shirt open at the collar, sleeves unbuttoned and rolled.

Physical labor suited him.

He'd told her that he went for a run every morning. What did he look like in a cotton T-shirt that clung to his sweaty skin beneath? How would a pair of nylon workout shorts fit his body? What of his legs?

With an audible snort, she gave herself a mental smack. *No, really, Emily. What about your boss's legs? Do tell. The professional ethics police would love to know.*

Unaware of Emily's indecent thoughts, Knox grabbed on to the oar handles and dipped the paddles into the water. Good. He was rowing her back to shore so they could end this awkward, oddly intimate boating excursion. Perched on the bench across from him, she let out a deep exhalation, infinitely relieved.

On his third stroke, Knox's attention shifted from the lake to Emily. "Can I ask you something?"

Small talk was definitely beyond her capabilities at the moment. Then again, if it helped pass the tense minutes until they arrived at the dock, she could handle a question or two.

"You can try, but I'm not sure I have any answers for you. We already agreed I'm not going to give you the dirt on Carina's family, and other than that, there's not much else I know. I'm just a chef."

She hadn't known such a sentiment was inside her heart until she'd said the words. *Just a chef.* It was true, though. She'd carefully constructed her life to be just this one label. She poured everything she was into her work, her chosen art. It was a singular identity that was both comforting and liberating.

Just a chef.

Damn right. Because if she was just Emily Ford, the chef, then she wasn't Rebecca Youngston, teen runaway. She wasn't that victim of abuse. She wasn't a *nothing*, adrift in the world with a fake name and a fake identity, with no family. So instead of all those things she didn't want to be, or couldn't be, she was Emily the chef. And a damn fine chef at that.

"I need you to tell me something honestly. And I don't know who else to ask," Knox said.

"I'm always honest."

He opened his mouth as though to speak, but ended up

grinning at her instead as he stroked the oars through the water. "That you are."

He shifted his focus back to the dark silhouettes of the hills. "I know we agreed that you wouldn't spill the dirt on Carina's family, but there's something I can't—" He stopped speaking, sighed, and then started over. "The fight between my dad and Ty and my grandfather, you had a word for it that first day we met in Ty's office, but I can't remember what it was. What did you call it?"

"The rift. Everybody at the resort who's been here long enough calls it that, Ty and Granny June included."

"The rift," he said slowly, as if weighing each word for import. "Do you know what the fight was about? I mean, really about?"

She didn't owe him answers. Her loyalty was to the Briscoes. But he'd disarmed her with his earnest, almost vulnerable tone. Implicit in the question was the admission that he didn't know the details of the decades-old family tragedy. Which was shocking, really. Hadn't Clint ever told his children why they never saw their grandparents or cousins? Hadn't the truth ever been revealed? Secrets that significant only went to the grave in soap operas and horror stories, or so she'd thought.

"I don't know any details. If I did, I would tell you because you deserve to know. Ty refuses to talk about it and so do Eloise and Granny June. I'm pretty sure Tyson was the same way, though he'd passed before I came to work here. I'm definitely sure no one ever told Carina or Haylie the truth because we've all sat around speculating about it together." She studied the frustrated set of his mouth. "You honestly don't know what happened either? Your dad never told you?"

His expression turned haunted. He broke eye contact with her and put his back into a stroke that sent the boat toward the far shore, the opposite direction of the dock. They were not headed back to shore as Emily had assumed. Knox pulled through another strong stroke and then another, turning them toward the bend in the lake, navigating the curve of the kidney bean-shaped lake.

She might have asked about where they were going, but she dared not interrupt his thoughts before he answered her question. Could it be that his father hadn't told him the reason behind the rift, the same way that Ty hadn't told his children? Would it be a secret that Ty and Granny June would take to their graves the way Clint and Tyson had? That was, if Granny June knew. In all the mentions of the rift that Emily had heard, never once was Granny June mentioned. Knowing her as well as Emily did, Emily seriously doubted Granny June supported Clint's exile.

But then why, all these years after Tyson's death, hadn't Granny June invited Clint and his family back into the fold?

"I do know the reasons," Knox said. "I mean, I thought I did. I thought it was about control of the resort's vision and who my grandfather's successor would be. But Granny June and Ty have said some things that don't jive with what my dad told me."

Knox's paddling took on a distracted quality, a rote movement to keep his body busy while his mind worked out the problem. Every stroke brought with it the sound of tinkling water and a fresh swirl of perfumed air, herbal and earthy. Emily watched her breath make a little cloud with each exhalation.

Emily made a point of relaxing back onto the bench and tipping her head to the side, inviting him to open up. "Like what kinds of things have Ty and Granny June said?"

At the question, Knox's even paddle strokes faltered. He shook his head. "Just . . . I don't know. They made it sound like it was about more than the business, but I can't imagine what else there could be that would be worth severing family ties like that."

Emily knew firsthand about the kinds of things that could make a person sever ties with their family, but none of them applied to the Briscoes. Other than the rift and Haylie's poor choice in husband, the family was stable and normal . . . boring, even.

She fixed her eyes on Knox, studying, learning. "What's your mom like?" she asked.

"My mom?"

"Yes. Does she still live in Hutchins, where you grew up?"

He seemed surprised that she knew that.

"I do my research," she added quietly.

"Yeah, she still lives in the Hutchins house, even though it's way too big for her needs now."

"Alone, or does she have someone new in her life?" Research had provided the answer to that question, but she wasn't asking because she wanted to know more about Knox's mother. She fixed her eyes on Knox, studying, learning.

His eyes lightened at the question. "Sometimes I wonder if she's seeing anyone, a nice man from church or the neighborhood. I hope she's out having fun, for her sake. She would never admit it to me and my siblings, though. I think, out of a misguided notion of respect for us kids' memory of my dad."

"Your father's been gone three years. That's a lifetime to some. But your dad's still very much on your mind, especially now that you're working at Briscoe Ranch."

"That's true. He is on my mind a lot. In a good way. Sometimes that three years feels like a lifetime, and others, it feels like yesterday. It's a hell of a thing, losing the person you loved and idolized most in this world."

"It doesn't sound like he's lost. It sounds to me like he's still watching over you."

Knox rolled his eyes heavenward, a wistful smile playing on his lips. "That's a very good point."

Emily couldn't tear her eyes from Knox and the fascinating play of emotions on his features. It was as though being on the water had completely disarmed him.

Seemingly unaware of Emily's focused gaze, Knox once again fixed his attention on the business of rowing. Not long after that, he skimmed an oar in the water, turning the boat. He nodded toward the shore. "Oh, wow. Look."

Emily had been so focused on their conversation that she was surprised to see that their little boat had rounded the bend in the lake. Briscoe Ranch in all its glory sat before them, rising up from the lakefront golf course like a castle on a hill. Lights blazed from the balconies and rooftops. The unlit golf course sloped down to the lake's edge. She followed the snaking trail of lights demarcating the pathways through the golf course and meandering to the main building. And there was the stable, its main arena lit with floodlights. She stared for a long time at the chapel on the hill behind the resort, the beating heart of the Briscoes' empire.

She often fought against complacency about her good fortune to wind up in such a beautiful, safe place as Briscoe Ranch. She fought not to take the fresh air and the sense of community for granted. It was stunning, all the many ways being homeless had scarred her, even now, after years of comfortable living and regular meals and career success.

Over the years, she'd gradually learned to trust that such luxuries would last, and that she didn't need to be so hyper-vigilant about her safety. She caught herself opting not to bask in every single sunset or smell every rose she encountered, secure in the knowledge that there would be another beautiful sunset the next day, more roses, more beauty.

Knox's plans for the resort jarred her from her security like nothing else had since the day she'd left home as a sixteen-year-old. She simply could not fathom a life away from Briscoe Ranch. He'd been correct that she'd missed chances by not apprenticing for accomplished chefs. But the peace of mind that life at Briscoe Ranch had brought her had superseded her need for prestige.

"It's so beautiful." The hitch in her voice surprised her. What a surreal, emotionally charged night this had become for both of them.

"It will be even better when I'm done with it." His words were loaded with ambition and confidence. In that moment, she believed him absolutely.

She pointed to the east side of the main resort building. "The restaurant I'm proposing would look out over the golf course and the lake."

It felt weirdly inappropriate to discuss business while immersed in the hushed majesty of the lake and the night, with the grand view of the resort before them. Granny June definitely wouldn't approve.

"I know. You want to put it on the southeast end of the main building, in the basement where housekeeping is right now. We would need to excavate around the basement to create the sunken patio you envision to create a subterranean feel. That's right under my office, so it'd have that same world-class view."

"You really did read my restaurant proposal thoroughly."

"It's been a little crazy these past couple days, but

yeah, I did read it. I told you I was going to give you an honest chance, Emily. I'm a man of my word."

She pulled her focus away from the resort to offer Knox a smile of gratitude but found him watching her with an earnestness that made her breath catch. As they held each other's gaze, the oddest sensation washed over her, as though her spirit, her very cells, were shifting toward him, reaching out, yearning for connection.

A puff of breeze brought with it the fragrance of the night once more. Their little boat rocked ever so gently in the calm water. Somewhere near the shore came the lone call of a duck. How would this strange and wondrous night translate into a meal? What flavors could encapsulate the scents and sounds of the lake at night? What textures and tastes could capture the complexities of the way she felt alone with Knox under the moonlight?

Culinary inspiration hit like an electric current zipping along her veins and over her skin, and with such force that she nearly levitated off the bench. Ingredients for a bourbon-glazed jambonette of duck tumbled through her mind with haphazard purpose. "Oh! That's it!"

"What's wrong? Did a bug get you?"

"I have to write something down about tomorrow's dinner. Give me a minute."

The spike of adrenaline turned her blood hot. She peeled out of her chef's jacket and draped it over the bench on which she sat. The white tank top she wore beneath it was damp with perspiration that turned downright cold in the night air. Goosebumps broke out on her arms as she took out her cell phone.

She felt his eyes on her as she typed away on the memo app of her phone, getting all her good ideas out of her mind before she forgot them. She barely noticed a splash of water hitting her arm, but she definitely noticed Knox's shouted curse and the slap of a large, slimy tail against her leg.

A massive fish had landed in the boat and was flopping around at her feet.

With a shriek, she dropped her phone and scrambled to her feet. She and Knox lunged at the panicked, flopping fish at the same time. The rowboat rocked precariously. Emily had to let go of the fish and pinwheel her arms so she didn't fall overboard, unlike the fish, who wriggled and flopped itself over the edge and into the water with a splash. It took Emily a moment to register Knox's hand on her hip, steadying her.

"Holy shit, that was crazy," Knox said through a laugh. "I think that was Phantom. I saw the same scar on its back."

Emily sank to the bench. "You were right. He really is an attack fish. It's too bad we couldn't keep it in the boat. I would've changed tomorrow night's dinner plans to fish."

Knox chuckled again, shaking his head. He draped a friendly arm around Emily's shoulder and gave it a squeeze. "I'm just glad you didn't fall overboard."

Too late, Emily noticed herself leaning into his touch, craving the contact. She'd long ago suppressed the need for another's touch, so much so that her unexpected appetite for it felt like an alien invader inside her trying to take over her mind and body. To yearn for the feel of her bare skin coming into contact with someone else's, with another's hands, with his mouth.

Just for a moment, just to satisfy the craving, she rested her cheek on his shoulder and nuzzled her face into his arm. She brought her hand up and splayed it over his chest. Goddamn, it felt good to be held. The only sounds she heard were the lapping of water against the boat, Knox's labored breathing, and the pounding of her pulse, so loud she wondered if Knox could hear it, too.

Knox's hand slipped from her shoulder to her waist. He held her close and released a stuttering breath that fanned over her neck. Chills wracked her body, and not only from the cold air on her damp skin. She allowed herself one last, long moment of touch. So inappropriate. So necessary. *How have I lived without this for so long?*

Stifling a groan, she pulled away and found her chef jacket on the floor of the boat. It was drenched with water and smudged with fish slime and dirt from their shoes.

"Is your jacket ruined?" Knox asked in a wooden voice, completely devoid of emotion.

"Looks like it. That's okay." She could only hope he wouldn't make a big deal out of that hug. Maybe they could both agree to forget it had happened.

She sat on the bench and wrapped her arms around herself, staving off the cold.

Knox took hold of the oars. "I'd better get you back before you freeze to death."

He turned the boat around. Within minutes, Briscoe Ranch disappeared again from view. This side of the lake seemed darker, now that their eyes had adjusted to the glow from the resort's lights. In the silence, there was nothing to do but consider what had just happened, and the raw, primitive need Knox had stirred to life within her with his touch. It hadn't been enough. If anything, she felt the craving for touch, for connection with a man building force within her.

She wanted nothing more than to put this new awakening back in its jar, close the lid tight, and toss it into a deep cave. She didn't want lust or men or physical need complicating her life. She was too busy for that, damn it all. The trouble was, she had a feeling that would be impossible. She couldn't ignore it any longer—and she wasn't sure she wanted to. She had a feeling she'd just learned the hard way that some things just wouldn't stay buried forever.

Chapter Seven

Thank goodness Knox was a master at compartmentalization. It was the only thing getting him through nightly dinners alone with Emily after that surreal boat ride earlier in the week. He still couldn't believe he'd embraced her like that. What the hell had gotten into him? He'd probably never know because he refused to think any more about it. From the moment she'd left his house that night, he'd vowed to redouble his efforts to walk the straight and narrow line as Knox Briscoe, successful businessman, and not Knox Briscoe, the emotionally unstable fool who went around getting teary-eyed with his grandmother over old memories and taking his personal chef for moonlit boat rides to name the fish in his lake.

Today, Friday, he had enough on his plate to distract him from any errant thoughts of Emily, what with Ty's mentorly advice and overeager attempts to bond, then a team of structural engineers scheduled to arrive that afternoon to determine the efficacy of the resort expansion plans and the structural integrity of the existing buildings.

Of course, Knox already knew the existing resort

buildings were foundationally unsound. A building in-
spector buddy of his had accompanied him to the county
records office, where they'd pored over the archived blue
prints, appraisals, and permits of the resort. After only
a few hours of looking, one thing became glaringly clear:
there was no way the original hotel that Tyson Briscoe
had built in the 1950s with his own two hands was up to
code, despite clear evidence that County Fire Marshal
Micah Garrity had taken Ty to task on various other building code violations over and over again throughout the
years. There were just some aspects of the Texas building
code that even the most vigilant fire marshal couldn't
determine, especially given the evidence Knox and his
buddy had uncovered that Tyson Briscoe—and then
Ty—had systematically paid off county building inspectors and structural engineers to feed the fire marshals
and county officials falsified data on the original building's hydrological and geological stability.

In other words, one of these years, after a particularly
rainy season, Briscoe Ranch Resort's foundation would
likely fail, sending it on a downhill creep toward the lake.
The resort guests weren't in any kind of immediate danger, but the overall valuation of the property was grossly
inflated. The resort was worth a fraction of what it was
valued at on paper. And even less when one considered
the slew of loans and refinancing funds Ty had taken out
over the years based on the inflated value.

So today was a very big day. Because the sooner the
building inspectors and structural engineers told Knox
what he already knew, the sooner Knox could have the
business's worth reevaluated and the sooner he could buy
his equity firm's investors' shares at a bargain-basement
price, making him the controlling partner, with Ty as his
subordinate.

Knox had always prided himself on his professional

ethics. He'd built his career on it, in fact, having decided during the first business ethics class he'd taken in college that he'd never stoop to being a shady businessman who took advantage of others—unlike his grandfather, Tyson, or his Uncle Ty. Everything Knox earned in this life, he'd wanted to earn by the rules, fair and square. No cutting corners, no backroom deals, no bribes or manipulations.

He still believed that, and still strove tirelessly to live by that creed—except that Briscoe Ranch wasn't just any business, and Knox's agreement to invest in the company wasn't just any deal. It was about justice for his father. And to accomplish that, he needed to beat Ty Briscoe at his own game.

With Shayla on speakerphone, calling from his house, working from her laptop, the two of them were in the process of reviewing the resort's previous year's profit and loss statements when Knox's office door opened. The scent of cinnamon and baked sugar had him tearing his gaze away from the computer screen to watch Emily enter the room pushing a stainless steel rolling tray that was laden down with a place setting, a carafe of orange juice, and a silver-lidded plate.

The room seemed to hum to life with her energy, jolting Knox's system awake.

"Hope you're ready for an apple pancake with mascarpone filling and maple sage sausage," Emily said as she positioned the cart in front of his desk, her eyes averted as though she was avoiding him. She'd rarely looked him in the eye since that boat ride, in fact. But maybe he was reading too much into that. Maybe she was just busy. And maybe she was just as skilled at compartmentalization as he was.

Over the phone, Shayla gasped. "Did someone bring you breakfast? Is that—"

Knox snatched his phone up and took the call off

speaker. "Yep, looks like breakfast." He offered Emily an awkward smile. She didn't return it; she was so busy bustling around the tray table.

"Your new girlfriend brought you breakfast," Shayla said in a singsong voice.

"Stop with that," he muttered.

"How late does she stay at your house after dinner? Does she linger over dessert? Or does she leave at all?"

"You're being ridiculous." To Emily, he added, "Not you. Though I am sorry you wasted your time again this morning. Like I tell you every morning, I don't eat breakfast."

"And as I told you yesterday and the day before and the day before that, I have the right to keep trying."

"Ambitious," Shayla mused.

His eyes tracked Emily as she plated a slice of thick, fluffy pastry oozing with baked apples. *Yes, she is.*

Shayla made a clicking noise, the same sound of disapproval their mom had made when they got in trouble as children.

"What does that mean?" Knox asked, though he regretted it immediately. He really didn't want to open himself up to any more of Shayla's teasing.

"I should be asking the same to you," Shayla said.

What he should have said was *I'll call you back later*, but what came out of his mouth was, "What the hell are you talking about?"

Emily walked to the back of the desk and unceremoniously stacked his paperwork off to the side in preparation to lay out a linen placemat. He waved her away. "I don't want breakfast. I swear."

"You have to eat in the morning," Emily said. "I know you get up early and work out. Even if you only think of food as fuel, you still need that fuel. And don't tell me you had a protein shake."

Too bad for her, that was the God's honest answer. "I had a protein shake."

Emily planted her fists on her hips and glared at him. "You and I have a deal. At the very least, you need to give me the chance to entice you."

In his ear, Shayla made that clicking sound again.

A deep pink color rose on Emily's cheeks. "To eat breakfast," she added with an exaggerated tone. With a shake of her head and a roll of her eyes, she unceremoniously set a plate piled high with sliced, cooked apples floating in a cinnamon sauce amid layers of dough and thick, oozing cream, and bracketed by a pair of succulent-looking sausages. With a mumbled excuse, she turned on her heel and marched with the tray from the room, closing the door behind her.

The apple pancake looked as decadent as it smelled. It also looked like the kind of meal he'd have to run a half-marathon after, to work off all the calories. He turned his attention back to Shayla.

"Okay, she's gone now. So what's with the clicking? What are you getting at?" he asked.

"What I'm getting at is that I saw the way you two watched each other the other night. And then she freakin' went on an evening stroll with you and Granny June. And she's at your house every night, just the two of you."

Guess he wouldn't mention that boat ride. "So?"

"So, you can't have it both ways," Shayla said. "You can't dangle this job opportunity over her head while you're also angling to sleep with her. It's one or the other, bro. That's called ethics."

Sleep with her? That was jumping to an awfully absurd conclusion. "I'm not planning to sleep with her. Or anyone at the resort, for that matter. The situation at the resort is complicated enough already. What I'm doing, apparently, is working Emily to death. God only knows how early she had to get up to make me this pancake breakfast. When she and I agreed to this arrangement, I challenged her to prove herself as a chef. So that's what she's doing. I've never seen such a hard worker. I admire her a lot. And that's the end of the story."

"She's seducing you."

Not even close. He was the one who'd crossed the ethical line. "She's not that kind of person, Shay."

"Everybody is that kind of person when they want something bad enough."

For a happy-go-lucky person, Shayla sure could get cynical. Though she had a point. With a pang of unease, Knox thought about the compromises to his professional integrity he was justifying to himself in the name of vengeance.

"You'll just have to trust me about Emily," he said.

Shayla made that clicking sound again. "I know you're a big believer in professional ethics, which is why you can't see it in other people. But trust me on this. She's ambitious and she'll do whatever it takes to get the restaurant. That line about enticing you may have been a Freudian slip, but I bet she did it on purpose. Part of her grand seduction plan."

"You've met Emily. Name one thing about her that's seductive?"

In answer to his own prompt, a hundred images of Emily raced through his mind. The flush of her skin when he'd caught her in his bedroom, the way her tank top had clung to her body in the rowboat, the way she bent over his arm every time she presented him with a plate of food, her unruly hair defying the bindings she tried to trap it in. The spark in her eye when she rattled off the ingredients of the dish she'd created. Everything she did was passion, perfection, and confidence. It was beautiful. It was everything.

He ignored the intense coil of lust tightening inside him, the same maddening sensation he was constantly battling to ignore every time he was in her presence. What an entitled jerk he was for even thinking bawdy thoughts about his employee. "Nothing about her, that's what."

"Oh, come on," Shayla said. "Doesn't she ever take off that bandanna and toss her hair around, all *Sports Illustrated* swimsuit model-like?"

If Emily were to do that, he'd never endure it with his professional integrity intact. "Stop. I've got a busy day. I'll talk to you later."

With his fork, he skimmed a bit of whipped cream off the top of the pancake and tasted it. There was no way he'd keep his resolve not to eat it as long as it was sitting in front of him. He buzzed Haylie. "Could you come on in?"

A moment later, she opened his door wearing a guarded expression. Maybe he'd interrupted her work with the typing app.

He pushed the plate in her direction. "Emily brought me breakfast, but I'm not going to eat this. I mean, it looks great, but I'm not hungry. Would you like it?

Haylie looked at him like he'd lost his mind. "Are you crazy? Emily brought me pancakes, too, and I'm telling you, they're OMG good. Rule number one is to always eat whatever Emily puts in front of you. She's the best cook ever." She paused, that guarded look returning to her face. "Even if nothing about her is seductive, her cooking sure is."

Whoa, shit. "You heard me on the phone."

"It's an old building. The walls are thin."

A knot formed in his throat. "Emily . . . did she . . ."

Haylie tucked her hair behind both ears. "No. She was in a hurry to get back to her kitchen, and it's a good thing she was because I think that would have sucked for her to hear you say that about her."

It would have been a disaster, and not just because his words had been unflattering, but because Emily deserved so much better than a skeevy boss who commented on her physical attractiveness in any way.

Haylie might not be very efficient or computer savvy, but as he always said, someone who'd give you their honest opinion, even when it was uncomfortable, was worth their weight in gold. "It's the mark of a good secretary, and a good friend, that you'd risk such an awkward conversation with your new boss to look out for Emily. And me, too. Thank you."

She preened a little at that.

"Hey, after you finish eating the breakfast Emily brought you," he said, "how would you feel about taking me on a tour of your favorite places around the resort, give me the low-down and catch me up on the gossip? I've got a little time this morning, and I'd like to take one last look around to orient myself before the structural engineers arrive."

"Oh, I already finished. It was too good to eat slow," she said with a wave of her French-tipped nails. "And I'd love to show you around. Nobody knows this place better than I do. I mean, except Carina and my mom and dad, and Granny June."

He had to smile at her, she was disarmingly genuine in a way he never would have guessed from the way she presented herself. That would teach him to judge someone before he'd gotten to know him or her.

A shadow filled the door behind Haylie. "Morning, darlin'," Ty said to Haylie. "Better stop that yapping and let the men work." He accompanied the quip with a wink to Knox, as though to say, *These frivolous women, am I right?*

The whole mentor/protégé dynamic was wearing thin

on Knox, as were the occasional sexist barbs Ty lobbed at Haylie whenever the mood struck him. He and Ty had only worked together for a week, but it had gotten to the point where all Ty had to do was open that big mouth of his, and Knox's teeth were instantly on edge.

Knox walked to his coat hanger. He shrugged into his suit jacket, then settled his Stetson on his head. "Something I can do for you, Ty?"

Ty moseyed up to Knox's desk and peered down at the apple pancake.

"Breakfast from Emily. You're welcome to it. I'm not hungry," Knox said.

To Knox's surprise, Ty took him up on the offer, picking up the fork and digging in. "I take it from your lack of interest in her cooking that things aren't going well with Emily?"

On the contrary, they *were* going well. A little too well for Knox's own good. "She's terrific. Talented, like you told me she was. But breakfast isn't my thing. No big deal."

Busy chowing down, Ty grunted in response. Little bits of cinnamon apple clung to his goatee. Knox decided he'd better get out of there before he let his disgust show on his face. "All right, Haylie. Let's get going."

Knox was halfway out the door when Ty asked, "Where are you two off to and can it wait? I thought we'd sit down today and go over the calendar for the rest of the year, make sure we're on the same page."

"Sounds good for another day. I've gotta check something out before this afternoon's building inspection."

The fork dropped onto the plate with a clatter. Ty's eyes narrowed. "What building inspection?"

Gotcha, you lying criminal. "With my team of structural engineers. The first step in our expansion plans."

If anything, Ty's eyes narrowed even more, so Knox added, "I must have forgotten to mention it. Guess you're right about needing to sync up our calendars."

Knox gave a little farewell salute, then brushed past Haylie's desk en route to the lobby, a man on a mission to get out of the office before Ty got on his nerves even more.

"Bye, Daddy," Haylie said, hustling to keep up with Knox.

As soon as they were standing on the far side of the Spanish-style tile fountain that dominated the center of the lobby, Knox slowed his pace for her.

"What do you want to see first?" Haylie asked.

"I thought we might start inside and work our way out and around the grounds."

"That's what I was thinking, too. We'll start at the spa on the basement level. And it's Monday, too, so my mom's probably there."

Oh, good. He'd finally get to meet the elusive Eloise Briscoe.

They headed to the grand staircase that curved from the basement through the ground floor and up to the second level. When they reached the basement, Haylie steered Knox right, through an *Employees Only* door and into a poorly lit hallway. "First, let me show you where all of Emily's magic happens. The catering kitchen."

Looked like he'd escaped the minefield of his office and was led right into another one. Given the disparate but equally unnerving feelings Emily and Ty stirred up in Knox, and their uncanny abilities to pop into his day at will, he was beginning to wonder if there were anywhere on the resort grounds that he could have a moment of peace. As Haylie pushed open the second door on the left, Knox girded himself for the sight of Emily.

The door opened into a sprawling, stainless steel

kitchen that was empty of people, but cluttered with used pots, pans, and ingredients amid a mouthwatering aroma that reminded him of the sausage Emily had served him that morning.

"This is the catering kitchen. We use it for special events, weddings, and things like that. It usually doesn't get busy with workers until closer to noon because most of the special events are in the evening. Emily's in charge of it all, and you can see her office right through that glass window on the far side."

Emily wasn't in her office, either, Knox noted with relief—as well as an unwanted shot of disappointment. He moved through the kitchen to study her office more closely. It was a bright space, or, as bright as it could be given that it was windowless. She'd painted the walls a cheery pale yellow and covered one of them with bookshelves. Most of the tomes looked to be cookbooks and other reference guides. Her desk was a massive, espresso-stained wood piece, tidier than he would've guessed, given her passionate nature and the current state of her kitchen.

"If you ever need Emily and she doesn't answer her phone, which she, like, never does because she can hardly ever remember to charge it, this is where you'll find her." Haylie pointed to a baby blue sofa along the near wall of the office that Knox hadn't noticed yet. "She sleeps here most nights, too, because she works such funky hours and lives far away."

"Huh." Did she crash on this sofa rather than make the trip home when she left his house every evening? She'd referenced her long drive home once, on the night Granny June joined them for dinner, but that was the only time he could recall her mentioning a home, and even then, he couldn't quite remember the circumstances surrounding that conversation, he'd been so overwhelmed with emotions that night.

He made a mental note to look up where Emily lived, then immediately rejected the idea. Overstepping an employee's boundaries was not a flattering attribute. If he wanted to know so badly, he'd have to ask her.

Haylie tugged on his arm. "Moving on. I want you to meet my mom, if she's at the spa."

"How do you know she's there?" Knox asked as Haylie led him down one hallway and then another in a seemingly endless maze of them.

"It's Monday, and that's the day she gets her hair done."

"Every Monday?"

Haylie pushed through a door marked *public* and they re-entered the guests' public space right in front of the spa entrance, comprised of a lovely atrium with a small fountain and some tasteful, low-light plants. "Why not every Monday? Hair on Monday, nails on Friday, massages or facials whenever. Keeping up her appearance is, like, her hobby. She's always been into fashion, even more than me."

And therefore, apparently, she availed herself of the resort's spa whenever she pleased. Haylie probably did, too. Knox was willing to bet the resort comped all the Briscoe women on their beauty treatments. That might have made sense when their family was a majority shareholder, except for the fact that the resort had been nearly bankrupt when Knox signed on. An occasional haircut was one thing, but unlimited use of the spa's facilities and its employees' time was quite another.

"Did you know Mama was crowned the Queen of Ravel County three years in a row?"

"I think I read that somewhere." Actually, he'd read that and more. After his first morning working at the resort, when the mention of Eloise's name and her absence from his warm welcome had dropped a blanket of tension over the room, he'd looked her up online.

Back in the day, Eloise Clark, as was her maiden name, had been a classic beauty. Flowing blonde hair, perfect bone structure, thin, and tall. After her run of local pageants, she'd set out for Dallas, where she'd won a single pageant before marrying Ty and reinventing herself as a housewife. In many photographs, even those from her high school days, Ty appeared alongside her. From the shot of them as prom king and queen as high school seniors to their wedding photo that had made the Home and Lifestyle section of the *San Antonio Sentinel*, the two seemed inseparable.

Haylie breezed past the receptionist, all the while spouting factoids about the spa and the various cutting-edge treatments it offered.

After a right turn at a wall of spa pedicure chairs, they arrived at a brightly lit hairstyling space. Only two customers were being fussed over at the moment, both draped in hot pink leopard print capes. Haylie walked up to the one with the long hair cascading down her back in shades of gold and white blonde.

"Hi, Mom."

Eloise's face brightened at the sight of her daughter through the mirror. Two slender arms appeared from beneath the cape and clasped together. Nearly every finger was dripping with jeweled rings. "Darling! What a nice surprise."

The hairstylist pivoted the salon chair so Eloise could face her guests. She did a double take when she saw Knox. Beneath her tan, her face paled. And then she sneered at him. An actual, ugly sneer that had Knox wondering what he'd ever done to piss her off or if this wasn't about him, but his dad. Had she hated Knox's dad? They'd all been schoolmates together. Was this about the rift? Knox's gut was telling him it was.

"Tracy, I need a martini," Eloise said. "Would you be a sweetheart and call the order up to the bar?"

"Mom, don't be so distracted. Come meet Knox. He's family. Plus, he gave me a job as his secretary, remember?"

She kept her focus on Haylie as she rose from her chair. "I do. But listen, honey, I'm late for my next treatment. When you're on your lunch break, maybe we could meet in the bar and catch up."

Knox decided to test Eloise's resolve in ignoring him. He stepped forward, almost getting in her personal space, his arm extended for a handshake. "So great to meet you, Aunt Eloise." Extra emphasis on the *aunt*.

She afforded his offered hand only the slightest glance before turning away from him. "Likewise," she tossed over her shoulder in an exaggerated Texas drawl as she strutted down the hall into the recesses of the spa.

"Your mom doesn't like me. Any idea why?" Knox said, curious about Haylie's take on the situation.

"Of course, she likes you. You're family. It's just that when she gets a couple martinis in her early, she's not herself." If her mom's before-noon martini swilling bothered Haylie, she did an ace job of hiding it. "Now, come on. I have so much more to show you on the tour. Next up, my favorite secret place to eat lunch. Our amphitheater."

As opposed to the spa or the catering kitchen, the shady, inviting amphitheater that was nestled against the southwest corner of the main resort building was humming with activity in preparation for a one-hundred-guest wedding that night, according to the resort's in-house wedding planner, whom they found on the amphitheater stage. She looked to be in her late twenties or early thirties and clearly knew how to command an amphitheater full of resort workers and wedding vendors. Knox approved of her immediately.

"Remedy Lane," she said, extending her hand.

"It's great to meet you, Remedy," Knox said, shaking her hand. "You've got yourself quite an operation here."

Remedy stood tall, pride and competence shining in her eyes. "We get the job done."

"I'll say. I'm discovering that weddings around here are a very big deal," Knox said.

Haylie leaned in towards him. "They're our cash cow."

Knox's analysis of the company's books had proven that to be true. The weddings at Briscoe Ranch had been the only thing keeping the place afloat. "How far out are you booking?"

Remedy nodded her agreement. "We're on target to break the resort record for number of weddings held here this year. Next year, as well."

"You already have projections for next year? That's good," Knox said.

"We're already booked solid for next year," came Remedy's reply.

God, the untapped potential of this place. If he could retain the charm, he could quadruple the profits in half the time proposed to the private equity investors. "What do you think it is about Briscoe Ranch that makes it such a popular destination?"

Remedy's attention was momentarily snagged by two workers who were stringing white lights across the top of the theater. She called out a directive to them.

"Magic," Haylie said to Knox, grinning broadly.

Remedy tore her focus from the workers. "Haylie's right. There's something magical about this place that makes people fall in love and stay in love forever. Especially if they get married at the resort during December."

How could there be magic in a place so full of dark

family history? He looked from Haylie to Remedy. "You're both serious?"

"I know what that sounds like. Crazy, huh?" Remedy said. "I was a skeptic at first, but now I'm the biggest believer in the magic of Briscoe Ranch. I'm getting married here in December."

"To Dulcet's most eligible bachelor, if I do say so myself," Haylie added. "Just like my Wendell was before we fell in love. And my sister met Decker here. And my parents met here, and my grandparents. Well, our grandparents, I guess. It's been a family tradition since Granny June and Tyson's wedding almost sixty years ago. Did your parents meet here?"

Knox searched his memory but drew a blank. "I don't think I know the answer to that. They got married here, though. But in November, not December like the family tradition." Which was just as well. There was nothing particularly magical about his parents' utilitarian marriage, and neither of them had ever pretended there was, so it wasn't as though they sat around basking in their romantic days of yore.

They loved each other in their own ways, and even though they'd bickered a fair amount, his dad had always waved it off by telling Knox and his siblings that they were just two very different people trying to make it work, just like all people who married. Neither had liked to talk about their wedding, and the only memento of the occasion they'd kept was a framed photograph tucked on a bookshelf in the family room. In the photo, the two of them were standing together after the ceremony at the altar, dressed in their Sunday best and looking as solemn as dust bowl farmers.

After Remedy Lane had excused herself to get back to the wedding prep, Haylie turned to Knox. "I was thinking we'd swing through housekeeping headquarters so you could meet the Martinez ladies, Yessica and her daughter Skye. Their family has been working for the resort for more than thirty years, so they're practically family. And then I thought we'd head to the golf course to say hi to Wendell."

Everywhere Knox went inside the resort and out on the grounds, he ran into members of the Briscoe tribe, as he was starting to think of the collection of Briscoes and people who'd worked at the resort for decades and were now more honorary family than employees. The property was starting to feel like a family commune as much as a tourist destination. "Everywhere we turn, we see someone you know. Is it always like this at Briscoe Ranch?"

Haylie beamed at him. "You bet. That was the fun of growing up here. It's like one big happy family." Her face fell. "No offense, I mean."

There it was again, the acrid taste of resentment creeping into his mouth. Briscoe Ranch Resort—one big happy family, except for the black sheep and his brood who would have starved in the streets, for all the rest of the Briscoe family cared. He fought against a scowl. "It's not your fault."

The opening notes of a horn honking *La Cucaracha* echoed through the amphitheater, followed by the hollered words, "Blessed serendipity!" in a now-familiar voice. Of its own volition, a smile spread on Knox's face at the sight of Granny June, sitting on her motorized scooter at the top of the amphitheater as though she was a queen and it was her throne.

"Hey, there, Granny June!" Haylie called back. She and Knox started up the amphitheater stairs in her direction.

"Didn't expect to see you two out of the office," Granny said. "I was just comin' to see if Remedy needed any decorating advice."

She said it as a jest, but Knox had to wonder if there weren't a grain of truth in it. Poor Remedy.

"We're on a tour," Haylie said. "I'm showing him all the good spots. But you've got great timing because we have a question. Did Knox's parents meet at the resort? He can't remember."

As Haylie finished asking the question, Granny June had pulled her smartphone from her pocket and started scrolling. She didn't look up or acknowledge Haylie's question, so Haylie touched her shoulder and repeated it louder, as though Granny June were hard of hearing. Which Knox was fairly certain she wasn't.

Granny swallowed hard. She tore her attention from the phone, but wouldn't meet anyone's eyes. For the woman who'd spent an evening availing Knox of story after story of Briscoe family history, she sure seemed uncomfortable. "They did. Yes. Your mama used to come around the resort to see my boys. Lots of local girls did."

His mom's oft-spoken refrain echoed through his mind, *Those Briscoe boys are charmers, always were.*

Haylie clapped, seemingly oblivious to Granny June's discomfort with the line of questioning. "Then the Briscoe magic continues! Tell us everything about Clint and Linda's romance. I'm sure Knox wants to know, too." She gently pushed Granny June's phone down and presented her with a well-practiced pout. "Don't make him wait and ask his mom."

"There's not much else to say. Linda was a grade lower than Clint. They went steady for more than a year before getting married in October of her senior year."

Haylie's eyes went wide. "When she was still in high school?"

Granny June stuck her nose in her phone again and scrolled through Facebook like her life depended on it. "It was a different era."

Knox was against causing Granny June any more anguish by questioning her further, but the need for the truth compelled him onward. "I thought they got married in November."

For a split second, Granny June seemed genuinely confused and panicked about it. After a series of rapid eye blinks, she seemed to regain her senses. "That must be it. Did I ever tell you that my memory's going? Maybe I did tell ya, and I can't remember. See what I mean?" She chuckled at her own joke and tapped her temple.

Knox gave her an indulgent smile. "I think that's enough of a walk down Memory Lane. Would you like to join us on the rest of our tour?"

Granny June sat back down in her motorized scooter and held the handles like she was getting ready to rev the engine, motorcycle style. "I'd be delighted. In fact, some folks around here consider me the ultimate tour guide. Did you know we've got the largest stable of horses south of Forth Worth?"

Emily was four hours into a whirlwind of a morning in her kitchen at the resort. New ideas for menus and meals for Knox were popping into her head so fast, she hardly had time to make note of them. She couldn't remember the last time she'd been so inspired. The more she learned about Knox, the deeper into his mind she delved, the more brilliant her creativity became. And the bonus was that the busier in the kitchen she kept, the less she thought about him or the bevy of inappropriate feelings he'd reawakened in her.

The trouble was, every time she slowed down or closed her eyes, she saw him watching her from across the boat with dark, heated eyes. She felt his hand on her hip, holding her close. She felt the erratic beat of his heart beneath her palm. Compounding that, she genuinely liked being around him, which was perhaps the most dangerously sexy thing about him of all.

But instead of wasting her brain space obsessing over what could never be with someone as off-limits as her boss, she would have to train herself to admire his many attributes in the same way one might crush on a celebrity or a cute delivery guy—from a distance and in small doses. Until she'd retrained herself, the logical solution was to not slow down or close her eyes. Easy as pie.

Or, better yet, maybe she needed to do all of that plus start dating again. It'd been more than two years since a string of dates from hell had helped her decide once and for all that there were no men in Texas worth the time away from her career, her friends, and her peace of mind. She'd not only sworn off men, but makeup, expensive haircuts, pedicures, and shaving her legs more than once every couple of weeks. She was still on the pill, but only because it kept her periods short, pain-free, and predictable. The choice to do away with all the frivolity of dating had been a liberating decision, to say the least. Or, at least, it had felt empowering right up until her new boss arrived, with the hard-bodied, polished virility of an NFL quarterback, to remind her that, at her core, she was still a woman with needs.

But maybe if she kept the ground rules simple—nothing serious; just someone she was only mildly attracted to, someone she wouldn't be tempted to invest her heart in—it wouldn't take up too much of her time or energy. All she needed was a casual hook-up. Or two or three. She could get the physical connection she needed without the emotional or professional baggage. Between that and her work, she wouldn't have time to sleep, much less slow down enough to think inappropriate, lusty thoughts about her boss.

Her embarrassing *entice you* comment to Knox that morning while serving breakfast had only made her more restless to get started on the solution to her dilemma. And what better way to start than consulting her best friend? Both of their dating skills were pretty rusty, but perhaps Carina was in the know about what the latest, greatest dating website or app was. Humming gaily, and with an admittedly almost manic skip in her step, she set off over the resort grounds.

She found Carina in the third place she looked, sitting in the bottom row of bleachers adjacent to the equestrian arena, watching Decker exercise a large horse the color of milk chocolate mousse.

When Carina saw her, her face lit up with a broad smile and she strummed her fingers absentmindedly on her massive belly. "Hey, you got my text."

Er, nope. "I don't even know where my phone is, actually. Haven't seen it today. You know how I get when I'm in the zone."

"I do. What I'd texted you about was that I'm getting the worst craving for your cheddar grits, but this time combined with that pickled shrimp and okra you made for the summer solstice cocktail reception last year. But this time, could you bread them and deep-fry them? Like, tempura style?"

Nasty. Then again, there was no accounting for a pregnant woman's taste and pickled shrimp had been a regular feature in Carina's cravings so far. "Sure. I can do that. Hey, listen. I decided something. I need to start dating again."

Carina blinked at her. "Say that again?"

"I need to start dating. It's been way too long."

Carina made cumbersome work of scooting her body around to face Emily head-on. "Let me get this straight.

You're in the middle of the most important month of your life, trying to convince Knox to give you the restaurant, and you want to start dating—for the first time in years?"

"That's correct. The sooner, the better. Tonight after I'm done with Knox's dinner, if possible."

"Are you familiar with the term *self-sabotage*?"

When Carina put it that way, the idea did seem self-sabotaging—but, then again, Carina hadn't been privy to the X-rated nature of Emily's imagination all week. Goddamn, she couldn't even think the word *X-rated* without her mind crowding with improper images. Knox rolling up his shirtsleeves. Knox pulling off his tie. Knox's muscles working while he rowed her across the lake in the moonlight. "Yeah, I need to get laid."

Carina eyed her like she was crazy. Which she was. Clearly.

"I'm sure there are plenty of men at the gym who would help you scratch that itch," Carina said.

Gross. "Not at Murph's. Haven't you heard the term don't fuck where you sleep?"

"The phrase is 'don't shit where you eat.'"

"Same difference," Emily said.

Carina braced her hands on Emily's shoulders. "Emily. Sweetie. You're going off the deep end. This challenge from Knox is messing with your mind."

"Tell me about it. Hence, why I need a man."

"Okay, if you could just stop for one second and look at me." She waited until Emily met her gaze. "Thank you. Now tell me, what's really going on?"

Nope. Carina was her best friend, but she was also Knox's cousin, and so the last person Emily wanted to confess her lustful thoughts to. "I'm a little stressed out at the moment."

"Clearly. You don't have to cook for me, if that's contributing. I can—"

"No, geez. That's not it. I love cooking for you. I love feeling like I'm helping to nourish your baby, in my own Auntie Emily way. It makes me feel closer to you than ever and I love it. I've told you that from the beginning."

"I know. I love it, too." She took Emily's hands and moved them to her belly. "He's moving a lot right now. Feel that?"

Beneath Emily's palm, Carina's belly undulated like a massage chair. "I feel it." To Carina's belly, she added, "Hi, Baby Decker. It's Auntie Emily again. You sure are making your mommy eat weird foods."

Feeling the baby move was all it took to put Emily's life and future back into perspective. She couldn't imagine not being near Carina and her new baby when it was born. She needed this job at the restaurant to work out. It had to. She couldn't resign herself to being some hotshot chef's line cook and she couldn't move to a big city in search of work. Briscoe Ranch was her home. After so many years fighting for a foothold in the world, she was loath to endure being adrift and poor again, away from the people she loved and who loved her back.

She rested her ear against Carina's belly and listened to the baby move, the reminder she needed to keep her eye on the prize. Getting laid and lusting over Knox and all other manners of self-sabotage were off the menu. From here on out, Emily was all business, all the time. To test herself, she thought the word *X-rated* again, and when an imagined vision of Knox's bare chest popped into her mind, she smashed it down like a Whac-A-Mole.

"So what gives? Why aren't you working today?" Emily asked. Carina's wedding gown design business had been booming since she'd opened it two years earlier, and with Briscoe Ranch's winter wedding season about to kick off, Emily was surprised to see Carina lolling about. Carina had never been a loller.

Carina shrugged. "Didn't feel like it, and I didn't have any pressing matters to attend to, so I gave myself the day off."

Good for her. "You and I were always workaholic twinsies, and now look at you."

Carina's eyes found Decker in the arena. Warmth and love radiated from her every cell. "I know. Look at me."

As though he felt his wife's eyes on him, Decker turned the horse around and cantered it across the arena to where Emily and Carina were.

As long-time employees at the resort, Emily had known James Decker, who went by his last name as a tribute to his late father, as long as she'd known Carina. He was the proverbial tall, dark, and handsome cowboy—who also took the prize for most reformed incorrigible bachelor at the resort. Back in his heyday, his reputation for hard drinking and partying was legendary in hill country. Emily had been a firsthand witness to his transformation to a family man who only had eyes for Carina, whom he doted on as though it were his life's work. "Hey, Decker."

"Hey, Em. What's new? You look tired. My wife running you ragged with her weird food cravings?"

"Emily has a new man to cook for," Carina said.

"Shut your pie hole," Emily said, giving Carina's ribs the gentlest of nudges.

"That would be your cousin Knox, right?" Decker asked. "Seems like a decent guy. He told me point blank that he doesn't plan on messing with my equestrian center in his expansion plan for the resort, so that's a good start."

"Definitely, and speaking of him," Emily said. "You know how to fish, right?"

"'Course I do. I don't get to go as often as I like, but sure. Why?"

"I need you to teach Knox. Lake Bandit has all these huge, aggressive fish in it, and at dinner on Tuesday, Granny June told Knox and me about how Clint and his buddy used to fish the lake all the time. Knox said he's never learned how to fish, so I suggested you as a teacher. I need him to catch a fish because I got this burst of inspiration about taking farm-to-table to the next level for Knox. I figure, if I can target his sentimentality by cooking with the same type of fish his father probably caught and ate a million times, then—"

Carina's smile turned knowing, so Emily clammed up. She *was* rambling, but that was nothing new. "What?"

"I love it when one of your clients bring out your passion. Yeah, it turns you a little crazy sometimes, but that's the price you pay for being a culinary artist. Who would've guessed my long-lost cousin would end up being your muse?"

Her muse? Damn it all to hell, Carina was right. Emily couldn't remember the last time she'd been so inspired. But admitting the truth wasn't going to help her keep that professional distance she so desperately needed. "I don't need a muse. My muse comes from within. I'm an island."

"Sure, you are," Decker said.

Emily ignored his ribbing and Carina's knowing smile. "Give me a break. My future's riding on this challenge, so I'd be worried if I wasn't inspired, given the circumstances."

Carina looped her arm around Emily's. "Maybe that's all it is. Maybe your muse is the challenge, not the client."

That was it. Had to be. Carina was a genius. All the horrible, confusing feelings Emily was experiencing had a logical reason. While it had been a while since she'd felt such a high level of passion for her cooking, it'd been even longer since she'd experienced anything akin to passion toward a man. No wonder her brain was confusing the two, especially since the challenge involved wowing a powerful, attractive man with her cooking in the privacy of his home, which demanded an intimacy she seldom experienced these days.

Carina shook Emily's arm. "Uh-oh. Look. Your muse is headed this way."

Emily bolted upright and followed Carina's line of sight. Sure enough, Knox was striding over the resort grounds in their direction with Haylie in tow and Granny June pacing them on her motorized scooter.

As always, every inch of Knox oozed with millionaire cowboy sensuality, from his perfectly tailored suit and confident stride to his ink-black Stetson and the lightly stubbled cheeks that gave him just the perfect amount of rakish charm. He was looking right at Emily, and when she returned his gaze, one side of his lips kicked up in a grin. Then a lock of his hair slipped from beneath his hat and fell over his forehead like he was friggin' Clark Kent.

Emily's body shimmered with heat and need.

Nope. That's not misplaced passion for cooking. That's lust, girl. Plain and simple.

She tore her gaze away from him. "Son of a bitch."

Carina's faint chuckle let Emily know she'd done a piss-poor job masking her true feelings from her best friend.

"Enjoying yourself?" Emily said through gritted teeth.

"Immensely, thank you."

"Oh, good."

"Haylie's with him," Carina said. "Has he said anything about how she's doing as his secretary? She hasn't been returning my texts lately, so I have no idea."

An unexpected tug of loyalty to Haylie had Emily holding her tongue about Haylie's shaky first day. "I'm sure she's doing fine. She's a lot more capable than she looks."

"Agreed. But not very many people see her potential other than you and me."

Haylie had only been seventeen when Emily came to work at the resort. At the time, Haylie and Carina didn't get along. Though Emily would never admit it outright, she resented Haylie's lack of ambition. Here she was, with the world handed to her on a silver platter, with a loving family and every possible opportunity, and all she'd done was squander her gifts while Emily had been scraping her way through life with no money or support system. In truth, it'd taken Emily a long time to grow into loving Haylie as part of her honorary family. But she had, and now Emily's life was all the richer for having Haylie in it.

Emily took another look at Haylie as she got nearer to the arena. Her collarbones were visible, her arms thin, her face showing the strains of her home life. Emily ground her molars together, swallowing her outrage lest it trigger memories of her own screwed up childhood. She had to believe that Haylie's job working for Knox was the first step to getting her confidence up to leave Wendell. From now on, Emily was going to bring Haylie breakfast when she brought Knox his. Not just Knox's leftovers, as she'd done today, but dishes tailor-made for her. What kind of food helped a woman find her power? What would nourish Haylie the most?

Chocolate. Definitely.

Emily caught herself holding her breath as Knox and his entourage drew closer, and so she stood, shaking off her sudden bout of nerves.

"Is this your first time seeing your man—I mean, your muse—today?" Carina teased.

Emily refused to acknowledge the ridiculous question as anything beyond the literal. "I stopped by his office earlier with breakfast, but he wasn't interested. He never eats breakfast beyond a protein shake, but that's only because he doesn't yet understand how determined I am to change his mindset. I was here at the crack of dawn stuffing sausage casings, so sooner or later, he's getting my sausages."

"Wait, what?" Decker said.

Carina hammed it up with a wink. "Just like you gave him your peaches?"

"*Tried* to give him my peaches. Also, FYI, you're driving me crazy turning everything I say into a double entendre."

"I can't help it! You're the master of them," Carina said. "Food and sex have so much in common. Both are decadent, when done right. A feast for the senses. People hunger for both on an elemental level."

"You tell her, babe."

Carina had no idea how close to home that observation hit. But there was just one problem. "You keep attempting to elevate sex to the level of fine cuisine, when the reality is that they're totally incomparable." That was her story and she was sticking to it.

"Have to agree with you on that. Totally incomparable." Carina hoisted herself up and leaned over the rail to plant a big ol' kiss on Decker.

Decker tugged her shirt collar, pulling her to him for a second kiss. "You're a sex-crazed pregnant woman, Mrs. Decker. And I love it."

Emily mustered a groan, though she secretly loved seeing Carina so happy. Her dating history was just as fraught with losers and disaster dates as Emily's, if not worse.

Granny June raced ahead of the group on her scooter, horn blaring as she hollered, "Slap my ass and call me Sally! Lookie here, it's three of my favorite people in one place!"

"Have I ever told you how much I love your grandma?" Decker said. "Little scared of her, too, but that's okay."

"Same here," Carina said. Emily helped her find her step down from the bleachers just as Knox and Haylie arrived behind Granny June's scooter.

Granny June snagged Knox's arm and stood, five-foot-nothing of proud, beaming grandma. "Haylie and I were just giving Knox a tour of the place and introducing him around."

"He and Wendell are going to play golf together next week," Haylie said.

"Ah," Carina said. "Lucky you," she added to Knox, without even a hint of the derision toward Wendell that Emily knew Carina was feeling, as she always did when his name came up.

After the requisite hugs, kisses, and handshakes all around, Decker caught Knox's attention. "Rumor is you want to learn to fish."

Knox gave Emily a pointed look. "That was fast."

What did he expect? "The clock's ticking. No time to waste, since you only gave me a month."

"Yeah, a month as my personal chef, not my activities coordinator."

He'd said it with light eyes, but still she couldn't help but wonder if she'd overstepped her bounds with that one. Too late now. "I can't cook Phantom for you if you don't catch him."

"Phantom?" Carina asked. "Is that a kind of fish?"

"It's complicated," Knox and Emily said in unison.

Right on cue, Carina's knowing smile made an

appearance as she glanced between Knox and Emily. "So I'm gathering."

"Of course, Decker'll teach you to fish, Knox," Granny June said with a wave. "That's what family's for. And speaking of activities we can all do together as a family, Haylie, you took Knox to see the amphitheater, but did you tell him about movie night?"

Judging by Haylie's sheepish grin, she had not. "I forgot. On the first and last Wednesday of every month, we hold a movie night for the guests in the amphitheater."

Granny June looped her arm around Knox's. "We're showing *Miracle on 34th Street* at the end of this month."

"Isn't it a little early for Christmas movies?" Knox asked.

Granny June waved away the critique. "Not at Briscoe Ranch. We kick off the holiday cheer in October and keep it going for three months. The more I think about movie night, the more I must insist you join us for it. It's the best way for you to see what we're all about here at Briscoe Ranch, and the guests love it when members of the Briscoe family put in an appearance. We're like celebrities around here. It's so fun! Sometimes, families from Dulcet come to watch the movies or participate in our activities along with the guests. It's great community outreach and it makes our guests happy, so it's a win for everyone."

Decker tipped his hat at Granny June. "Great idea. If Carina hasn't popped, then we'll try our best to make it."

"Me and Wendell, too. I mean, if he doesn't have to work," Haylie said.

Knox demurred. "You know, it sounds great, but uh . . . Emily had had a point earlier. I only gave her four weeks for this personal chef challenge, so it wouldn't be fair for me to deprive her of any opportunities."

"Agreed. Thank you," Emily said. Movie Night was nice and all, unless a person happened to be an introvert with a strong aversion to crowds and who was presently in the midst of a time-consuming culinary challenge.

"Oh, pish. You young people and your excuses. Ain't nobody knows how to have a good time anymore. Going to bed early, staying in to watch television. It's a shame. We're raising a generation of fuddy-duddies. Emily can just as easily pack your dinner up in a picnic basket. You can eat it during the movie. Lots of folks do that, too. In fact, our family restaurant, Texas Table, offers a family style to-go meal for those attending the movie. Right, Emily? You can pack up his dinner. Maybe you can join us, too. It's been too long."

"I'm very busy," Emily said meekly. Going against Granny June was definitely not a strong suit of hers.

Granny June whipped out her smartphone and started typing.

Carina cast a worried look at Granny June. "What are you doing, Granny?"

Granny June ducked her head and typed even faster. "There. It's on our Facebook page now. 'Next Sunday in the Turtle Doves Amphitheater at the showing of *Miracle on 34th Street*, meet our award-winning chef Emily Ford and the rest of the Briscoe family, including the newest executive on our team, Knox Briscoe.' "

Knox tried valiantly to hide a wince.

Granny June's face shone with delight. "Oh, look at that. We're already getting likes and comments on the post. You can't disappoint our guests, Knox. You either, Emily. You're both on the hook now. Together."

Emily was impressed how Knox managed to turn his wince into a smile. She, on the other hand, was still recovering from the shock that she'd been unwittingly roped into yet another of Granny June's matchmaking schemes.

Like moths to a flame. "Subterfuge," Emily muttered under her breath. "Unbelievable."

Before Emily could recover her wits, Granny June pulled her close, with one arm around her and the other around Knox. "By golly, it's a date."

Chapter Eight

"I'm not self-sabotaging. I'm not self-sabotaging. I'm not . . ."

Emily had chanted that mantra during most of the hundred-plus mile drive to the small town of Hutchins, Texas, on this brisk, but sunny Sunday morning. If only chanting something made it true. But all Emily could hear was Carina's voice in her head, reminding her that this was the most important month of her life, so she'd better not screw it up by making dumb-ass choices. Not exactly Carina's words, but close enough.

She ran a finger along the conservative neckline of her charcoal gray knit dress, ruing the fact that nothing was quite so unbecoming as stress sweat. All she'd wanted to do was swap recipes over the phone with Knox's mother, Linda. That in itself was crossing a professional line, since she'd contacted Linda Briscoe on Saturday afternoon without Knox's permission. It hadn't taken much sleuthing to locate her. Her address was plainly written on the envelopes of the old letters and cards Granny June had presented to Knox and his sister, which now sat on the desk in Knox's den. It also hadn't taken much for Emily to rationalize the decision because the payoff would be worth it if she could wow Knox by presenting him with her take on his favorite childhood dishes. Or, better yet, his father's favorite foods. After all, what was a little line crossing when Emily's career was at stake?

But she couldn't quite figure out a way to rationalize her split-second decision to accept Linda's invitation to join her at Father of Light Lutheran Church the next morning. Emily had done a lot of things in the name of culinary excellence, but attending church was a first. True, Linda had refused to share any personal details about Knox over the phone, insisting Emily join her for Sunday worship. Emily couldn't decide if Linda had insisted because she was lonely, or because bringing a newcomer to church might make her look good to her fellow congregants. Or maybe she just wanted to double-check Emily's standing with God before revealing the secret ingredients in her barbecue sauce recipe.

Regardless of the reason behind the offer, Emily had agreed to Linda's terms because she couldn't shake the notion that the more she'd gotten to know what made Knox tick, the better her meals had become and the more impressed he was. Carina's assertion that Knox was Emily's muse had been a tough pill to swallow, but she'd been right. He was. And now it was time to take that inspiration to the next level.

Unfortunately, the more Emily considered how many lines she was crossing, the more certain she was that Knox was going to be royally pissed when he found out. She wasn't sure there was a meal profound enough to assuage him. She swallowed hard. Guess she'd find out.

The charming, two-story brick and light blue house that Knox had grown up in sat in the middle of a long, unassuming residential street and was easily the nicest and most well kept on the block. The front yard was impeccably landscaped with a lush green lawn and perfectly trimmed hedges. Little touches of whimsy were everywhere Emily looked, from an autumn-themed flag showing a pumpkin pie declaring *Pie Season!*, to a family of painted wooden rabbits staged in the flowerbeds beneath the front windows, and a painted wooden sign near the front door reading *Frog parking only. All others will be toad.*

Despite Emily's nerves, she had to smile at that. Maybe Shayla got her love of groan-worthy puns from her mom.

The front door opened before Emily could ring the bell. Linda Briscoe met her on the front steps with a bright wide smile and open arms. She wore a busy orange Halloween sweater featuring pumpkin buttons, dangling crow-shaped beads, and felt applique scarecrows, but it somehow seemed to go perfectly with her petite, slim figure, short, salt-and-pepper hair, and upbeat energy that reminded Emily very much of Granny June.

Emily stuck out her hand in greeting. "Linda? I'm Emily."

Linda threw her arms around Emily and gave a hearty squeeze. "It's so good to meet Knox's girl!"

"Thank you. But, like I said on the phone, I'm his personal chef, not his—"

"If you say so, dear." The next thing Emily knew, Linda had pushed a Bible into her hands. "Off we go. I'll drive. It's been ages since I've gotten to shuttle a young person around. My kids insist on driving me everywhere. It's so obnoxious! As if I'm senile. You wait here. I'll lock up and open the garage."

Before Granny June's injuries in the chapel fire the year before, she'd always insisted on driving Emily around, too. The last of Emily's misgivings about meeting up with Knox's mother on the sly evaporated. This was bound to be a great, if hair-raising, adventure. Not more than a couple of minutes later, Emily buckled into the passenger seat of Linda's newer model hybrid hatchback.

Linda put on a pair oversized, round-framed sunglasses and backed out of the garage, pumping the brakes too hard and way too much. Emily braced her hands and tried to hold her neck steady so she didn't get whiplash. No doubt about it, this was going to be a wild ride, the kind of hair-raising, pedal-to-the-metal ride that Granny June used to take her on in her tricked-out golf cart.

"Okay, here we go. Now, look over there at Glenda's house as we pass," Linda said, gesturing to a small, yellow-trimmed house on the right as they crawled down the street at a solid fifteen miles per hour. The car drifted right, as though pulled by Linda's attention. "It looks like her oranges are almost ripe. Last winter, I helped her pick them and we managed okay for two old ladies, but let me tell you, the juicing was another—"

Emily glanced straight ahead in time to see Linda's car nearly bumping the curb and headed straight for a parked car. "Watch that car!"

"Oops." Linda jerked the wheel left to avoid the car, though she managed to tap mirrors with it. Not that she seemed concerned. "As I was saying . . ."

Rattling off her story, barely pausing for breath, Linda rolled them down the street, hugging the gutter, and occasionally swerving to avoid parked cars and trash-cans. Emily hugged the Bible she'd been entrusted with, lest she be tempted to take over steering the car as they crawled down street after street, barely pushing twenty miles per hour.

When they'd arrived at the Father of Light Lutheran Church parking lot, nearly twenty minutes later, the numerous horn honks they'd received echoed in one of Emily's ears and Linda's non-stop storytelling in her other. On Linda's fifth attempt to straighten the car in a parking spot, Emily realized that she'd dug nail marks into the leather cover of the Bible. She rubbed the leather, trying to work out the impressions. As she stepped from the car, she realized both her legs had fallen asleep, probably due to the sheer effort it'd taken not to stretch her foot across the cab and stomp down on the gas pedal herself. Linda Briscoe was a crazy driver, indeed. Crazy slow with a fondness for listing right.

And she'd gabbed the entire drive, from the story of juicing oranges to remarking about birds she'd seen in her backyard and the rising costs at her favorite deli and so much minutiae that it seemed as though she needed to voice the words that had been building inside her for so long, waiting for a sympathetic ear to share them all with. As though she'd invited Emily to church not because she was trying to save her soul or make her jump through hoops, but because under all her unbridled zest for life, Linda was lonely.

And while Emily didn't mind being that sympathetic ear—as long as eventually the conversation turned to Knox's childhood and his father, and both their favorite foods—it was a relief to enter the church's courtyard. Not only because they were out of the car with their lives and limbs intact, but because she could simply stand there, smiling, while Linda introduced her around and gushed about Emily and Linda's children to her friends. Even if Linda kept calling her Knox's girl. Even if she kept fabricating half-truths about what a big shot chef Emily was. If that's what the lonely, effervescent Linda needed to tell herself and her friends, then so be it. At this point, Emily was just along for the ride, so to speak.

Once the service got started, Emily relaxed back into the wooden pew next to Linda, the Bible still in her arms. Emily had grown up attending a see-and-be-seen upscale church in Chicago with her parents, and so she'd always equated it with the lies of wealth that masked her family's dysfunction. The concept of a Heavenly Father reminded her too starkly of her own father who had damaged her beyond repair and the mother who'd warped the idea of forgiveness into a justification for staying married to the monster, keeping both her and her daughter in harm's way. Redemption, that grand Christian concept, had been a dream Emily had prayed for as a child—her father redeemed, reborn a good man through Emily's and her mother's and God's forgiveness. It'd taken a lot of pain and years for her to realize that the Holy directive to turn the other cheek didn't mean she had to be a punching bag for the Devil.

She heard the words of the sermon, songs, and prayers differently today. She could hear the hope and the sense of peace in those around her. The sense of trying to be good people and lift themselves out of the darkness in their lives. Like Emily had, and like she was still striving to do. After the final hymn, the pastor directed the congregation to bow their heads. Linda took Emily's hand in her bony one and they bowed their heads together. For the first time since she'd been sixteen and on the street, Emily prayed. The last time she'd prayed, it'd been for food, and for a warm, dry place to sleep.

It worked then, didn't it? The cynic inside her wanted to scream *no*. But that would be a lie. She had found shelter and food, not always right away, but it'd happened. And then, not too many years later, she'd found Briscoe Ranch and the place of peace and love she'd always longed for.

Her prayer today wasn't so different from that last one. She prayed for Knox to give her the restaurant, for a chance to stay at Briscoe Ranch among her chosen family. Tears crowded her eyes, though she couldn't quite fathom why she felt so humbled and raw.

In a fog, she shuffled out of the church behind Linda, her eyes on Linda's black orthopedic wedges. Now and then, she shook hands with and offered plastic smiles to the parishioners she'd been introduced to. Some asked her to give Knox their greeting while others patted her hand and gave her blessings and told her how proud they could tell Linda was to have such a nice young lady in her son's life.

Emily thought about her own mother. Had she stuck it out with Emily's father after Emily had left? Was she lonely like Linda, too?

"You'll come with me back to my house now, right? And we can swap recipes. I'll fill you in on all Knox's favorite dishes, and maybe throw in some embarrassing stories you can tease him with," Linda said with a wink.

"Of course. I'll stay as long as I can. Maybe you'll allow me to fix you lunch."

Linda smiled. "Now there's a fancy idea. My own personal chef cooking Sunday supper. I'd love that. I've got a pot roast going in the crockpot, but maybe you can help dress it up a bit."

Emily considered offering to drive home, but Linda had seemed excited to be the one behind the wheel, shuttling Emily to church. She climbed into the passenger seat again. "You and Clint were high school sweethearts in Dulcet," she prompted once they were on the road.

"That we were," Linda said wistfully. "I miss Dulcet sometimes, especially this time of year. My favorite. The countryside's so pretty in the fall. Are they doin' okay, then? All the Briscoes?" A hint of longing tinged Linda's tone, as though Emily had conjured her grief with the question. She definitely didn't seem angry about the rift, as Knox or Ty did.

"Everyone's doing great. Ty's daughter Carina is pregnant, due in a couple weeks."

"Oh, how nice. Ty's gonna be a grandpa. Hmph. I can't imagine. Well, maybe it'll soften that temper. How's his wife? How's Eloise?"

Odd, the affectation in Linda's tone when she enunciated Eloise's name. The loneliness vanished and stiffness entered her voice, as though she and Eloise were long-standing enemies rather than long-lost friends or neighbors, though they'd grown up in the same small town of Dulcet, in the shadow of the resort, both classmates with Clint and Ty.

"She is. As beautiful as ever." Thanks in part to availing herself of the many services at the resort's spa as well as the occasional cosmetic surgery down in San Antonio. "Were you two classmates in high school, as well?"

She clicked her tongue at the question, a motherly sound of disapproval. "How about Granny June. I always liked her. She's still healthy?"

Interesting. "Healthy as a horse."

Linda smiled. "Good for her. I hope my children inherit her longevity."

There was an odd sort of hard-edged haunting in her tone that reminded Emily of Knox's expression when he spoke of his family's exile.

"With Knox as part-owner of Briscoe Ranch now, you should come visit," Emily said. "I'd fix a great meal for the two of you. Maybe we could invite Shayla and Granny June, too. Maybe Ty's daughters, Carina and Haylie. You'd love them."

A slight shudder passed through Linda, though her smile remained in place. "No. That's sweet of you, but I could never; I'm sitting fat and sassy right here in Hutchins."

Emily's heart sank as Linda turned onto her block at the sight of a familiar Chevy truck parked out front of Linda's house.

"Well, glory be," Linda said. "I thought he wasn't coming now that he moved so far away. What a pair you two are, surprising me like this. You sure do keep a good secret, missy."

Emily swallowed as they pulled to a stop behind the truck. "Well, I mean, I didn't exactly tell him . . . he's been busy and I . . ." Jesus, she couldn't even tell a decent lie these days to save her own ass. Get her within a hundred yards of Knox Briscoe and her composure fell apart like a soggy tortilla.

Linda was unfazed. "Then God must be smiling down on us for this happy accident." She walked from the car as Knox stepped out from the house onto the porch where several bags of groceries sat, one with a bouquet of flowers sticking out of the top. When he saw Emily, he froze, one hand reaching for a grocery bag. His gaze shifted between Emily and her car, parked in front of the neighbor's house, which had been the only spot available at the time. Even from the street, she could see his expression morph from shock to confusion to fury.

Linda practically skipped up the front walk, her arms open wide, reaching for a hug. "Knox, honey! Bless your heart, you brought me groceries. You're always such a good boy like that. Your daddy would be so proud."

Emily followed Linda onto the front steps. Knox kissed his mother on the cheek and hugged her tight, but his eyes remained locked on Emily. No doubt about it, he was livid with her. On top of everything else that church had dredged up within her, she wasn't equipped to deal with his anger, too.

"This is most unexpected, Ms. Ford."

Ms. Ford? Shit.

Emily grabbed several bags of groceries and walked into the house, Linda and Knox on her heels. "It was supposed to be a surprise. I've been wanting to fix you a dish or two from your childhood, so I thought, why not go to the source? I didn't think you'd mind."

Emily's shoulders stiffened in anticipation of his rebuttal. She chanced a look at Knox. He was working hard to hide his anger, probably thanks to Linda's presence.

"Nonsense," Linda said. "Of course, he doesn't mind. I think it's a capital idea. And it's been a gas for me to have her around for the morning. She got to meet my friends at church and she's going to help me spruce up the pot roast for supper. It isn't every day I can get tips from a professional chef. Isn't that delightful, Knoxy?"

"Yes, delightful," he said mechanically.

"And now you're here, which is another wonderful surprise. What a blessed day!" With that, Linda launched into a detailed retelling of their morning to Knox.

If Knox got his way, Emily would be gone from the house as soon as he could gracefully manage. But there was one last place she wanted to visit, to at least glean some knowledge from the trip since she'd never gotten the chance to swap recipes with Linda. Knox's childhood bedroom. Perhaps it'd be as inspiring to her culinary imagination as his current bedroom had proven to be.

As Linda held his attention in the kitchen, Emily slipped back to the entryway. Her heart pounded against her ribs and in her ears. After a last look over her shoulder, she stole up the stairs.

Chapter Nine

Emily paused in the second-floor hallway, temporarily distracted by a row of sepia-tinted collages of old family photos behind dusty glass frames. Two rowdy boys and a tomboy sister on horseback. A teen Knox being presented with a belt buckle at a rodeo. His brother, Wade, feeding a goat at a petting zoo. The whole family clustered together on a beach, the boys with bowl cuts and Shayla in pigtails.

Emily was struck once again by how similar in appearance all the Briscoe men were. They all looked related, but Knox was the spitting image of young Ty and Knox's Grandpa Tyson, down to the stiff jaw and ambitious gleam in his eyes, while Wade's face was rounder, more closely resembling Clint and Granny June, and then all with echoes of each other, including Carina and Haylie. No doubt about it, the Briscoe bloodline was strong. Emily couldn't wait to see how that lineage manifested in Carina and Decker's baby boy.

Knox and Wade's room was marked with a sign taped to the door that looked like it had been printed out on an

old dot matrix printer, the perforated edges still attached.
Knox and Wade's Private Lair—Enter at Your Own Risk.

After another look over her shoulder, Emily pushed
the door open.

The room was divided in half, much like a college
dorm room, with each side containing a twin bed and a
desk. One of the two boys had been into comic books and
WWF as a kid, as evidenced by the posters of oiled-up
musclemen in costumes and masks that plastered his wall
and the rows of colorful comic books that lined his bookshelves. The other side of the room had been done up in
a rodeo motif. There was even a line of cowboy hats
hooked on the wall, as well as a line of trophies on bookshelves, all with Knox's name, all declaring him a junior
rodeo champ. What a nice, sweet life they'd all had in
this house.

Jealousy hit her hard, as though it had been waiting
quietly in the shadows since the church service, ready to
pounce. For all the material wealth Clint's family lacked
compared to Emily's own upper-class youth, they'd had
something far richer than she'd ever known. Real, famil-
ial love. There was a time she would've given anything—
anything in the whole world—for the unconditional love
of her parents, to go to bed without being terrified of being awoken in the middle of the night by her drunk father,
to not have suffered her mother's emotional distance and
half-baked rationalizations.

Knox's childhood home was filled with the same sort
of authentic love that Emily had been chasing her whole
adulthood through her cooking. Her hand closed over a
framed photo on Knox's desk of him and his father. She
couldn't stop staring at the pride in Clint's eyes. *The goddamn fatherly pride*. No wonder Knox held his father's
memory in such reverence. Emily was certain that no one
had ever looked at her like that.

There was nothing more for her to learn in this house tonight, not with bitterness and jealousy and the ache of longing that was bulldozing over her professional detachment. There was no room in her mind for her muse to work. She was straightening the framed photograph in preparation to leave when footsteps behind her caught her attention.

"You had no right to come my mother's house. No right at all."

She cursed internally, because, of course, Knox's anger was justifiable. With nowhere to run or hide, she pulled a cowboy hat from the wall and turned, then set the hat on his head. "Are you sure your mom's okay with you being alone in your room with a girl?"

He ripped the hat off his head and tossed it on the bed. "Don't play cute. I refuse to allow you to use my mother."

"I'm not trying to."

"I sent Mom to the store for wine to have with dinner. That gives you plenty of time to leave."

Emily's heart sank, even though she'd known that was coming. "I didn't mean her or you any harm by doing this. I wanted to learn more about you and—"

"Then you should have asked me instead of dragging my mother into your . . . your . . ." He waved a hand at her, as though her mere presence articulated plainly enough the point he was getting at.

"My what? My evil plan to succeed at the challenge you've laid out for me? My dastardly intention to tap into your love for your father by fixing you his favorite meal? Buttering you up with nostalgia?" A wry huff escaped her lips. "But guess what? The trick's on me. I'm the one who let sentimentality get the best of me today. This room, your mom and her church, the love in the house itself. I can feel it in the walls and in every room. It's nothing that money can buy. I know you feel like you were cheated out of the life you were owed by being cut out of the Briscoe fortune, but you have to believe me when I say that money can't buy everything. It can't buy love. It can't—" Wincing, she closed her eyes and fought to get a grip. She'd already said too much and taken the conversation way past the boundaries of professionalism.

She raised her lashes again. Knox was standing close, watching her with those dark, enigmatic eyes that drew her in every time.

"You shouldn't have come here," he said quietly.

No, she shouldn't have. "But I am here. Why does that scare you so much? What are you trying to hide?"

He stepped even closer, so near that his shoes bumped hers. His lips parted as though he were on the verge of speaking. She chanced another look in his eyes, but flinched back at the presence of anguish in them—anguish that mirrored her own.

Her attention dipped to his neck, and to the press of his shirt collar against his Adam's apple as he swallowed hard. How could he breathe in that choker of a suit? Her fingers twitched with the urge to undo the button at his neck and unmake him in the same way he'd shed his business attire in his bedroom on that first night of their agreement. That was the man she wanted to feed, the man free of his armor, the one who drove his father's old truck and named the fish in his lake. The one whose eyes glowed with warmth when he looked at his grandmother. Emily wanted to feed the former rodeo champion who brought flowers to his mom on Sunday morning. The tender, loving soul behind the fierce Briscoe name and CEO title.

Without thinking, she reached out and touched his tie. The back of her hand scraped against that ever-present five o'clock shadow on his jaw as she loosened the knot, then unfastened the top button of his shirt. Needing to feel

his skin, she flipped her hand over and cupped his cheek.
And then the whole world unraveled before her eyes.

Different bedroom. Same woman. Same crushing hunger
for her that had swept through him that first night she'd
cooked for him, when he found her lying on his bed.
What was it about Emily Ford that drove him to the brink
of devastation every time he was in her orbit?

If he were honest with himself, that was the real trouble
with getting that text from his old friend wondering why
Knox's mom was flaunting his 'girl' Emily around church
without him. As though they were an item. As though she
really were his to flaunt around his hometown.

When she'd skulked up to his bedroom, he'd followed
her, prepared for a confrontation. He hadn't expected the
tinge of sorrow behind her eyes or the glimpse into her
soul that she'd shared. It was a sorrow that mimicked the
grief he'd struggled with after his dad's passing. When
her eyes had turned glassy, he'd wanted desperately to
draw her into his arms and take on the burden of her sorrow, whatever the source. In that instant, it was tempting
to see her as a different person from the confident chef
who'd flung soup into his lap, but she was exactly the
same woman as that fateful day—with the same heart
on her sleeve, the same impetuous passion. He'd never
met anyone quite like her, and the intertwining of their
lives that had happened in the days since had only whet-
ted his appetite for more.

With fingers that trembled against the sensitive skin
under his chin, she loosened his tie, then unfastened the
button at his collar. The release of pressure from around
his neck left him gasping for air, as though he'd been
holding his breath for too long without ever being aware
of it. Then she touched his face. After a life spent perfecting the art of never losing control, with one touch, Emily

transformed him into a man enslaved by his urges, erasing a lifetime of discipline.

With stiff, stilted movement, he snared her waist with his arm and drew her up against him. The sheer force of the emotional storm raging inside him rendered him incapable of smooth moves or intelligible thoughts. She came willingly and brought her other hand up to his face, cradling his cheeks as she released ragged breaths against his neck. Cupping her neck to lock her against him, he pressed his lips to her forehead and breathed his need into her skin.

Her hands roved over his body, as though memorizing the shape of him by feel. His chest, his arms, his waist. As her hands moved, her lips touched his jawline, sending electric currents sizzling through him. He gritted his teeth, enduring the sensations, and yet needing so much more.

He willed his arms to move so he could match her movements. His hands molded against her back and down over the flare of her hips. The dress fabric was thin, but still a burden. He needed her skin under his grip. He bunched the fabric of her dress until the hem was high enough that his hands could reach her leg. At the first contact of his palm splaying over the back of her thigh, he heard a guttural growl in the back of his throat. On a whimper, she melted against him. He slipped his hand higher, breaching the hem of her panties and filling his hand with soft, supple flesh. Her hands sank from his chest to his waist. She gripped his belt and tipped her head back, eyes closed, and gave herself over to his touch.

"I need . . ." she began as a whisper. Her fingers delved behind the waistband of his pants, letting him know exactly what she needed.

"More," he finished for her.

She tipped her head up. Her eyelids were heavy with

desire, her cheeks flushed, a goddess of sensuality, the sexiest goddamn woman he'd ever seen in the whole of his life. "Yes. More. Now."

At her words, everything Knox had thought he was, a man of reason and purpose and control, surrendered irrevocably to the drumbeat of raw, primitive need. He reached between her legs and grazed his hand over her panties. On a whimper, her body shifted, and she pressed herself more fully into his touch, sinking his fingers against the wet fabric. He groaned along with her at the intimate contact. She gripped his belt tightly as her body undulated against his hand.

Her lips parted in a silent cry. She released a hand from his belt and molded her fingers over his still-clothed erection. The caress rocked through him so intensely that his knees buckled. He collapsed back into the desk chair, pulled her down to straddle him.

With her curly brown hair cascading in waves around her face, she unlatched his belt, then his pants. He watched her work, marveling that the same hands that were so capable and confident in the kitchen were so unsteady now. He leaned back in the chair to give her more room to work, but bumped the chair back into the desk. Something tumbled from the desk to the floor. A *Dukes of Hazzard* action figure, reminding Knox where they were. Not his current house, not his apartment in Dallas either. His mother's house. Which meant . . .

Shit.

He forced the fog of desire to clear from his mind insomuch that he could speak. "I don't have . . ." Damn it, he couldn't get his mouth to form words. "There's no protection here." Every sound had to be forced out from a sandbag tongue and concrete jaw. "So I'll need to . . ." The sentence dissolved into an almost angry growl of pleasure as she tugged his briefs down, freeing his heavy, swollen cock. He couldn't think past being inside her, past achieving that profound connection with Emily—this maddeningly intense, ferocious, singular woman who was so much a reflection of his own famished soul. *Right the hell now.*

She wrapped a hand around his girth with a reverently whispered curse of approval and need. Then she met his gaze again, her expression pleading. "I'm on the pill. If that's . . . if you . . ." Her eyes turned glassy again with unshed tears. "I need this. You."

He searched her eyes, weighing her words. As if it would've made a difference if she'd been lying about the birth control. Their needs were too intense to be ignored, regardless of the cost.

Panting, he moved his hand between her legs again and slid her underwear out of the way. He parted her folds with a single finger and swirled his knuckle gently around her clit. She writhed against him, her head back and lips parted, lost in her pleasure. The slick heat of her body was intoxicating. He swayed with her, drunk on the feel of her flesh.

He considered himself a good lover, smooth and confident, with a practiced touch. Not today. Not with her. Every flex of muscle was a battle between logic and lust. The knowledge that he was violating so many boundary lines that, professionally, he may never recover was at war with the howl of his most primitive, atavistic instincts warning him that if he didn't join with Emily right now, right here, then his inner self—his very soul— would perish.

Her body went rigid in his arms. She clutched the back of his neck to steady herself and rose, positioning herself over his cock. Her body was wet and ready for him, but still, he spit onto his hand, then stroked his erection.

She sank onto him with excruciating slowness. Her

tight, silky flesh gripped him, drawing untold pleasure from him, setting his nerves on fire. Her hands gripped his neck and shoulder too hard, as he was probably gripping her hips too hard. But he couldn't seem to get his limbs to ease up their hold. It was all too much. He gritted his teeth and surrendered himself to Emily, body and soul.

The moment Emily seated herself to the hilt, a harsh gasp vibrated up from her throat. Her soul shattered, as though her ribs had ripped open, exposing her beating, damaged heart to Knox. She'd never felt so raw or vulnerable. In the distance, muffled and far away, she heard him cry out, too. At the sound, at the realization that he felt it too, the profoundness and pain of it all, the tears crowding her eyes spilled over.

She turned her face away from him so he wouldn't see, but he wasn't having it. His hand took hold of her chin and forced her back to lock gazes with him. She complied, allowing him to see her tears, knowing now that hiding anything from him was useless. For better or worse, he was seeing all of her today.

Eyes fixed on each other, they moved together with jerky, harsh thrusts and arches, drugged by the pleasure and desperate for release. Their foreheads came together, contracting the universe down to the two of them. She clutched at his neck, as he was clutching hers. At least he didn't try to kiss her; she couldn't have borne it on top of everything else. When the first stirrings of her release started to gather pressure, she snaked a hand between their bodies to stroke her clit as they moved, pushing herself right over the edge of the cliff.

She came so hard that fresh tears burst from her eyes. She threw her head back in a silent, open-mouth cry as her body violently quivered. Knox tightened his hold on her and buried his head against her chest, his lips and nose pressed to her breastbone. When he found release a few heartbeats later, he nearly levitated them both off the chair. Beneath her thighs, she felt his quads tighten, his pectorals, his arms, his whole body. His warm breath fanned over her like a salve for her raw, aching heart.

The arm wrapped around her waist tightened to the verge of pain, but she didn't try to loosen his grip. She knew what it meant to need to hold on to something so tightly that you risked crushing it. So rather than fight it, she wrapped her arms around him, buried her face in his hair, and, together, they quaked until both were wholly spent. Still, they remained locked together. Her quiet, persistent stream of tears slid over her cheeks and into his hair.

"Jesus, Emily. What have you done to me?" he whispered on a breath.

Done to him? What about what he had done to her? What he had done to the simple, straightforward fabric of her life? Every time she was near him, she felt like she was on fire, burning uncontrollably. Her brain, her heart, her body. She'd never been so inspired professionally, yet so completely out of control emotionally.

Downstairs, a door closed with a bang. Both Emily and Knox tensed and lifted their heads.

"You two still here? Hello?" Linda called.

Oh God. His mother was home. And Emily had slept with Knox. And nothing was ever going to be the same. And . . . *oh God. What the fuck had she done?*

Knox cleared his throat. "We're upstairs. Be right down." He voice was husky, drained. He sounded like Emily felt.

She swiped at the lingering tears in her eyes as she disentangled her body from Knox's and stood. She walked to the window, righting her clothes as she moved, and stared out at the darkness. The lights were on in the house across the street. A black cat sat in the living room window. In the sky, the lights of a plane blinked as it crossed the horizon. So ordinary a night. From behind her came the sound of rustling clothes, the zip of a zipper, the clang of a belt buckle. The chair creaked as Knox stood.

There was no escaping the room without facing him, and when she did so, she wasn't surprised to see his face curtained by a stoic mask, the same warrior's mask she'd donned before turning around. They both needed the masks now, as much as they'd needed the intimacy only moments earlier because they'd both seen too many intimate details of the other—their hearts, their weaknesses, and their deepest needs.

"You wanted to know why you scared me," he said in a tight growl of a tone. "Do you have your answer now?"

She opened her mouth, meaning to tell him, *Yes. I get it. And you're right. We're both terrified of each other for good reason*. But no sound came out. Maybe that was for the best. She closed her mouth again, made sure her pride and dignity were on full display, and walked from the room.

Chapter Ten

Dinner the next several nights was one gastronomic wonder after another, served in Knox's dining room on fine china. By Haylie, who was apparently acting as Emily's assistant. The better for Emily to avoid him by lurking in his kitchen, as she'd been doing all week. It was hard to hold it against Emily, though, because he'd tied himself into knots trying to avoid her, too. He simply couldn't figure out what he felt, much less what to say to her.

On this night, after the first course of asparagus soup with a poached duck egg, he glanced over the cardstock menu next to his place setting that described in great detail the four courses he'd be served. Up next would be sous vide salmon.

Every element of the meal was a technical culinary marvel. Perfectly prepared, perfectly seasoned. Totally void of Emily's passion and personality. Just as the tropical smoothie she'd presented him with—via Haylie—for breakfast had been, as the deconstructed salad nicoise had been for lunch, all the meals had been that week. Before this week, he never would've guessed it possible to use food as a tool of distance, but he felt Emily's retreat from him in every empty bite he took.

When Haylie delivered the salmon—a work of art with a yin and yang of vibrant green basil oil and vivid red pepper sauce, and radishes so finely minced, they sprinkled like confetti over a perfect fillet of deep orange fish—she did a little curtsey.

Knox gave the fish the side-eye and poked at it with his fork. Maybe this was part of Emily's strategy—prove her culinary skill by getting him addicted to her meals, then yank them away. If she'd been hoping he'd go into withdrawals, then she would have been right.

Something in him snapped. He couldn't stomach one more technically perfect, heartless meal. It was time to face up to Emily and the damage he'd done by taking advantage of her at his mom's house.

He caught Haylie's attention just as she reached the door to the kitchen. "Haylie, would you send the chef out, please?"

Haylie paled. "I don't think that's in your best interest. She's, like, way stressed tonight."

I'll bet. "Please. I can handle her." The lie of the century. He'd already demonstrated he could no more handle being alone with Emily than a puppy could be trusted alone with an ice cream sundae.

Haylie returned with Emily, and the pair stood at the far side of the long table, with Haylie's carriage that of a bodyguard, though it was unclear whether she was there to protect Knox or Emily.

"Haylie, leave us," Knox said.

She looked to Emily for approval.

Emily nodded, and Haylie scurried back to the kitchen.

"Will you sit?" he said.

"No."

There was no way he was going to call to her from across the long table. He pushed out of his chair and walked her way. With each step nearer, her body grew more rigid. The pink stain on her skin spread and deepened.

"Stop right there," she said, holding her palm out. "Me first. The other day—" The swinging door to the kitchen creaked. Both their eyes swung in its direction. The shadows of two feet were visible in the space beneath it. Emily stepped closer to Knox and lowered her voice. "The other day, at your mother's house, that shouldn't have happened. I shouldn't have been there, and we shouldn't have slept together."

The word she'd left out was *barely*. They'd *barely* slept together, in the loosest definition of the term. They hadn't kissed or spoken or removed their clothes. In fact, the more time went by, the hazier the experience got in his mind, and the more he wondered if it had only been a dream. "If that's what you want to call what we did, then fine."

She wrung the kitchen town folded over the belt of her chef jacket. "What else would we call it? A hook-up? A quickie? Fucking? You tell me, Knox."

"How about momentary insanity?"

He read the debate on her features, the head of steam too stubborn to dissipate. She finally answered him with a curt nod. "Sounds about right."

On a huff, he raked a hand through his hair. "Look, I called you out here to tell you that I'm sorry. As your boss, I should have never put you in this position. This is all on me, and I can assure you that it won't happen again."

"Damn right, it won't. When you give me the restaurant, it will be because I earned it with my skill in the kitchen and nothing more. I refuse to sleep my way to the top. Even if it was . . ."

Her voice trailed off, but he could've easily finished her sentence.

Even if it was the most profound release he may have ever had.

Even if, when their bodies had connected, the electric force of it was nothing he'd ever experienced before.

Even if he still wanted her so badly that it wasn't healthy or wise or reasonable.

His mind filled with all the things he would never have the chance to say to her, *do* to her, with her—thoughts that were too dangerous even to think. That same atavistic coil of lust flared to life inside him again. Disgusted by his visceral reaction, he took a step back, then turned and walked to the wall of windows overlooking the lake, his hands in his pockets to obscure his ill-timed arousal.

"For the record, it had never occurred to me that you had ulterior motives or were trying to win me over . . . that way." As he'd told Shayla, when she'd voiced the same concern, it would have been insulting to Emily for him to think that about her. Not to mention how insulting it would have been if any other employee—yes, she was an employee, a fact he needed to start keeping in the forefront of his mind—had suggested that Knox would be so corrupt as to coerce her. That went against everything he stood for. But Emily was perilously close to being correct. "But I agree that it certainly has that appearance."

She stepped to his side, her eyes on the view, and splayed a hand out on the windowpane. "Which is why it can never happen again."

Restraint and lust warred in his blood. He could reverse the conversation with one touch. He could pull her into his arms, carry her to his room, and spend the rest of the night ravishing her. He could once again ease that deep well of longing that only she could temper. "No, it can't."

"Are you enjoying dinner?"

His gaze traced the line of her jaw to her delicate earlobe. A curl of her hair snagged in its ridges. His fingers itched with the urge to free it. "It's horrible."

She flicked a glance in his direction. "I tasted it. It's perfection."

"It has no soul. It's not you. And it's not me." When had that become the touchstone? What happened to the notion that food was fuel? How could ten days in Emily's orbit set fire to such a fundamental philosophy—a symbol of the way he calibrated his life with precision. With control. Always playing by the rules.

My God, how had he allowed himself to go so far off course? Especially now, when he was so close to having everything he'd ever wanted? What would his father think of his behavior?

"Emily . . ." God, he hated the strain in his voice, the telltale weakness. The prayer infused in her name. Enough was enough. Time to put out the fire raging between him and Emily before it burned everything he'd staked his life on to the ground. He peeled away from the window and resumed his seat at the table. "You're right. I was being sarcastic about dinner being horrible. The truth is, it's exceptional and healthy and lean. Everything I look for in a meal. Great job. But I'm afraid this salmon's getting cold, so if you'll excuse me."

He lifted his fork and forced his vision to tunnel to his food.

Still at the window, Emily's chef jacket rustled. She released a slow, jagged exhalation loaded with tension. He ground his molars together, tamping the urge to look her way. She had to know this was for the best. She had to agree. Neither of them wanted so much as a shadow of controversy in their lives. Neither of them could afford one.

Her footsteps sounded in retreat to the kitchen.

"Emily? I really am sorry."

She stopped with a hand on the door. "Don't call me Emily. As if you know me so well. Let's keep it Briscoe and Ford from now on."

With a proud carriage, she pushed through the kitchen door. He memorized the swish of her ponytail and the curve of her back, keenly aware that this was probably the last time he'd see her for a while.

On Friday, Knox woke up knowing that the day was special. He put a little extra verve in his steps during his morning jog, and he'd dressed with meticulous purpose. His father's cufflinks. His lucky hat. Not that he needed it because this morning, one week after their initial visit, the structural engineers were returning to the resort to have a second look before presenting their findings to Knox and Ty, and this time, they were bringing a geologist along. Fancy that. Wonder what findings they'd present at their meeting with Ty and Knox afterward.

He slid his truck key into the ignition with extra care, then turned his eyes heavenward. "If you were ever going to let your truck drive onto the resort, today's the day. You could have a front row seat to see the look on Ty's face."

He turned the key.

Click. Click.

He banged on the steering wheel. "Really?"

Too agitated to sit, he jumped out of the truck, fighting to keep his good mood in place. "Why? You wanted this to happen. You told me over and over that you wanted this for the resort, and for me. Why not support me now?

What am I doing wrong?" On a whim, he leaned on the side mirror as Emily had done, talked to it as if it were an ear. "Dad, this is a good thing. The next step toward justice. Your brother's a criminal, your father was a criminal, and they both screwed you over. It's time to make things right."

With a decisive crack, the mirror snapped off, sending Knox stumbling for footing. When he regained his balance, he glared at the mirror, dangling by its wires. "What the hell kind of sign is that?"

Of all the possible days, today he didn't have time to interpret whatever random message his dad was sending him from the great beyond. He whipped out his phone and called Haylie's cell phone number. She had to be on her way to work, too. But she didn't pick up the line. Unwilling to waste time running through his contact list, he accessed his Cab'd app and made a request.

Ten minutes later, a car pulled around Knox's driveway. This was not Ralph in the Cab'd luxury sedan, but a dull maroon economy car carrying a rounder, middle-aged gentlemen with a pencil mustache, slicked-back, black hair, and a slightly manic smile that reminded Knox vaguely of Gomez Addams from *The Addams Family*. Knox looked at his app's read out. Paco. The name sounded vaguely familiar, though he couldn't recall where he'd heard it.

Paco stuck his head out his open window. "Hey, I know you! You're June's grandson! Climb on in and let Paco take you for a ride."

All right. No problem. He assumed the front passenger seat. "Thanks, though it's not much of a ride. We're only going to Briscoe Ranch."

"Oooh, it's my lucky day. Maybe I'll park and take a look around, see if I can find June." He smoothed a hand over his hair. "How do I look?"

"Er . . ."

Steering with his knee, Paco unwrapped a mint and popped it in his mouth. "June, you know, she's a classy lady. I've definitely had to up my game."

Knox didn't usually think of *classy* and *Granny June* in the same sentence, but Paco's gushing opinion of her was kind of sweet. "Are you two dating or something?"

Paco let out a belly laugh. "Only in my dreams."

Okay, that was a little less sweet, and a bit more creepy. Also, way more information than Knox needed to know. Thankfully, they arrived at the resort's circular drive in record time. Knox tossed a twenty on the seat as a tip. "Thanks for the lift, Paco."

Paco rolled down the passenger window and dipped his head to smile at Knox. "Wish me luck with your grandma!"

Yeah, no. Knox braced his hands on the car door. "How about this instead? You treat her right and I won't have to kick your ass." He'd never threatened to kick anyone's ass over a woman's honor, because Shayla had never needed his help, and neither had his mom, but it felt good, having family to protect for a change. Ironic, given the way the day was going to unfold, but nice all the same. He smiled and tapped his brow in a two-fingered salute to Paco, then tipped his hat to the worker manning the valet booth as he walked through the sliding double doors.

Haylie was not at her desk. Her arrivals in the morning were getting later and later. Add to that her frequent lunches that often ran much longer than an hour, and which she sometimes returned from reeking of cigarette smoke, and the picture of her job performance wasn't a pretty one. He liked Haylie a lot, but it was time to crack down.

He rounded the corner into his office to see Ty sitting in Knox's chair behind the desk.

"This again?" Knox said, refusing to be ruffled by the surprise.

"You and I need to talk."

Knox set his messenger bag on the floor next to the desk. "I thought we were already doing that, all day, every day."

"Your engineers are back this morning."

No wonder Ty was sweating. "Good. They're early."

Could have been an optical illusion, but Knox swore he could see the sweat sprouting on Ty's cue ball head. "We don't need them. I've got my own team of inspectors I usually use. A top-notch company, one that knows the area. How 'bout I give them a call and we send your city boys packin'?"

Knox eyed the bottle of scotch near the door. Was it too early to celebrate his victory? *Nah.*

He poured shots into the two lowball glasses that shared a tray with the bottle, then handed one to Ty and settled into one of the chairs across from the desk.

"What's this for?"

Knox's response to that question could go in so many different directions. Hard to pick just one. "To help calm your nerves."

"What do you think I have to be nervous about?" Ty snapped.

A knock sounded at the door.

"Mr. Briscoe?" It was one of the engineers, looking deadly serious. "I know it's early, but there's something you're going to want to see."

Perfect timing. Knox gave his best fake look of concern. "Is everything all right?"

"Well, no, actually. We've found a problem. A big one. It's why we brought Ron, the geologist, with us today, to double check that we were drawing the correct conclusions."

Ty tossed back his second serving of scotch.

"Come on in. Give it to us straight," Knox said.

The engineer took a sheepish step into the room. "The problem is, the original structure should never have been placed where it is. The make-up of the soil and the proximity to the lake could have supported a single-family dwelling, but not a building this size. The hill that the building is built on cannot support its weight, hydrologically or geologically. In fact, the building has already started to creep downhill. We found evidence deep in the foundation. All it would take was one big storm or, worse, a measurable snowfall, which has been known to happen in these hills, historically, and y'all could be in real trouble."

The situation was even worse than Knox and his engineer buddy had estimated. Excellent.

"Will we be able to save the buildings?"

"We think so, but it'll cost you."

"That's hard news to take," Knox said.

"I know that, sir, which is why we'd like to show you for yourselves what we're talking about, if you'd just follow me."

Knox made to stand, but Ty gestured him back down. "Tell us where. We'll meet you there in a minute," Ty said, sounding far more composed than Knox knew him to be.

As soon as the engineer had left, Ty sloshed the scotch back, then rose from the desk. He closed the door, then refilled his glass with scotch. "You have no idea the damage you've done bringing those fools in."

What Knox had done? Oh, please. Knox stepped around his desk until he was behind it. As discretely as possible, he clicked the record button on his computer's camera. "What are we going to do about this? The inspectors say the building's sinking toward the lake. They say the foundation's cracked."

Ty swabbed his brow with a cocktail napkin, then took a seat in a guest chair, seemingly unaware of the musical chairs they were playing. "We can make this go away. We'll get a second opinion. The guys I told you about. I've been working with them for decades, and they're amenable to persuasion."

"You think we should bribe them? Are you insane?"

"No, but you've proven to be disappointingly naïve. This is the way business works 'round these parts. The Briscoe way. If you don't like it, then just close your eyes. I told you I'd take care of everything. And I will."

Oh, hell, no. "But what if the building failed? What if guests got hurt? You heard the guy. One bad storm and the resort could slide into the lake."

"The Briscoes have been on this land for nearly a hundred years, first my grandparents as a farm, and then my parents when they turned it into a hotel. My father had an unorthodox building style, but he got the job done. The hotel he built has stood the test of time. We've never had a problem and we never will. The land is solid."

Time to go for the jugular. "You've known about this land problem all along, haven't you?"

"Would it matter if I did?" Ty said.

"You duped me," Knox said. "You duped me and my investment team. We paid a premium to buy into the resort, and come to find out we flushed millions of dollars down the toilet because you inflated the value of the property with your scam."

"I didn't dupe you. I was protecting my business. My family. Our family. Like you should be doing right now."

Our family? That was funny. "Now you want me to collude with you on this new lie? You want me to break the law and put hundreds of guests and employees at risk. Is that seriously what you're asking of me?"

"You sit there pretending that you can compartmentalize business and family, but this business was built on the backs of our family. It's all about family, and always has been, and I won't let you bastardize what we've created. So I'm asking you, man to man, Briscoe to Briscoe, to shut up and follow my lead. I'm still the CEO of this business, so the call is mine to make."

"For the record, you and I are not family in any way that counts. And you're only the CEO for now. And that call is Briscoe Equity Group's to make, as the controlling partners. That's my company, in case you'd forgotten, so I'm pretty sure they'll heed my recommendation to fire you."

Just like that, the last vestiges of their mentor/protégé illusion, along with any semblance of civility, shattered.

Ty rose again, looming over the desk. "You ungrateful son of a bitch."

Knox tipped back in his chair and propped his boots on the desk, inches from Ty's nose, forcing him to back off. "I'm ungrateful? So, what, you expected me to go along with your plan because we're family? Briscoe to Briscoe, like you said?"

"That's right," Ty growled from behind clenched teeth.

"You're counting on me to stand in allegiance with you, to break the law with you, because we're family, and family doesn't let a business divide them." Knox tipped his head back, face to the ceiling. "You hear that, Dad? Ty thinks I owe him a pledge of solidarity because we're family."

Ty's head was so red and filled with so much steam, it was a wonder his eyes didn't pop out of their sockets. "Don't you dare bring him into this."

Knox finished his drink, then spun the glass onto the table near his boots. "What do you think all this is about? Me, being here." He pointed to the ceiling. "I'm here to deliver a big *fuck you* on behalf of my dad."

"You'll never get away with this."

Looks like they were on to the empty threat portion of the conversation. "Get away with what? I could sue you for falsifying documents. It's in the contract that I could. Hell, I'm pretty sure I could have you arrested, using this tape I just made of our conversation as evidence." He made a show of stopping the recording.

All that bright red color drained from Ty's face. "You wouldn't dare."

"Why not? Let me hear you say it this time." Knox cupped is ear. "Because we're family?"

"You bastard. What do you want from me?"

Knox ignored the question while he uploaded the recording to a zip drive, then pocketed it. He brought his legs to the ground, then stood and shook them out. "Good question. And we'll get to that. But, first, the engineers are waiting, so let's get going." He adjusted his hat, then buttoned his sports coat. "One last thing. I won't sue you, Ty. I've got better things to do with my time. And I won't tell your family or your employees just yet, either.

"All I ask is that you remember that I didn't take anything from you. You did this to yourself. You were bleeding this resort dry, overextending your assets. But it's okay because you invited my colleagues and me to this party and we'll take it from here. Your pride's wounded, but you know this is the right move. I'm the future of this company, not you. The sooner you get on board with that idea, the easier your life will be. And I'm sure we can come up with a great retirement package for you when you're ready."

Ty blocked Knox's passage to the door. "You show up here with your entitlement, but you're not entitled to shit. I will not be defeated so easily, boy."

Lucky for Knox that he'd never expected Ty to make it

easy on him. "You're afraid, but that's natural. Change is hard."

"What's your long game?" Ty said in a low rumble.

Know squared a look at him. "You sure you want to know?"

With a growl, Ty whirled around and smacked the scotch bottle off the table. The glass shattered and the room filled with the noxious fumes of evaporating alcohol.

"I'll take that as a yes. It's simple, really. I'm going to bring the resort back from the brink of disaster and make it greater than it's ever been."

"And then what?"

Knox debated coming clean, then decided there was no harm in it. "And then, I'm going to strip *Briscoe* from its name and I'm going to sell it to the highest corporate bidder."

"You wouldn't dare," he whispered.

Knox sniffed. "Do you ever miss Clint? He was your sole brother, only a year and a half apart in age. You could've had each other's backs, but you turned your back on him, and on my mom, and on me and my siblings. You did that, you and Tyson. When Tyson died, my dad didn't get a penny. He had to scrape his way through life to make ends meet. And now you want me to show you mercy? You want me to pretend that I care what happens to you a year from now? Two years from now?"

The only sound in the room was Ty's angry breaths taken through flared nostrils.

"What did you think was gonna happen when you brought me here, Ty? What'd you think?"

Ty seemed to collect himself all at once. The rage in his eyes transformed to determination. "Nothin's happened yet." Proud words, though his voice betrayed him by cracking once.

Knox didn't think he'd ever had a more satisfying business meeting in all his life. This moment and the look on Ty's face, along with the desperate quality to his voice, were going to sustain Knox for a lot of years to come. Long after he'd remodeled the resort and sold it away.

Chapter Eleven

Friday night, Emily was stirring a pot of grits in Knox's kitchen when the doorbell rang. Carina, who'd texted Emily an hour ago begging for grits and pickled shrimp again. She hoped Knox didn't mind her inviting Carina to his house without his permission. Ever since Knox and Emily's momentary insanity at his mother's house, Emily had done her best to play by the rules and keep her distance from him. She'd even managed to keep her unwanted lusting to a minimum, thanks to Haylie's help serving dinner every night.

But even if Knox would've minded Carina's presence in his house, it was early enough in the workday that he'd probably never find out, and Emily wasn't willing to make Carina wait to have her crazy cravings satisfied.

She opened the front door to Carina, who was showing off her baby bump in a body-contouring royal blue sweater dress. Judging by her wide-eyed, awed expression, she was impressed by the grandeur of Knox's digs. She entered the foyer, her head on a swivel. "So this is his house."

"This is it."

"I've never been on this property before. I didn't realize so much space was back up in these hills. And this house . . . it's so modern. I can see why he bought it. It reminds me of him."

"How so?" Emily asked.

Carina lifted a shoulder in a shrug. "Some might call it sleek and sophisticated, but I think it's kind of cold and detached."

That's what Carina thought of Knox? Cold and detached? On what planet? "I don't get that vibe from him at all. Quite the opposite."

Carina leveled a teasing look at Emily, tapping a finger on her chin. "Let me guess. What's the opposite of cold? Oh yeah, you think he's hot."

Carina had no idea how right she was, and Emily wasn't about to fill her in. "You're really getting a lot of mileage out of that joke."

"I do my best. I smell something yummy other than my grits. Is that chili?"

"Frito Pie. It was Knox's dad's favorite and I got ahold of his family recipe. Not that I'm sticking to it very closely."

"Genius idea."

"Let's hope Knox thinks so, too. Come on into the kitchen. Your grits are about done."

Carina rubbed Emily's back as they walked. "You're not only a genius, but a life saver."

Emily sat Carina at the kitchen table and placed a steaming bowl of grits in front of her. While Carina looked on in rapt wonderment, Emily grated aged cheddar over the grits.

"Sure you don't want any shaved black truffles on that?" Emily asked.

Carina licked her lips. "Uh-uh. This is perfect."

"Great. Your pickled shrimp will be right up." While

she dug in, Emily pulled the jar of pickled shrimp from the fridge, then set to work chopping parsley to garnish it with.

She was nearly done when Carina's cell phone rang. When Carina saw the read-out, she let her spoon fall from her hand. It landed on the table with a clatter. "Oh, please, no, God . . ."

The shift in Carina's mood was lightning-quick, calm to panic in an instant as she accepted the call. Emily set down her knife and listened. Her pulse quickened, though she had no idea what was happening.

"It's Haylie's neighbor," Carina said, answering. Her face turned white as she listened to whoever was on the line. "Is the yelling still going on?"

Dread sank like a rock in Emily's stomach. "What is it?" she whispered.

Carina ignored the question. She reached a hand out and gripped Emily's sleeve. "Breaking glass? Are you sure?"

The tone of Carina's voice, the call from the worried neighbor, yelling and breaking glass . . . Emily knew what those signifiers meant.

"Mrs. Cordera, would you go knock on their door? See if you can disrupt it," Carina said. "I'm calling 9-1-1. I'll be there as fast as I can."

Emily couldn't decide where to direct her anger—at Wendell, at Carina, or at herself for, apparently, not being good enough to be trusted with the information. Clearly, Haylie and Wendell's marriage wasn't just dysfunctional. This went way beyond Wendell having control issues and Haylie needing to learn to stand up for herself, as Carina had led her to believe. "He's hurting her, isn't he?"

Carina dialed 9-1-1, then turned terrified eyes on Emily as the phone rang. "Yes, hello, um, I think my sister's in danger. I just got a call from her neighbor about a fight between her and her husband, and I have reason to believe it's getting physically violent."

Emily's heart sank. Hearing the words, calling the police. This was real. This was happening. While Carina filled the dispatcher in on the details, Emily grabbed her purse from its spot in the pantry, then gathered Carina's purse and keys. At the last moment, she remembered she had dinner on the stove. She turned off the heat, but didn't bother to do anything to preserve the food. None of that mattered now in the face of Haylie's danger.

"I'll start the car," she mouthed to Carina.

Emily climbed into the driver's seat of Carina's car, which was newer and faster than Emily's. Carina didn't question the choice. In a daze, she sank into the passenger seat, gripping her cell phone too hard. On the drive, Carina dialed Haylie's cell phone and texted her over and over, to no avail.

"I don't understand what Haylie's doing home, anyway. It's the middle of a workday," Carina said.

"She was in Knox's office, cleaning up broken glass when I delivered Knox's breakfast around nine. I guess the bottle of scotch tipped over. Or maybe Haylie bumped into it. She didn't say. Anyhow, Knox was already out and about with some building inspectors, she told me. Maybe he let her go early because it's Friday." After a moment's deliberation, Emily added, "This isn't the first time, is it? There's a reason you have Haylie's neighbor's number programmed into your phone."

Carina's attention slipped to the window. "No. This isn't the first time."

Emily pushed Carina's car even faster and gripped the steering wheel harder so she wouldn't shake like Carina. She wished she could be mad at Carina for misleading her about Haylie's situation. It would be so much less scary to be angry at her friend than at a monster like

Wendell. But focusing her outrage and fear on Carina would only be deflecting. Still, she wanted to know why Carina hadn't felt comfortable being honest.

"I would've been there for you and Haylie," Emily said. "I would've tried to help even. I wish you would have felt comfortable confiding in me."

"I'm sorry. I've only known for a couple months, and not because Haylie told me. I saw bruises on her arms. You know I've been trying to get her out of the situation, but she won't leave him. Heck, she won't even admit he's abusing her. She keeps swearing that they're happy and everything's okay. I don't know what to do. She's desperate for no one to know. I realized right away that I couldn't tell anyone because if it got back to my dad, he'd make the situation even worse."

That was the truth. Emily could easily imagine what Ty would do if he found out that his little princess was being abused. "He'd kill Wendell. He'd storm in and shoot the bastard dead."

"He would. And then he'd go to jail for murder. Or, if he didn't succeed, he'd make Wendell look like the victim in Haylie's mind. She's so brainwashed that she'd do anything to defend Wendell, like she does to me anytime I suggest he's less than a perfect husband. Even worse, if my dad or I spooked Wendell, what if he left Texas and took Haylie with him? You know he would. They'd disappear, and then what could I do to try to save her? Nothing. It seemed safer to keep them here and try to convince her to leave him."

Emily hadn't considered the possibility of Haylie and Wendell leaving, but Carina was right. That would be devastating for everyone and put Haylie in even more danger.

Carina continued, "I've been trying everything, reading books on how to help battered wives leave their husbands, trying to get Haylie into therapy. I've contacted shelters and gotten information about how to get Haylie out of the situation when she's ready, but I don't know what else to do. She has to find the courage to take that step. I can't make her save herself."

Emily reached across the seat and took Carina's hand. "You're doing the best you can."

"So many times, I tried to tell you, but with your history with your father, I wasn't sure if that was the right thing to do. You hate talking about your past and I didn't want to trigger anything. And I didn't want you to spring into action and spook Wendell into taking off with Haylie. I've been so scared."

"Does Decker know?"

Carina shook her head. "No. He'd confront Wendell as fast as my dad would. I just can't . . . The situation is too delicate to bring too many people into the fold."

"Except now, you called the cops. Your dad's golf buddies with the Sheriff."

Carina squeezed her eyes closed. "I know. I only had a split second to decide that. Haylie's going to hate me, but I love her too much to let him . . ." She swallowed hard and gripped Emily's hand. "What if he kills her?"

Fear squeezed her ribcage. It was a legitimate possibility, one that Emily had borne as a kid, every time her parents fought, a fear she still entertained whenever she thought about her mom continuing to stay married to him. She had to believe that if her father had killed her mom, she would've heard, somehow. Wouldn't she? Despite that she had long ago severed all the ties to her former life and her blood relatives—so thoroughly that no one from her old life should be able to reach her—a part of her still wondered if, somehow, a daughter could sense her mother's murder.

"It's okay," Emily said. "I get why you didn't. I know

I don't like to talk about my past, but that's just because I've moved on. My father doesn't have the power to trigger me anymore." Emily took Carina's hand. "Calling the cops on Wendell was the right thing to do. Maybe they'll catch him in the act and arrest him. That would be the best outcome."

Carina's eyes closed. "Drive faster, will you? I'm going to pray."

She released Emily's hand and clasped hers in front of her face, mouthing a silent prayer of her own. Heart pounding and her head dizzy with fear for Haylie, Emily turned her focus back to the road.

Haylie and Wendell's apartment was a twenty-minute drive from the resort, though both places were located in the same small town of Dulcet, in the heart of Ravel County. The apartment was tucked into the backside of a complex one block removed from Dulcet's Main Street, behind Delbert's Grocery Depot and two blocks from the firehouse.

Ty had invited Haylie and Wendell to live in the family's compound on Briscoe Ranch after they eloped two years earlier, even offering to remodel Carina's former office above the garage into a granny flat so the newlyweds could have privacy, but Wendell had insisted they strike out on their own. It made sense now why Wendell had done that. An abuser's first job was to isolate his victim from her support network.

Emily and Carina arrived at the apartment complex to find a crowd gathered in the doorways and parking lot, all eyes on the spectacle on the second-floor walkway. Haylie was standing outside her open apartment door, dressed in a gray skirt and silky blue top, barefoot, and shouting at the top of her lungs while gesticulating wildly at the two sheriff's deputies who stood next to their cruiser in the parking lot.

As she took in the scene, Carina sucked in a pained breath. "Oh, no."

Emily ran a visual scan of Haylie's body for damage. Her face was red, her hair was tangled, and the top two buttons on her blouse had pulled from their buttonholes, with one missing and the other dangling by a thread. Other than that, her body showed no visible signs of injury. Though her arms were covered by the blouse's long sleeves, she seemed to be moving them fine. Her legs looked strong and bruise-free. Her lips weren't swollen, and neither were her cheeks.

Emily patted Carina's knee as she double-parked behind a line of cars. "She doesn't look hurt too badly. We can handle this."

Haylie bent down and grabbed a potted succulent from a cluster of plants near her front door and held it over the railing, looking ready to hurl it at the officers. "Fuck you! No one asked you to come here. This is private property!"

The deputies perked up at that. One of them made a calming gesture with his open palms. "Ma'am, please. Set the plant down or we'll have to take you in. You can't be destroying property and threatening an officer."

Carina scrambled to unfasten her seatbelt and open her door. "Let's get over there before she gets herself arrested."

When Haylie spotted Carina and Emily, the eye roll she gave them was probably visible from space. With the plant in her hand, she threw both arms in the air. Potting soil and dried leaves rained over Haylie and fluttered to the first floor walkway below her. "And look who it is now! The guardian fucking angels I never asked for."

Carina's steps faltered for a moment before continuing on her route up the concrete stairs at the end of the building. Emily followed, keeping quiet and letting Carina take the lead. "Are you okay, Haylie?"

Haylie stabbed one of her long, acrylic nails toward the deputies. "Did you call them? I told you to stay out of my fucking business!"

Carina stopped at the top of the stairs, several apartment doors away from Haylie. "We can't stay out of it. We love you too much."

Haylie snarled. "Do I look like I need your help?"

Yes, she did. Emily's gaze went to the mangled potted plant. Carina's must have, too, because Haylie looked down at it in her hands as though realizing for the first time that she was holding something.

With proud, if stilted, movement, Haylie set the plant down, then rose to her full height, her chin high. She extended the middle fingers of both hands and held them out to Carina and Emily. "How about now? Do I look like I want you your help now?"

"Is he here?" Carina asked. There was no need to clarify who *he* was.

Haylie huffed. "No, which I'm sure frustrates the fuck out of you, seeing as how you were trying to get him arrested."

"We want you to be safe. That's all," Carina said, staying calm.

Haylie released a hard bark of laughter. "No, I'm pretty sure you just want him to go to jail, but nice try. You've had it out for him since the first time he asked me on a date. You won't be happy until I'm alone and he's gone so you can keep your status as the perfect one. You don't think I know what you're all about?"

"Haylie, please. This isn't about me."

But Haylie was having none of it. She spun on her heel, flung her apartment door open, and slammed it again behind her.

A silver-haired neighbor poked her head out of the door and looked at Carina with wide, frightened eyes.

"Wendell took off before the cops got here, right after I got off the phone with you. I hope she's not mad I called you. If you could not tell her it was me who got in touch with you, I'd be much obliged. And a tip for my troubles wouldn't hurt nothin' either."

Carina nodded. "I won't tell, but you did the right thing by calling me. Thank you, Mrs. Cordera." She rifled through her purse and pulled out a handful of twenty-dollar bills. Mrs. Cordera took the offered money and tucked it into her pants pocket. "I can't take it anymore, the two of them at each other's throats all the time. I feel for that girl because she's got a nasty dog for a man, but there's no peace around here anymore."

"I know. I'm sorry."

"We're working on it," Emily added.

With a harrumph, Mrs. Cordera disappeared behind her closed door.

It took longer for Carina and Emily to smooth the ruffled feathers of the sheriff's deputies. They didn't seem to have processed that Haylie Halcott was a Briscoe, or who Carina's high-profile father was, which was all for the better. Anything to keep Ty from making the situation worse.

In the end, the deputies agreed not to charge Haylie with any crime, and to swing through the apartment parking lot whenever possible, to keep an eye on the situation. After many thanks, Carina and Emily mounted the stairs again and let themselves into Haylie's apartment.

The place smelled of cleaning products and the savory scent of braised meat and tomato sauce. It was also dark, which wasn't surprising. When you lived with an abuser, you tended to keep the curtains closed. Even Emily's parents' two-story penthouse apartment with expansive views of Lake Michigan had the ambiance of a cave unless company was present.

Other than the darkness, Haylie's apartment decor looked like so many acquaintances' apartments where Emily had bunked down after she ran away from home. Dull white paint on the walls punctuated by the occasional plastic-framed poster print, and decorated with a mish-mash of worn furniture, inexpensive white bookshelves, and colorful plastic storage solutions and beanbags that looked better suited for a college dorm room.

Magazines were strewn on the short, tightly woven brown carpet as though they'd been knocked off the coffee table. Broken shards of a crystal vase were scattered over the living room floor near the TV stand, with carnations, daisies, and baby's breath strewn among the pieces.

Emily could feel Haylie's manic effort to appease Wendell and keep up the appearance that she was a happy wife. Nausea tightened her throat and tingled her sinuses. She knew that behavior. She'd grown up watching her mom tie herself into knots to keep the peace in their house.

They found Haylie in the small kitchen, looking out the back window and absentmindedly stroking the ear of the tiny, black and white dog in her arms—Twinnie, the teacup puppy Haylie's parents had gotten her and Wendell as a housewarming gift.

"Get the fuck out of here," Haylie said without turning around.

"No," Carina said, gently but firmly.

With a haughty sniff, Haylie tucked Twinnie in the crook of her arm and walked to the refrigerator. From deep in the recesses of the lowest shelf, she pulled out a chocolate candy bar. Emily took note of her trembling fingers as she unwrapped it and bit off a huge chunk. She closed her eyes, as though the chocolate's medicinal effect was washing through her.

"He's going to come back for dinner and you can't be here," Haylie said, her eyes still closed.

So tempting to start in on a lecture about how Haylie deserved better than a man who would be upset to find Haylie's family and friends visiting. Instead, Emily said, "We won't stay too long."

Carina looked like she wanted to say all the same things Emily was holding herself back from pointing out, but instead, she lifted the lid of the crockpot next to the stove. "Is this beef stew? It smells wonderful. You've really become a great cook."

Emily opened a drawer in search of a spoon. "Mind if I try it? I'm always on the hunt for new stew recipes." Which was a total lie, but it was a relief to have a neutral topic to cut through the tension.

"Don't taste it," Haylie said. "I spit in it."

Carina's eyes went wide. "You *what?*"

Haylie shrugged, then set Twinnie on the floor. "I came home on my lunch break to put dinner in the crockpot and caught him watching porn again, so this is what he gets."

"That's what you two were arguing over? Porn?"

Haylie's face blanched. "No. That wasn't it. I would never call him out for that, but—" She seemed to notice that her façade of being in control was slipping, and straightened. "I'm not into getting mad; I'm into getting even. Like this . . ." She walked to the crockpot, lifted the lid, shifted her jaw as though gathering her saliva, then spit right into the bubbling broth.

Emily recoiled internally. Nothing was more disgusting than perfectly good food being defiled, even if a part of her was cheering Haylie on for her quiet defiance. Maybe that was a first step towards finding the strength to stand up for herself by leaving.

Carina, on the other hand, burst out laughing. "Ew, sis. That's so gross." But when Haylie made to set the lid down, Carina took it from her. "Allow me to help," she said with over-formality before added her spit to the pot.

Haylie's face cracked into a grin. "See? You're nasty, too. Must be a Briscoe thing."

They both looked to Emily. Carina tipped her ear toward the crockpot. "Care to help season Wendell's dinner?"

Spitting into food was not her jam, but she would never do anything to dim the renewed luster in Haylie's eyes. Without looking into the pot, she said, "Maybe it needs some special pepper." And then, before she could talk herself out of it, she took off her clog, held it over the crockpot, and tapped it until bits of dirt sprinkled down. Squelching her subsequent gag of revulsion was tough, but Emily managed.

The last vestiges of Haylie's armor vanished. With a look of devilish delight, she skipped to a cupboard. "I have a better idea. I think the stew needs more meat in it." She held out a can of beef-and-gravy premium dog food.

"Hell, yeah, it does," Carina said.

As the dog food oozed out of the can and into the crockpot, Emily swallowed back another retch by imagining Wendell sitting down at the kitchen table that night and digging into a steaming bowl of Haylie's special stew. She tried not to think about the chili for the Frito Pie she had sitting on Knox's stovetop.

As if reading Emily's mind, Haylie said, "Don't tell Knox about this. Please. I need that job. It's the first time I've—"

"You don't have to say any more. I know." Emily had no plans to breathe one word to anyone, especially Knox. There was too much humiliation involved in being abused to take on the additional shame of it being made public.

She would never forget the looks she'd gotten the next day at school from two friends who'd been at her house and witnessed her dad losing control, drunk and stumbling, calling her a piece of shit before passing out on the sofa. Those friends never came back to her house. No friends did. Eventually, Emily stopped inviting them. The risk was too great.

Haylie looked at her phone, then crumpled. "Oh, shit. Look at the time. My lunch break ended an hour ago. Shit. Knox is going to fire me for sure."

"He won't," Emily said, believing it.

"Let me hug you," Carina said, choking up. "Please."

Haylie picked up Twinnie, then allowed Carina to envelop them both in a hug. "You're too good for him, sis," Carina said.

"He and I belong together," Haylie croaked.

"Stay at my place tonight, would you? That would make me feel so much better."

Emily cringed. Carina didn't realize it, but she was undoing their efforts to gain Haylie's trust because Haylie wasn't anywhere near ready, emotionally, mentally, to take such a leap as to sleep over at Carina's house, even if only for a night. That would mean admitting there was a problem.

Sure enough, Haylie pushed out of Carina's arms and threw a protective arm over Twinnie, as though Carina might snatch the dog from her hands to use it as leverage. "Are you kidding me? So you can spend the night judging me and begging me to leave him."

"But it's true. You need—"

Emily stopped Carina's well-meaning, but ill-conceived plea with a hand to her shoulder. "Go wait in the living room. Give us a sec."

Carina looked between Emily and Haylie. Emily tried to tell her it wasn't personal and they weren't shutting her out, but Emily and Haylie needed a moment—survivor to survivor.

Emily waited for Carina to leave, then reached onto her keychain and took off her apartment key. "My apartment is open to you, anytime, day or night, no questions asked and no lectures given. I'm rarely there, I don't have any roommates, and it's safe. Nobody knows where it is except Carina and that's just the way I like it. Tell the guy at the front desk that I gave you a key and he'll give you passage into the building."

Emily pulled a paperback thriller from her purse and flipped to page 100. With Haylie looking on, she scribbled detailed directions to her apartment, right over the text. Better to write the instructions out longhand instead of a mere address so Haylie wouldn't have to look up directions on an internet search engine if she decided to go, since Wendell could find her that way. And Haylie could keep the book close to her, in her car or purse, without anyone being the wiser. She tucked the key inside, then walked to a bookshelf she'd seen in the living room.

Carina was busying herself using the side of a magazine to push the broken vase pieces into a pile.

With Haylie watching, Emily slid the thriller between two other paperbacks.

"Where's your broom and dustpan?" Carina said.

Haylie hurried to her side and took the magazine from her hands. "I can finish on my own. You two have to leave. He'll be back any time."

Carina stood, her eyes welling with fresh tears. "Please come with us, Haylie. Please."

Haylie looked past her sister to Emily, as though Emily were her only ally—the only one who understood her plight. Yes, they were both survivors, but the truth was Emily didn't understand, not deep down, not really. She would never be able to understand on an elemental level why a battered woman remained in her abusive situation. She only knew what she'd seen with her mom. Emily had rejected her abuse and fled as soon as she was old enough to survive on her own. She didn't know what it meant to choose to stay.

Emily looped an arm around Carina's shoulders and pulled her out the door. "You know how to reach us if you need anything," Carina told Haylie. "I'll be pissed if you don't call us."

"No more cops," Haylie said.

Emily wouldn't promise that, and judging by Carina's silence, neither would she. At the car, Emily pulled Carina into her arms as her friend's silent tears gave way to wrenching sobs.

Emily held her tight. "We're going to get her out of there. I promise. She's going to get through this. Someday, she's going to be the strongest badass of all badasses that ever were. She's going to rise and she's going to live a wonderful, happy life pursuing her dreams. She's going to soar."

"Like you did," Carina croaked.

Emily wasn't soaring yet, but she was getting there, one meal at a time for Knox.

Chapter Twelve

With the heady aroma of simmering tomato sauce filling the air, Knox stood in his empty kitchen and surveyed the mess. It looked like Emily had paused mid-dinner prep. An unopened bag of Fritos chips sat on the counter, along with a cold bowl of grits topped with melted and cooled white cheese. On the island, a glass jar sat, the shrimp inside visible through a layer of condensation. More ingredients were strewn over the counters.

The pan on the stove was cool to the touch. He opened the lid and found chili, cold. His eyes again found the bag of Fritos. *Frito Pie? Really?* That was hardly the obvious choice for an accomplished chef.

Then again, Emily was no ordinary chef. Frito Pie had been his father's favorite meal. No doubt Knox's mother had given Emily the idea, but he no longer cared that she'd used his mother for insider information because the relief that his exile to Gastronomyville was over superseded all annoyance over her methods.

The question now was, where was the chef? The house felt empty, but Emily's silver hatchback sat squarely in the driveway, right in front of the steps leading up to the main entrance as though she owned the place, so she had to be around somewhere. Asleep on his bed again, perhaps?

Doubtful. That was a slippery slope that neither of them dared start down.

He walked through the house calling her name, then stepped out to the deck. The evening was blustery. Wind whipped at his hair and dried leaves scuttled across his deck. The time change was a couple of weeks away, so the glow of dusk still saturated the hills, even at the dinner hour. He strode with purpose along the deck, then down to the lake's edge, peering in the boathouse and along the trail that led to the lookout point on the hill above his home. It was as though Emily had vanished into thin air.

Back in the kitchen, he texted her. *Where are you?*

He held the phone, awaited her reply. Nothing.

He felt like a whiny, 1950s-era husband. *Where's the little woman and why isn't she in the kitchen ready to serve me dinner when I get home from work?*

Yes, she was probably still furious about their momentary insanity at his mom's house, but there was no way she'd go from creating culinary masterpieces to brushing him off with a lowbrow dinner cooling on the stove. Impossible that she'd leave the kitchen such a mess. She was a professional, and she wanted the restaurant too much. The truth reminded him that, as opposed to a whiny husband, he was her boss. He was entitled by their arrangement to expect her here, cooking for him, every night this month.

And what of next month? he caught himself wondering. Then fear jolted him out of his selfishness. What if something were wrong with Emily—an emergency, an accident? Could she have been kidnapped? Impossible. But what if?

Are you okay? he texted.

The minutes ticked by. Nothing.

Rather than text again, he called, but her phone flipped to voicemail instantly. He called her office next, but the phone in her office at the resort rang on and on.

He was about to call Carina when the kitchen door opened and Emily trudged in. Her face was drawn and her eyes red-rimmed.

Knox hurried to her and braced his hands on her shoulders. "What happened?"

Eyes downcast, she wrenched her body away and walked to the stove. "I was hoping you weren't home yet."

He strode after her, but ground to a halt a few feet away and stuffed his hands in his pockets. The way she hunched away from him, stiff and private, reminded him anew that he had no business imposing himself on her personal life and he certainly had no business touching her. "No such luck. Your car was in the driveway, so how did you get here? Did you walk from somewhere?"

With a shake of her head, she picked up the chef's knife, then set it down again, as though she couldn't quite remember what she needed it for. Her hand lighted over the jar of shrimp, then touched the rim of the grits bowl. He'd never seen her frazzled like this, not even at his mother's house, after they'd . . .

He shook the thought away. A little tough to establish professional distance when his thoughts kept sliding back to that night.

"I got a ride from a friend," Emily said. "Sorry that dinner's going to be late. It couldn't be helped." With that, she turned the burner under the pot on.

"What happened tonight? What's wrong?"

She turned to face him, but her haunted expression only left him with more questions. All he knew was, he wasn't going to let her cook. She was too distracted to be anything more than a hazard to herself. What she needed was TLC, not to serve him. "Forget the Frito Pie. And forget cooking, too. I had a great day and I'd love to celebrate. With you. Let's go out to a restaurant instead." *Jesus, man. So much for keeping a professional distance.* "It would be an informative exercise," he added in haste. "You could choose a restaurant that's the critics' darling right now and critique it for me. Explain how you would do it better."

"Briscoe Ranch is out in the boonies. The hottest restaurants in Texas are hundreds of miles away and probably booked solid since it's Friday night."

A legitimate point, one he should agree with so they could move back to solid, professional ground. "One, I have access to a helicopter. And two, Shayla's an expert at last-minute reservations for everyone at the equity firm. She has yet to be turned down for a reservation on my behalf."

"I forget that you're a billionaire."

"Multimillionaire. I'm still a little less than halfway to a billion in assets and investments." And didn't he sound like the biggest douchebag in history, clarifying that for her? "But most of it is tied up."

Her eyes lit, sharp with humor. The only trace of her former distress was the red rimming her eyes. "So you're an underachiever, is what you're saying? Okay. But just so we're clear, I'm definitely judging you on that."

"Oh, had you stopped judging me for a moment there?"

She inhaled slow and deep through her nose, as though waking up and drawing life and hope into her body once more.

He filled a glass with water and delivered it to the counter next to her hand. "Name the restaurant and I'll give Shayla a call."

She lifted the glass and drank deeply of the water. Her hand trembled with the effort. Perhaps she hadn't rebounded as swiftly as she wanted him to believe. "A friend of mine is in an abusive relationship. There was an incident today and I tried to help. That's why I'm late."

He wasn't sure what he'd been expecting the reason for her absence to be, but that sure wasn't it. "Is she out of the situation now?"

Emily set the glass down too hard. Not because she seemed angry, but as though her storming emotions had robbed her of complete control of her body. "No. She won't leave. She's stuck there, believing she deserves it. That's the way it is, you know? You absorb the shame of it until you're nothing. That's the most horrible part about abuse. For most victims, there is no rock bottom. It's a well that never ends."

She shuttered her expression again and turned away, her gaze on the lake through the window.

Knox didn't know the first thing about abusive relationships, but Emily had spoken as though she did. She couldn't be talking about herself, could she? The inimitable Emily Ford was no victim, and as far as he knew, she wasn't involved with anyone. God, he hoped not, on both accounts. Then again, how could he be sure? He knew practically nothing about her outside of her culinary skills and her friendship with the Briscoes. The realization floored him. He'd slept with her, she had a key to his house, she knew his father's favorite meal, and yet she was a complete enigma to him.

"I wish there was a way to help your friend," he said.

She sniffled, then released a long, slow exhalation. "I might hold you to that offer someday."

The possibility rose in his mind again that she was the one in trouble. "I hope you do. And in the meantime, where should we dine tonight?"

She only had to think for a moment. "The Smoking Gun."

He raised an eyebrow in question.

"It's a restaurant in Austin," she said. "You'd love it, if Shayla can get us in, which would be a huge *if*. They've been booking more than a month out."

"That won't be a problem."

She smoothed a self-conscious hand down her front, the white T-shirt stretching over her curves. "I guess I'd better borrow a dress from Carina."

Another dress . . . He wasn't sure his heart could take it. Would she let her hair down? Would she be true to her bold streak and wear comfortable flats or slip her feet into delicate, strappy high-heels? The thrill of discovery coursing through him should have been enough of a warning flag to spur him to cancel.

He watched her lift the glass of water for another drink, her hands steadier now. At least his dinner plan had succeeded in calming her nerves, though a weary sheen settled over her eyes once more.

"I'll meet you at the resort's helipad in an hour," he said.

According to Emily, this was her first time in a helicopter. If the idea of death-defying height and the careening through the sky in something barely larger than the size of her car had made her anxious, she didn't show it as they boarded the helicopter that Shayla had called for them from a private airfield in San Antonio.

Even if Emily had been on edge, there was no way it compared to Knox's nervous anticipation of sitting across the table from her in a candlelit restaurant. Especially with her looking so extraordinarily beautiful tonight. She'd worn her curly hair down so that it skimmed her shoulders and brushed against the black dress that seemed perfectly molded to her every curve. Keeping his eyes on her face was proving a Herculean task.

Ty had watched their every move from a golf cart at the edge of the heliport. For all Knox's determination not to give the impression of impropriety with Emily, he sure was failing at that tonight, whisking her away for a nine o'clock reservation, right from their place of business out in the open for all to see.

"It's a rush, isn't it? Having that much money at your disposal," she said once they were in the air.

"It has its perks."

"It's no wonder you weren't impressed with my lowly, no-name credentials when you first came to Briscoe Ranch. Why would you be when you can dine on meals created by the finest chefs in the world with the snap of your fingers?"

He wasn't sure what to say to that that wouldn't get him in trouble. She was correct on all fronts, but her analysis was only part of the story. "Then what does it say about your charisma and your skills that you've made me see how narrow my vantage point about food was?"

She smiled a little at his words, then settled back to enjoy the view.

A car was waiting for them at the private airfield where they touched down. Knox insisted on helping her jump out of the helicopter, which she probably only allowed because the strappy black heels she wore looked precarious indeed. Her hand was small and cool to the touch. But still, he found the willpower to release it when she was safely on the ground.

She allowed for his help again when they reached the restaurant. This time, after he pulled her from the car, he didn't let her hand go, but tucked it into the crook of his arm, shocked all over again that she would allow it.

Perhaps, just for this night, they could leave their baggage and careers behind in Dulcet and simply be two friends out on the town. It was worth a try, anyway.

The Smoking Gun was a molecular gastronomist's take on a traditional Texas barbecue joint—a hipster paradise in the heart of hipsterville itself, Austin's Warehouse District. The mood was electric, the dining room crowded and noisy. They were seated at a relatively intimate window table and immediately attended to by a youthful, goateed server in skinny jeans and an even skinnier tie.

As soon as they'd ordered a bottle of Syrah and the server left, Emily tore a corner off a piece of Texas toast from the basket on the table. "You said you had a great day. What happened?"

She would, of course, learn the results of today's battle of wills in due time, probably along with the rest of the resort staff when it was announced that Knox was replacing Ty as the CEO, but not tonight. There was no way he was going to interfere with the warm sweetness that had returned to Emily's face or the casual, intimate manner with which she'd asked the question, as though this were merely one of thousands of nights that they'd come together over dinner, reviewing their day. He'd missed that this week, since she'd relegated him to the dining room to eat dinner alone.

So, instead, he told her simply, "I met with a team of structural engineers today about the expansion. It's great to see my vision for the resort starting to materialize. Hey, here's a question for you, since you've lived in Dulcet for quite a few years. Tell me stories about it snowing at the resort. I heard it doesn't happen often . . ."

To his delight, she regaled him with stories of flurries and miniature snowmen scraped together from the occasional light dustings of snow that Dulcet experienced in a normal year. After that, they poured over the menu, with Knox pausing to quiz her about various techniques and ingredients he'd either never heard of or been curious enough to ask about, and none he'd probably remember if he'd been tested, he was so fixated on Emily rather than their meal choices.

Their wine arrived, with Emily doing the tasting honors. At the first sip, her body swayed and her eyes fluttered closed for a long moment. A smile curved her lips. "Oh, wow."

The dim mood-lighting played on her body the same way as the moonlight had on the rowboat ride they'd taken. The glow kissed her skin and reflected off her hair like gold flecks. It glittered over her lower lip and played in her eyes like lightning. And just as he had on that boat ride, he couldn't take his eyes off her.

While the server filled their wine glasses, Knox ordered one of every dish that had caught their eye, eager to expedite the server's interruption so he could have Emily to himself again. When the server left, Knox took his wine glass in hand. "So, it's good?"

"Better than good. I can think of six different dishes to cook for you that I could pair with this wine."

"Why? What does it taste like?" Anything to keep her talking.

"You." Her smile fell. With a shake of her head, she pinched the bridge of her nose. "That came out wrong. What I meant was, it reminds me of you. Complicated, peppery, with a touch of sweet berries and notes of leather and tobacco that remind me of your rodeo days and that black hat you're so fond of."

He took a sip. The flavors burst against the roof of his mouth and tingled over his tongue. "I'll have to order a case for my house."

That sly smile returned. She swirled the wine in her glass. "Funny, I was just thinking about how I'll have to order it for my new restaurant."

Yes, she would. But he couldn't think of a way to answer her that didn't jump the gun about making his decision. Because as soon as that happened, then their deal was done and he wasn't prepared to give up the pleasure of coming home to her every night. So instead, he cleared his throat. "Decker and I were able to hook up for a fishing lesson earlier this week. It was fun."

Her only acknowledgment of his abrupt change of topic was a brief flicker of her eyebrows. "Did you catch anything?"

"A few small bass."

"No sign of Phantom, though?"

Knox rolled another sip of wine over his tongue. "That sneaky fish didn't even jump out of the water to make his presence known. I told Decker the story about Phantom attacking me, and he thought I was bullshitting him."

"Keep trying to catch it. Once Decker sees Phantom, he'll believe you."

"That's the plan. Decker loaned me his fishing gear, said he wasn't going to need it for a while with the baby on the way, so if you feel like trying your hand at catching Phantom, be my guest. It's in the boathouse. I could even share the pointers Decker told me, if you'd like. Maybe between the two of us, we'd stand a chance at catching Phantom."

He could imagine himself and Emily sitting on his dock, spending an afternoon fishing and chatting amicably like they were tonight. The intense need for physical connection still crackled in the air between them, but rather than being a hindrance, it served to sharpen his awareness of every little detail of her, from the way she pressed the wine glass to her lips or tucked her chin and cast her eyes down when she smiled to every story she told and the inflection of her voice.

To the suggestion that they fish together, she raised her eyebrows in a show of skepticism. "Maybe we should try chumming for him from the dock. I just so happen to have a spoiled pot of Frito Pie at your house. It's your dad's favorite dish, and I get the feeling Phantom and your dad might have known each other, way back when, so who knows. Maybe the fish has a soft spot for Frito Pie, too." She wrinkled her nose. "I know that probably sounds crazy."

It did, but she was in sympathetic company. "Come on, you're talking to the guy who thinks his truck's haunted."

"Well, it is haunted," she deadpanned.

They shared a conspiratorial smile as their server laid out the dishes they'd ordered, a sampling from every section of the menu. In companionable silence, they dug in, critiquing the dishes as they went. After one bite of the pecan wood-smoked pork, Emily pushed the plate away.

"Uh-oh, you look queasy," Knox said.

"That's not queasiness, it's disgust. What a waste of an opportunity. This pecan wood is muddling the flavors of what should have been a complex profile. And, by the way, what's up with the chef adding a pecan-sage cream sauce to pecan wood-smoked pork—how is that, in any way, a cutting-edge flavor combination?" She scooped a bit of the cream onto her spoon and held it out to him. "If you lick this and let it roll around in your mouth, what do you feel?"

Before he knew what he was doing, he'd leaned across the table and let his lips close over the spoon as she held it, as though she were feeding it to him. Their gazes locked, making the back of his neck tingle with the electric shock of their connection. She snagged her bottom lip with her teeth as her gaze dipped to his mouth. God, he could imagine it, what it would feel like to lose his hands in her hair as he kissed those full, strawberry lips.

"Now use your tongue," she said.

Shit.

Her eyes went wide and her mouth fell open. "To taste

the cream sauce, I meant. Spread it over the roof of your mouth to release the flavors."

He couldn't very well swallow past the tightening of his throat, so he did as he was told, squishing the sauce against the roof of his mouth. A woodsy sage flavor bloomed over his tongue. Tasty, but rather flat. The flavor faded fast. "Nutmeg," he said.

"But how do you feel?"

Was that a trick question? How he felt at that moment, sitting across the table from Emily Ford, had absolutely nothing to do with the pecan sage cream sauce. All he could manage was a shrug.

Emily threw her hands up. "There you go. A shrug. The worst review a chef could get."

He could see how someone as passionate as she would be averse to mediocrity and bland feelings, especially given that every dish of hers he ate resulted in one big tempest of emotion. He took another bite of pork, redoubling his efforts to keep their night platonic and easy. "All I can think about now is you serving up your version of smoked pork. What would you do differently?"

She paused, considering the question. "Nothing I could say would capture the taste. You'd have to experience it."

He felt the smile her answer elicited from him all the way to his heart, as a kind of delicious ache. "Okay, when? And don't say, when you have your restaurant."

"Okay, then. When I'm good and ready," she said in a playful tone.

He would never tire of the give-and-take battle of their conversations. Never. "I've been thinking of hosting a dinner party next weekend for my equity firm partners and their wives. Smoked pork would be perfect. I mean, assuming you'd agree to cater it."

"Only if you don't make me hobnob with the dinner guests."

The condition made him smile even bigger—made his heart ache even more deliciously—it was so *her.* "Not a big fan of schmoozing clients?"

"I don't do small talk. I'm terrible at it."

It came as no surprise that for as confident and capable as she was in the kitchen, she was insecure about being the person in the spotlight. "It scares you."

She cast him a wary look. "Yes, it scares me," she said finally. "But who said we have to do everything that scares us? Humankind evolved to have fear for a reason, so why would we suppress it? Because some inspirational poster with a tightrope walker tells us that facing our fears is a virtue? That's bullshit. Maybe we're scared for a reason. Maybe we don't have to be great at everything. That's such a stupid American construct."

"There you go sounding like you're rationalizing your choice to labor in obscurity at the resort. How can we evolve if we don't conquer what scares us?"

She set her glass down and leaned forward. The fire in her eyes was something a man could get addicted to. "There is a noodle maker in Hong Kong who's been making noodles the same way for sixty years, the same way his father did, the same way as generations before him did, bouncing on a bamboo pole. That's it. That's his life. That's his skill. He has perfected noodle making. Do you have any idea how few people in this world ever perfect the art of anything?"

Almost no one, ever. Which begged the question, which struck more fear into hearts—spending sixty years on a single goal or accepting mediocrity for the manufactured concept of personal growth? It was a point Knox had certainly never considered before. And the fact that Emily Ford was telling him the noodle maker story, that she dared to strive for a level of perfection that might take a lifetime to achieve, made her the most fearless person in his life right now. Possibly, in the whole of Texas.

"I rendered you speechless," she said.

"I was thinking about how it is the rarity of diamonds that makes them so valuable."

She rolled her eyes melodramatically. "Oh my God, it's like you're an inspirational poster come to life. The point is, I am a culinary artist. That's what I'm striving to perfect, and I'm not going to waste my time pretending to be someone I'm not or learning a skill that useless for me, like making vapid small talk at dinner parties when I'd rather be in the kitchen honing my art."

Knox pushed the plate nearest him in Emily's direction. "Here's another dish that misses the mark, like that pork." The dish was a deconstructed mole involving two quail breasts floating on pasilla chili-chocolate foam, surrounded by caviar-like gelatin balls, each containing a different spice used in the sauce. It looked and tasted like a gastronomical chemistry experiment gone bad.

"The mole? I loved it, but I knew it would leave you feeling empty. Remember, I told you that when I ordered it?"

He hadn't put that all together, but she was correct. "How did you know?"

She pulled a bite of quail meat from the plate with her fork and dredged it through the caviar gelatin. "Because deconstructed mole is not what you need."

What he needed to do was slide his fingers through her unruly curls of hair. What he needed to do was call for the bill so they could leave this loud, pretentious restaurant and he could have her to himself. What he needed to do was kiss—

Stop it, you dirty bastard. She is not your wife or your lover or yours in any way. A ten-minute fuck in your childhood bedroom does not a personal relationship

make. And even if that could have been the start of
something, it would all come crashing down the moment
she learned of Knox's eventual plans for the resort. And
then she'd probably never speak to him again.

Regret knifed through him. Suddenly, acutely. He'd
thought his strategy for revenge was flawless. He would
have never guessed that a small-time chef would prove to
be the chink in his armor.

But never mind that tonight. He wouldn't allow
anything to interfere with this one perfect evening with
her. He had to reach back, struggling to remember the conversation at hand. Ah, yes. The mole that left him empty.
"All right, then, what do I need, if not mole?"

She met his gaze with a triumphant smile. "I've been
trying to show you since day one. You keep resisting. Are
you ready to surrender? Are you ready to let me feed you
like you need to be fed, every meal, unequivocally?"

He'd never heard a more erotic line of questions.

Their server appeared tableside. "How's everything,
folks?"

Emily sat back in her chair. Knox did the same. Both
of them watched the server pour more wine.

"You can take the smoked pork," Emily told the server.
"It didn't satisfy us."

"I'm sorry to hear that. Would you care for something
else?"

"Yes," she said. "We'll look at some menus."

Damn this interruption. He still hadn't gotten his
answer from Emily, and he suddenly, quite desperately,
needed to know what it was that Emily thought he needed.
Then again, perhaps a better question was why was he
intrigued by the idea that someone whom he'd only just
met would know what he needed better than he would. He
already knew what he needed. He forged his own path.

He didn't take advice from anyone outside his close circle of advisors. And Emily was not in that circle.

Maybe she should be.

And there he had it, the answer to his own question. What he needed, more than anything, more than smoked pork or mole or Frito pie, or even peach soup, was her.

He studied her as she perused the menu, feeling like he was seeing her for the first time all over again, marveling at his epiphany. *She's what you need, what you've always needed but could never find.*

"What should we get?" she said without looking up.

He had to clear his throat before speaking. "Anything you want."

She shone her bright green eyes at him. "I like the sound of that."

So did he. "Tell me, Emily. What are you feeding me next?"

Her expression turned saucy. She gave a toss of her hair as she signaled the waiter. "I guess you'll have to wait and see. But I think you're going to love it."

"I think I already do."

Chapter Thirteen

For the first time since moving to Briscoe Ranch, Knox didn't sleep a wink. Rather, he'd lain in bed, replaying every moment he'd spent with Emily in his mind. He'd never seen it coming, how deeply he'd grown to feel about her. He'd come a long way from the restlessness and lust that had led to their brief, intense sex in his childhood bedroom.

Oh, the lust was still there, all right, but it had evolved into so much more. When they'd returned to the resort after dinner, it had been torture to walk her to her office, where she'd insisted she needed to go in order to make notes about upcoming menus she was planning, and leave her there—when all he wanted to do was press her to the wall and kiss her. He wanted to gather her up in his arms and cart her off to his bed where they could dissolve into a naked, sweaty mess of passion, then lie in the dark and talk for hours about Hong Kong noodle makers and wines and fishing until the sun rose.

Are you ready to let me feed you like you need to be fed?

Yes, by God, he was.

At dawn, Knox gave up the fruitless pursuit of sleep and dressed in his running clothes and shoes, then stepped outside into the foggy morning. He stood a long time and stared at the lake, considering his next move. Usually, no matter how late he'd gone to bed the night before, or how fitfully he'd slept, he loved the shot of energy being up this early infused him with. The illusion of beginning at the starting line of the day instead of coming in during the middle of the race gave him a better sense of control. But he couldn't get Emily out of his head.

After a brief stretch, he took off jogging down his driveway. As he turned onto the road, he touched the sign indicating that Briscoe Ranch Resort was three miles ahead. The perfect distance for a morning jog. Perhaps putting in a few hours at the office would give him a much-needed reprieve from his wayward thoughts about Emily. And there was plenty of work to be done, especially since the equity firm had approved a plan for repairs that would keep the resort open, before launching into a three-hundred-room expansion and complete remodeling of the main building, and the bids would be coming in any day on revamping the golf course into a competitive one that rivaled the best in the world.

The resort office was as quiet as one might expect on an early Saturday morning and smelling faintly of brewing coffee. Knox snagged the spare suit he kept in his office, then detoured to the employee locker room on the basement level for a shower.

He couldn't help but glance into the catering kitchen as he passed. Emily's domain. On a whim, he ground to a stop. With a look over his shoulder, dogged by the illogical feeling that he was trespassing, he stepped inside.

The kitchen was a sea of spotless, gleaming stainless steel—a blank canvas for Emily's artistry. How late had she stayed the night before, scribbling notes? She'd had to be exhausted when she finally went home. He glanced through the window into her office. In his mind's eye, he could see her at her desk, bent over her computer, typing out ingredient lists and flavor profiles with the passion of a mad genius.

Setting his spare suit on the nearest counter, he took a step closer to her office. The top edge of her sofa came into view. Haylie had told him during their tour of the resort that Emily slept there often. At the time, he'd thought of that as evidence of Emily's ambition. But that was before he'd seen the world-weary look in her eyes the night before, when she'd spoken of the abusive relationship her friend was in. The words she'd chosen and the look on her face made it clear that her knowledge of battered women's mentality was rooted in personal experience.

What if she didn't sleep in her office because of the long hours she worked? Rather, what if she worked those long hours and slept in her office because there was someone at her home from whom she was trying to escape? What if she were asleep on the sofa right now?

Heart racing, he crept closer, torn between a heady desire to discover what she looked like as she slept and the hope that the sofa was empty and his instinct about her home life was wrong.

The breath caught in his throat at the sight of her bare knee poking out from beneath a quilt. *Damn it.*

Something definitely wasn't right, and he intended to find out what it was. Yes, Emily deserved privacy. She deserved better than a boss who snooped into her personal life. But she also deserved a good home situation instead of working herself to the bone and bunking in her office night after night. He grabbed his suit from the counter and tiptoed out of the kitchen.

He showered and changed with mechanical indifference, his mind a swirling stew of questions and ideas on how to go about his search for answers.

When he passed the door to the kitchen again, his steps faltered at the sight of her office lights on, the door open. He swallowed hard. Talking to her now would be a mistake. He couldn't take the chance of letting on to her about his concerns, not when he wasn't even sure there was something to be concerned about.

He kept walking and didn't stop until he was in his office with the door closed. Emily's personnel file was easy to find in the company's human resources database. He typed her address into an internet search engine.

The address came up as a business, not a residence. Murph's, a boxing gym in a dead-end town forty-five minutes from the resort. He clicked the street view on the map and stared at the two-story building, a banner splashed over a window advertising that it was open twenty-four hours, seven days a week. The ground floor was dominated by a boxing ring surrounded by free weights and pulley machines, while the floor-to-ceiling windows on the second floor revealed empty fitness classrooms with walls of mirrors.

It didn't make sense.

On a whim, he started a new search, this time for her name. There were several *Emily Fords* in Texas, and it only took a few clicks for him to decide that wading through the Facebook pages and high school photos of random *Emily*s was a poor use of his time. Instead, he navigated to a private investigation database he'd once seen Shayla use to research a potential employee for the firm.

The first mention of an *Emily Ford* with her birthday and social security number happened thirteen years earlier, the year she'd started culinary school when she was eighteen. She'd never owned property, never purchased or leased a car. She had a credit card, with a credit history also beginning at age eighteen, as well as a bank account. Before that, there was no record of her in Texas or otherwise—not even a birth certificate or a high school transcript. It was as though she'd materialized from thin air when she turned eighteen. That's when he noticed that the social security number on record had also belonged to another Emily Ford, one who'd died more than fifty years ago.

After nearly an hour of digging and crosschecking the information he found, he could no longer deny what his findings were telling him. Whoever the woman who fixed his meals each day was, her real name wasn't Emily Ford.

He thought back to their first encounter when he'd cut her down with questions about why she was holding herself back, why she hadn't made a name for herself, if she was such an extraordinary chef. Now it made sense. Whoever she really was, she must have had a good reason to forge all identifying information about herself and disappear into the hills of Texas to toil away anonymously at a resort as a catering chef, careful not to draw too much attention to herself.

It didn't take him long to connect the rest of the dots. He could think of only one reason that a woman would forge her identity as Emily had. Escaping an abuser. No wonder she'd sounded so intimately familiar with the domestic abuse her friend was suffering.

He stood, his instincts urging him to immediate action. He scribbled Emily's address of record onto a sticky note, then stuffed it into his pocket. He strode from the room, summoning a Cab'd driver using the app on his phone as he walked. Of all the days to have left his truck at his house.

Ty stood in the doorway to his office across the hall as though he'd been waiting for Knox to emerge. Ever since they'd clashed after the meeting with the structural engineers and their mentor/ingénue illusion had fallen away, Ty had watched Knox like a hawk, all day, every day. Knox wouldn't be surprised if Ty were rifling through Knox's desk drawers every chance he got. Knox tried to take Ty's overbearingness for what it was, the last, gasping power play of a defeated man. Soon enough, Ty would be gone, and Knox would have free rein of the place.

Ty nodded to Haylie's empty desk. "I've been meaning to talk to you about Haylie. You've got to rein her in. Maybe you haven't noticed, but yesterday was her third late arrival since you hired her, and that's not even mentioning how many days she's taken an extended lunch. I love that girl to death, but I told you she's the type to take advantage of a situation if you let out too much leash."

Given Ty's imperious ways and the all-consuming distraction that Emily had become, Knox had forgotten all about his often-absent secretary. Though he chafed at Ty comparing his own daughter to a dog on a leash, that didn't mean Ty wasn't right about Knox needing to hold Haylie accountable as he would any other employee. As soon as possible, he'd sit her down and lay out some ground rules. But not today. Not when Emily's possible danger crowded his every thought.

"Where ya headed?"

Knox closed his office door and kept moving. "I'm going to lunch."

"It's nine in the morning."

That late already?

"Breakfast, then," Knox tossed over his shoulder as he pushed out the door to the lobby. His Cab'd app said a driver was still ten minutes away, but maybe the wait would give him time to figure out what to do or say to Emily now that he knew the truth.

Chapter Fourteen

Knox pulled his truck in front of Murph's Gym and confirmed what he knew he'd find. That there was no apartment to be seen either behind or above or next to the gym. Even if there had been apartments for rent, there was no way a resort executive lived on this rundown shop-lined street of a lower-income San Antonio suburb. He knew what Emily's salary was.

He leaned against the hood of his truck and feigned casualness as he watched the smattering of men—and one woman—bust their tails in the sparse, no-nonsense gym that had nary a circuit training machine in sight amongst the free weights and pulleys and punching bags. Two men sparred inside the boxing ring. He busied him-self watching them while he pondered what an idiot he'd been to cross the line and spy on Emily.

Thankfully, she'd never find out.

The rumble of a bus engine caught his attention and he looked down the street. As the bus pulled away from the curb, Emily came into view, walking in his direction on the sidewalk across the street three blocks down.

He jolted to his feet, cursing, his heart racing. He flung

the truck door open and dove in. In all his idiocy, he hadn't considered what he'd do if he saw her. For a man who prided himself on always having his shit together, he sure was spiraling into a reckless fool. Over a woman, of all the pedestrian reasons. Men only fell to pieces over women in fairy tales. Not in real life, and definitely not a man such as Knox. Even in high school and college, with his dangerous combination of immature teenage brain, surging testosterone, and insatiable sexual appetite, he'd chosen his girlfriends and bedmates prudently and had never spiraled out of control. Never.

Except that now, Emily was driving him to the brink of insanity. He'd entertained more foolish thoughts and crossed more ethical and moral lines in the past two weeks than the rest of his life.

He turned the key in the ignition, but all the engine did was click.

He threw his back against the seat and looked to the truck roof, as though Heaven itself were hovering over him like a cloud. "Really, Dad? Because she can't catch me here, okay? Let me start the truck and get out of here."

Holding his breath, he turned the key again. *Click.*

"Damn it, Dad. What do you want from me?"

He looked down the street. Emily was a block closer. Any moment, she'd spot him and then what? What could he say that wouldn't make him seem like a creepy stalker?

Nothing, because that's exactly what you are. Idiot.

So this was what it was like to hit rock bottom. He needed to remember the way this felt so he could never fall into the same well of shame again.

Closing his eyes, he gave the ignition one more try, praying as he turned the key. Nothing. When he opened his eyes again, the meathead who'd been standing behind the front desk at the gym was standing outside his door, now with a pair of dark sunglasses sitting atop a crooked nose that gave the impression he'd spent his fair share of time in the gym's boxing ring. The embroidery on his gray polo shirt read *Murph*.

Tamping his impatience to have to field questions from a stranger when what he really needed to do was get the hell out of there, Knox rolled down the window. "Yes?"

"Sounds like you gotta problem with the truck," Murph said in a pack-a-day New Jersey accent.

"It won't turn over. Happens all the time." At least, all the time since he'd moved to Dulcet.

"Let's pop the hood and have a look."

That seemed his only option at the moment. Perhaps if he had his head buried under the hood, Emily would walk right past without noticing. He popped the hood, then stepped out of the truck. "You're Murph, the owner here?"

"That's me. I saw you poking your eyes around the gym. You looking for someone in particular?"

Emily was closer, only a block away.

"I was, actually." Because what was the harm in telling Murph about his misunderstanding? Surely the man had never heard of Emily.

Another pink-faced, no-neck meathead drifted out from the gym, this one sweating like a roasted pig and with dirty white bandages wrapped around his knuckles. "Is that an '85 Chevy, there? I had one of those back in the day. Lemme take a look with you, Murph."

"Thanks," Knox said, glancing around. Emily had vanished. He felt his shoulders relax a little and drew a full breath for the first time since he'd turned down this street. "I've got some jumper cables in the back, if either of you could offer your battery."

"Who'd you say you were here looking for?" Murph asked. "Either me or Big Tommy, here, probably knows the guy."

"Actually, it's a woman. I'm looking for Emily Ford."

Murph stopped fiddling with the engine. He rose to his full height, a few inches taller than Knox's six-one. Murph's face was stone hard. He cracked his knuckles while sneering at Knox, a totally different man than the one who'd come to help him with his truck, a violent man. Whatever his opponents in the ring had done to his nose, Murph had messed them up exponentially more. "Who the fuck are you and what do you want with her?"

Knox opened and closed his mouth, thrown for another loop. Murph knew her? "We're friends."

The other man, Big Tommy, shoved Knox's shoulder. The next instant, he grabbed Knox's shirt and twisted as he slammed Knox's back against the side of the hood. In the corner of Knox's vision, he saw a handful of other men walk out of the gym to watch the spectacle. "How 'bout you give us your name and we'll tell her you stopped by."

Knox raised his hands in the universal signal of surrender. He could've fought these guys and gotten away relatively uninjured, but he definitely wouldn't have won. "Wait . . . she lives here? At the gym?"

Big Tommy gave him a shake that rattled his teeth. "I smell bullshit." He slammed Knox's back against the truck again. "I'm pretty sure a friend would know where she lives."

"Damn straight," Murph said.

"Murph, she told us this might happen someday," one of the men standing behind Big Tommy said.

"That *what* would happen?" Knox asked. Had Emily predicted that someone would come around the gym asking about her? Is that why she had bodyguard-types looking out for her? The bodyguards combined with her fake identity gave Knox a sick feeling in his stomach. *Who are you running from, Emily?* Before he could really contemplate that question, Murph brought out a cell phone and snapped a photo of Knox, then walked to the back of the truck and snapped a photo of the license plate.

"Knox?" came a woman's voice behind the crowd. Emily, dressed in jeans and a snug red sweater was walking along the sidewalk in their direction. Her hair was down and tumbled over her shoulders in waves of curls. In her hands she cradled a paper coffee cup. "What are you doing here? How'd you find me?"

No sense in lying about that one. "Personnel file."

"Are you . . . stalking me?"

Murph folded his arms over his chest. "Looks that way to me."

Knox shoved Big Tommy's hand away from his chest and stood tall. "No. Yes, actually." Because he was kind of stalking her, even if his motivation was noble.

"Want me to make sure this creep never bugs you again?" Murph said.

Emily sipped her drink, pretending to contemplate the offer, then cast Knox a side-eye coupled with a sly smile that filled him with heat, like a gust of hot wind that swept through him and pulled him along in its wake, dragging his awareness closer to her until the world around her fell away. It was unlike any lust Knox had experienced before and he hated it. Never had he felt so pathetically out of control. Rock bottom, indeed.

He curled his toes and swayed, resisting the magnetic pull of her.

She took another drink, then tossed the cup in the trashcan next to the gym doors. "Thanks for the offer, Murph, but I have a soft spot for this particular creep."

She did?

"If you're sure," Murph said. "But say the word and I'll make sure he never looks at another woman that way again."

Until that exact moment, he hadn't been aware of

looking at her any particular way. He balled his hands into fists in his pockets to keep from swabbing his face as he forcibly tried to relax his expression.

"Thanks, Murph. I've got your cell on speed dial, so keep it close in case I need to take you up on it," Emily said, winking at Knox.

Knox huffed. What the hell kind of alternate universe had he stumbled into?

Big Tommy and Murph, along with their buddies, executed a slow, menacing walk back into the gym, fierce scowls on their faces and their eyes boring into Knox.

Knox smoothed a hand over his shirt and straightened his tie, trying to reclaim a fraction of his dignity.

"So, what brings you out stalking on this fine day?" Emily asked, that sly smile in place.

That now familiar electric heat slid up his spine again and wrapped around his chest and throat, squeezing the air from him every time he looked at her.

Are you ready for me to feed you the way you need to be fed?

Yes.

No. It could never be that way between them. Once had been too dangerous for both of them.

He shook the errant thoughts from his head and decided he was out of options except to give the truth to her straight. "The way you talked about your friend's abusive relationship yesterday made me think you know a thing or two about what she's going through. And Haylie mentioned that you sleep in your office at the resort most nights. After I saw you sleeping in there this morning, I got concerned about you, so I looked up your personnel file and violated just about every privacy law on the books because I needed to know if your situation at home was bad. Like your friend's."

The sly smile vanished as her expression went completely neutral. Was she pissed or flattered? He couldn't tell.

"Hence the stalking," she said.

"Yeah, I own that. Because then I got even more worried when I looked up the address from your personnel file and it came up as this gym."

"I rent a studio on the second floor from Murph. As far as why I sometimes sleep in my office, I work long hours. Sometimes, the extra hour of sleep I get by sleeping there instead of commuting back and forth is worth it."

A studio apartment above a gym? He knew what she made as an executive chef at the hotel, and she could certainly afford better than that. Which brought him back around to the question of why she used Murph and his tough guy friends as bodyguards. "So then I looked up your name and social security number, to search for clues about where you lived from another angle. There was no Emily Ford born the year you were. The information you provided Briscoe Ranch was falsified."

Her face went white. "You're over the line."

"I know." He was over the line, in too deep, and out of control in every way when it came to her.

"Don't do this to me," she said so quietly that he might have doubted she'd spoken at all if he hadn't watched her lips move. Her gaze shifted to the gym. Specifically, to Murph.

Knox stepped to the side, blocking her line of sight. "I'm not going to do anything with that information. You can trust me on that. But I have questions." He had so many questions crowding his mind, and he couldn't seem to articulate any of them. He wanted to know if Emily was her given name, how she'd come up with the last name 'Ford,' where she'd grown up, why she didn't live somewhere nicer, closer, than above the gym. But those were mere details, immaterial compared to the most important question of all. "Actually, I only have one question. Are you safe?"

She blinked at him as though stunned. In the moment before she wrenched her face away, he caught a glimpse of pain, as though he'd wounded her with his concern. It took her a long moment to infuse her features with her indomitable strength again. Knox caught himself holding his breath awaiting her reply, praying she hadn't been in some unseen danger the whole time he'd known her, something that he could have protected her from sooner.

"Keep my secret," she finally said.

"Yes. Forever."

"The discrepancies in the information about me that you found online, was it an easy puzzle to piece together?"

The dread in her voice made his ribs tighten. He wished he had a better answer for her. "For anyone mildly interested and with access to the internet, it would be simple."

Closing her eyes, she muttered a curse under her breath.

The gym rat's words came back to him. *Emily warned us this might happen someday.*

Who was after her? A man, but who? She'd been eighteen when she forged a new identity. A violent ex? Her father?

"I'm sorry. For everything. I took advantage of you. And I put your job in jeopardy by invading your privacy. What can I do to make things right? What do you need? You have the keys to my house. Stay as often as you'd like, for as long as you like. If you need a new identity, if you need to go underground again, I can help with that, too. I can—"

She placed a finger over his lips. Her expression softened. "Thank you for being worried about me. Would you like to come upstairs, see my place?"

That was a terrible idea. He'd already crossed too many lines tonight, and together they'd crossed even more.

Their relationship didn't need any more complications. The only correct answer would be for him to decline politely, then get in his truck and see if it'd start, then drive away and put her in his rearview mirror. And he should give her the restaurant straightaway so he could be done with the out of control feeling he had when he was around her. But his mind and heart weren't seeing eye-to-eye at the moment. "Yes. I'd love to see your apartment."

Chapter Fifteen

Knox followed Emily through the gym doors and past a silently snarling Murph. The glares of dozens of meat-heads followed them up the stairs at the back of the room. The second-floor fitness rooms opened in front of them and to the right, but they went left, down a hall to a door labeled with a bronze plaque that read *Employees Only*.

The door opened to a clean, white-walled studio, sparsely decorated and with a tiny kitchen. She led him to a two-seat table near the kitchen and sat him down, then walked to the fridge. It looked as empty as his had been before she'd filled it. From the door, she took out a mason jar of jam and a glass carafe of milk. While she busied herself on the counter with her back to him, he took the opportunity to study the apartment closer.

A corner of the space was devoted to metal garment racks stuffed with clothes and framed by sheer curtain panels. A light blue folding screen separated a king-sized bed with a fluffy white duvet from the living room area. His attention landed on the beige, overstuffed sofa that dominated the living room, his thoughts drifting back to the night before and to the stop by Emily's office on Haylie's tour of the resort. "Do you sleep on the bed or the sofa?"

Jesus H. Christ. Everything he said to her was inappropriate, over the line. Since the day they'd first met, he hadn't been able to stem the tide of dumb shit coming out of his mouth when he was around her. He pinched the bridge of his nose. "I'm sorry. Would you forget I asked that?"

The shadow of a smile appeared on her lips. "No, it's okay. Where I sleep depends on my mood. When I'm stressed or feeling out of sorts, I like to tuck into a sofa and burrow under a heavy quilt. Otherwise, I sleep right in the middle of the bed and take up all the space."

She appeared at his side and set a plate in front of him. Two peanut butter and jelly sandwiches on white bread with the crusts off, both cut into triangles. She reached towards his face. He froze, unbreathing, bracing for her touch. Her fingers did not settle on his face, but his tie. She worked the knot loose, then popped open the top button of his shirt. "You and these suits. Always so constrained." She stroked a hand lightly over his hair, sending chills over his skin.

He was milliseconds away from lifting his hand to cup her hip and drag her up against him when she stepped away. She returned a moment later with two tall glasses of milk, then assumed the seat across from him.

"Eat," she said, lifting a half sandwich to her lips.

He hadn't known he was hungry until he looked at the sandwiches. Bright red jelly with chunks of strawberry oozed from the triangles and pooled on the plate. He couldn't remember the last time he'd had a peanut butter sandwich, especially one with the crusts cut off. What he was sure of was that he'd never seen a better-looking meal, or enjoyed one with better company.

The peanut butter was thick and salty on his tongue, the jelly tartly sweet. He washed down his first bite with a long drink of the milk. It was bracingly cold and as dense as cream. His last memory of drinking whole milk was from his grandparents' ranch, his mother's people, when he'd been thirteen. What a summer that had been.

"I ran away from home when I was sixteen and never looked back," she said, as casually as she might have commented on the brand of peanut butter she'd used.

Knox couldn't think of anything to do but nod as he processed her words. She'd been a teen runaway. Sixteen. So young. An onslaught of questions raced through his mind. Why had she needed to run? Abuse at home? Is that how she knew what her friend was going through or was there more to Emily's story? Did her nightmare end when she ran away or was that the beginning of a new nightmare?

"You never returned home?" he asked.

"No. I've been on my own since then."

"And you grew up in Houston. You're not that far from home. Weren't you worried your parents would find you?"

She finished her bite of sandwich and washed it down with milk before answering. "I lied about Houston. Rule number one about assuming a new identity is learning how to lie."

Every detail she revealed only created more questions in his mind. Sixteen, alone. How did she not end up dead or on drugs or mixed up with the wrong crowd? "How did you survive? How did you start there and become an executive chef at a world-class resort by the age of thirty? It doesn't add up."

"At first, wherever I could find work or bunk down. Eventually, I bought an old car off my friend's older brother. I worked my ass off, juggling every odd job I could find. I lived in that car for three years while I worked and got my GED. Sometime during those years, I got it in my head to be a chef because food . . . it's life and comfort and makes people feel good. And I was always so hungry. When I went to the culinary academy, it was on a scholarship for teen runaways, but I still couldn't afford a place to stay most months. That car was my lifeline, my best friend, until I graduated from the culinary academy and Ty Briscoe took a chance on me."

No wonder, was all Knox could think. No wonder Emily was so loyal to the Briscoes. No wonder she hadn't sought out mentorships with renowned chefs or traveled to a culinary mecca like New York City to seek her fortune. Whatever abuse had happened in her household growing up, it'd been bad enough that she'd opted to live on the streets and assume a new identity at an age when most kids spent their time worrying about crushes and loitering at malls, spending their parents' money. No wonder she'd structured her whole life around keeping her true identity a secret and not drawing too much attention to herself.

Her attention drifted to the small window over the sink, as though she was deliberating what more to tell him, if anything. He held his breath, waiting.

After clearing her throat, she met his gaze again. Her eyes were sharp with challenge. "I changed my last name to Ford, after that car. Emily was the name of my imaginary friend when I was little. I spent all the money I'd brought with me when I left home on that car and on buying the highest quality forged identity available. I had to, to survive and to stay hidden." Her jaw tightened, pulling her tight lips into a frown. He doubted she was aware that she was gripping the edge of the table so hard her knuckles had gone white. "And now you have the power to ruin me. No one's had that power in a long, long time."

Ruining other's lives was not a part of who he was. *Except Ty Briscoe, except . . .*

He extinguished the errant thoughts immediately. His goal at Briscoe Ranch to seek justice for his father was a different situation entirely. That was business. That was justified retribution. That was not anything remotely like holding the fate of an abuse survivor in his hands.

"Then I'm giving that power back to you. I don't want it." He dragged his chair toward her, then covered her hand with his. "Your secret will die with me, Emily. On my life, I will never do anything to put you in danger. I promise you that."

She peeled her fingers away from the edge of the table and threaded them with Knox's. "Thank you," she breathed.

"But do you believe me?"

She stared into his eyes, beyond his eyes, searching for something. He held still, his hands still entwined with hers, and let her look. Finally, she nodded. "I do."

He could think of no other action than to fold over their joined hands and kiss her knuckles. He lingered there with his lips on her soft skin, even when he felt her kiss his hair and nuzzle her face against it.

They may have remained locked like that for eternity had her cell phone not rung. But ring, it did.

To his disappointment, she raised her head and pulled away from him. "I have to get that," she said, her voice cracking once. "It's the ringtone for the catering kitchen, and there's a big wedding tonight."

While she took the call, Knox walked to the living room area to look closer at the shelf of framed photographs that included numerous ones of her and Carina, her and the whole Briscoe family, and one with a younger her and a group of other men and women all wearing chef's jackets that had to be from her years at the culinary academy. He sank into her plush sofa and let her story and her struggles drift through his mind as he listened to her impassioned tone on the phone with her employee.

She really was an incredible woman. No wonder he'd been drawn to her. No wonder she held him under her spell.

A yawn came from out of nowhere. Fatigue from this whirlwind of a month finally rearing its head. The deep sofa, the warmth of the room, the richness of the sandwich and milk turned his lids heavy. He turned his head to the side, closed his eyes, and inhaled against the overstuffed cushion. It smelled faintly of Emily's sweet, herbal scent. Everything in this apartment did. Emily, Emily. He mouthed her name. It wasn't enough. He languished with the need for more, for her, for everything he couldn't have.

He inhaled again. *Yes . . .*

Emily stared down at the sleeping man on her sofa. She'd knocked him out with a PB&J. Guess there was a first time for everything.

She perched on the coffee table, the better to study his sleeping form, as tenderness for this impossible, strikingly handsome, brilliant man flowed through her. What the hell was she going to do about him? And about everything he made her feel?

Even though it had scared her how easily he'd discovered her secrets, despite her valiant and ongoing effort to conceal her past, there was no denying the relief in opening up about everything she'd hidden and had never shared with anyone other than Carina. Just as there was no denying the restlessness he'd awoken within her—a need so deep and hidden, it had no name.

All she knew was, no matter how hard she tried, she was incapable of keeping a professional distance from him. She couldn't get their one, brief lovemaking out of her head. She couldn't stop wondering what a full night in his arms would be like. What kissing him would be like. And, it seemed, given his presence in her apartment, he was having the same problem keeping his distance from her.

Maybe it was time to stop trying so hard to resist the pull of him. Maybe it was time to let herself feel this— whatever *this* was.

She reached out and touched his knee.

The next instant, his hand encircled her wrist. As she gasped in surprise, his eyes opened. "You're watching me."

Though his hold on her wrist was gentle, the sensation triggered too many unpleasant memories from her childhood. She let her arm go limp and concentrated on breathing evenly, pushing past the triggered emotions. Knox wasn't going to overpower her or restrain her in a sinister way. He wasn't. He was never going to hurt her.

Through that fog of residual fear and memory, she picked her words. "I thought you were sleeping."

He sat up straighter, his grip on her wrist inadvertently tightening. "Napping is not a skill I've mastered."

Her attention lowered to his hand on her wrist. *You're safe, you're safe, you're safe.*

He must have caught her looking because he opened his hand immediately. Before she could think better of it, she retracted her arm and cradled it against her chest.

"Who wants to hurt you?" Knox said.

The question caught her off guard. Suddenly restless, she stood and returned to the kitchen, putting some distance between them. "My father. My mother, too. They'd make my life a living hell if they found me. But, Knox, you're not making life easy on me, either. Dredging all of this up, making me fight for my worth at Briscoe Ranch, my chosen home. My life was easy before you came along. I knew what I wanted and how to get it. And now . . ." At a loss for words, she shook her head. *And now what?* And now she wanted something that terrified her even more than her parents, even more than exposure as a fraud.

He followed her to the kitchen and crowded behind her, close enough that she could feel the heat of him against her back. If she pivoted in place, he'd be close enough to kiss. Damn it all to hell, she'd never wanted anything more.

His words vibrated against her neck. "And now you don't know what you—"

"I know what I want," she snapped.

And then she did turn. She took his face in her hands, rocked up onto the balls of her feet, and took what she needed.

She angled her lips against his. That first shock of contact sent a sizzle of electricity racing through her that made her whole body quake. On a groan, he wrapped his arms around her and took control of the kiss. There was no tentative exploration, no gradual build. She opened her mouth and gave herself over to the taste and feel of Knox's commanding mouth, to his hard body, to the wet, greedy kiss that went on and on.

She ripped his shirt open and dragged her hands along his bare shoulder. She couldn't get enough of him, body or soul.

As it turned out, that deep need that she'd thought was so ancient and foreign that it had no name, had one. She just hadn't acknowledged it until now. She needed kissing and sex and intimate touch. She needed connection in a way that superseded friendship or family or coworkers. She needed Knox—and she needed him in a way that was not polite or easy.

He'd turned her into an immoderate beast stripped

bare for him to see the fathomless depths of her soul, her rawest edges. Fuck him for crippling her power with this unbearable yearning for connection with him. Only him.

She tore her lips away, so angry at herself for becoming this person she didn't recognize.

"Fuck you, Knox." She startled at the hitch in her words. She couldn't even speak without shards of emotion piercing her voice. "Fuck you for what you've done to me, for turning me into this."

He panted through gritted teeth. "What I've done to you? Why don't we talk about what you've done to me?"

His fists closed around the hem of her sweater. He yanked it over her head, then molded his hand to her breast as his eyes raked over her body. A growling groan reverberated from his throat. "You think I like feeling this way? You think this is what I want? This isn't who I am." His hand closed in her hair. He tipped her head back and grazed her neck with his lips. "But I'm hungry, damn it. I'm starving for you, Emily."

"Then take me," she said between panting breaths.

He rose to his full height. The heat in his gaze nearly singed her. His fingers slid down her arm and took her hand. Together, they walked in charged silence from the kitchen to her bed.

At the foot of the bed, she turned in his arms and kissed him again, hard and deep. She felt his hands on her back, and then her bra fell away. Her pants went next. In a haze of lust, they stripped each other bare, kissing and touching as they went.

When they were naked, Emily broke the kiss. She needed to see the body she'd fantasized about so often. Little had she known that the reality would be even better than her wildest dreams. His body was carved to perfection. Tanned and toned. Every exhalation accentuated the cut of his abdominal muscles and the trail of fine, dark hair that cut a path to his fully aroused cock. Everything about this man was powerful and perfect. And today, he was hers. The realization summoned a pulse between her legs.

"You're so beautiful," he crooned, snapping her back to the present. He lightly cupped her breast and pressed her nipple between his thumb and finger. "I've never seen anyone like you in all my life."

That couldn't be true. She'd seen media photos of him with gorgeous blondes on his arm, women light years more conventionally attractive than Emily, but the way he'd said it coupled with the way his heated gaze drank her in, Emily believed him.

On another kiss, they sank onto the bed, Knox's heavy body caging hers below him in a hot press of flesh on flesh. He kissed his way down her body, often lingering to tease every drop of pleasure from her. Then his lips burrowed into the thatch of hair above her pussy, making his intentions crystal clear.

Even at the height of her dating years, she'd rarely allowed men to perform so intimate an act. Nothing felt more vulnerable than his lips and tongue on her swollen flesh. But one caress from Knox's tongue between her folds instantly stripped her of her power to resist him. He held her down on the bed with nothing but the force of his desire and the almost painful pleasure that his mouth wrested from her body.

He brought her right up to the first tremor of release, then stopped. It was all Emily could do to lie there, a tightly coiled band of unbearable tension, afraid to move lest she spontaneously combust.

"Can you have more than one?" he asked in a husky voice.

It took a few beats for her to wrap her mind around his question. She didn't often have multiple orgasms in a night, but that said more about her partners than her body's attributes. Today, with Knox, she was limitless in every way. "Yes," she said.

He buried his face between her legs again. Fingers breached her entrance and curled to rub her G-spot. She groaned with the sweet torture of this new pressure point. On the first swirl of his tongue, she broke wide open. He rode her release out with the ease of a masterful lover, and then before she could even catch her breath, his erection nudged at her opening.

"I need to taste your cock," she murmured in protest.

He almost smiled, but intensity kept his features torqued into a grimace. "First this. I need you too much."

He sank into her on a muttered curse. And he was right; the acute relief of their bodies locking together felt even more profound than the orgasm. A deep, satisfying shudder rocked her to her bones. She wrapped her legs and arms around him and teased his lips until he covered her mouth with his as he began to move. This, right here, was where she needed to be. Knox Briscoe inside and all around her. Sharing an endless kiss as rippling waves of sensation accompanied each rolling thrust.

When, finally, they collapsed side by side, Emily was tender and glowing from her second release. She snuggled close to Knox, absentmindedly tracing the edge of his pectoral muscle with her finger. This is what it felt like to be lost in time. Free. Sheltered in his arms, she felt softer, somehow. Cherished.

Fuck.

She bolted upright.

Cherished? What the hell does that mean? She was not that woman.

Knox pushed up onto his elbows. He looked as thoroughly worked over as she felt. "What?"

She didn't recognize either of them for their loss of control. "Who are we right now?"

He flopped back again, pulling her down with him. "I have no idea. Not ourselves, though." He stroked her back. "But could we wait until later to regret this? Please? I feel like I can breathe for the first time in weeks."

She raked her nails over his abs, then took his softening erection in her hand. "Then allow me to change that. Assuming you can come more than once."

He propped a hand behind his head and rewarded her with a rakish grin. "Guess we'll find out."

It took Emily a second to register the jiggle of the front door lock. Even then, she wasn't quick enough to do more than utter, "Oh, shit!" before the door swung open.

Haylie yelped and put her back to the room, even as she clamped her hands over her eyes. Knox grabbed a pillow and jammed it in front of him. "Haylie? What are you doing here?"

"I didn't see anything," Haylie said. "Oh my God, I'm so sorry. Emily said I could come over any time I needed to, but I didn't know that she was . . . that you two were . . ." She groaned. "I'm leaving now."

Emily leapt from the bed and grabbed the bathrobe hanging on the wall. Her only concern was for Haylie. She wouldn't have come to Emily's apartment without ample reason. Pulling the robe on, she rushed to Haylie's side. "No. Don't go. Are you all right? What did he do to you?"

Haylie stepped away from Emily and hugged herself. Was she favoring her left arm? Was she in pain? Emily couldn't tell.

"I'm fine. He . . ." Haylie shook her head, then tipped her face in Knox's direction, though she didn't chance a look. "I thought you'd be at work. I needed a place to—" Another tip of her head toward Knox. "To be."

Emily whirled to face Knox, wondering what she could say to make him leave. Haylie's need for a safe haven trumped everything else.

Knox was already on his feet, dressed, though his clothes were disheveled and his shirt unbuttoned. His focus shifted from Haylie to Emily, and in his eyes, she saw dawning understanding. "Uh, I was on my way out."

Emily could have kissed him for that. "Yes, you were. Okay. Good. Haylie, come on in."

"No, please," Haylie said. "I'll go. I'm so sorry I interrupted. I was just looking for a place to be alone. It's silly of me, honestly. I don't know what I was thinking."

Emily all but threw herself in front of the door. "No, Knox is right. Actually, we were both leaving."

Haylie eyed them both warily. "You're not just saying that?"

"Nope," Knox and Emily said at the same time. "We've got to get back to the resort. Too much to do," Knox added.

Haylie inched farther into the room. "If you're sure."

"Absolutely. Stay as long as you want. All night if you want. I'll be working late. And after work, I might be, um, busy." With Knox. At his place. Lord, was that even a possibility? Could he want that, too? Her hunger for him wasn't even close to being sated. She put her hand on the doorknob but found Knox's hand already there. "Oops. Okay. We're out of here. Call if you need anything."

Emily preceded Knox out the door. She didn't realize until she was on the landing halfway down the stairs, that she was only dressed in a semi-sheer bathrobe. "Oh my God, I forgot clothes."

Just as panic set in, Knox showed her the bundle of fabric in his hands. Her clothes. "I think I grabbed them all."

"Well, that's about the luckiest thing that's ever happened to me. Thank you."

"Besides the part where you actually got lucky a few minutes ago, you mean?" He extricated her black thong from the pile and dangled it in front of her face. "Here."

He made careful work of watching her slip into it. "What's going on with Haylie?"

What could Emily do but shake her head? Anything more would be talking out of turn. From the clothes pile, she pulled her jeans. "I can't tell you that."

But Knox would not be deterred. "She's the friend you were telling me about, isn't she? The one in the abusive relationship." His mouth screwed up as though he'd eaten a slice of lemon. "Wendell's hurting her."

"Knox, come on. It's not my place to say. It's really not."

Rather than hand her the bra, he held out the straps so she could slip right into it. "I'm already keeping some of your secrets. What's one more? Especially if it helps Haylie."

He had a point. There had to be a line in which Haylie's safety trumped her privacy. No one had ever crossed that line for Emily. Who knows what might have changed in her life if they had?

She shrugged out of the robe, then slipped her arms into the bra and adjusted the cups as she turned so Knox could latch it closed. That accomplished, she turned to face him again, modulating her voice on the off-chance that Haylie might be listening in on the other side of the door. "You're right. He hurts her. I wasn't sure until yesterday. I've always thought he was emotionally abusive, which is bad enough, but it's so much worse. Haylie's done an ace job of covering it up so her dad won't find out. Carina, too. She's known for a while.

"They're both afraid Ty would kill Wendell if he found

out, and they're probably right. Carina and I have been trying to get Haylie out of that situation since his true colors showed themselves right after they eloped, but she's . . ." Frustration choked out Emily's remaining words.

Knox wrapped his arms around her, offering his strength so she could finish her thought.

"It doesn't take long for a battered woman to stop believing she's strong enough or valuable enough to save herself." She heard the edge of personal testimony in her voice and knew he heard it, too, but she no longer minded him seeing her at her most vulnerable.

Though she could have managed on her own, Knox helped her into the sweater, then smoothed it down over her. "Thank God I'm getting rid of his worthless ass."

Such a noble gesture. "I wish that were the answer, but I'm afraid that if you fired him, Haylie would stick by him, even if we all know he'll take his humiliation out on her. If anything, firing him might make the situation worse."

She dared a look at Knox again. His eyes had turned troubled and distant. When he caught her looking, he gathered her more tightly in his arms and kissed her hair. It was such a relief to be comforted in his sure embrace.

"I might not have a choice about laying him off," Knox said. "It's already in the works, actually. He and about fifteen other employees who aren't pulling their weight. I don't know if I can justify stopping it."

"But you're the boss."

"Yes and no. The minute Ty signed that contract with me at my equity firm, Briscoe Ranch Resort stopped being a family business. Every decision I make, I'm answerable to a group of investors who have committed more than fifty million dollars to this property. Until I buy out their shares, they're the majority shareholders. I work for them, and they're already skittish because of some structural problems my building inspectors found at the resort."

"Structural problems?"

"A story for another time. The point is, the pressure's on me to turn a profit, and if I can't demonstrate to them that I'm taking action, then they're not going to sell to me and, worst case scenario, they vote to shut down the resort or sell it off, and then Granny June and Carina and all the Briscoes wouldn't have a place to live. And there wouldn't be a five-star restaurant to offer you. I'm not going to let that happen. I can't."

Well, shit. "I get that you're under a lot of pressure, but be that as it may, you can't go on pretending—" She bit her lip. That line of thought was taking it too far. Stupid, big mouth.

"Pretending what?"

So much for playing it cool. That really wasn't her style, anyway. "Pretending that this is about your father anymore. Pretending you don't care and this is all just business. I know you better than that." And wasn't that astounding in itself? She knew Knox Briscoe, inside and out. She got him and what made him tick, more than any other man she'd ever been intimate with.

His only response was the rippling of his jaw.

She knew what that meant, too. She'd hit a bullseye with her observation, though he was yet unwilling to admit to his shifting motives.

She melted against the stairwell wall and closed her eyes, suddenly exhausted by life. "I don't know where we go from here. You and me, Haylie, the resort. No idea what should happen next."

After a stretch of silence, he said. "I do. I'm going to delay the layoffs and find another way to appease the investors until I'm ready to make my buyout offer. And I'm going to offer Haylie a job at my Dallas office. A steady job with good pay might get her confidence up enough to take care of herself. And then, I'm going to invite the partners in my firm to that dinner party next weekend that I mentioned at The Smoking Gun. You're catering it. It'll be the best way to introduce you to them and show-case your skills as the secret weapon of the resort's future."

She'd been following just fine right up until that last part. *Could he mean . . . was it possible?* She searched his eyes. In them, she read desperation and tenderness. "What are you saying?"

"I'm saying you were spot-on when you warned me the day we agreed to the challenge that by the end of the month, I'd be begging you to take the restaurant. You were right. You're a genius. I've known since the first meal you cooked for me. Hell, I've known since you over-turned that bowl in my lap. Looking back at it, that was the day you wrapped me around your little finger. The restaurant is yours, Emily. Anything you want, it's yours."

Chapter Sixteen

Wednesday was another lucky hat day. And not only because Knox had settled things in his mind with Emily. Their relationship was still up in the air, but now that they were no longer challenging each other over the restaurant, he felt free to pursue her. Which he fully planned to do. But, today's donning of his lucky Stetson had everything to do with business.

Because today was the day Ty and Knox were flying to Dallas for a meeting with the Briscoe Equity Group investors—the day of Ty's reckoning, the day Knox would ask them to vote him in as CEO. The day that Ty Briscoe would officially lose all power. God, Knox wished his dad were there to see it unfold. Hopefully, he would be watching from up on High. Because Knox had no doubt that it was going to be epic.

Since Ty's and Knox's confrontation over the structural engineers' findings, Ty had spent his days stomping around the office, silently fuming and pretending that Knox didn't exist. Which had been fantastic. Without Ty looming over his shoulder, trying to be buddy-buddy with him, Knox was free to run the resort and forward his expansion plans as he saw fit.

When Knox arrived at the office to put in a few hours of work in advance of their midday flight, Ty had already shuttered himself away in his office, the blinds down, the door closed. No surprise there. In fact, the only surprise was the sight of Haylie at her desk, far earlier than she usually rolled in. She was hard at work typing up a memo for the retail division that he'd left on her desk the evening before. The word *overcompensating* sprang to mind. Or perhaps, instead, enthusiastic denial of the professional boundaries they'd inadvertently crossed the Saturday before at Emily's house. Enthusiastic denial was a solid plan, but not one Knox could go along with if he wanted to consider himself a good boss.

He paused at her desk when she didn't acknowledge his arrival, the same as she'd done every day that week. "Bright and early, I see. I appreciate that."

"There's a lot to do," she said without tearing her eyes away from the computer screen.

"Right. Too true. But if you would be so kind as to join me in my office, there's a matter we need to discuss." And there he went again, in full stodgy butler mode. What a ridiculous affectation. "What I'm trying to say is that we need to talk about what happened on Saturday at Emily's house."

"Oh, that's okay. Really."

"I know, but I need to. Would it make you more comfortable if we talked cousin-to-cousin instead of boss-to-employee?"

Then she did look at him, her eyebrows pursed. Then she sighed. "Actually, I think boss-to-employee would probably be better in this case."

He tapped the edge of her desk with his knuckle. "Good. Come on into my office. Shut the door behind you."

He gestured to the chair across from his desk and waited while she assumed a seat, her back rigid and her expression wary.

"I just want to say right off the bat that I'm sorry," he said. "I'm sorry you saw what you did, I'm sorry I've put you in an awkward position."

She seemed to relax a little. "That's what I was going to say, word for word. But I mean, like, seriously, you and Emily? I had no idea."

"Yeah. It came as a surprise to me, too."

She tilted her head and eyed him quizzically. "Although . . . now that I'm thinking about it, your whole *there's nothing seductive about her* line makes sense now. You were trying to throw your sister off the scent."

Knox was unsuccessful at stifling a cringe. "I forgot I'd said that. If you could forget about it, too, that would be great. Because obviously, you're right about why I said it. In fact, if you could just keep it to yourself that Emily and I were . . . that we are . . ." Whatever the hell they were at the moment. Knox had no idea, and even if he did, he wasn't about to go sharing it with Haylie.

She waved her hands. "I won't say anything. You have my word. As long as you don't tell anyone you saw me at Emily's apartment, either. I really need that to stay a secret."

Her request conjured Knox's frustrated anger all over again. Goddamn that animal, Wendell, for whatever he was doing to Haylie that made her need a secret, safe haven from him. "Understood. You have my word, too."

"Thank you. I know I said I wanted us to talk boss-to-employee, but I can't help it. I hope you don't mind me saying that I like you for Emily. I hope you're not just using her because she needs someone who appreciates her unconventional style."

There was that refrain again, that Emily and Knox's

relationship was mercenary. Someday soon, people would
get it that Emily and Knox weren't just using each other
for material gain. "I do appreciate it, and her, very much.
And, no, I'm not using her. But until she and I decide
to make something public, I'd rather it not get spread
around."

Haylie pretended to zip her lips closed.

Knox tapped a pen on his desk as a new idea occurred
to him. "You know, your dad and I will be leaving for
Dallas around noon to meet with our investors. We char-
tered a private jet. I know it's last minute, but is there any
chance you'd like to tag along and shadow Shayla in the
office for the afternoon? It might be fun to get out of town
for a few hours, and maybe you can pick up some tips."

Haylie pulled her face back, clearly taken off guard
by the invitation. "Oh, wow. That would be cool, but I'd
have to check with Wendell. He likes me to have dinner
on the table by six. Would we be back in time?"

Knox ground his molars together and took great pains
to school his features and his tone before answering. "Probably not, but I'll make sure you get overtime pay. He
wouldn't have a problem with a little extra money,
would he?"

Her eyes rolled to the ceiling and her mouth bunched
up as she considered. Finally, she nodded. "You're right.
He wouldn't. Sure, I'll go. That would be fun."

Knox clapped his hands. "Great. Then if you'll excuse
me, I'd better get on with my workday."

Haylie sprang up, full of energy, but she lingered at the
door, her hand on the handle and her back to him. "And
Knox? Thank you. Thank you for giving me so many
chances."

"You're welcome. But really, it's self-serving. You're a
terrific secretary. I'd love to steal you away from this
place for my Dallas office someday, if you ever wanted a

change of scenery. We always need more qualified help at Briscoe Equity. Shayla, in particular. She's been looking for an assistant office manager for ages. And I have an empty condo just sitting there. I'd be happy to give you a good deal on rent."

He pressed his lips together, annoyed with himself for taking the offer too far, too fast.

Haylie's head dropped. "I don't know what Emily told you about me and why I was using her apartment, but she's wrong. I'm fine. I'm happy. Thanks for the offer, but my life and my family are here."

Damn it. Him and his big mouth. "Understood. Just . . . there's no time limit on the offer, so if you ever change your mind, just say the word."

She opened the door and stepped out. "I won't."

Roger Healy tossed his copy of the structural engineering report on the conference table in Briscoe Equity Group's meeting room. He pulled his glasses off his nose to chew on the earpiece while he glared at Ty. "This report is troubling in more ways than one."

Seated next to Knox, Ty sat a little straighter. "Agreed. I'm sure no one was more surprised than me at the extent of the problem."

Linda Yamaguchi, one of the firm's lawyers, cleared her throat. "We evaluated several of the property assessments you provided before we invested. None of them indicated even the possibility of an issue, including the sections of the reports specifically about hydrological and geological integrity. Are you saying that every one of the reports got it wrong?"

"Yes, ma'am."

"Then how do you explain the proof Knox provided that you were the one who orchestrated the false documentation?"

"Excuse me?" For the duration of the meeting, Ty's expression had remained blank, his posture unyielding, as the investors and lawyers took him to task on the report. But at this new information, Ty blanched. His façade cracked.

Yamaguchi slid a bound stack of papers across the table. "Along with the structural engineering report, Knox provided us with an evaluation by a second team of structural engineers and geologists of the appraisals and inspection documents you've provided the county records office and loan officers for years, comparing them against blueprints of the resort. The picture they paint isn't pretty. Or legal. But whether the erroneous information was a result of willful negligence on your part or the purposeful falsifying of documents and bribery is something for a judge to decide."

Ty very deliberately removed his Stetson and set it on the table in front of him as he seemed to be carefully picking his words. "It was a different time. And there was no harm done. It was an honest mistake. Despite what it looks like today, I would never endanger the people at my resort—the employees or the guests."

The investors shifted uneasily at that. Healy slid a copy of the proof and analysis of Ty's misdeeds across the table. The stack of papers displaced Ty's hat. Ty eyed it as one might regard at a poisonous plant.

"By inflating the value of the business, you've swindled us out of millions," Healy said.

Ty crumpled the brim of his hat in his grip. "I can make this right. You have to give me a chance."

Boris Sandomir tipped back in his chair and laced his fingers over his ample waist. "Are you suggesting that you'll return the money from our initial investment?"

"I don't have it to return," Ty stammered. "You know that."

To Knox's dismay, it was not as enjoyable as he'd

expected to watch Ty get taken to task. For all his faults and lies, Knox had come to know Ty's humanity these past few weeks. Despite his flaws, he was still a human being with feelings—a father, a husband, an uncle—but there was no way Ty was leaving this meeting with anything resembling pride. Knox tried to remind himself that Ty had brought this on himself, that Ty had not shown compassion to Knox's dad when he exiled him from the family. But, try as he might, Knox couldn't shake the feeling that this dressing down was unnecessary. Stripping him of his title and ownership of the resort was enough.

"But I do," Knox said. All eyes turned to him. It was a relief to have the floor once more, to shift the tone of the meeting away from berating Ty and back to Knox's plan to exact justice for his father.

Healy snorted, clearly unimpressed. "I'm not sure anything you say is going to carry much weight. This investment was your brainchild. You convinced us that this was a short-term, high-yield investment. But we were misled. Whether or not you were a party to this deception, it doesn't make you come out smelling like roses."

"I understand." In fact, that had been one of Knox's worries when he'd originally devised the strategy to take over Briscoe Ranch so he could sell it off. But the potential rewards eclipsed the risks, turning Knox's plan of justice into yet another high-stakes gamble, the same kind he'd based his career on. At least, in that way, he was on familiar ground. "Even with all of this . . . unpleasantness, the selling points of the resort haven't changed. Its ideal location, its international reputation. And both teams of engineers I've consulted with think the hydrological and geological problems are reversible. The bottom line is that we could all still make a lot of money. The only difference is that it will take more time than we'd previously allowed for."

Healy strummed his hand over his copy of the report. "I think I speak for all of us when I say that this is a headache we're not interested in. I say we shut it down, sell the land, and recoup our investment, profits be damned. We've done that before when deals went sour."

The grumbling around the room affirmed Healy's opinion.

Knox kept his cool, outwardly, but his pulse was beating out of control. In his zeal to stick it to Ty, he hadn't seen this possibility coming. But if he couldn't convince them to wait out the problems with the resort instead of writing it off as a loss, there wouldn't be any restaurant in need of a brilliant, passionate head chef. There would be nowhere for Granny June and the Briscoe family to live. Sure, eventually, Knox still planned to sell the resort off, but not until it was a success. Not until he'd had time to ease the Briscoe family into the idea.

But if the investors sided against Knox, then they'd all be out on the streets before Christmas.

"I see your point, but I'd like you to consider mine. I've given this a lot of thought." *More than any of you will ever know.* "Here's my plan. Vote me in as the new CEO. Ty will retire quietly, immediately. After we have the value of the business reassessed to reflect these new hydrological and geological issues, Ty will sell me his shares at that new, lower price. He'll walk away a rich enough man, with his reputation intact, and I'll be the majority stakeholder in Briscoe Ranch. I'll shoulder the costs of repairing the damage, and then our plan to expand the resort will be back on track.

"I'll take care of everything. All the risk will be on me. All you have to do is hang tight. We've done that before, too, when deals went sour. In this case, your headache goes away, and the original plan, with the original profit projections, still stands. May I remind you that we have potential buyers already lined up, but they're no more ready to buy today than we are to sell at a loss. We've done this before, gentlemen. We know how to turn a sinking business into profit. The only difference now is that this business is quite literally sinking."

The joke earned him a few halfhearted chuckles around the room. Other than Healy and Yamaguchi, most of the investors and lawyers seemed to warm to Knox's plan.

Ty braced his hands on the table and made a show of standing, his speech face in full force. "This business has been in my family for generations. There is so much more at stake than a bunch of millionaires adding to their bank accounts. This is my family's ancestral home. My grandparents and my father are buried on the property. My wife and I, my daughters, and my mother all live there. Our blood has been soaked into the very ground on which the resort stands. Don't do this."

It was unbearable, hearing this once great man, the ruler of a kingdom, beg for mercy. Knox hoped his dad really was watching on High, because this was it. Justice achieved. Knox couldn't stomach any more. The thirst for revenge had completely left him.

He stood in a show of solidarity with Ty. "If the investors will give me a chance, then the property will stay in the family, at least for a few more years until I can make it even greater than it ever was in its prime. As for the chapel and the family burial plot, I'll bequeath that land to you and your daughters as a gift. That's always been my plan, so you don't have to worry about the graves of your—our—family being desecrated."

Ty was composed.

Healy frowned, but Sandomir nodded. "I'm going to trust you on this, Knox. Like I've done so many times in the past, and you've always come through. Besides, our investment in Briscoe Ranch is already a sunk cost, so what's the harm in a few more years? Especially if you'll take the burden of the extra expenses on yourself."

"Thank you, Boris," Knox said.

"I'm with Sandomir," Richard Gorman said. To Ty, he added, "Retire. Enjoy your family. The business will be in good hands with Knox."

The skin of Ty's face tightened like he was holding back a grimace. "And if I decline your offer to retire?"

Knox clapped him on the back. "Then you can still be a part of this company in some capacity. I'm sure we'll find a suitable role for you." As long as it didn't involve any decision making or managing. Maybe he could be chaplain. HR was just telling Knox that they were in the market for a new one.

Ty shifted to square a look directly at Knox. "You can't do this to me."

You did this to yourself, Knox considered saying. But he was over the urge to turn the screws any harder. "It won't be so bad."

Ty huffed at that. "Then I guess you leave me with no choice. I accept. I'll sell you my shares. And I'll retire. On one condition." He swallowed hard. From his pocket, he pulled a handkerchief that he used to wipe his brow. "Nothing we discussed here today leaves this room. And I'll be the one to break the news to my family."

"Of course," Knox said. Disquiet tugged at his conscience. Not guilt or regret. Just . . . this didn't feel as satisfying as he'd thought it would. Especially given the euphoria he'd initially felt at pulling the rug out from under Ty with that structural engineering report. Healy took control of the meeting again. "We've got to take an official vote about making Knox CEO and staying the course, and the lawyers have to draw some contracts up. For the record, I don't like this, but I'll cede to the wishes of the room."

"Excellent. Make me CEO and you won't regret it. I promise you that. In the meantime, I hope you received my email this morning about coming to the resort for a dinner party next weekend to celebrate."

"There's not much to celebrate," Healy grumbled.

"A show of force, then. Once you see the resort first-hand, you'll see what I mean about it being a special place, worth all the effort we're putting into it. I'll have more details for you on my plans, so you can rest assured that I've got everything under control."

Ty gave a huff of protest that Knox ignored. He thrust out his hand for Ty to shake. "Uncle Ty, it's been a pleasure doing business with you."

Ty glared at Knox's outstretched hand. "What happened with Clint and Linda and me, it was the darkest time in our family. I have regrets. A lot of them. But bringing you to Briscoe Ranch wasn't one of them until now."

And Linda? "What did my mom have to do with the rift?"

Ty sniffed, then side-eyed the rest of the conference attendees. "Doesn't matter anymore. Any of it. You're the keeper of the Briscoe legacy now and that's what counts. You do right by our family name and I won't have to kill you." Hard to tell how serious that threat was. Knox certainly wouldn't put it past him.

Ty turned away from the table, thumping Knox hard on the shoulder as he walked toward the door. "Don't hold the plane for me. I'll find my own way back to Dulcet."

If Haylie minded that Knox was more quiet than usual on the flight home, she didn't mention it. She prattled on about all the things she and Shayla had in common and what they'd talked about. Certainly, Knox had noticed after the meeting ended how cozy Haylie and Shayla had looked sitting side by side at Shayla's desk, discussing some reality TV show called *Celebrity Matchmaker.* Two peas in a pod.

He'd even gotten a text from Shayla after he and Haylie had departed for the airport.

OMG, how could you have kept H from me all this time? She and I were separated at birth.

Now that he thought about it, they really did have a lot in common. They were both into fashion and celebrity gossip, they both talked a mile a minute and had a generally cheery outlook—and they looked strikingly similar with those strong Briscoe genes in their blood.

It was amazing, all this family that Knox and Shayla—and Wade, if he ever deigned to visit—never really knew about all these years, but that lived only a couple of hours away. Knox was eternally grateful that the board had voted to give Knox a chance to turn the resort around. He didn't want to contemplate how devastating it would have been had Knox had to tell the family to pack their bags because they were losing everything.

It was after dark when the Cab'd driver dropped him off in front of his home. Emily's car in his driveway caught his eye. The sight brought a smile to his lips, despite the draining day he'd had. He hadn't told her the purpose of the day's meeting, wanting to wait until he had concrete news to share with her, but he loved the idea of coming home to her, of holding her and kissing her and letting the rest of the world fall away.

When he didn't find her in the house, he started his usual search around the property and found her in the first place he looked. Sitting cross-legged on the dock of the lake, under the floodlights mounted to the roof of the boathouse.

"Picnic for one?"

She smiled up at him as he kissed the crown of her head. "No. This is my version of fishing."

Knox took another look inside the bowl, then at the bag of chips on the dock next to her, and laughed out loud. "You're actually chumming with Frito pie, like you said you would."

"You bet I am. And check this out."

She lobbed a spoonful of chili into the water, then tossed a handful of Fritos in after it.

Knox snagged a chip from the bag and popped it into his mouth. "Nice touch. I suppose if you're going to entice fish with Frito Pie, you've got to give them the whole experience."

"Just wait. You'll see."

Knox lowered to the deck next to her.

The water rippled, and then out of the dark depths, a huge gray carp appeared, swirling just beneath the surface.

Knox looked into its ancient eyes as it opened its mouth and gobbled up a chip. And there it was, the scar on its dorsal fin. "Hello, Phantom."

"It's him, isn't it? Hey, buddy," Emily said. "You like Fritos?"

As if in response, Phantom sucked another chip into its mouth.

"If you could find a gaffe in the boat house, we could be eating him for dinner," Emily said. "But I don't know. That kind of makes me sad. He looks like a survivor."

So much had changed for Knox since his first day at Briscoe Ranch when Phantom had become his cold-blooded nemesis. Ty had been his nemesis, too. No longer. Knox had purged himself of the need for competition. He no longer had anything to prove, except to himself. And to Emily, if she'd have him.

He reached into the chip bag and pulled out a handful, then sprinkled them into the water. "I agree. He does seem like a survivor. Plus, this guy and I have history. I'm officially taking him off the menu."

He felt Emily's eyes on him, searching. Then her fingers stroked his temple and his hair. "Something's different with you. Something's wrong. Is it us? Is it because of what happened at my apartment?"

He tore his attention from Phantom to regard her. Her hand still stroked his hair, so he turned his head and kissed her wrist. "Nothing's wrong. Everything's great, actually. Including what happened in your apartment. That was a very good thing."

"You flew to Dallas today for a meeting. You and Ty."

"And Haylie. She came, too. She and my sister hit it off."

"It's not hard to hit it off with your sister," Emily said.

"That's a good point. So, about the meeting today. Don't share this with anyone yet, including Carina, but you're looking at the new CEO of Briscoe Ranch."

Emily's hand fell. "What?"

For a breathless, wild moment, Knox was seized with fear that Emily wouldn't support his move because of her loyalty to Ty. But whether she did or not, the act was done, and all he could do now was be honest with her. "The equity firm voted me in today because Ty has decided to retire. And he'll do so in style, I might add. With a pension that will ensure that he and his wife will never want for anything, especially given the extra revenue he's going to get by selling me his shares."

Emily blinked fast, processing. "I don't understand. I mean, I'm happy for you. That's . . . wow. But I had no idea Ty was thinking of retiring. I guess that makes sense. I knew there was a good reason he brought you in that didn't have anything to do with the resort's debt."

He nodded to the bench that sat against the wall of the boathouse. "Come sit with me and I'll start at the beginning."

They bid goodnight to Phantom, then grabbed the bag

of Fritos and walked to the bench. Once they were settled, Knox did what he'd been waiting to do all day. He gathered her in his arms and kissed her slow and deep, until she softened into him and wrapped her arms around his neck.

"I could see you and me necking on this bench all the time," he said in a gruff voice once the kiss ended.

A shadow passed over her features and was gone before he had a chance to study it. Maybe she was just concerned about Ty. "I like that idea," she said. "I never expected this, with you. I never saw it coming."

"Ditto. But I wouldn't change a thing."

There was that shadow again. Could there be a chance she wasn't feeling their connection as deeply as he was? Maybe she needed time to catch her breath. Then again, maybe after she heard the story of how he came to be CEO and controlling shareholder of Briscoe Ranch within a month of signing on as part-owner, she might not want anything to do with him. It wasn't a matter of testing her loyalty to either Ty or him, but whether she could accept Knox, warts and all, including the thirst for justice that had plagued him for so long.

He sat back, took her hand, and then told her everything—about his father's predictions that Ty would run the family business into the ground and his dying wish that Knox would seek justice against Ty, about how hard Knox had worked to position himself as the person Ty would turn to when he ran out of revenue, as his father had predicted. He told her about the structural and land problems plaguing the resort and about Ty's lies and the overvaluation of the business. And then he told her about the meeting today, sparing no details.

It felt foreign, laying it all out for her like that, but he needed Emily to know. What good would it be to try to win her over if there were secrets between them?

For the most part, she listened quietly and attentively, asking clarifying questions every so often and expressing bewilderment that the resort was sliding toward the lake.

They sat in silence for a few minutes, watching the moonlight-kissed water ripple in the breeze.

"You still plan to sell."

"Eventually. At this point, anyway. It was the best deal I could strike for now, given that my investors were ready to shut the resort down and take the loss. At least this way, we have a few years to figure out what to do next. That's enough time for your restaurant to establish itself. You've worked too hard for this. I'm ready to roll up my sleeves and make Briscoe Ranch thrive, including your restaurant. We can set it up so that you're leasing the space as a separate company, that way, if the next resort owners decide to go in a different direction, you'll still own your brand. You can relocate or expand as you want."

"Hmm," she said, her eyes still on the lake.

"What does that mean?"

She shrugged. "Or maybe you won't sell the resort at all. Maybe you'll make it so wildly profitable that you'll buy out the investors' shares, too."

His heart squeezed. She wanted him to stay. "Let's celebrate my new job title. Unless you already made dinner. I wouldn't want to stomp on your plans for the night."

She clapped her hands on her knees. "I had no plans. I wasn't sure when you'd get home tonight. What did you have in mind?"

"It's the last Wednesday of the month."

Emily groaned. "You want to go to Movie Night at the resort? That's how you want to celebrate all this? I don't even like *Miracle on 34th Street*. That girl is too precocious. It gets on my nerves."

He grinned; she seemed so nettled at the idea. Just as he had been when Granny June had announced that they'd be attending. It was tempting to give in to Emily's protests so he could spend the night alone with her, but he was trying not to rush things with her, to show her through his actions how committed he was to her and to Briscoe Ranch. He leapt to his feet and brought Emily up with him. "We can't let Granny June or her Facebook friends down. And I want the employees to know I'm committed to them and to the resort, quell any buyout or layoff rumors that might be floating around."

She melted into his side with a groan. "Ugh, you have too many good points. You're going to make me go to Movie Night."

By the time they arrived via Emily's car to Movie Night at the resort's open-air amphitheater, the movie had already begun, and the place was packed. Families and couples lounged on blankets and in lawn chairs amid the scents of fried chicken and chips and colas. Children ran around with friends, laughing and playing, and only about half the people there seemed to notice a movie was playing at all. Knox squeezed Emily's hand. "See? Not so bad."

Emily sighed through a smile. "You're right. And I see Carina and Decker about halfway up on the left, sitting next to Granny June and Haylie."

Looking over the faces in the crowd, Knox saw other faces he recognized. The hairdresser whom he'd seen styling Eloise Briscoe's hair chatting with a group of women, several of the employees from human resources, and even the maintenance worker who'd once helped him push his dad's truck to the shoulder of the road just outside the resort's property line. The air crackled with happiness and togetherness. Love. He looked at the woman by his side as Haylie's words the day of his first tour of the resort came back to him. This place really was magic when it came to finding love. Thank goodness Knox had convinced the investors not to sell. It would have broken his heart.

Briscoe Ranch really was one big family—a family Knox was now an inextricable part of. The keeper of the family legacy, Ty had called him.

But until tonight, he hadn't realized what an honor that was. It was a job he wouldn't take lightly. He was going to take all that private, hidden rot under the building's foundation—all the rot from the past and the wounds of the generation that had come before his—and he was going to restore the integrity of its foundation. He was going to make Briscoe Ranch thrive again. He'd never been so proud to be a part of something.

And maybe, just maybe, he'd have Emily by his side while he did it.

For the first time since his dad's passing, he felt completely at peace. He looked to the heavens. *Dad, I don't know what part you've played in all this, but thank you. Thank you for leading me back here, back to where I'm supposed to be.*

He took Emily's hand and kissed the back of it. "Come on. Let's go say hi to our family."

Chapter Seventeen

Like most great chefs, Emily thrived under pressure. When a culinary performance was do-or-die, Emily did her best work, churning out extraordinary, show-stopping dishes. None of that explained why she'd spent the week before the Briscoe Equity Group dinner party on the cusp of a panic attack.

While it was true that this was her debut performance for Knox's business partners, he'd already promised her the restaurant, so her growing sense of dread was completely illogical. In all, they'd be hosting nearly thirty people in the private dining room at the resort's steakhouse, including Knox's business partners and their spouses, Ty and Eloise, and the other executives at the resort. No problem. She'd handled far larger groups than that. The menu she'd created for the night was outstanding, her staff was on their A-game, and she'd spent every night that week in Knox's bed. And yet, she woke every morning feeling like she'd built a house of cards and that it was now on the verge of collapse.

An hour until show time, Shayla breezed into the kitchen. Though she was decked out in a sophisticated turquoise and black knee-length cocktail dress, it was her broad, genuine smile that made her ensemble truly eye-catching.

"Emily! I'm sorry to interrupt."

Emily wiped her hands on a towel, then hugged Shayla. "No problem. You look fantastic, by the way."

"Really? I always feel like such an imposter when I wear dresses. I'd rather have my running shoes and a sports bra on." She took Emily's hand and pulled her into the walk-in pantry just off the auxiliary kitchen in the steakhouse where they were operating tonight. She shut the door, then turned her high-wattage smile back onto Emily. "I just wanted to pop in and tell you how happy I am that things are working out with you and the restaurant you want to open. Knox already has me looking for a publicist to make sure it gets the international hype it deserves when we launch it."

"Oh, wow." International hype. Shit. She battled back a shock of fear at the idea of her parents recognizing her, of finding her after all these years and so many precautions taken to prevent them from ever discovering her. What good was a disappearing act if she let a publicist splash her image all over the globe? Guess she'd find out. It was yet another threat to her ever-more-precarious house of cards.

"Knox is really taken with you. I know I'm talking out of turn, but we're all adults here, right? I just hope that even though you got what you wanted, that you give my brother a real chance. I like you two together. You definitely have my blessing. I mean, not that you need it." She shook her head. "Listen to me ramble. Sorry. Anyway, congratulations again."

Even though you got what you wanted. Words that evoked that gnawing sense of dread in Emily's gut because they were exactly what had been on her mind all week.

She hated that it appeared as though Emily had slept with
Knox to get the restaurant. Check that. It didn't merely
appear that way. That was *precisely* what had happened.
Knox's decision to give her the restaurant wasn't about
Emily's cooking. Not even close.

Emily swayed, dizzy and lightheaded. She didn't want
this. She didn't want him like this. She didn't want the
appearance that she'd slept her way to the top. If Knox's
sister, arguably the person who knew him better than anyone, had drawn that conclusion, then what would the rest
of the world think? More importantly, what would the
food critics and bloggers and foodies who were merci-
less to new, overhyped restaurants—to female chefs as a
whole—think? Her restaurant could be ruined before it
got off the ground.

"It's all right. And thank you for the congratulations,"
she said. She even managed a smile.

"Okay, I'd better let you get back to work. I can't wait
to eat your food tonight. The menu looks great."

Emily watched Shayla's retreating form, stunned anew
how everything had gone so horribly wrong. She drifted
to the prep table where her knife sat and picked it up,
chopping parsley in an attempt to soothe her nerves.
But she couldn't stop replaying Knox's words in her head
from the week before about how she'd wrapped him
around her little finger before he'd tasted a single bite of
her cooking. She wanted to be with him, but not like this.
What happened when their affair ended? What happened
if he changed his mind about running Briscoe Ranch?

Or, the better question, why the hell was she hinging
her future, her home, and her career on a man?

A zinger of pain shot up her arm and she yelped. She'd
sliced the tip of her middle finger. A spray of blood smeared
over the chopped herbs and cutting board. Horrified, she
stared down at the mess, barely cognizant of the pain.

She dropped the whole cutting board into a trashcan, then headed to the sink to flush out the cut. Her hands shook under the hot water as she scrubbed them clean. No wonder she'd cut herself. She was turning hysterical.

Nori, her sous chef, appeared at her side. "You okay, Emily?"

"I think so. I've had worse. Do you mind taking over for a little bit while I get this bandaged up?"

"Take your time."

If anyone could talk Emily down from her panic, it would be Carina. She stole down the stairs and through the hall, racing to her office. When she stepped inside, she dug into her desk drawer for a bandage, which she applied to her still-dripping cut before pulling her phone from her pocket and dialing Carina's number.

Carina answered on the second ring.

"I can't do this," Emily said in a quiet voice.

"Do what? Cook for the dinner party? Don't go there, Emily. You know how you have a tendency to sabotage a good thing. Remember?"

"I know." That was exactly what Emily had done. She'd sabotaged her success by sleeping with Knox. She'd let herself down. She thought about her crew of dedicated, talented sous chefs. She'd let them down, too.

"If this is out of loyalty to my dad about his retirement, then I'm going to stop you right there. It was his idea to retire early. He told us that this was for the best, so Knox could run the resort without feeling like my dad was looking over his shoulder all the time. He said it was to right the wrong from the rift so our family can move forward."

To right the wrong from the rift.

Emily knew the next step in Knox's plan to right the injustices that were done to his dad. She knew he was going to sell the resort as soon as it started turning a profit again, and then Emily would have to either find another location to move her restaurant or put her fate in the hands of the resort's new owner. One thing was certain, she may never live down the reputation that she'd gotten this break because she was banging the boss. The restaurant world was cutthroat, and every perceived weakness—especially with female chefs—was exploited accordingly.

"Look, Carina. I need to tell you something. I did something—"

A knock on the glass interrupted her. Emily whirled around and nearly dropped the phone at the sight of Knox, dressed handsomely in a black suit with his lucky black Stetson secure on his head.

So much for Emily's grand confession. "Carina? I'm going to have to tell you later. I've got to go."

"Okay. I'll be home all night, if you want to talk after the dinner party. Try to have fun. This new direction for the resort is a good thing, remember?"

Emily was trying to believe that, even though her success had come at the expense of her professional integrity. *Jesus.* When she thought about it like that, the situation felt even worse.

Knox gave her a sweet, lingering kiss. But even though none of her employees were likely to discover them, the display of affection still made her heart sink.

"Hey, there," he said. "Nori told me you might be down here patching up a wound. Are you okay?"

She held up her bandaged finger. "Just a slice. You're looking mighty fine," she said as she straightened his tie.

"You're looking mighty fine, yourself," he crooned, tipping his hat to her like a good and proper cowboy. "Would now be a good time for me to whisk you out to the dinner party to meet my partners? I'd love for them to put a face with the chef before the meal begins."

She was way too wound up at the moment to cope with

vacuous small talk and artificial smiles. "You know small talk isn't my thing. I'm the noodle maker, remember?"

"How could I forget? But listen, it would be great to have my partners' support about your restaurant. I'm asking you to do this for me."

She hesitated. "I thought the choice was yours, as the controlling partner."

He shrugged. "It is, and I could overrule them if necessary. But their backing would be infinitely helpful to both our causes."

She swallowed back a groan. She was going to have to do this. Shaking hands and kissing babies like a friggin' politician. "Can't my food speak for itself?"

He raised an eyebrow, then took her hand and tucked it into the crook of his arm. "I'll be right there next to you. And I'll make a deal with you. Do this, and then I'll take you fishing in the dark after the party breaks up tonight."

She let him tug her towards the double doors leading to the stairs. "Is that a euphemism?"

A rakish grin spread on his lips. "I guess you'll have to wait and see."

The private dining room in the steakhouse had been designed with the charm of an old hotel lounge, complete with brass fixtures, and elegant wood paneling. Lush velvet curtains were drawn back to allow access to a veranda that looked out over the gardens, with their strolling resort guests, and boasted a breathtaking view of the golf course and Lake Bandit. It was the perfect setting for Knox's business partners to experience firsthand the magic of Briscoe Ranch after dark.

As they moved toward the nearest cluster of guests, Emily ruminated on the impressive wealth represented in the room, as she'd done so many times as a teenager at the dinner parties her parents dragged her to. No wonder

Knox had had the confidence to sweep into Briscoe Ranch and assume control. This was the world he lived in, a world Emily had shed when she'd left her parents' cavernous penthouse at sixteen. No doubt Knox could have privately financed Emily's dream restaurant as easily as he'd arranged their dinner at The Smoking Gun. He could have rejected her proposal just as easily. No doubt about it, she was at the mercy of a powerful, wealthy man—a position she'd vowed to never find herself in again.

Knox still held her hand tucked in the crook of his arm, so she pulled it away. Tonight, in front of the equity firm investors and resort executives, they were nothing but boss and employee, despite the wicked, wonderful things he'd done to her body that very morning. Oh God, what a terrible corner she'd painted herself into.

She wiped her clammy palms on her chef's jacket. "I can't do this."

It felt like she was saying that a lot that week. And every time she did, she was struck by the terrible sensation of being on a runaway horse, clinging to it by only her fingertips.

Knox stopped short of the guests and gave her a studying look. "You're really nervous, aren't you?"

He had no idea. All she could do was nod.

"I'll tell you what. Let's scrap this idea. I can make your grand introduction when you serve dessert. How does that sound?"

"Divine," she choked out.

He leaned in as though in preparation for a kiss. Emily stopped him with a hand to his chest. "We can't."

"They'll know soon enough," he countered.

And that, right there, was the whole problem. "I'm going to get back to work. Enjoy the evening. I'll see you at dessert."

The dinner service and the dishes she'd crafted for the party were flawless, just as she'd known they'd be. Between her and Nori and the rest of her top-notch staff, there wasn't a menu she could design that they wouldn't master. The trouble was, the night was flying by. Every course served brought Emily closer to dessert, and to facing the crowd of all of Knox's business partners to announce that she'd been tapped by Knox to open a restaurant.

Well, maybe *tapped* was the wrong word. "Damn double entendres," she grumbled as she pulled a cart of individually crafted desserts from the refrigerator.

Dessert was a riff on another dish she'd served Knox, and that, in itself, only dog-piled onto her stress. When she'd originally designed tonight's menu, it had seemed the perfect gesture to show him how taken she was with him—but that was before she'd gotten an extreme case of cold feet. Or self-sabotage, as Carina would tell her.

But it was too late to change course, and so, at eight-thirty on the nose, she and Nori plated thirty chocolate bombes filled with chilled peach soup.

"Go ahead," she told the servers. "I'll be right out. I'll make a grand entrance."

When she walked into the dining room, the crowd applauded. All except Knox, who was staring at the bomb in front of him as though it were an actual bomb.

When she reached his side, she whispered, "Is something wrong?"

The question seemed to shake him from his trace. He refocused his eyes on her, and in them, she read tenderness and heat. "It's peach soup," he said almost reverently.

She nearly stroked his cheek before thinking better of it. "I thought that might be a nice touch. Kind of brings everything full circle, you know?"

"It's more than a nice touch. It's perfect." He stood and took her hand, lacing their fingers together. Then he leaned in close to her ear. "Thank you for giving me a second chance to try the peach soup."

Grinning, Knox faced the crowd. "Ladies and Gentlemen. I'd like you to meet Emily Ford, the mastermind behind tonight's fantastic dinner and the chef of a future five-star restaurant here at the resort that we're installing as part of the resort's renovations. Didn't she do a fantastic job tonight?"

Shayla led the room in another round of applause. Emily smiled and nodded her appreciation, but only until she noticed one of the dinner guests leaning back in her chair, her eyes on Knox's and Emily's joined hands.

Panic struck, swifter and harder than ever before. They'd basically just told all of Knox's investors exactly how intimate she and the company CEO were. Her eyes flashed wide as she pulled away from him, but the damage was done. She read it on enough faces in the crowd.

What a pretzel she'd contorted herself into for this job—for this man. He'd dared her to prove her worth and she'd tried. Like a mindless drone. He'd snapped his fingers and she'd performed for him. And now she was falling in love with him on top of it all. He held too much power over her. Her career, her heart. He knew her deepest secret and her greatest weaknesses. He controlled every aspect of her life.

Because she'd let him.

That wasn't love, not in any way that would last. If she ever hoped for a future with Knox, if she ever wanted them to have a chance at something real, then they'd have to come together as equals. Not boss and employee. The power differential was too great. There was no way for her to consider what to do, much less breathe, with Knox right there by her side clouding her judgment, even as he signed her paychecks. Instead of bending to another's will, instead of living in fear of discovery by her parents, timid in the face of the unknown, it was time for her to rise, secure in her bones. The only person she should have been trying to prove her worthiness to was herself.

There was only one way out of this spiral into disaster. One of them had to be strong enough to say *enough*. She'd been the one to say enough when she'd run away from home, and she needed to be that strong again.

She looked at Knox. His eyes glowed with pride for her. Then she looked at the roomful of investors who were watching her, assessing her bankability and waiting for her to speak to them.

She opened her mouth and said the two most important words of her career and love life. "I quit."

The dinner guests' only responses were quizzical stares.

Knox stepped in front of her, angling into her line of sight. "Say that again?"

Though her mind was buzzing with a thousand different topics and she could barely focus her eyes, she tried to hold his gaze. She owed him that much. "I can't work for Briscoe Ranch anymore, and I can't work for you. I don't want the restaurant. I quit."

And then she did the only other thing she could think of. She ran. Out of the restaurant, down the hall, and through the door to the employee staircase. She'd taken two steps down the stairs when Knox's voice called to her. "Emily, wait! Stop!"

No, she would not stop. Eventually, she owed him an apology and explanation for humiliating them both in front of his investors, but she was going to do it on her terms, after she'd had the chance to lay out the broken pieces of her life and figure out what she felt and what she wanted to do. But that wouldn't be tonight, and certainly not because he was commanding her to stop. She picked up her pace down the stairs, though she heard his footfalls fast approaching.

He caught up to her as she reached the stairwell entrance to the lobby and slammed his hand against the door, holding it closed. For a moment, all either of them did was breathe.

She closed her eyes. "I'm sorry. I'm so sorry for everything. But Knox, please, let me go."

He touched her chin in an attempt to shift her gaze to him, but she jerked her face away. She couldn't bear his touch lest she lose her nerve to walk away.

"What happened back there? You earned the restaurant and now you've got it. I don't understand what's wrong."

The phrase *careful what you wish for* came to mind. "The only reason I earned it was by sleeping with you."

His jaw stiffened. "You know that's not why you got the job, so don't insult us both by claiming otherwise."

"Then tell me what happened, Knox, if this isn't because we were lovers."

"*Were?*"

God, this hurt like hell. But she had to reclaim her life. She had to put herself back in the driver's seat and that would be impossible with Knox holding sway over her. She pinched the bridge of her nose. "Past tense. For now, until I can think straight again."

He swallowed hard. His focus slipped to the empty space past her shoulder. "Okay, then I'll tell you what happened. I challenged you to make me think about food as more than fuel. You did that and so much more. You made me crave things I never knew I needed. You brought me to life. You opened my eyes to so many aspects of living and myself that I'd been blind to. You're brilliant, Emily. You're the most brilliant light I've ever seen."

How could he say that after she'd embarrassed him in front of his business partners? "You've opened my eyes, too. You've helped me see that the thing that's been holding me back all the time has been me. I've let fear of my parents and fear of the unknown dictate every single choice I've made since running away. I feel like a bird who's never exercised its wings for fear of falling. And now, instead of flying on my own, I'm using you and Briscoe Ranch as crutches."

"Not crutches, support. There's a difference. Everybody needs a support system. Even you, Emily."

"Knox, please don't argue semantics. Phrase it any way you want, but the truth is the same. I was letting you dictate the terms of my life. And I have to knock that shit off right now before it drowns us both. I can't be with you if it's not as your equal."

He clamped his lips together. Because, clearly, he knew she was right.

All these years, she'd convinced herself that she didn't need love and companionship, but now she knew that had been her fear talking. Knox had helped her see that she needed both. And, not only that, but he'd helped her realize that she was strong enough to risk her heart to love. Maybe from Knox, or maybe from someone with whom she didn't share such tangled connections.

There was only one way for her to find out, and that was with space and time and distance. "I have to go."

With a stunned expression, he lowered his hand from the door and stood aside so she could pass. Emily flung the stairwell door open and raced through the lobby. She no longer heard Knox's footfalls or voice, but she continued to push herself faster until she burst into the night through the main doors—escaping her past, escaping her fears, and escaping the sheltered box of a future that would have only held her back while she finally learned to fly.

Chapter Eighteen

Emily pounded on Carina's door for a second time, ready to spill the confession she'd been poised to share with Carina before the dinner party. Knox had been right about one thing: Emily did need a support system, and hers was her best friend. She wasn't sure what advice she hoped Carina would give her—to support her quitting or encourage her to go groveling back to Knox and his investors—but either way, Emily was bound to come out of their talk with a clearer idea about what she felt and what she wanted to do.

At the sound of the door unlocking, Emily drew herself up, trying to look poised and in control of her faculties. Decker opened the door, looking sleepy in a pair of tattered sweatpants and flannel shirt with a day's worth of stubble on his cheeks. When he saw it was Emily, he flicked his eyebrows in a bored greeting and stepped aside for her to enter. "Can't you womenfolk powwow in the morning? What is it with you two and these late-night gabfests?"

It wasn't that late, only ten o'clock, but for a rancher like Decker who woke before the crows to tend to the horses, the hour was well past his bedtime. Emily darted past him into the house. "Sorry. I need to talk to Carina."

She found Carina sitting on the sofa watching TV, her belly protruding between her bent knees as though she were wearing a watermelon under her pajamas. "What's wrong?"

What a question. What *wasn't* wrong? There was only one place to start the story. "I slept with Knox. A lot."

Carina gasped, then made a cumbersome attempt to leap to her feet. Decker snatched his cowboy hat from a peg near the door. "Okay, that's my cue to scram. I'm gonna go check on the horses."

Emily had never seen a man disappear so fast.

Carina waited for the door to close behind Decker, then smacked the sofa cushions in time with her words. "You what? You what?"

Emily let the humiliation wash over her. She knew this was the worst Carina had ever seen her, but their love was unconditional, so she had nothing to hide from her friend. "I slept with Knox," she repeated, more slowly this time.

"By *a lot*, do you mean a lot in one night? Or . . ."

"More than one night. A lot of nights. My place. His place." Emily cringed and closed her eyes. "His mother's place."

"Oh my God, Em. How?"

Restless and agitated, Emily started to pace absent-mindedly in front of the sofa. "What do you mean *how*? You're the one who's pregnant. I think you're plenty aware of how it's done."

"You know what I mean! I need details. You . . . and Knox . . . you two—" Carina's words were cut off by a grunt of pain. "Ow. Damn it."

"What happened? The little guy's kicking harder?"

"Well, yeah. But this was just another Braxton-Hicks contraction. Don't mind me. I need details, now! I can't even picture you and Knox as a couple. He's so . . . so . . . reserved. And you're . . . you."

"We're not a couple. The thing between us isn't even physical," she said, almost to herself. It was a nutso idea. Of course, their attraction was physical. They couldn't keep their hands off each other. "I mean, it is. He's so hot, I can't even deal . . . I mean, that body . . . and the sex is . . . wow . . . but it's not . . ." But when Emily thought about everything she loved about Knox, the aspects of him that had captured her heart, his eight-pack abs didn't even make the list. It wasn't his body. It wasn't infatuation or lust. Her feelings ran so much deeper than that.

Carina groaned. "You're driving me crazy. Spit it out already."

She whirled to face Carina, fully aware that her horror was showing on her face. "I think I'm in love with him. I think that's what this is. Love." She nearly choked on the word, it was so foreign a concept. She grabbed fistfuls of her hair. "This is horrible. It feels terrible. I can't sleep and food doesn't taste good at all and I feel like my life's spinning out of control and all I can think about is him."

Carina was back on her feet. "You're *in love*? You've only known him for a month."

"I've practically been living in his house for that month. I've been studying him for a month. I climbed inside his mind and his soul, and then I let my guard down and I let him climb inside me."

Carina scrunched her face up. "That doesn't sound all that romantic."

"Huh? No, not like that. I mean, yeah, but—" A frustrated growl. "Double entendres are the bane of my existence! You know how I get when I want to fix someone the perfect meal. I get inside their heads."

Carina snagged Emily's hand and tried to drag her

down onto the sofa next to her. "That's what makes you such a great culinary artist."

"Yeah, well, I got inside Knox's mind and I learned everything about him. And then he got inside my head, too. And I fell in love." *Holy shit.* She was in love. Her throat tightened even more. She gasped, struggling to draw a full breath. "I ruined my career over a man. Over love, of all the goddamn terrible things." Dizziness made her sway. This time, she allowed Carina to pull her down onto the sofa, where she pressed her hands over her eyes. "What have I done?"

Carina rubbed her back. "Your career's not ruined. Knox is a professional. He's not going to let—"

"I quit, Carina. Tonight, in front of all the partners at his firm. I quit the resort. I turned down the restaurant because I can't live like this anymore. He has too much control over me and my future." Her throat tightened. "He boxed me in."

"Whoa, whoa, whoa. Slow down. You quit your job here?"

"It was the only way."

"You don't have to do this, Emily."

Emily could see shades of Knox in Carina's expression and tone of voice when she spoke the words that echoed his. How fucked up was that? She'd slept with her best friend's cousin? Knox was practically family. That was how low she'd sunk. "Yes, I do. I don't have a choice. He left me with no other options."

Carina pulled Emily into a hug and released a long, slow exhalation that prompted Emily to do the same. "I've got you," Carina cooed. "Everything's going to be okay."

A knock sounded at the front door.

After exchanging looks, Emily pulled away from Carina to peer through the peephole. When she saw who it was, her heart gave a painful squeeze. "It's Knox," she whispered. "I can't talk to him. I need time."

Carina wiggled and scooted her butt to the edge of the sofa then held out her hand. "I'm going to tell him that, okay? Let me handle it. Just help me up first." Emily pulled Carina to standing, then hustled to the shadows of the kitchen as Carina opened the door as wide as her body.

"Is she here?" Knox said.

The sound of his voice sent a shiver down Emily's spine. Tears pricked her eyes.

"Yes," Carina said.

Emily looked in his direction to make sure he wasn't trying to push past Carina to get in, which he wasn't, and found him watching her. She met his troubled gaze, pride forcing hers not to turn away.

"Emily," he rasped from behind clenched jaws.

"Give her time to calm down, okay?" Carina said.

Knox's nostrils flared. With his attention locked on Emily, he offered a terse nod.

Decker appeared behind Knox and set a firm hand on his shoulder. "Tomorrow's as good as tonight, man. You want to go grab a beer with me?"

Knox scowled, the contortion of his lips reflecting the monumental effort it was taking for him to remain poised. "Can't. I have a restaurant full of investors waiting for me to return with an explanation about why the talented chef I've been telling them about just quit. I wanted to ask her one last time if she'd reconsider."

Shit. She'd embarrassed him in front of his colleagues. Yet another way their relationship had messed with her judgment. She walked toward the door, prepared to apologize for putting him in such a terrible place. "That's what this visit is about? Your investors?"

"Of course, it's not," he growled. "It's about you and

me and whatever the hell happened back there. But more than that, I want you to—" his voice broke. "I want you to succeed in your career, with your passion. I'm trying to be your support."

"Tomorrow," Carina pressed. Decker's hand appeared on Knox's shoulder once more.

Knox's eyes remained steadily on Emily. "Tomorrow."

Emily swallowed and turned away from the door. Then tomorrow she'd need to be long gone.

Chapter Nineteen

He was going to fight for her. After too many sleepless nights alone in bed spent playing the events of the past month over and over again, this was the one truth Knox kept circling back around to. He refused to lose Emily over this decision. And though he was no closer to understanding why she'd quit, he was going to fight for her presence in his life.

Starting today.

This was bigger than the restaurant, bigger than the resort. He was going to fight for the woman he loved because the two of them deserved a chance to try for something real. And so, at dawn on the seventh day—seven days of unanswered voicemail messages to her, seven days of her being AWOL at the resort—he hoisted his gym bag into the back of his truck.

He pushed the key into the ignition, then paused. Ever since he'd been voted the new CEO of Briscoe Ranch, he'd felt his dad's presence all around him every time he was in the truck. What was his dad's spirit's opinion on everything that had gone down with the resort and with Emily?

Did it matter anymore what his dad thought? Knox was feeling less and less that it did. Knox had made enough decisions in his life with the goal of making his father proud, and he was starting to reach the conclusion that it was time for him to grow the hell up and stop worrying about his father's judgment.

He rested against the seatback, his vision softening as he pictured his father sitting in the passenger seat, as they'd done so many times in their lives, beginning when his dad had taught Knox how to drive. "Dad, my life can't be about revenge anymore. I did this for you, but I never expected her. I'd love your support, but either way, I know what I want now, and I'm going after her. And I'm not sure what that's going to mean for my plans for the resort. I'm not sure I can sell it off anymore."

He'd never expected the way Emily had changed how he thought about passion and family and love. Just like he'd never expected to care about his grandmother or cousins the way he did. The idea of displacing them when he sold the resort made his stomach churn.

One thing at a time, man. Nothing was going to happen with the resort for a couple of years, until the renovations were complete, so he had time to figure out how to handle the sale in a way that would keep the Briscoes on their property while keeping Knox's investors happy.

All he knew now was that there was more to life than revenge. And that he was in love with a woman worth fighting for.

He half expected his truck to break down on the way to Murph's Gym.

It didn't. He sent up a silent prayer of thanks to his dad, then grabbed his gym bag and headed inside. Murph didn't look up from the game of solitaire he'd dealt himself on the counter. "She's not here."

Knox had figured as much.

"She hasn't been here for a week."

Panic made Knox's heart squeeze painfully. "She's coming back, isn't she?"

Murph shrugged. "She said she was, but I wouldn't hold her to it. People who've been through what she has, they're light as a feather. Doesn't take much of a storm to blow them away."

Knox had to believe she'd be back. If nothing else, then for the birth of Carina's baby. He dropped his credit card on the glass countertop. "I'd like to become a member of the gym. And I'm going to need a personal trainer, someone to teach me kickboxing."

Murph flicked the credit card back toward Knox. "What is this about? What's your move, here? You stalking our girl for real this time?"

"I'm in love with her." It felt weird to say aloud, as the truth often did.

"Doesn't make you any less of a stalker."

He wasn't going to get anywhere with Emily unless he could win over the men who protected her and show them that he was a stand-up guy who valued her as much as they did. "True. So run my ID and credit card, look me up online, start a file on me. Meanwhile, you can train me. I'll even let you or any of your guys try to beat the shit out of me in the ring."

Murph's stone-cold expression cracked with a snort of laughter. "Need me to go over the rates?"

"Nope."

"Pay by the month?"

"Let's do a year. Or two," Knox said. "Whatever max amount your system is designed for."

"That would be the lifetime membership."

Sounded about right to Knox. He planned to stick around for as long as Emily would have him. A lifetime, even. "Sign me up."

Murph raised a single eyebrow. "You want to hear how much that costs?"

"No. But get on with it. I could use a good fight this morning."

Chicago, Illinois . . .

For the fourth day in a row, Emily sat at a café across the street from the building that had housed her parents' penthouse apartment, wondering if that was even their place of residence anymore. She supposed she could have made her life easier by looking them up online, but that ran the risk of discovering a gushing society page article about their participation in a charity gala or news of her father's latest business deal. She didn't want to see their pictures on the internet. That wouldn't do her any good.

When she'd set out on the trip, she hadn't been clear on why she was driving twelve hundred miles north, or what she'd do if and when she saw her parents. All she knew was that fear of them—and fear of who she really was—had held her back for far too long. As she had when she'd quit the resort, with this she knew that the only way to change the trajectory of her life was to ignore her misgivings and force change to happen with sheer will.

It wasn't until she crossed the state line into Illinois that she'd figured out her purpose for traveling there. She wanted to look into the faces of her parents and remind herself that she'd done the right thing by leaving. All she needed to do was see them, if only from across the street. There was no need for words to be exchanged, or for them to even know she'd been there.

Seeing them in the flesh was the only way she could bring them back down to the status of human beings rather than the larger-than-life, all-powerful monsters she'd created in her imagination. And then, once she'd corrected the image of them in her mind, she'd let go of all the fears and resentment she'd been harboring so she could move on to the next phase of her life with a clear heart.

The trouble was, she was running out of time. She had to get back to Texas soon because Carina's baby was due any day. As important as it was for her to discover what had happened to her parents, being there for her best friend was priority number one, even though it meant apologizing to Carina's family for leaving her job so abruptly. Even though it meant that she might see Knox before she was ready.

After her second day of fruitless surveillance, she'd debated approaching Louis, the doorman, who'd been watching over the building and the tenants who called it home for as long as Emily could remember. But she couldn't quite convince her legs to walk across the street. For reasons she didn't need to analyze, she needed a four-lane buffer between herself and her old life.

Of all the things she missed from her old life, Louis topped the list. Often, when her father would be dragging her along beside him, handling her too abrasively or quietly berating her, Louis would find a way to distract her dad and slip her candy. He was always ready with a smile and a willing ear when she got home after school, to listen to her expound about playground drama and the lessons she'd learned in class. Most importantly, he'd always kept her secrets, and was the last person to talk to her on the day she ran away with nothing but the clothes on her back and a full backpack, though he didn't know she was leaving for good at the time. He'd held the door open for her that day and had slipped her a twenty-dollar bill, explaining that he didn't have much, but he wanted her to go buy herself a sweet treat.

In the early afternoon on this fourth day of watching and waiting, Emily stood, once again trying to work up the courage to walk across the street and talk to Louis. She busied herself collecting the trash from her table, sweeping up crumbs from the muffin she'd eaten and bussing her dishes, as she tried to talk herself down from her fear. He was just a man. A very nice man. She had nothing to be scared of.

But what if her parents walked out at that exact moment? What if they saw her before she could hide? She shivered at the thought, a reminder of how far she had to go in order to exorcise the residual fear about her parents from her heart.

The next time she looked up, Louis was no longer standing at his post near the door. She pressed her face to the glass and scanned the sidewalk in either direction but didn't see him. It was too early for his shift to be over, but maybe he'd had to use the restroom or make a phone call or something.

"Rebecca Youngston."

She nearly leapt out of her skin at the sound of her old name said in a man's baritone voice. She'd always assumed that if anyone called her by her given name again, it would either be her parents or the police. She whirled around to find Louis smiling down at her. "You saw me here?" was all she could think to say in her panic.

"For four days now. Did you forget that I know everything that happens in these streets? Especially when it comes to my very favorite tenant," he said with a kindly wink.

Emily forced herself to take even breaths, then commanded her shoulders to drop and her pulse to slow back down. "I did forget that, yes."

Louis's smile broadened, crinkling the edges of his eyes. "I knew you'd be back someday. I prayed for it. And here you are, Praise Jesus." He opened his arms wide in an invitation for a hug.

She indulged his invitation and wrapped her arms around the kind soul who'd been such a steady, calming force in her childhood. As they hugged, she felt the broken pieces of her spirit healing. She felt the fear melt away. "It's so good to see you, Louis."

"Likewise you, darlin'. Especially seeing you look so good." He held her at arm's length and looked her over, the same way Granny June sometimes did. "You must have done all right for yourself."

"I have. I'm a chef."

He chuckled at that. "You? You never cooked nothing in your life when you lived in my building."

She couldn't help but smile. "I know. I didn't learn to appreciate the art of cooking until later." When scrounging up enough food became one of the most important elements of her survival.

Louis's smile fell. "I'm sure you're here looking for your parents."

All she could do was nod.

"As happy as I am to see you, it's now my burden to let you know that your parents are no longer with us."

"What?" The possibility had never crossed her mind. She really had believed that if they'd died, she would have sensed it, somehow.

"Your father of a heart attack not too long after you left. Your mother moved out of my building soon after, but she kept in touch with me. I learned a couple years ago that she'd passed on. Cancer."

Emily went numb, cold. They were both dead. Had been for years. She dropped into the nearest chair. All this time, she'd been so fearful, so vigilant about concealing her identity. And for no reason. If she'd ever bothered to conduct that internet search, she could have spared herself years of unnecessary worry. "I don't know what to say."

Louis eased into the chair across from her. "I bet you have a lot of questions, about your folks and where they're buried and other details about their passing, but I'm not the one to ask. They don't tell me nothing because I'm just the doorman. But I know someone who can help you." He pulled a business card from his jacket pocket and handed it to her.

The name on the card was Charles Welk. Her parents' closest friend and lawyer. "How did you . . ."

"Mr. Welk has been convinced, just as I was, that someday you'd be back. Every time he comes around, he gives me his card. He said that if you ever came back, that you should go talk to him because he's the executor of your parents' estate."

Emily fingered the corner of the card. Her stomach churned with dread at the idea of presenting herself to her parents' closest friend, of coming out of hiding. Whatever her parents had left her in their wills, she didn't want it. She wanted no ties to them, nothing to make her be-holden to their memory. Then again, what if it was a letter, an apology? Her eyes pricked with moisture at the thought. Did she dare hope?

Louis patted her hand. "You have a lot to think about. I hope you go see this Mr. Welk. Don't give yourself something new to regret by leaving this stone unturned."

Emily stood with Louis and embraced him once more. "Thank you."

"Darlin', you just made my year, finding out that you're alive and well. All the thanks goes to Jesus for bringing you home."

Home. Not by a long shot.

She watched Louis cross the street and reassume his position at the door, then she walked through the café, out the back door and through the alley where her car was parked. On her phone, she pulled up directions to Charles Welk's office on the twenty-fourth floor of a building on West Jackson Blvd, downtown, and hit the road.

Welk's office was a cheery space, and quiet, with large windows affording a partial view of Lake Michigan. The secretary, a slim blonde who looked to be in her fifties smiled at Emily and waited for her to approach her desk before asking, "May I help you?"

Emily flashed the business card Louis had given her. "Mr. Welk isn't expecting me, but I was told to pay him a visit if I ever came back to Chicago. Is he in today?"

"He is. Let me see if he's available now. Who may I tell him is here?"

"Emily." She huffed. Not today, she wasn't. "No, wait. He would know me as Rebecca. Rebecca Youngston."

She disappeared through a door behind her desk. Emily walked to the window and settled her gaze on a sailboat that was little more than a white speck in the vast blue-gray water.

In a matter of moments, the door opened again. "Rebecca, could that really be you?" said a male voice.

Emily turned, but she was too nervous to smile.

Charles Welk had gone gray since she'd last seen him and now sported a neatly trimmed salt-and-pepper mustache, but she would have recognized his lanky frame and moneyed air anywhere. He looked like maybe he wanted to hug her, so she thrust out her hand between them, which he accepted.

"My God, I can't wait to hear where you've been and what you've been up to."

Not so fast, buddy. If he wanted to catch up for old time's sake, then he was going to be sorely disappointed because Emily had too much on her mind to make small talk, not that she was any good at it anyway. "Could we talk in your office?"

If he was startled by her abruptness, he showed no sign of it. "Of course. After you. Sheri, hold my calls, please."

Welk's office afforded the same stunning view of the lake, but Emily forced herself to sit in one of the chairs facing his ornate French Provincial desk rather than distract herself with the view.

"I was told by Louis, the doorman at my parents' apartment, that they'd passed away. He gave me your card."

"Louis always did have your family's best interests at heart. He's a fine man."

Oh, the urge to take Charles Welk by the lapels, give him a good shake, and command him to stop dancing around with small talk and spit it out about why he'd wanted to talk to her. "He said you wanted to speak to me, that you had something for me."

Welk took a long, studying look at her, clearly deliberating whether to keep pursuing a chatty conversation or indulge her by getting straight to the matter at hand. "You father died shortly after you left home," he said. "I'm not saying that so you'll blame yourself. He and I were friends and colleagues, but he was a hard man and he never did right by you or your mother. Everything that happened to him, he brought on himself."

Truer words had never been spoken, though the news left her surprisingly angry all over again. Not at her father, but at herself, for expending so much energy and thought evading her parents only to find out it was an imagined threat. Nothing but a ghost. "And my mother?"

For the first time, Welk's expression shifted away from cheery professionalism. "Breast cancer took her from the world, from me, too soon. Two years ago." He fiddled with a wedding band on his left ring finger.

Had her mother remarried her father's best friend? Charles Welk had always seemed like a decent guy. It felt nice, imagining her mother finding companionship and enjoying a few happy years after her father died. "You two were . . . close?"

"In the years after Bernard died, we took solace in each other. We were a good match. Married for four years."

"Then I'm sorry for your loss." What an ironic world she lived in, to comfort a virtual stranger about the loss of her own mother.

Welk nodded. "Thank you. And to you. I like to think I made her happy. I did my best to help her achieve that goal every day, even after the diagnosis. Life really is so short. Happiness is the only thing that makes the brevity bearable. But she never got over losing you. She'd want me to tell you that we never stopped looking for you."

"That's . . . I don't know what to say." Emily dropped her chin, not sure how to feel about that. The safest thing seemed to be to put that kernel of truth in a locked box in her mind to deal with later.

"You don't have to say anything. I'm sure this is all quite overwhelming. We finally concluded that you'd changed your identity because there were no Rebeccas in the country, living or deceased, who matched your age or description."

"I did change it, yes," Emily said.

"Then may I congratulate you for a job well done because we searched long and hard for you, using the best experts in the country, for any possible aliases. And always came up completely empty." He punctuated the words with a genuine smile of respect.

"Thank you." She'd always known that the pricey forger she'd hired had been well worth his fee. She'd poured the vast majority of the money she'd stolen from her parents and withdrawn from her savings account into that forged identity. She hadn't merely wanted to hide, but to recast herself as someone entirely new and sustainable. Emily Ford was a tax-paying, social security contributing, upstanding member of society.

"Is there anything you want to know before we get down to business?"

"No, thank you."

"Fair enough." He perched a pair of reading glasses on his nose. "Your mother left a substantial sum of money for you. From the sale of properties, both your parents' retirement funds, and their investments. She trusted me to hold on to it for you and to issue payment if you ever emerged from hiding."

The words made her skin tingle. She really had been hiding all these years. Not only from her parents but also from herself and the world. It had taken Knox and her feelings for him to push her out of her safe little nest.

Welk flipped through the leather-bound pages of an old-fashioned address book. "Her instruction was to transfer the money to you under whatever alias you now identified with, not as an inheritance, which we both felt you might have trouble accessing under your new identity without attracting the attention of the government, but rather through an offshore account. All I have to do is make you a signer on the account and the money is yours, I've been investing the inheritance to great results. I think you'll be pleased."

Pleased wasn't the right word. How could she be pleased about receiving a gift from the people who'd made her life hell? After all this time, she was finally on the verge of being free of them. The money felt like yet another shackle.

"If it's all right with you, I'd like to clear my afternoon schedule so that we may pay a visit to my lawyer today,"

Welk said, tapping an entry in the address book. "He'll handle adding your name to the account with the necessary discretion. I assure you that you can trust him, as you can me."

Maybe she would donate it all to a shelter for battered women and children. Maybe she would pass it to Haylie so she could escape. All Emily knew was that she wanted to keep her options open so she could decide what to do with the money in her own time instead of being forced to make a decision while her emotions were running so high. No more flights of chaotic passion. "That sounds good. Thank you."

Welk removed his glasses again and sat back in his chair, studying her. "May I ask what your name is now?"

She drew a tremulous breath. Speaking it aloud in the presence of her parents' closest friend felt like leaping over a great divide. It was time to trust herself not to fall. It was time to trust that no matter what happened next, she was going to be all right. "Emily Ford."

With a smile, he stood and walked around the desk. He extended his hand to her, his eyes welling with unshed tears. "Well, Emily, it's wonderful to meet you. It is my profound pleasure to fulfill your mother's final wish. Thank you."

Emily returned to Texas on a cold, rainy night two weeks after she'd left. Like a beacon, the ever-shining lights of Murph's called to her as she stepped out of her car and stretched. Chicago had looked closer to Dulcet on paper. The drive had been a real slog, but she'd needed the time and the open road to think.

She pulled her suitcase from the back seat, then stood for a moment staring down at the two manila envelopes Charles had given her. One for her future, containing the offshore account information and recent bank statements, the other containing the final remnants of her past. Rebecca Youngston's driver's license, her birth certificate, her social security card, an expired passport, and photographs her parents had used in their search for her.

There was something volatile about that envelope and the information therein. A secret she no longer needed to protect, an identity she never wanted to use again. She didn't even want the envelope crossing the threshold of her apartment. She shoved it under the driver's seat as far as it would go, where it would have to stay until she decided on the best way to dispose of it. Then she tucked the envelope with the bank information into the front pocket of her suitcase. As soon as she was locked behind her apartment door, she'd have the solitude to process that particular grenade, and she didn't plan on making any hasty choices. That was what old Emily might have done. New, self-composed, thinking-with-her-brain-and-not-her-heart Emily was going to take her time and consider her options.

Murph was in his usual spot behind the front desk, playing a game on his phone. A handful of regulars were sweating through their grueling workouts to the sound of a classic rock tune playing over the gym's speakers. She pulled her suitcase behind her, smiling. It was good to be home.

Action in the boxing ring caught her eye and she gasped at the familiar face—the last person she could handle seeing tonight. Knox, who'd evidently taken up mixed martial arts. His shirt was off and his skin and hair were slick with sweat. His hands were protected by wraps, and his lips puffed out around a mouth guard. And he was circling his opponent, none other than Big Tommy. Emily's eyebrows shot up at that. Big Tommy was often described as the toughest guy at the gym. He kicked ass and took names from anyone foolish enough to take him on.

Slack-jawed, she ground to a halt just outside the door and watched them spar.

Knox was good. Fast on his feet. Tough. His eyes gleamed, sharp and dangerous. Every ripple or flex of muscle drew her attention to his lean, hard body. She'd made love to this man. She knew how he moved, how he kissed. She knew what all those bulky muscles felt like against her skin. A slow burn of desire settled low in her belly.

Yeah, Knox was definitely the worst person she could've encountered tonight.

"Hey, Em. You're back," Murph called. "You need help with your suitcase?"

She shook herself out of her daze and sidled up to the counter, where she stole a peppermint from the tin Murph hid behind the pen holder. "I'm back. And, nah, I've got it. It's just the one."

Murph nodded to the ring. "Your stalker's here."

Her gaze found Knox again. "I can see that."

"He's not so bad."

Emily's heart squeezed, painfully. "That's the problem."

"You probably need to know he's been here twice a day, every day, waiting for you, going on more than a week now. Letting anyone who will get in the ring with him kick his ass. I will say one thing about him—he can take a beating. 'Course, that's not happening as much anymore. He's getting better."

Every day? Another surprise.

That now familiar longing for connection with him reached out from every cell of her being. As drained and raw as she was from her trip to Chicago, nothing sounded better than taking Knox in her arms and clinging to him tightly enough to block the world out, along with the pain, the heartache, and the impossible choices. But she was determined to make a clear-headed decision about her future, not return from discovering that her parents were dead only to fall right back into her old pattern of letting passion and desire rule her choices.

When Knox noticed Emily, he turned and took a step in her direction. His eyes swept over her from head to toe, but his inspection didn't last long. Taking advantage of his distraction, Big Tommy clocked his chin with a right hook. Knox staggered into the ropes. He shook his head as if trying to dislodge a stubborn mosquito, though he was probably trying to clear the stars from his vision.

"Get your head back in the match," Big Tommy bellowed, knocking his fists together. "You're better than this. I don't care who just walked in. You've got to see your commitment through. And right now, that's in the ring with me. Let's go."

Knox's focus swung back to the sparring match. He and Tommy squared up again. In a flurry of movement, they punched and blocked and kicked. Tommy attacked with a left jab that Knox evaded by spinning into a round kick that connected with Tommy's gut. This time, Tommy was the one staggering back.

Knox seized on the opportunity to pounce. He swept his leg under Tommy's feet and knocked him to the ground. Tommy didn't stay neutralized long. With a scissor kick, he brought Knox down to the floor with him. And in a few short moves, he had Knox pinned in a chokehold.

When Knox tapped out, Murph snorted. "Not bad, but the guy still has a lot to learn. We've got to work on his floor game. Lucky for him, he sprang for a lifetime membership."

Emily flinched at that. "Lifetime membership?"

"I guess he really is sweet on you. I only sold it to him with the understanding that I'd revoke it if you had a problem with that."

It was yet another decision she needed to postpone until her head was clear. "I'm not sure yet."

"You keep me posted, sweetheart." Murph nodded toward the ring. "Heads up. He's headed over. I'm going to go stand by the phone and pretend that I'm not listening to your conversation."

Emily watched Knox push the ring's ropes down and vault over them to the floor, then tore her attention away to smile at Murph. "You're a doll, Murph."

He winked at her. "Don't I know it."

Knox stopped in front of her, breathing hard, a towel slung around his neck. Sweat dripped off his nose and beaded on his chest. "Hey. Hi." He opened and closed his mouth, and she could see the wheels turning in his head, as though he couldn't decide on the next thing to say.

"You looked good up there," she said by way of breaking the ice.

"Yeah? Felt like I got my ass kicked." He glanced at her suitcase. "I'm glad you're back. I'm glad you're safe. I was worried."

Before she realized what she was doing, she hugged herself. She'd wanted to present herself as strong and self-composed to him, to prove to herself how she was evolving, but the way he looked at her, it was as though he could already see past her bravado. "Safe, yes. But tired. And confused. And scared."

He mopped his face with the towel. "What are you afraid of?"

"You. Well, you and me." She'd already made herself vulnerable to him, so there was no sense in holding back now.

He released a heavy sigh, his eyes on hers. "That works both ways. But there's something you should know."

"What?"

"I miss you. And the food around here sucks."

She let out a breathy laugh. "Yeah, it does."

He nodded toward the stairs. "Will you invite me up to your apartment?"

"I don't think that's a good idea tonight, what with all that tiredness and confusion and fear."

"May I at least carry your suitcase upstairs?"

"I'm pretty sure I can manage." She drew a fortifying breath, then asked him the question still plaguing her. "What are you doing here, Knox? Here, at the gym, with a lifetime membership?"

His expression turned intense and tender all at the same time. "I go after what I want."

Wrong answer. "I'm not a business you can acquire."

"I'm aware." He brushed past her and took her suitcase handle, then started up the stairs with it. Rather than fight him on that, she followed. "Isn't it ironic, though, that that's exactly how this whole mess started? You came to my office demanding a chance to prove how valuable a business investment you would be. And you were right."

He set her suitcase as far into the hall as he could reach, but he remained rooted on the top stair, as though to let her know he didn't plan on pushing any farther into her personal space.

Angling around him, she crested the stairs and faced him, no longer fearing the intensity or heat of his gaze. He was such a strong man, so proud and unequivocally male. She brushed her thumb over a bead of sweat at his temple. "I can't work for you."

"That's not what I want from you anymore. The other irony of this all is that in accepting your challenge to prove your culinary worth, I discovered that you are far more valuable to me than a business investment."

His words left her breathless with longing to feel that inexplicable electricity that thrummed between them whenever they touched. She was not emotionally equipped to hash things out with him yet. Soon, but not tonight, not with that grenade of an envelope to open and process. But maybe just one hug before she went inside. One hug to sustain her while she sorted through the paperwork in the envelope Charles Welk had given her. She cupped Knox's neck and pulled him to her, nuzzling in close. Her whole body shuddered with relief at the feel of his strong arms enveloping her.

She smooshed her lips and nose against the cold, sweaty skin of his chest. "I can't do this tonight, Knox. Soon, but not tonight. I need time. Space."

The heat of him radiated against her skin. He burrowed his nose into her hair. "I know, and it's okay. If you'll allow it, then I'd like to keep training with Big Tommy. I've had a lot on my mind. It's been good to fight it out. I don't think I understood how much anger I was carrying around, at Ty, at the situation, until I started to unleash it in the ring."

"I'll allow it."

His arms tightened around her back and he brushed a kiss across her cheek. "Thank you," came his whispered words. "You were right to quit, by the way. That's something I figured out this week. You were right that we can only be together as equals."

That was just about the last thing she'd expected him to say. She backed up so she could tilt her face up to look at him.

"I held your future and your career and your home in my hands. I was controlling you without meaning to. That's my comfort zone. Control all the odds, control the outcome. I can't control how I feel about you. I can't control what this is. You have humbled me, Emily."

She knew what she felt for him, but it had never occurred to her that he might have feelings for her that mirrored her own, or even come close. "And what is it that you feel?"

There was no hesitation in his reply. "I'm in love with you. Desperately."

A rippling ache of longing coursed through her, visceral enough that her body swayed with the effort of resisting its force. She was in love with him, too. Just as desperately. But life had taught her the hard way that love wasn't enough, not if it compromised a person's autonomy and happiness. Her eyes pricked again, perilously close to shedding tears. "Knox . . ." she started, though it was the only word she could push past the lump in her throat.

"You don't have to say anything tonight. I know you're weary from your trip. You once called me out for being impatient—right before you spilled peach soup all over me, if memory serves. But I want you to know that I'm going to be patient about this. When you're ready to deal with us, you let me know, okay?"

"Okay," she croaked.

He brought his hands up to her face and touched his fingertips to her cheeks, tipping her head back enough to slot his mouth over hers. She closed her eyes and opened to him, giving herself over to the salty taste of his lips and the warm caress of his tongue.

"Goodnight, Emily."

And then he released his hold on her and started back down the stairs.

She stood stock-still, focusing on the lingering sensation of his kiss, until the sound of his footfalls faded away. Willing her body to function again, she dug through her purse for her keys. She didn't release her exhale until she'd closed the door of her apartment behind her, her thoughts warring between disappointment and relief that he hadn't pushed her to come inside.

She reached into the external pocket on her suitcase and pulled out the envelope. Bracing her back against the door, she slid down it until she sat on the floor. She ripped the envelope open and pulled out the bank statement, her eyes zooming in immediately on the total.

All those zeroes. Seven of them.

She was a multimillionaire.

Closing her eyes, she let the papers fall to the floor beside her as she imagined the possibilities. She could donate it all to a center for teen runaways and wash her hands of her parents once and for all. Or she could use it to open the restaurant of her dreams.

The devil and angel on her shoulders shouted over each other for her attention.

Take their money. They owe you.

While the other one said, *Don't surrender. Don't let them poison your life with their blood money.*

The trouble was, keeping the money would change her life in all the ways she wanted.

She wouldn't need the Briscoes' or any investors' help to make her dreams come true. She would never again be tempted to twist herself into a pretzel for a job or a man. For the first time in her life, she would be utterly and completely free.

Chapter Twenty

Early Friday morning, after a particularly brutal and unsuccessful sparring session with Joe Boy, one of Big Tommy's closest associates, Knox was striding across the resort grounds en route to the office from where he'd parked his truck just outside the gate when a text from Shayla sounded on his phone.

Head's up. You got an offer on Briscoe Ranch. Healy and Sandomir are headed your way.

He dialed Shayla's number.

"An offer? From whom? We weren't looking for an offer."

"Hey, bro." She dropped her voice to a whisper. "It's chaos around here. People are going nuts, choosing sides and talking shit about you and Healy when they think no one can hear them."

What the hell happened? Knox thought everything was in the bag, though the paperwork for the transfer of Ty's company shares to Knox had yet to go through while all the lawyers vetted the deal. "The offer, Shayla."

"Right. Sorry. It came in about an hour ago. Not that any of the partners told me, but they've been locked up in the conference room and I'm a hella good eavesdropper. My money's on the theory that Healy went behind everyone's back to tip off Lux Universal that the business was up for grabs. He was pretty vocal against your plan."

Knox ground to a stop. "The offer's from Lux Universal? Please tell me you're kidding."

Lux Universal consistently ranked in the top ten property management companies in the world in net worth. They specialized in beachfront luxury condos and timeshares. Briscoe Equity Group had sold them a property a few years back, a high-rise hotel perched on a sliver of beachfront in the Florida Keys that Lux was going to repurpose as timeshares. Doing business with them had been a cakewalk because once Lux decided they wanted a property badly enough, they were willing to throw buckets of money at the buyers, making their offers nearly impossible to refuse.

"I wish."

A niggle of fear started in Knox's chest. "What could they possibly want with Briscoe Ranch? It doesn't fit their profile at all."

"That was my thought, too. And none of the investment partners have contacted you yet?" Shayla said.

"No." Could it be that his own equity firm was trying to box him out of ownership of his family's business by going around his back to accept a better offer? Like Shayla, he wouldn't put it past Healy to pull something like that. Hell, for all he knew, Healy and the rest of the partners were trying to box him out of Briscoe Equity Group, the company he'd founded. It happened in the business world often enough. Carl Karcher, Steve Jobs, and Jerry Yang of Yahoo were three examples that sprang to mind.

Knox held his phone out to check the time. Still early

in the day. "You said Healy and Sandomir are on their way to Dulcet?"

"Yes. They're taking Sandomir's private jet. They wanted to talk to you in person."

Knox let his gaze roam over the resort grounds. If Healy and Sandomir wanted a fight, then he'd give it to them. The resort was worth it. It was time to look his colleagues in the eye and make the case once more for giving him a shot at restoring the resort to a profitable business. "Thanks, Shayla. I'll be waiting."

"You've got this, bro. Call me afterwards, okay? And good luck."

Three hours later, right on schedule with the ETA Shayla had texted him, Knox met Healy and Sandomir in front of Briscoe Ranch Resort's lobby. "Gentlemen, I wish I could say I'm surprised."

Healy offered him a smile that wasn't at all friendly. "Good. Shayla called. We wanted you to be ready."

Did they? "You sure have a funny way of showing it." He tipped his head toward the building. "Let's head straight to my office. I'm eager to hear about this deal."

Healy sneered at the Spanish-style fountain in the lobby, then stopped to pick at a chipped tile. "This place is a money pit."

He wasn't far off, but neither profit nor revenge was Knox's bottom line any longer. "Be that as it may, this is my family, which makes it about more than money to me."

Sandomir harrumphed. "That's a change of tune from our last meeting about Briscoe Ranch, when you convinced us to hold tight until we sold for a profit."

Knox ushered them around behind the front desk and through the glass door leading to the offices. Haylie was at her desk, reading a magazine that she tried valiantly to hide when she noticed Knox's approach.

"Morning, Haylie. Hold my calls and see that we're not disturbed by anyone. You remember Roger Healy and Boris Sandomir from my Dallas office?"

She wiggled her fingers at them, which Knox supposed was as deferential and business-like as Haylie had it in her to be at the moment.

"Right this way," Knox said, leading the way into his office, then closing the door firmly behind Healy.

Healy headed to the floor-to-ceiling windows that looked out over the golf course and lake, while Sandomir sank into one of the chairs opposite Knox's desk. "As I was saying," Sandomir said. "You changed your tune, Knox."

Knox assumed a seat at his desk. "You're right. I did. I never expected this business venture to become so personal." Which was a total lie, if he really thought about it. Investing in the resort had been personal long before he'd ever brought his team of equity partners on board. It was only the nature of Knox's personal bias that had changed. The vendetta that had once consumed his thoughts of the future had been replaced by hope. As corny as it would sound if he said it aloud, he'd been changed by love.

Healy turned from the window. "The problem is, to the rest of us, this is still just business as usual. It doesn't bring us pleasure to go against your wishes or evict your family from their homes and place of business, but this is the nature of the beast with private equity firm investments. You know that. If we got heartsick for every employee we laid off or underperforming company we shut down, we'd be in the wrong business."

Healy had a point, but that didn't give him the right to run roughshod over Knox's change of heart. "You're right. The business hasn't changed, and I didn't expect any of you to, either. But I have. And I would have thought that I earned more consideration from you for my position after all these years. And my position right now is that I want Briscoe Ranch."

Healy strolled to the empty chair next to Sandomir and took a seat. "You might not have a choice. Look, Knox. Lux Universal made us a generous offer. And the lawyers are still hashing out the details of your buyout arrangement with Ty. Nothing's been signed yet. You're the minority partner in this situation still. I'm speaking on behalf of the majority of our investors when I say that we want out of this money pit. Lux Universal is giving us that chance."

Frustration and panic churned in Knox's stomach and tightened his throat. They weren't hearing him out. They'd already made up their mind, which was frustrating as hell. "You're not in this particular money pit that deep, Healy. It's nothing you can't afford. You probably wipe your ass with more money than you've personally sunk into this place."

"They're offering seventy-five million dollars for the land and the business," Sandomir said.

Jesus H. Christ, that was a lot of money. Way over the resort's true valuation. "You told them about the geological and hydrological issues? The cracked foundation? And they still made us an offer like that?"

"We told them, but they don't care about any of that. They've decided the location is worth more than the business, and they're right. They're going to raze the whole place and start over. Part of a new direction for their company. A high-end retirement community, timeshare, and golf course, one of those mega-complexes that they like to build, but this one for seniors. It's all the rage right now, or so they said.

No doubt, anything Lux Universal built would be modern and grand and packed with luxury. But it wouldn't be Briscoe Ranch. A place renowned for its romantic magic—a magic Knox had discovered to be true. If he allowed the resort to be sold to a company that would level it to the ground, he'd lose Emily for good. He knew it as sure as he knew his own name. She may have quit her job as the executive catering chef, but this place was still her home. It was his cousins' home, his grandmother's. People he'd grown to care about. His and Emily's family.

He couldn't sell. There had to be another way. "Give me time to match their offer."

"You can't match this offer, Knox. You don't have enough liquid assets to draw from."

No, he most certainly did not have ready access to that kind of money. "You're not my accountant or my stock broker, so don't pretend to know the intimacies of my finances."

Sandomir sighed. "Fair enough, but you know as well as we do that when Lux sets their mind on a property, they don't take no for an answer."

He did know that. They liked to keep upping the bid until they'd choked out all their competition in a not-so-subtle show of might. But Knox had to take this chance. "You owe me the chance to try before you sell out my family business to a company that wants to destroy it and put hundreds of people out of work."

Healy arched a brow. "Do we?"

Knox ground his molars together. "Give me one week."

"Forty-eight hours," Healy countered. "Good luck, Knox. We'll show ourselves out."

Knox was going to need a lot more than luck. Divine intervention was more like it. He raised his eyes heavenward, then caught himself. This was not about this dad. This was no longer about the rift or revenge or trusting in ghosts.

This was about Knox doing what he had to do to preserve what had become hallowed ground for him, and for the extended family he'd never known he needed. To save the home of the woman he loved. And he couldn't do it alone. It was time to call in every favor and cash in every stock. More than anything, it was time to swallow his pride and get the job done because he refused to be the person to disband the Briscoes' and Emily's entire world.

Thus resolved, he grabbed his messenger bag and headed to the door. He had a lot of calls to make and he didn't care to make them in his office, with its thin walls and eager ears. He threw the door open and stopped short at the sight of Haylie, Wendell, Ty, and Granny June gathered at Haylie's desk, wide-eyed horror playing on their faces.

Knox looked past them, to the other workers who were starting their day. Some were preoccupied, but enough of them were paying close enough attention to the Briscoes that they posed the risk of starting a company-wide panic, fueled by rumors. "Into my office, all of you."

Even once Knox closed the door and gestured to the chairs, nobody sat down. Even Granny June rose up off her motorized scooter to pace the room with the aid of her cane.

"Please don't tell me you were all eavesdropping on that meeting."

Haylie raised her hand. "I'll cop to it. There's no way to not listen in with these walls. It sounded important, so I called my dad over. And then Granny June and Wendell were just passing through. They do that a lot."

So Knox had noticed.

"You got an offer to sell?" Granny June asked in a tremulous voice.

Ty threw up his arms. "Didn't you hear what those equity douches said? It's over. Briscoe Ranch Resort is over. Thanks to Knox, here, it's going to be leveled and rebuilt as senior living. Senior goddamn living!"

Damn these paper-thin walls.

Wendell's face was growing redder by the second, as though he was feeding off Ty's agitated energy. "I knew it. There have been rumors flying around the golf course since you got here that you're going to sell and we'll all be laid off. Frankly, it's no surprise to me that you're the dick who's selling out." He emphasized the insult by getting up in Knox's face.

"Wendell," Haylie warned.

"Shut up, Haylie. Don't you see what's happening here? Or are you too busy jet-setting with him to Dallas on his private plane like a proper whore?"

Ty stepped between Wendell and Haylie. "Don't you dare talk to my daughter that way."

"Daddy, please. You're not helping." Haylie stepped around Ty and touched Wendell's sleeve. "I'm not sleeping with Knox. I don't even like him. I mean, not like that. He's my cousin. You're the only man for me."

With a forty-eight hour deadline, Knox had way too much to do to stand there and placate an overgrown toddler like Wendell. "I'm going to try to stop the sale, so there's no need to panic." *Yet, anyway.* "Since you were listening in, you heard that they're giving me a chance to make a counter-offer."

"We heard," Granny June said. "Do you think it's possible?"

Ty snorted. "Hell, no, it ain't. We heard that part of the meeting, too."

This would have been so much easier had Knox simply invited them all to join him in the meeting. "I have to try, which means I need to leave and make some calls. You're holding me up."

Wendell took hold of Haylie's arm. "Come on, babe. Let's get out of here. Guess I've got a new job to find."

Knox registered a flash of fear on Haylie's face before she masked it. She did not want to go home with Wendell, as riled up as he was. Knox wasn't the only one who'd noticed the manic look in his eyes.

"Can't we stay and hear what Knox has to say about his counter-offer?" she squeaked.

"Don't matter what he has to say. He's nothing but scum. A Judas." This time, when Wendell got all up in Knox's face, he flicked the black Stetson off Knox's head. "Let's go, Haylie. Now." And he snapped his fingers.

If Wendell took his anger about Knox and the Lux Universal offer out on Haylie, Knox would never forgive himself. "Wendell, why don't you go on ahead? I'm going to need Haylie's help, as my secretary. Her workday's barely gotten started."

"No way. She quits, too. We're out of here. Haylie, kiss this lame-ass job goodbye."

Granny June dropped onto the seat of her scooter and surged forward, rushing Wendell with her cane out like a jousting lance. "I don't know what game you're playing at, but Haylie does what she wants. She don't respond to no man snapping his fingers at her like she's a dog."

Wendell pushed the cane aside and chuckled at her. "Well, ain't you cute as a button, Granny? Pretending to be all mighty like that. In case you didn't notice, Haylie's my wife, so this is none of your business."

"She may be your wife, but I'm not," Ty said, stepping between Granny June's scooter and Wendell. "And my mother's right. You don't get to snap your fingers and order my little girl around. If I ever hear you do that again, we're gonna step outside and I'll personally teach you some manners."

Haylie took hold of Ty's arm and tried to pull him away from his staring match with Wendell. "Dad, butt out. Please. All of you, just back off. You have your own problems to deal with. Stop taking them out on Wendell. He's right. We're husband and wife, and what we do is none of any of your business."

With that, she took Wendell by the hand and marched with him toward the employee exit. Behind his back, Wendell held up his middle finger.

They hadn't made it to the door yet when Ty's, Granny June's, and Haylie's phones all chimed with a text. Granny June was the first to read it off. "It's Decker. Carina's water broke and they're on their way to the hospital."

Haylie pulled away from Wendell's arm. "Oh, cool. She's three days early! Change of plans, Wendell. We'll meet you guys at the hospital."

Wendell snared Haylie around the waist with his arm. "Naw. No change of plans. We're going home. I'm sick of your stupid family and I'm ready for a beer."

Knox had never felt more helpless—to rescue Haylie, to save the resort, to win Emily's love. He stared down at his hands, stunned by the swift, sharp fall over the cliff his life had taken. And now, in the midst of it all, Carina was giving birth.

Granny June's cold, wrinkled hand settled on Knox's forearm. "I'll ride with you. We got a lot to discuss."

Knox did not have time for this. The best gift he could give Carina was to save her home. "I think you should ride with Ty. I'm pretty sure I won't be welcome there and I've got a lot to do."

"Nonsense. I know I've done a lousy job teaching you this, and I can't blame your mama and daddy, but the whole point of family is to weather storms together. I failed you on that point too many times. I'm hoping you'll give this old bat one last chance to show you the strength of our bonds. Like it or not, you're a part of our family, Knox. I'm not letting you go this time. No matter what."

Chapter Twenty-One

When Knox and Granny June walked through the entrance of Cambridge Memorial Hospital, Emily, Ty, and Eloise were already there, sitting in chairs near the main desk. Ty hunched toward the women, speaking what looked like harsh words while Eloise cradled a small pink leather flask in her hands, looking millions of miles away, Emily hugged herself as she watched Ty speak, her expression one of disbelief.

Knox's heart sank. He'd been hoping to get to Emily first, to tell her the straight story before Ty was able to spin some gross distortion of the truth.

"Lord help us all," Granny June muttered, sagging over her cane.

Knox wasn't sure what the Lord could do to help the situation unless he dropped fifty million dollars into Knox's bank account so he could match Lux Universal's offer.

When Emily noticed Knox and Granny June standing near the entrance, she stood and dropped her hands to her sides. It was all Knox could do to restrain himself from stomping over, taking Emily in his arms, and running with her to some quiet corner of the world where he could tell her what had really happened and come up with a solution together.

Granny June's hand touched Knox's. "We'll figure this out, Knox. Don't give up on this family, yet. Emily, neither. And don't let her give up on you."

He didn't plan on it. But he might not have a choice if he couldn't come up with the money to make his investors an offer that topped Lux Universal's. He tugged Granny's hand. "Come on. Looks like I've got some explaining to do."

Emily's face seemed to pale as Knox approached. "Is it true? About the offer for Briscoe Ranch? Ty told me." She whispered the words, as though she ran the risk of making the offer real by voicing it out loud.

Knox looked from Ty to Eloise before settling his gaze on Emily. "Let's talk in private."

"Too late. The damage is done," Eloise muttered, slipping the flask back into her purse. Knox ignored her, his only thought of making things right with Emily.

"You were serious about selling. I mean, you told me, but I was hoping you'd change your mind. I thought—" Emily shook her head. "Never mind. It doesn't matter what I thought."

"Emily, please. Give me a chance to explain."

She wrung her hands, then caught herself doing so and tucked strands of hair behind her ears. "Yes. That's a good idea."

He reached his hand out and she laced their fingers together. For the first time since Knox had gotten the news about Lux Universal, he drew a full breath. They'd only taken a step before the closed door adjacent to the reception desk burst open and Decker stood in the door. His chest heaved and his wide, scared eyes were rimmed in red.

Eloise was the first person to reach him, Emily not far behind. "What's happening? You don't look good," Eloise said.

Decker staggered a few steps into the lobby and sagged against the wall. He grabbed fistfuls of his hair as he bent forward.

"My God, Decker. You're scaring me," Emily said.

Decker shook his head. "They couldn't find the baby's heartbeat, and then they could, but it was irregular. And then Carina's blood pressure crashed. They're taking her in for an emergency C-section. I've got to get back in there but I wanted you to know. They're going to let me be in there with her for support, so I—" Dropping his hands to his knees, he gasped, as though the explanation had used up all his oxygen. "Sweet Jesus, I've never been so scared in my life."

"She's in good hands," Eloise said. "The doctors probably see this kind of thing all the time. She's going to be okay. She has to be."

Ty swayed, then braced a hand against the wall, clearly terrified.

"Eloise is right," Granny June said. "Carina's a fighter. We'll pray and God will make sure she and the baby are fine. End of story."

"I hope to God you're right. That's my wife in there. That's my baby boy."

Emily rubbed Decker's back. "We know. We love her, too. Granny June's right. They're going to be fine."

A nurse appeared in the doorway. "Mr. Decker, we're ready for you. And if the rest of the family can move to the waiting area, that'd be great. We need to keep this doorway clear. I promise you that either Mr. Decker or I will come out to tell you what's going on as soon as possible."

Decker hugged each person in turn, then followed the

nurse down the hall. Granny June, Ty, Eloise, Knox, and Emily stood staring at the closed door for a beat.

Then Emily sagged against Knox's chest. "She and the baby have to be okay. They just have to."

Behind her, Ty snorted. "Look at you two, playing like you're part of this family. What the hell are you even doing here?"

Emily pulled away from Knox. "Not now, Ty."

But Ty wasn't having it. "No time like the present. You stand there acting like you care one whit about my daughter, even as you're planning to sell our home out from under us and let some corporation bulldoze it to the ground."

"That's not my plan," Knox countered. As scared for Carina as Ty clearly was, as out of control as it must feel to have his child's and grandchild's lives at risk, it came as no surprise that he'd unleash his feelings on Knox.

Ty prowled around him, forcing Knox to pivot in order to keep eye contact. "Bullshit. You did this. You ruined our lives. And I'm sure that was your plan all along. Revenge for Clint, am I right? You have no place in this family. Consider our blood ties broken."

Granny June tugged on her son's arm. "Ty, no. He's family. He's your—"

"Like Wendell said, he's nothing to me but a Judas," Ty snapped.

Eloise's flask was back out. She held it aloft in a mock toast. "Like you were to Clint, all those years ago?"

"Woman, don't you dare play that card here, now."

Eloise drank deeply from the flask, then licked a drop off her lower lip. "Oh, please. It's time. The rift was more than thirty years ago. Enough with the damn secrets. I kept them for you because I loved you. More than that little whore ever did, but this might be the only way to save our home."

A tingling started on the back of Knox's neck. *Little whore? Who?* And what did that have to do with the rift? What did any of it have to do with the Lux Universal sale? "What secrets?"

Eloise opened her mouth, but Ty thrust his open palm in front of her face. "Stop or I will make you stop."

Granny June sagged into her cane, tears in her eyes. "No. Eloise is right. Enough with the lies, even though it was for the best, all these years."

Eloise whirled on her mother-in-law, sloshing liquid from the flask onto her hand. "The best for whom? For you and your precious family legacy?"

"I'm warning you. Stop this now." Fists clenched, red-faced, and nostrils flared, Ty looked like a bull that was ready to charge.

Afraid Ty might actually physically assault his wife, Knox stepped between them.

"For Knox," Granny June said. "All of this—the secret, the rift—Tyson and I knew it was best for Knox, and that was the only thing that mattered."

Knox had just about had enough of them talking about him like he wasn't there. "Someone had better fill me in—now."

Eloise pulled her flask from her purse and unscrewed the lid. "What's your birthdate, Knox?"

"August fifteenth."

"Which means you were conceived in November. Do the math."

What the hell was she getting at? "I've done the math, so I'm not sure what point you're trying to prove. My parents eloped on the second of November, right after the rift, and my mom got pregnant with me a couple weeks later."

Knox wasn't putting it together, the importance of his birthday and Eloise's vitriol about *that little whore* and laying claim to Ty. What did the rift have to do with Knox and what was best for him? He hadn't even been conceived yet.

"November, hmm? Not December? Have you seen their marriage license?" Eloise said.

No. No, he hadn't ever seen their license.

Granny June's color blanched. "It wouldn't matter, Eloise. Chaplain Roberts fudged the date."

"Are you're trying to tell me that my mom got pregnant before they were married? Is that the big secret? I mean, I'm only half-surprised because that helps clarify why they had such a low-key wedding." And, if they got married because his mom was pregnant, then that helped clarify why they'd never seemed much in love.

Eloise said, "Don't you ever wonder what the rift was all about? Why Clint and Ty would have killed each other that night if Tyson hadn't gotten in the middle of it with his shotgun?"

"Of course I have." A terrible foreboding made Knox's stomach churn, even as anticipation sped his pulse. This was it. The revealing of a thirty-five-year secret. Eloise was going to tell him what the rift was about. He turned, searching out Emily, and found her behind him, obviously hanging on every word, as Knox was. He took her hand firmly in his. "It's time for the truth," he told Eloise. "Spit it out."

Ty surged forward, knocking Knox and Emily out of the way. "Damn it, woman. Don't you dare."

Granny June's cane came up and rested against Ty's chest. "I raised you better than this. Get back and stop threatening your wife."

Eloise gestured to Granny June with the open flask, sloshing clear liquid onto her hand. "Thank you, June. And, Knox, here's the truth. Thirty-five years ago, in early December, Clint dragged Ty out to a field in the middle of the night and beat him up pretty bad. Probably, he would have killed him had Tyson not intervened, and it's hard to blame him because it turned out that Linda, the sweet little Christian girl Clint was dating, got herself knocked up on the night of the Sadie Hawkins dance, and Clint wasn't the father."

The rush of blood in Knox's ears sounded like a gust of wind as he was sucked backwards, forced to helplessly watch the scene in front of him as though looking through a long tunnel. He swallowed back his revulsion. "No. Impossible."

Emily slipped between Eloise and Knox and cupped his cheeks in her hands. Her gaze bounced between Ty's and Knox's faces, then tears crowded her eyes. "My God."

"The resemblance is uncanny, isn't it?" Eloise's every word dripped with poison.

Knox closed his eyes, unable to bear the truth and horror in her expression. His pulse pounded in his throat, in his ears. None of this was real. None of this was happening. The rift had been about business. Nothing more. Had to be. Knox's mother was a devout Christian, there was no way she would have . . . The thought died in his mind, the idea was so unthinkable.

"It doesn't matter what happened," came Ty's growling drawl. "You are not my son."

Knox's eyes flew open at that. "Goddamn right, I'm not." Knox's whole life was *not* founded on a lie, with everyone from his mother and father to his grandparents complicit in the deception. *No.*

Knox raised a hand to his mouth, but it was shaking. The corners of his vision were narrowing. Anger whipped through him, frenzied and powerful. His dad's command echoed through his mind. *Never lose control.* Oh, but he was perilously close. He refused to desecrate his father's memory by violating his number one rule. His father—the man who'd taught him everything and loved him until his last breath, the man who was watching Knox from on High. The man who haunted his truck.

Emily's hands had slid down from Knox's cheeks to rest on his chest. He couldn't quite bear to look at her, but he took her hands in his and held on tight, the better to steady the trembling.

Eloise flattened her back against the wall and glared at Ty through slits of eyes. "Did you think the truth wouldn't come out? You brought him here. Isn't this what you wanted? Your bastard son to take over our family business, to steal everything we hold dear? I told you this would happen, but you didn't listen to me. You never listen to me." Her voice cracked. A ripple of raw emotion shimmered through her and was gone just as fast. She swallowed, the sneer returning to her lips. "It was always her, wasn't it? It was always Linda. I guess it's time for me to get out of this marriage and get my slice of the pie while there's any pie left. I'll wait for Carina to get out of surgery somewhere else. June, call me when the baby's born." With a dignified shake of her hair, she pushed away from the wall and walked toward the exit.

Knox was a lot of things, but he was no man's bastard son. No way had Ty brought him to Briscoe Ranch as some sort of gesture of atonement or to reveal himself as Knox's fa—. *No.* He refused to think the word.

Ty chased after Eloise. He grabbed at her wrist, but she jerked her hand away and sped her pace. "Eloise, don't go. Not now. We have to stick together now. For our girls, for our grandbaby," he shouted after her. "I was a stupid kid. You know that's all it was. Linda meant nothing to me. She never did."

But Eloise was out of there. Granny June sped past them on her scooter. "I'll go talk to her," she said. "We've got to make this right. For everyone in the family."

Knox watched his grandmother leave, while all the while Ty's words rang through his mind, loud and clear. *You know that's all it was. Linda meant nothing to me.* Ty really had slept with Knox's mother. My God.

Ty whirled to face the room, zeroing in on Knox. "Linda never meant anything to me and neither do you. You're not my family anymore than she is."

Emily squared a searing look at Ty. "Stop this. Right now. Before you say something you can't take back."

Snickering, Ty jabbed a finger at Emily's face. Her flinch was unmistakable. "That's rich, you giving me advice. You stay out of this, girl. You have no dog in this fight."

"Like hell, I don't," Emily said.

Ty's attention dipped to Knox and Emily's joined hands, then gave a bark of mad laughter. "Because you're fucking him? You think I don't know? You think we all don't know what's been going on between you two, you little slut?" Every word was hurled at her like shards of glass, meant to wound.

That cleared the fog from Knox's mind right good. "Don't you dare speak to her that way."

Emily went rigid, though her expression was one of pure control. "It's okay, Knox. I can handle this." To Ty, she said, "You think that insult is new? You think you're the first man to call me that? Do you have any idea of the number of bruises I carried on my body as a child?" She held her index finger out like a sword and stabbed Ty hard in the shoulder. "So many of them fingertip-shaped bruises. But I'm not a kid anymore, and I don't have to take shit from anyone. Not even you."

Ty rolled the shoulder she'd jabbed. The expression in his eyes turned rageful enough that Knox took a step back, pulling Emily with him.

"You were nothing when I took you in, you ungrateful

bitch," Ty bit out, looking more rabid by the second. "Homeless, jobless. I gave you a chance at a real life. I opened my family to you. But look at you now. All these years, it turns out you were just using my family's good fortune, and then, when the next moneybags showed up, you moved on to him. Could you be any more transparent? You were nothing before you came begging me for a job. And you're nothing now. Nothing but a user. My God, it's embarrassing to watch."

"Shut up," Knox said to Ty. To Emily, he added, "Let's get out of here." He needed space to process everything Ty, Eloise, and Granny June had revealed. He'd wanted to be there for Carina and Decker, and he knew Emily would want to be there, too, but Ty had turned the experience too toxic for either of them to withstand.

But Emily wasn't ready to back down. "I'm so tired of these . . . these powerful men projecting their anger onto me. All these monsters clawing at me, trying to drag me down, telling me, *You're nothing,*" she said, mimicking Ty's deep voice. "I'm not nothing. I'm a goddamn phoenix, reborn from the ashes of a childhood hell. I remade myself completely and I've got the scars to prove it."

Knox tugged Emily's arm. "Come on. Please. Let's leave. I need air."

"Not so fast," Ty said. "You're just as bad as her. I brought you both into the Briscoe Ranch family. I vouched for you. I tried to do the right thing for you in my own way. I trusted you. Both of you. And I guess the joke's on me because you're both a disgrace. A disgrace for everything the Briscoe name stands for. And you, Knox, will never, ever be a son of mine."

Before Knox knew what was happening, Emily raised her hand, wound back, and backhanded Ty Briscoe across the face.

A hush fell over the room and time seemed to stop.

Even Ty froze, his lips slack as a pink stain spread on his cheek.

"I get it now. This is how it works with you." Emily said. "The minute your back's up against the wall, you turn on people to protect yourself. Is that what happened when Linda got pregnant? Is that why you abandoned her and your baby? What a coward."

With a curse, Ty lunged at Emily, his hands up as though he was going for her throat.

Knox didn't think. He didn't plan. He released Emily's hand, made a fist, and punched Ty in the gut. The release of anger felt so damn good, that he ducked his head and went at Ty again. This time, he slammed Ty against the lobby wall, using the skills Big Tommy taught him in the ring. He raised his head, ready to tell Ty off, right in his face, but when he looked up, he was looking into the eyes of his father.

His father. Holy shit.

In that moment, Knox's anger seceded to compassion. Ty had lost everything. The business, his self-respect. His wife, most likely. Which meant Knox had accomplished what he'd set out to do from the day he first stepped foot on Briscoe Ranch Resort. He'd ruined Ty Briscoe in the name of revenge.

Except that now, Knox didn't want any part of it. He didn't want revenge; he didn't want the resort or any profits from it. Had that been what his dad was trying to tell him by preventing the truck from driving onto the resort? Knox could almost hear his dad's voice. *Don't do this. It's not too late to turn this truck around. There are things you don't want to know.*

Damn right, there were. And if he could, he would've scrubbed it all from his memory. The knowledge of what Granny June's laugh sounded like and that Shayla and Haylie shared the same eyes. He didn't want to be aware of Carina's new baby and the life she and Decker enjoyed on the resort grounds, each pursuing their dream careers—businesses that would be torn down if the sale to Lux Universal went through. He didn't want to know that the father he loved with his whole heart and whom he spoke to every damn day had lied to him. That his father and mother had been lying to him his whole life.

Mostly, his temper howled at the heavy weight of responsibility pressing on him. He held the Briscoe family's future in his hands—their legacy, their livelihoods. The future of people who'd lied to him, who'd marginalized him. The biological father who'd rejected him before he was born, and who rejected him now. Someday, Knox wanted to find out why. But he couldn't think past his outrage at the corner he'd painted himself into.

If he wanted to save the resort, he'd have to put his reputation and career on the line to drum up enough money. He'd have to pour his entire net worth into this place and these people who'd betrayed him. Did he even want to? Maybe selling to Lux was the right choice. Maybe he needed to let it all burn to the ground. Like Emily had so many years ago, the Briscoe family legacy could rise from the ashes of a sordid and cruel past into something new and beautiful. Maybe it was time to let Briscoe Ranch go.

He let the fury of betrayal seize hold of him. With a curse, he slammed Ty into the wall again. "Were you ever going to tell me the truth? Were any of you?"

Ty shoved him back. "No. Never."

"Knox, let him go," Emily said. He felt a tug on his belt, as though she were trying to pull him away. But Knox was nowhere near done. He could hear that she was trying to talk him down, but he could barely make out the words over the rush of adrenaline in his ears.

"Why not?" Knox spat at Ty. "Why cover up the truth

in the first place? I have a right to know who I am, god-damn it."

"Knox!" Emily called again. "The police!"

No sooner had he registered her words than strong, male arms looped around his chest, dragging him back. A loud voice barked at him to get back before he was charged with more than just assault. The Sheriff's department had arrived. *Just fucking fantastic.*

"It's about time," Ty said to the deputy. "Thanks for getting that animal off me."

Knox flexed his fist. Fuck it all; prison would be worth getting another good punch in.

"Yes, sir, Mr. Briscoe. We're just happy we got here in time," the deputy said.

Ty brushed imaginary dust off his shirt, the picture of civility. "When you get back to the station, be sure to give Sheriff Mendez my regards." To Knox, Ty added, "You might think you hold all the cards, but guess again. You're about to find out what my longstanding reputation in this community is worth."

"I'm assuming you want to press charges?" the deputy who was restraining Knox asked Ty.

With harnessed anger and pride, Emily stepped between Ty and the deputy. "Don't. Do. This. You're his—"

"I'm his nothing. Yes, I'm pressing charges, Deputy Thurman. Nobody assaults me and gets away with it."

Seething that his own biological father would have him arrested within minutes of the truth coming out about his parentage, Knox played the last card he had as the deputies dragged him out of the lobby. "If they arrest me, I can't stop the sale."

Ty followed them out, strutting like he owned the place, Emily on his heels. "As if you would stop it," Ty said. "As if you haven't been trying to stab me in the back since I brought you on board. I'm done with your lies."

The fragile strings of Knox's composure snapped all over again. "My lies? You're done with *my lies*?"

"Sweet Mother of God, Ty. Knox. What the hell's going on?" A pale-faced Decker jogged to meet them at the curb, where they stood next to an idling patrol car. "Knox, are they arresting you? What happened?"

Emily braced her hands on Decker's shoulders and shook them until she had Decker's attention. "Are they all right? Carina and the baby, did they make it out of surgery okay?"

Decker cast a sideways glance at Knox as a deputy strong-armed him into the backseat of the cruiser. A tentative smile kicked up at the corners of his lips. "I've got a son, and he's good, strong. Eight pounds, probably thanks to all that good food you fixed for Carina. And as for Carina, she's a tough one. They have her in a recovery room and the baby's taking a brief detour to the NICU since his heartbeat was so erratic in the womb. But that's just a precaution, they said."

Ty took off back in the direction of the lobby.

Knox bit his lip, disgusted that his only option out of this pissing match was to swallow his pride and beg Ty to direct the officers to release him. Was he really prepared to invest the bulk of his wealth to take on full ownership of a resort with crumbling foundation that would need a complete overhaul? Was he really willing to risk everything to be a part of the family that shunned his and lied to him about who he was?

Don't do it for them. Do it for Emily.

"Ty, the sale. I'll stop it if you don't press charges. I'll find a way. Do it for your girls," Knox called, careful not to infuse the word with a single iota of desperation.

At the door, Ty stopped and shot Knox a look over his shoulder.

"What sale? And why would Ty press charges?" Decker said, looking more confused by the second. "Did you two get into a fight or something?"

There was no way Knox was going to interfere with Decker's happiness. "Let's just say tensions were high," Knox said from behind gritted teeth.

Emily must have agreed with Knox's decision because she told added, "Don't worry about it. It was a misunderstanding. We're handling it. You go back in and take care of Carina. Let her know I'll be there as soon as I can."

Decker only hesitated for a moment before nodding, then pivoting on his boot heel and fast-walking back inside, bypassing Ty on the way.

"Knox is right," Emily said to Ty as soon as Decker was gone. "Tell them to let him go. Do it for Carina and Haylie. For the new baby. Don't let Knox's arrest and the subsequent destruction of the resort be the final word of the Briscoe legacy."

Those must have been the magic words because Ty's hard gaze flicked to the officers. He swallowed hard enough that his Adam's apple bobbed and his jaw rippled. "Let him go."

The next thing Knox knew, Ty had rushed him, wearing a sneer that bared his teeth. "But you hear me out, boy. With these deputies as my witnesses, if you sell the resort out from under my family, I'm going to kill you with my own two hands. And that is not an empty threat."

And then Ty stormed back into the building.

Chapter Twenty-Two

Knox had borrowed a company car to drive Granny June to the hospital. He parked it in the nearest employee parking lot at the resort and left the keys inside, then set off at a run toward the fire road where his truck was parked. Nothing short of a full-out sprint could match the rage pumping through Knox's veins at the betrayal by his dad.

His dad. What a big fucking joke that Knox still thought of him as that. *Guess what, chump? The man who taught you to hate your grandparents and your uncle—no, your real father—is really your uncle. Surprise!*

He'd tried, in the only way he could, to prevent Knox from learning the truth about the man he'd groomed Knox to believe was the enemy. Ty, the greedy uncle who'd cheated Knox's dad out of the family fortune. He was the reason they'd grown up scraping the barrel for enough money every month to get by, the reason Knox and his siblings had grown up as the poorest kids in their neighborhood. Ty was the reason Knox's dad had rarely been able to hold down a steady job, the reason he'd let his anger rot his insides until, finally, his body responded with a fatal heart attack.

"Mom always did say those Briscoe boys were charmers," Knox muttered as he ran. But Knox hadn't put it together until today that she'd been talking about both brothers.

Mom, what did you do?

But Knox already knew the answer. She'd lied to Knox. Just like his dad had. And his grandmother. The whole lot of them. What a fool they'd made Knox out to be.

Seeing his dad's truck parked on the edge of the dirt road just beyond the resort grounds pushed his festering rage out of control. No wonder his dad hadn't wanted his truck to drive onto the resort. No wonder his dad had tried to thwart Knox's every effort.

Knox pounded on the glass of the driver's side window with the side of his fist, over and over, relishing the shot of pain radiating up his arm until his thirst for destruction grew. He grabbed his pocketknife and without extending the blade, pounded the window with the hilt until the safety glass shattered into a flimsy sheet of tiny beads.

"Fuck you, Dad. You coward." He tipped his head back and bellowed directly at the heavens. "Me coming here was never about getting justice for what the family did to me or Mom or Shayla or Wade. This was all about you, you selfish son of a bitch. And not even for a real fucking reason. You used me to get revenge on your brother for sleeping with your girlfriend! Of all the goddamn things! But you know what? I'm not your goon anymore. I'm not Ty's goon, either. You all lied to me. Every last one of you."

He cleared the broken glass with the knife hilt, then picked the shards off his seat and got behind the wheel. The truck started on the first try. He threw it into gear, then barreled down the hill in the direction of his house. He was so far out of control that the road was blurry, but he kept his foot pressed on the gas pedal all the way down.

What was a little danger now, after everything? He had nothing left to care about anyway. The resort was going to be sold off, Emily was going to hate him, and his family had screwed him over in the worst possible way.

"How am I going to face Mom?" he growled, strangling the steering wheel in his grip. "Did you think about that, Dad? How am I going to look at her and not hate her for this? She's my mother, goddamn it. How can our relationship ever recover?"

In one mighty swoop, he'd lost his mother, his father, his career. Everything he held dear.

It was all gone. He hit the steering wheel with his open palm and ground his teeth together, fighting the urge to scream.

At the lake, Knox stopped at the very same place the truck had backed into the water on Knox's first day at the resort. Leaving the engine on, he rolled the passenger window down, shifted into neutral, and stepped out. "Is this what you wanted all along, Dad? Is this what you were going for? Holding me back, taking what I cared about? Ruining my fucking life?"

The words echoed off the surrounding hills. Somewhere nearby, a flock of birds took flight.

"I worshipped you, old man." A bubble of hysterical laughter escaped his throat. "And you're not even my father. You're my goddamn uncle."

With that, he gave the truck a shove, putting all his weight into it until the wheels rolled forward. As it had that first day, the truck gathered momentum down the hill to the lakeshore. It splashed into the water and kept rolling. And like last time, much to Knox's anger, the wheels snagged on the rocks. Another bubble of hysterical laughter had Knox doubling over. "Fine. I'll do it myself."

He dropped to the ground and took off his boots, then

shimmied out of his pants, ready to brave the cold water to finish the job he'd started and push the truck all the way under. He had one foot in the water when the sound of splashing as a fish jumped out of water caught his attention. Phantom.

Yes.

That would satisfy his howling thirst for destruction far better than trying to dislodge the truck from the rocks. With his mind nothing but a storm of rage and hurt, he ran up his driveway and into the kitchen. Emily had caught Phantom's attention with Fritos, so that's what Knox would use. He found a partial bag in the pantry, then raced to the boathouse and threw his fishing gear into the rowboat.

It felt good, being at the top of the food chain again. Controlling the outcome, instead of playing the chump. Maybe he'd burn the boathouse down after this, rid it of his dad's carved name, that symbol of innocent boyhood before betrayal and vengeance had poisoned his life and the lives of his children.

After so much hard work and planning, Knox had nothing to show for all his ambition. Healy was right; the resort was a money pit, the land beneath it worth more than the business ever could be. It was time to stop fighting fate. It was time to give up on the resort and walk away to start fresh somewhere else. Maybe razing the buildings down to nothing was the answer. Maybe then, Knox would find the peace that had eluded him all his life.

The hospital room's clock struck eleven, but Emily was anything but tired as she sat in a chair in Carina's hospital room, holding the most perfect little human being she'd ever seen. Samuel James Decker, born at one p.m. and clocking in at eight pounds right on the dot. Eight pounds that Emily liked to believe she had a lot to do with.

Throughout the afternoon, she'd kept her distance from Ty, watching him with his family from afar and waiting for them to leave before slipping into Carina's room. Hence, why she was still there long after visiting hours had ended, rocking in the slider next to Carina's bed, holding the baby while Carina dozed. The whole world seemed to go quiet, save for the whir of machinery and muffled nurses' voices from the hall.

Decker returned to the room with a cup of coffee in a paper cup. He smiled at Emily behind a thick coat of stubble, then crossed the room and perched on the glider arm.

Emily would never forget the sight of Decker's tears or the look of fear on his face when the baby's heartbeat couldn't be detected. One of the strongest men she'd ever met brought to his knees in terror, and then again in reverence at the sight of his son in the NICU, where he'd been taken for observation, though all his vitals were normal and he clearly had a healthy set of lungs on him.

Seeing Samuel, and Decker's reaction as a father, had put Ty's cruel behavior to Knox into stark focus. There were so many awful fathers in the world that wore their anger and pride like heavy yokes across their shoulders. Decker was a reminder that it didn't have to be that way. That even out of a dark and toxic situation, there was hope to be found, and good men who took care of their families in gentle, loving ways.

Decker stroked a finger along Samuel's cheek. "He's perfect, isn't he?"

"He is."

Without warning, Emily's eyes welled with tears. She sniffed and wiped her cheek against her sleeve.

Decker pulled a tissue from the box on the bedside table and handed it to Emily. "Everything okay?"

"Of course. Carina's healthy, Sam's healthy. It's just been an emotional day."

"That it has. I haven't been immune to tears, myself."

She offered a weak smile. "I noticed."

"I'm crazy about that girl," he said, nodding to the bed.

"I noticed that, too."

He winked, and for the first time since Carina had gone into labor, his cowboy swagger started to return. "Before Carina and I got together, I thought my life was headed down a very specific path. I thought I knew where I was going, but God had other plans. I never saw it coming."

"Saw what?"

Decker's gaze glowed as he looked at his son. "Love. How it changes everything. When I realized Carina was the one, it blew all my grand plans to smithereens. And then this guy . . . I feel like everything I thought I knew about myself and the world is changing again. I didn't know it was possible to love something this much."

Love. It really did change everything. Not too long ago, Emily could have said with certainty where she was going and what it was going to take to get there. But now she knew better. Charles Welk had gotten it slightly wrong. Happiness alone didn't make the brevity of life bearable. Love did. Holding the baby, knowing she was part of this beautiful creature's journey was such an honor. But as grateful as she was for being a part of someone else's story, she wanted her own story. With Knox.

When Knox had come to Briscoe Ranch, looking every inch the wolf in a Prada suit, she'd been terrified that he'd send her packing from the only home and job that had ever mattered to her. She'd been terrified that he'd blow her grand plans all to hell. She'd never expected to fall in love with the wolf. Her fear had convinced her that loving him meant holding herself back, submitting to the will of another at the forfeit of her independence. But that couldn't be further from the truth. Loving him wasn't a chain of bondage, but the chance to become more than she could ever be alone. Rather than hold her back, his love helped her fly.

Knox needed her tonight, more than Samuel did. So, why, then, was she hiding out in Carina's hospital room instead of going after her own happiness with the man she loved?

She slowly sat up, then gently transferred the baby to Decker's arms.

"Leaving already? Was it something I said?" Decker asked.

"Yes, actually. In the best possible way." She kissed his cheek. "I've got to go."

Chapter Twenty-Three

Emily sped through the quiet, dark streets until she hit Dulcet, impatient to find Knox. Not only to help him through whatever emotional storm he was weathering after finding out that Ty was his father, but also to let him know how deeply she'd fallen in love with him. And that she might have the means to save the resort. She couldn't imagine a better use for her inheritance than to save the place that had been her safe haven and the family that had made her one of their own.

On Main Street in Dulcet, Emily slowed her car as she passed Haylie's apartment building. Haylie hadn't been at the hospital all day, which didn't bode well. Haylie would have definitely been there for the birth of Carina's baby, if she'd been able. Dread washed through Emily.

She pulled into the parking lot, then took her phone out of her purse, deliberating on whether or not to reach out to Haylie, despite the late hour. If Haylie were hurt, if Wendell had snapped, given Knox's news about the offer on the resort, then there existed the very real possibility that Haylie needed immediate help.

Emily was still considering her options when move-

ment on the second floor caught her eye. She looked up
to see Haylie stealing down the stairs, an overnight bag
in her hand and one eye looking over her shoulder.

Relief at the sight of her made Emily's heart squeeze.
She turned off her engine, then jogged to the base of the
stairs to meet Haylie.

Haylie startled at the sight of her. "Emily? What are
you doing here?" she whispered. Even in the shadows,
Emily could see her black eye and split lip plainly enough.

"I was passing by, going to Knox's house. What's
going on?"

Haylie drew herself up proud and tall. "I'm leaving."

The words, said in a tone of pure conviction, sent chill
bumps skittering over Emily's skin. Good for her. "Do
you know where?"

"I have no idea. I'm not coming back." It had been that
way for Emily, too. When she'd snapped, she snapped for
good.

"I'm proud of you. Will you let me help?"

Haylie cast a wary eye at her apartment door. "I don't
have time. I have to go while he's still passed out."

"I know, but I've been where you are. I don't know
what Carina's told you, but I left home at sixteen and
never looked back. I changed my name and started a
whole new life."

That pulled Haylie up short. "You did?"

"Which is why I know you can do this because you're
a survivor like me. It's why I also know what you need to
make this work." Emily held out her car keys. "So, here.
Take it. It's paid for. He'd have a harder time tracing it than
your own car. And under the driver's seat, you'll find an
envelope with everything from my old identity. Rebecca.
My ID, a birth certificate, and more. I don't need the name
anymore. I'm not that person. But you could be, if you
wanted. If that would help."

Nothing had ever felt so right in her life as passing Rebecca to another woman in need, paying it forward.

"Rebecca," Haylie murmured as they walked to Emily's car, as though rolling the idea around in her head.

Emily grabbed her purse off the passenger seat, then took out her wallet. She handed over all the cash she had, her credit card, and her ATM card. "The code is Carina's birthday, six digits. In a month or so, I'll tell the credit card company and bank that I lost them somewhere in my house. That'll give you time."

"You don't have to give me your money, too."

"I really do." She pulled Haylie into a hug. "You have to go now."

In Emily's arms, Haylie trembled. "Tell my sister I love her. Tell her I'm sorry I can't be there for Samuel."

Emily held her at arm's length and smiled her best supportive smile. "I'll let her know. She'll understand. So will Samuel someday."

Haylie tossed her bag into the back seat of Emily's car, then took the driver's seat. "I know I can't stay gone forever because my family's here, but right now I just need to get out of town."

She was right. No one could stay gone forever. The past would only stay buried for so long before it demanded its day in the sun. "I know. Go breathe. Figure out who you are and who you want to be. You're going to fly, Haylie. I just know it. You're going to soar."

Haylie's attention drifted to the empty street. "It's Rebecca now."

A knot formed in Emily's throat. She pressed her lips together, staving off an onslaught of tears. Rebecca Youngston—that daring, big-hearted, wounded girl she'd been—had truly come full circle. Hearing the name on Haylie's lips was the final piece of the puzzle in Emily's journey to make peace with her past. "Drive safe, Rebecca. We'll meet again someday. I know it in my heart."

After a last look at her second-floor apartment, Haylie closed the car door and started the ignition. Emily managed to hold back her tears until the Pontiac's taillights disappeared around a curve in the road down past Main Street.

Then she let out the breath she'd been holding in a half-laugh, half-cry. She scrubbed her hands over her face, letting the tears fall freely. What a day it had been. And there was one thing left to do. A date with destiny.

On her phone, she opened the Cab'd app. The nearest driver was only ten minutes away. Must be her lucky night. She summoned it to meet her in front of the firehouse around the corner. No sense in lingering near Haylie's apartment on the off-chance that Wendell came to.

Ten minutes later, a red compact car rolled to a stop at the curb in front of the firehouse. Paco rolled down the passenger window and beamed at Emily. "Hey, it's June's young friend! I'd do anything for June. How is my favorite lady?"

Emily opened the passenger door and climbed in. "She just became a great-grandmother tonight."

Paco threw up his hands. "How is that possible? She's in the prime of her youth! A beautiful lady like that can't be a great-grandmother yet."

Guess Granny June hadn't been exaggerating when she'd said Paco was sweet on her. "You be sure to tell her that next time you see her. I'm sure that'll win you some points."

"Count on it. Where are we headed on this fine evening?"

Thank you, Paco, for not caring why I'm out on Main Street so late at night. "To June's grandson's house, near the resort. You dropped Granny June off there once, if memory serves."

He started down the street. "With a smile like hers, I would take that beautiful lady anywhere she asked."

Paco never stopped extolling Granny June's virtues for the entirety of the trip. Which was kind of a relief, as it left Emily free to let her thoughts drift through the events of the day.

Emily saw Knox before she'd even left Paco's car. She walked to the dock and watched him drift on the lake in his rowboat, his back hunched, his head bowed, and sitting ever so still. She ached for him. Of all the people hurt today, Knox had sustained the biggest blow. Carina and her baby were safe and healthy, and now Haylie would be safe, too. But the damage done to Knox by the lie of his parentage and Ty's rejection of him as a son couldn't ever be undone.

"Knox," she called gently.

He raised his head and looked at her for a long time. She half expected him to tell her to leave so he could be alone, but he didn't. After a while, his hands reached out and took the oars, and then he brought the boat to shore.

It wasn't until the boat had reached the dock that she saw a crumpled up Fritos bag on the bottom of the boat next to a gaffe and net. "Were you looking for—"

"Phantom." Anguish oozed from the word. "I was going to kill it. I was so angry, I couldn't think past the need to destroy every link to my dad," he said, not meeting her eyes. "But then Phantom surfaced and he just sat there looking at me, waiting, like he knew what was coming and wasn't going to fight it. And I just . . . I couldn't. I can't let this be how it ends for me and my dad. I don't know how to make peace with all of this, but I do know that I can't erase him from my past or my heart.

Killing Phantom would have just been another waste of life."

He turned his stricken eyes on her. "I'm in love with you, Emily. I don't have anything to offer you, certainly not any kind of secure future, but you're the only true thing in my life right now. You're the only thing that isn't a lie or a waste. You, and the way I feel about you."

Nothing that had happened in the last month had been a waste—not Emily quitting, not Knox giving Haylie a job, and not even him learning the truth about Ty. "I'm in love with you, too. But you're wrong. Getting closer to the truth and discovering who we really are is never a waste. Love is never a waste."

Nodding, he closed his eyes as a torrent of tears fell over his cheeks. Emily stepped into the boat. She threaded her fingers into his hair and kissed every one of his tears away.

"Ty is my real father."

She'd been there, heard it all, which he knew. Which meant this announcement was to himself as much as anything. Perhaps it was the first time he'd voiced it. The truth sounded so different, so much more final, when said out loud.

"You believe them about that?"

"There's no reason not to. Tomorrow, I'm going to go see my mom. I need to know the whole truth about what happened before I can try to forgive her."

Emily gathered his hands into hers and cradled them. "You will forgive her, in time. If not for her, then for you, so the resentment won't eat you up inside."

"You know, when I think about it, that was a lesson my dad never taught me, and one he never learned, either. I had to learn it the hard way, coming to Briscoe Ranch," Knox said. "Resentment will eat you up if you let it fester."

"My parents both died. That's what I learned last week when I was gone. I went to their apartment in Chicago. I needed to see them for myself, to remember that they were humans and not these grandiose monsters that I'd built them up to be. The doorman recognized me. He'd been waiting for me all these years so he could hand over a message from their lawyer. My father went first. Of a heart attack. My mom two years ago of cancer."

He looked at her a long time. "I'm so sorry."

About her mother, so was Emily. But even that didn't compare to the relief she felt at being freed. "All this time, I've kept one eye looking over my shoulder, waiting for the other shoe to drop. I feel like, now, I can finally be at peace. I have nothing to run from anymore."

"Do you still want to be Emily Ford?"

The question brought a smile to her lips, thinking of Haylie, one of the bravest women Emily knew, out there on the road, ready to forge a new life. "Yes. I can never go back to who I used to be. I wouldn't want to."

"It's the same for me. I would never go back to the man I was before all this. But I still don't know if I want to stop the sale of the resort. Would you resent me if I didn't? All the hate and the secrets . . . that place is toxic."

A tendril of fear snaked through her at the thought of losing Briscoe Ranch. "It's my home, my family. We have to save it."

He brought her hand to his chest and pressed it against his heart. "Let me be your home. Let me be your family. We don't need this place. And what if all this is happening exactly like it's supposed to? What if I'm supposed to fail? You called yourself a phoenix, and the imagery of that stuck with me. What if Briscoe Ranch Resort is meant to be razed so we can all have a fresh start?"

She'd never thought about it that way, but she remained unconvinced. "This resort has been in your family for generations. Instead of believing that there's a reason you should fail, what if you believed there's a reason you're being made to fight so hard? What if all these trials are to help us all clarify what really matters? I know it has for me, and for Haylie and for Ty. Heck, even for Eloise." She took his hands in hers. "Nothing worth having ever comes easy. Isn't that the saying? Maybe all this is really about learning to fight for each other. Maybe we don't need to burn the past to the ground before we can rise strong, together."

His shoulders relaxed and his expression went distant as he considered her argument.

Taking his hand again, she stood, bracing her legs apart as the boat rocked. "I'm going to try to save the resort. Will you help me?"

He rose, though his eyes were troubled. "I don't think we can. Every way I figure it, every calculation I make about the money I could raise in a day, falls depressingly short of the mark. Seventy-five million is a lot of money to collect in forty-eight hours. Twenty-four, now."

"How much are you short?"

"Twenty million, give or take." A wry smile spread on his lips. "Any chance you've got that lying around?"

Wild, crazy hope buzzed through her. She took both his cheeks in her hands. "Knox, baby, buckle up. Do I ever have some news for you."

Chapter Twenty-Four

Neither Knox nor Emily currently owned a functioning vehicle. Which made their trip to Knox's mother's house the next morning slightly more complicated. Knox got Shayla on the job of calling for another tow truck to pull his truck out of the lake—again—while Emily summoned a Cab'd driver to take them to the resort, where they could borrow a company car.

They'd slept in a tangle of sheets and limbs in his bed, not so much making up for lost time as getting their future off to a magnificent start. Despite all the strife and pain of the day before, or perhaps because of it, they'd both woken up optimistic and ready to face their futures together. Which was a very good thing because there was much to be done that day. First, Knox needed to pay a visit to his mother, followed by an afternoon meeting with the resort's lawyers, who were already busy composing a buyout offer, and Knox's team of structural engineers.

But while, yesterday, he'd dreaded the confrontation with his mom, today he knew that it didn't matter what she said or how she reacted to the news of Knox finding out the truth because he'd already forgiven her. It had been a simple choice, namely that he refused to start his life with Emily while rotting with resentment, the way his father and mother had started their marriage.

His mom met them at the door of her house before they'd even had a chance to knock. Her face was drawn, her eyes red-rimmed.

"Hey, Mom. Is everything okay?"

She pushed the door open wider. Behind her stood Ty, his expression hard as ever.

Knox's heart sank. So much for an easy conversation. As ready as he was to forgive his mom, Knox had no idea how he felt about Ty. None at all. He wasn't angry, per se, but he wasn't at peace, either. The fact remained that Ty had brought Knox to the resort. As Ty had said the day before, he'd tried to do the right thing by Knox, in his own way. Knox was going to have to give that point a lot of thought.

Knox nodded at Ty, who merely blinked in response.

"You know the truth," his mom said. Her whole body trembled with the words. All Knox wanted to do was throw his arms around her and tell her everything was going to be okay. Except Ty was right there, clouding Knox's judgment. Had she loved him? Was his dad her second choice?

Instead of a hug, Knox bussed her cheek, then squeezed her hands. They were ice-cold. "You remember Emily, right?"

"I don't think this is going to be a conversation fit for company," his mom said, casting a worried look at Emily.

"She's not company," Knox said. He shot a look at Ty. "She's family. And I'm planning to keep her by my side for a very long time, so I'd like her to be here with us today. Let's go inside and talk, shall we?"

He took Emily by the hand and followed his mom into

the house. Ty stepped aside to let them pass, but he held Knox's glare. It'd been that way since the beginning—two alpha dogs circling, sizing each other up, planning a strategy of attack. They were so alike. In looks, in the way they came at the world with a unique Briscoe brand of brash confidence. Father and son.

Fucking hell. Who would've ever guessed?

His mom bee-lined for the kitchen and flitted around them, wringing her hands. "Knox, can I get you a coke? What about you, Emily? I don't have any beer, but I could . . . I mean, I could run to the store, if you want."

"Linda, sit down," Ty said, taking a seat at the head of the table.

She did as she was told. Knox and Emily followed suit.

Knox had zero interest in distressing his mom any more. He reached across the table and captured her hands. "I love you, Mom. I'm not mad."

Her mouth screwed up and her eyes turned glassy. "Oh, Knox," she croaked.

"Damn it, woman, get ahold of yourself," Ty said in a low growl.

Knox shot him a warning glare before turning his attention back to his mother. "Don't cry, Mom. Everything's okay." Beneath the table, Emily set a supportive hand on his thigh. He took a fortifying breath, then continued. "I'd just like to hear some details. I'd like to know how it happened. That would help me sort everything out in my mind. But I'm not upset and I've already forgiven you."

She pulled her hands away and extricated a tissue from the sleeve of her sweater. "I'm not proud of what I did. Praise God for having mercy on sinners like me because I am not worthy."

"Mom, please." He wasn't sure how to move the conversation past her transgressions against God. For the

whole of Knox's life, that had been her way during times
of stress and grief. She took solace in boiling a situation
down to black and white, good and evil, the sins of man-
kind clashing with the divinity of the Holy Father. "You're
worthy. You did the best you could."

"No, I did not. I let myself become an instrument of
Satan. Your father might as well have been Job for how
cruelly I tested him."

My father Clint or my father Ty? With Ty's eyes on
him, Knox bit back the question, asking instead, "Tested
him how? Please. What happened?"

"I was too young, and the Briscoe boys, they were
charmers, both of them."

Knox's patience was fraying. "Mom, come on. Please.
You dated Dad in high school, I know that much. So how
did you end up sleeping with Ty? He didn't . . ." There
was no way he could voice the word *rape*. This was his
mother. His sweet, fragile mother.

Emily's hand moved to his back, sharing with him her
strength.

Ty cleared his throat. "Linda, the boy wants answers,
not blubbering. Are you gonna tell him, or should I?"

"Ty, thank you," Emily said, in the calm, neutral voice
of a moderator. "Help us understand."

Ty ran a hand over his bald head. "Of course, I flirted
with Linda in high school, but I never expected her to
take that seriously. Back then, me and Clint had a healthy
rivalry. My father was a good, good man, but he had a
thing where he liked to pit us boys against each other. He
had a phrase he used with us. He said our responsibility
as brothers was to push each other to greater heights. In
his mind, there wasn't anyone better to compete with than
your own brother. I don't suppose he ever expected us to
take that as far as we did."

"You two were always neck-and-neck, in sports, in

academics," Knox's mom said. "It was a big joke in the neighborhood. When one of you had a girlfriend, the other one did. When one of you got a job that paid two dollars an hour, the other would get a job that paid four. And on and on. I remember my own mama talking about you two and all your ambition. It was why I went after Clint in the first place. I liked myself an ambitious man."

Knox looked between Ty and his mom. "So you slept with Mom because she was your brother's girlfriend?"

"She was the one who came after me, not the other way around," Ty said.

That stunned Knox silly. He sat back in his chair, mouth agape.

"You see, I graduated a year before Clint, and my buddies and me had a habit on the nights of the high school dances to grab some beers and some girls and make our own party out in Chicory Hollow. It was the night of the Sadie Hawkins dance during Clint's senior year when out of the blue, Linda showed up at our party, all hopped up like someone had lit a fire under her feet. She was all over me, and I didn't bother to ask what she was thinking since she was Clint's girl. Competition took hold of me and I lost my good judgment."

"Mom? What happened? Why go after Ty when you were already dating Clint."

She shook her head, while her hands teased off bits of fiber from the tissue in her hands. "That's the sinner in me. At the Sadie Hawkins dance, Clint and I had a fight, a real bad one. He'd been flirting with Patsy Burleton, so I thought, two can play at that game. Back then, I didn't know Christ like I do now. I was blinded by sin. I knew where Ty and his boys were drinking, so I ditched Clint and I . . . I sacrificed my virginity to the Devil." She crumpled over her hands.

"It's okay, Mom."

Ty stood. "You know, I don't think it is, Knox. We're the ones who should be comforting you instead of the other way around. We're the ones who should be asking for your forgiveness for keeping you in the dark all these years. Linda, stop hiding behind your religious safety blanket and talk straight with our son. You tell him why you took him away from me. You tell him why you forced me to lie to him all these years."

Holy shit. "Mom?"

"I was getting there," she shouted in dramatic indignation. "When I found out I was pregnant, I told my mother, who told my father. And I let them believe their assumption that the baby's daddy was Clint. Before I knew it, they went to Tyson and June. Nobody asked my opinion. Nobody asked me what I wanted."

"My dad thought Clint was the father, too," Ty said. "But I knew it was me. And as soon as your parents left, I told my folks and Clint as much. I tried to do the right thing. I offered to marry you, but you wouldn't have me."

"The one sin was enough."

Ty's spine was rigid, his face a stone mask. "You think you were the only one being pressured by your parents that night to do the right thing? I was prepared to make you an honest woman, but you chose this shit-poor life with my mediocre brother over what I could have given you."

"Clint gave Knox what you can't, you heartless sinner. He gave him a real daddy, with love and a Christian upbringing and enough food on the table to never go hungry."

Ty's careful façade cracked with a derisive huff. "That wasn't love. It was revenge, pure and simple. My mother was ready to set up a nursery in the family compound. But Clint and your parents had you so brainwashed, you couldn't think for yourself. You didn't want anybody to know what you'd done with me, your folks included. And Clint preyed on your weak-willed vanity. Your shame. He married you and deprived me of my own son out of revenge against me for sleeping with you. Like he's using Knox now to ruin my business. Even buried six feet under, he's still controlling you all."

Unimaginable hurt threatened at the corners of Knox's conscious thought. Ty had wanted to be a father to him. He'd wanted Knox to be a part of the Briscoe Ranch legacy. Knox pushed the hurt away and locked it up tight. There would be time enough later to unpack this conversation and work through the pain in a rational, constructive way.

"My husband was a hero," his mom said. "He took me back, the worthless sinner I was, and forgave me in the merciful spirit of Jesus Christ."

"Shut up with that religious garbage, woman."

Knox stood. "She may have made some mistakes, but you don't get to talk to her like that."

Ty grimaced. "You think it was easy for me to give you up? I would've cast aside Eloise for you—I would have given up everything to keep you—but your mother, she wasn't going to leave Clint and he wasn't gonna let her go, so I didn't have a choice. All that Briscoe pride running through Clint's veins . . . there was no reasoning with him. As my father reminded me that night, business at the resort was just starting to boom, and our family's reputation was on the line. He was right that no good would come of speaking the truth about Linda's baby, not for our family business and not for you, since Clint was hell-bent on eye-for-an-eye revenge. I took what belonged to Clint the night of the Sadie Hawkins dance, and so he took what was mine."

Knox felt himself swaying. It was all too much. Then Emily was behind him, her arm around his waist and her strength fanning out over them both like a protective shield.

"I thought bringing you to work for me was righting a wrong," Ty continued. "I thought I could be in your life, finally. I was prepared to pass my legacy to you as my only son—the son I was cheated out of parenting. But Clint got the last laugh, didn't he? Using you from the grave for his revenge. I never factored in that Clint had raised you to believe all that eye-for-an-eye bullshit. And now you're selling our family's hallowed ground out from under us. How does it feel to be a puppet for a dead man?"

Emily waved her arms. "Both of you, stop. Can you even hear yourselves? Talking about your son like he's your greatest sin, your greatest regret. I can't . . ." She pressed her fingers to her temples and closed her eyes. Everyone in the room waited in collective silence for her to regroup and finish her thought.

When she opened her eyes again, she looked at Knox's mom. "Thank you for Knox. For raising him to be such a good man." She turned her attention to Ty. "And thank you for bringing him back to Briscoe Ranch. And for asking me to provide lunch for your meeting that first day. You two created a miracle together and I'll forever be indebted to you."

She turned and faced Knox. Their eyes met. "I love you. And I'm so grateful that our lives unfolded exactly as they did so we could be here together right now."

All the pain and anger melted away as he looked into her eyes. She was right. He wouldn't change a thing. "I think it's time you and I bought some property together," he said.

The edges of her lips kicked up into a dreamy smile. "We'll be partners, in every sense of the word."

The thought left him giddy. "Emily Ford, are you proposing to me?"

Her eyebrows flickered up and her smile turned impish. "If only I had a ring to offer you right now."

"What's happening?" Linda said. "What property?"

Knox put his arm around Emily and faced his mother and Ty, steeped in the power of the truth—the power of his love for Emily. It flowed from his heart and all around him. He felt his dad watching him from on High and harnessed that power, too. Nothing could stop him, nothing could hurt him. He was above it all, with her.

"You'll see," Knox told his mom and Ty. "Soon enough. You'll all see. Now, if you two will excuse us, we've got some money to move."

Epilogue

One month later . . .

With a blanket wrapped around them to stave off the chilly late-November air, Knox and Emily sat in the bed of his newly repaired Chevy and watched the stars come up over Briscoe Ranch Resort from their favorite lookout point on the fire road right at the edge of the resort where Knox always parked his truck. Somewhere, a group of carolers sang *Joy to the World* to the merriment of the resort guests. Knox didn't think he'd ever been happier than he was in that moment, surveying the hill country kingdom he shared with the woman he loved.

In so many ways, tonight was a night of celebration. Not only because the Chevy was finally back in working order but also because today marked the finalization of their purchase of Briscoe Ranch. In the end, with the help of Knox's crackerjack team of structural engineers and geologists, it hadn't been too tough to convince Lux Universal that Briscoe Ranch wasn't worth the sandy, ever-shifting ground it sat on. Certainly, it wouldn't be a safe bet for senior housing.

But even though Lux withdrew their offer, Knox and

Emily decided to buy out Briscoe Equity Group's shares of the resort anyway. There was no sense in risking another near-catastrophe, not when Knox planned to spend the rest of his life at Briscoe Ranch by Emily's side.

He turned to kiss her and found her grinning from ear to ear. "What's that smile about?"

She snuggled in closer to him. "I've never owned anything before, nothing of value. I love that this is ours now." Her hand roved lower on his chest, then dipped to his jeans. "But as happy as I am watching the stars with you, I think I'm ready to get to the necking part of the whole sitting at a lookout point experience."

He gave her a kiss on her nose. "Are you sure you are? Because my neck is definitely not down there. Besides, Movie Night's going to start soon. Carina and Decker are bringing Sam. I told them we'd be there."

She teased the corner of his lips with hers as her hands roved over his body. "We might be a little late."

"You want to christen the truck? All right, then. That would be one way to celebrate it getting fixed up after two plunges into Lake Bandit."

Emily bolted upright, her eyes wide and a sly smile on her lips. "Forget necking. I've got a better idea to christen it."

"Well, so did I. I thought we'd do a lot more than just neck."

"No, no, no. I have a plan." She threw off the blanket and stood.

He loved it when she got this way, so caught up with passion for a new idea that she barely remembered that the rest of the world existed. Usually, though, she only got that way about cooking, and now that she was on the verge of opening up her restaurant, Subterranean, those light bulb moments were hitting her faster than ever. "Do tell. The suspense is killing me."

"I think we should try to roll your truck onto the resort property."

Knox groaned and rolled his neck. "That's your big idea? We've tried that. A lot. It doesn't work."

"We haven't tried it since everything came out about Ty being your dad. We haven't tried it since we bought the resort. There's something in the air tonight. I feel like this is our shot. I think your dad's ready to stop haunting your truck."

Knox eased up to standing, then patted the roof of the cab. "That would be a shame. I'm pretty fond of having a haunted truck."

"Well, then, maybe it's time your fatherly ghost knows it's time to stop holding you back."

He lassoed her into a hug. "I like the way you think."

"I know." She tapped her temple. "I like the way I think, too."

Full of love, he took a good long look at the woman he was going to marry. "Emily, I have a question for you."

"What?"

He pecked a kiss on her lips. "Do you want to drive or push?"

She let out a triumphant whoop of laughter. "I'll drive."

"You know how to start it by popping the clutch?"

She leapt over the side of the bed and onto the ground. "Done it a million times."

All Knox could do was laugh; she was so single-minded in her enthusiasm. He jumped out of the truck and watched Emily get settled in the driver's seat. "See if you can get it right to the edge of the hill before it dies. Sometimes it's generous to me like that."

She flashed him a thumbs-up and started the engine.

Knox moseyed behind the truck as she eased it to the property line and stopped. It took a second for Knox to register the chug of the engine. It hadn't died.

Emily looked at Knox through the side mirror, a questioning look on her face. "Knox, are you seeing this?"

Hope bloomed in his chest. "Let it go forward a few more inches."

She let up on the brake and the truck rolled forward—and remained on.

Holy Mother of God. "Keep going. The engine doesn't seem like it wants to die." He watched in awe as she slowly rolled the truck all the way over the property line, where she hit the brakes again.

The next time Emily looked at him through the mirror, her smile could have lit up the night. "What the hell's going on, Knox?"

"I have no idea."

She threw her head back and laughed. "Don't just stand there," she called. "Get in! Come drive this truck of yours around your newly purchased luxury resort. I'll slide over."

Feeling like he was in a dream, Knox walked the length of the truck, listening to that *chug chug chug*.

He stopped at the driver's door, but before opening it, he bent down and used the side mirror as an ear. "Thank you."

When Knox climbed behind the wheel of the truck, his heart busting with pure joy. He didn't realize he was crying until he felt the wetness on his cheek. A glance at Emily told him she was getting weepy, too.

"Do you think this means your dad's gone?" she asked quietly.

His dad. For all his faults, Clint Briscoe had been Knox's dad for thirty-two years, and he'd done the very best he could. Knox knew he'd never stop calling him Dad, just as sure as he was that his dad was watching over him from on High.

Knox's relationship with Ty was still awkward at

times, but they were working on figuring out their place in the other's life, and in the month since the truth had come out, they'd managed to settle into a mostly comfortable peace. Really, it was impossible to stay angry with the man who'd lost his business and was in the process of what would probably be a costly divorce. Not to mention that Ty had lost a daughter, as well.

In truth, the whole family was grieving Haylie's absence. At least she was safe. She'd called Emily a couple of times to check in, though she would never say where she was. At least the calls had managed to set the family's minds at ease and had given Emily the opportunity to tell her that Knox had made short work of firing Wendell. The last Knox had heard, Wendell had gone to live with his mother in El Paso. Hopefully, that was far away from wherever Haylie was putting down new roots.

Knox rolled his eyes heavenward. "I don't think my dad's gone, but I do think it means he's resting now. He's at peace."

Emily reached across the seat and took his hand. "You set him free."

"I'm the one who's been set free, Emily. By you." Unsatisfied with merely holding her hand, he reached over and pulled her right alongside his hip and stretched his arm around her. "That's better."

Her gaze roved over the resort. "This is ours now. I still can't believe it. We're the keepers of the Briscoe legacy. And I'm not even a Briscoe yet."

"Sounds like we'd better get that ring on your finger this December instead of waiting."

"December? Does that mean you're a believer in the resort's holiday wedding magic now, too?"

"Consider me a new convert about how much magic's in the air around here."

She settled back in his arm and cupped his cheek, then

gave him a slow, sweet kiss. "Who would've thought Knox Briscoe, businessman, self-made millionaire entrepreneur, would believe in ghosts and magic?"

"On the other hand, not everyone is lucky enough to drive a haunted truck, so I consider myself lucky to have been enlightened in that way. Ready to go meet our family for movie night?"

Emily sighed. "Ready as I'll ever be, but how about we take the long way around, give this old truck a tour of the place? Plus, I'm not quite ready to share you yet tonight."

With his arm still around Emily, Knox eased up on the brake and pressed the gas. The truck rolled forward, just as it was supposed to. He took his time going down the hill, feeling the breeze in his hair and soaking in every moment. He took a left at the bottom of the hill and drove them along the water, which had turned golden in the setting sun. Somewhere near the middle of the lake, movement caught his eye. He looked in time to watch a familiar silver carp splash back into the water.

Rising behind the hills, the moon shone down on the crystal clear night. And all around them, the sights and sounds and smells of Briscoe Ranch's holiday season were in full effect. Laughing and cuddling, they kept driving, taking a slow, back road tour of their home, sweet home. Life just didn't get any more magical than that.

Read on for an excerpt from
Melissa Cutler's next book

ONE WILD NIGHT

Coming soon from St. Martin's Paperbacks

Chapter One

If only Skye Martinez could run a fever on command. Or, after a few bites of the eggplant parmesan that Mrs. Biaggi of Vito's Eatery just delivered to the table, maybe she could fake food poisoning. *Anything* to get her out of this disaster of a blind date, the latest in a string of them. That was the trouble with living in a small Texas town. All the good men were taken—along with most of the bad ones too.

"And here's your meatball, Sweetums," Mrs. Biaggi said.

Sweetums, in this case, was Vince Biaggi, Skye's date—and Mrs. Biaggi's son.

Yeah.

Skye was gonna kill Granny June for this one.

"It looks great, as always, Mother," Vince said, digging in. With a mouth full of meatball, he poked his fork in Skye's direction. "Now you see why I wanted us to eat here. There's no sense paying for dinner when we can eat for free."

Naturally.

Mrs. Biaggi gave Skye a nudge and a wink. "Vince brings all his first dates here. It gives his Pops and me a chance to check out the merchandise."

And now she was merchandise. Good to know.

She took a despairing glance at her phone, which she's positioned strategically at the opening of her purse. Twenty minutes until her sister Gloria was scheduled to call, in case Skye needed to fake an emergency and escape. When she raised her gaze, it was find Vince and his mother beaming at her.

"Go on and try the eggplant parmesan," Mrs. Biaggi said. "It's been Vince's favorite since he was just a little squirt."

Skye made slow work of slicing the eggplant cutlet as her mind scrolled through possible ways to make Granny June pay. Maybe she'd reprogram the horn on Granny's riding scooter to play chicken noises. Or set her up on a blind date disaster of her own. God knew there were plenty of toothless or senile senior men at Skye's church. Or maybe Skye could get her mom to whip up one of her old world curses to turn Granny's hair bright blue.

Then again, probably Granny June would approve of that one.

Granny June Briscoe was the matriarch of the family-owned Briscoe Ranch Resort where Skye's family had worked for almost four decades, and where Skye worked in housekeeping. Usually, Granny June had a knack for matchmaking—which was the only reason Skye had agreed go on a date with the son of one of Granny's Bingo buddies. Well, that, and the fact that Skye had made a decision to abandon her rebellious nature and settle down like the good Catholic woman she was raised to be.

She had a bite of food halfway to her lips when, miracle of miracles, her phone chimed with an incoming text. It was all she could do to hide her relief.

"Oh Gosh, I'm so sorry. I didn't realize I'd left the volume on. Excuse me," she murmured with a smile of apology as she set her fork down and lifted the phone.

The text read, *This wedding is bananas crazy*.

It wasn't from her sister, but from her friend Remedy, the head wedding planner at Briscoe Ranch. In Skye's ample experience at the resort, all weddings fell somewhere on the crazy spectrum, so tonight's affair would have to be extra gonzo for Remedy to text something like that.

Skye waved her phone at Vince. "Sorry, it's my mom. Just a sec." Oh, how the lies rolled off her tongue. But she couldn't find it in her heart to care as she let her fingers fly over the touch keys.

Crazier than the date I'm on? she texted.

Looking at Mrs. Biaggi and Vince, she forced her smile to stay apologetic while waiting for Remedy's reply. It came a minute later.

Better hurry if you want to see the maid of honor doing tequila shots from the best man's belt buckle flask with no hands.

That did sound bananas crazy—and exactly what Skye needed to salvage her Saturday night. A zing of delicious, addictive adrenaline pulsed through her veins. It was only a small fix of her preferred vice—nowhere near enough to satisfy the rebellious streak she'd been cursed with— but it was way more of a thrill than she'd expected out of the night.

"Aw, shoot," Skye said, taking her purse handles in one hand and waving her phone in the other as she stood. Her napkin fell from her lap to the floor, but she didn't dare risk losing momentum by stooping to pick it up. "My mom needs me. My dad, with his bad back . . . he fell again and he's stuck. She can't get him off the floor on her own." Which was kind of the truth. Sort of. He'd fallen a few times lately and had needed Skye's help to hoist him up again.

She sent up a quick mental prayer for forgiveness for

using her dad's disability as an excuse. Then she dashed off a second prayer for forgiveness about lying in the first place, covering all her bases. One thing she *wouldn't* feel guilty about was running out on their free meal.

Vince looked as lost as a boy who was just told his dog had to visit a farm far, far away. He poked at his half-eaten meatball. "But our date's not over."

Yeah, buddy, it is. "I'll text you."

Another lie, another prayer. Such was life.

Skye grabbed a dinner roll from the table, nodded to a still agape Mrs. Biaggi, and dashed through the front door. She'd driven herself to the restaurant, a rule she'd learned the hard way a few years back while on another excruciating blind date. In fact, she'd come to think of inviting a guy to pick her up at home for a date as a big relationship step—one that the men she'd dated had seldom made it to.

Racing the clock, hoping to catch the maid of honor's and groom's belt buckle antics, Skye arrived at Briscoe Ranch Resort's in record time. After tossing her car keys to her cousin Marco who was working valet that night, she hot-footed it through the lobby and ascended the grand staircase, headed to the ballroom on the second level.

What she saw as she crested the stairs didn't disappoint. With a small crowd surrounding them, Remedy and her assistant Tabby were pushing a luggage trolley through a small crowd of onlookers. Seated on the base of the trolley was a very, *very* drunk young woman who slumped against one of the trolley's brass poles as her eyes fluttered open and closed. The voluminous yellow bridesmaid's dress she wore billowed out around her like she was being eaten alive by Pac-Man.

Skye's mouth fell open at the sight, but she sprang to action again when the yellow dress caught in the trolley's wheels, and rushed over to free the material. "Is this the maid of honor?"

Remedy flashed a wry smile. "Oh, yes. And it's time for her to turn in for the night." She patted the woman on the top of her elaborate, hairspray-crispy updo. "Sound good, Kimberly?"

Kimberly groaned. Her head lolled to the side.

"I think it's a little past time," Tabby muttered.

With Skye clearing the crowd from their path, Remedy and Tabby wheeled the trolley to the elevators, where Remedy got on her phone to request that someone meet them at Kimberly's room with the master key to let them in, since they hadn't snagged her clutch purse during their hustle to get her off the bride and groom's sweetheart table and out of the ballroom.

"So, your date was a bust?" Remedy asked Skye once they were in an elevator, headed to the fifth floor.

Skye pressed her fingers to her temples. "This guy was even worse than the last one. Remember him? He kept steering the conversation back to his plant collection and making double entendres about propagating succulents."

Remedy snorted out a laugh. "This guy was worse?"

"He took me to dinner at his parents' restaurant so he wouldn't have to pay and so they could scope out the merchandise."

Remedy gave her a playful hit on the shoulder. "Ew!"

"Right? I know I said I wanted to settle down with a nice, vanilla, Catholic guy, but Vince Biaggi was a little too vanilla. I have to believe that in the danger-and-drama spectrum of Vince on one end and Mike the Mistake on the other, there's got to be some middle ground."

Mike the Mistake was Skye's ex-husband. Except she couldn't quite get the word *ex-husband* past her lips. Partly because, eight years later, she was still reeling in disbelief that she'd ever been that out-of-control twenty-year-old who'd allowed the thrill of rebellion to intoxicate her into marrying a lion keeper with an international traveling circus—even if they'd only lasted for three months. And partly out of respect for her faith and her parents, both of which strictly forbid divorce. That three-month marriage had caused her nothing but pain and had resulted in the greatest sin of her life—a sin she could never afford to make again. Which was why she had to get it right next time when it came to choosing a mate, because next time would be forever, for real.

On the fifth floor, they rounded the corner and found Skye's mom leaning against the wall just outside of Kimberley's hotel room door. Clad in the resort's standard-issue middle management uniform of a burgundy skirt suit, she held herself with the noble bearing that came with being the fierce loving, no-nonsense heart of both the resort and the Martinez family. She'd put on some pounds since Skye's dad's health had deteriorated a few years earlier, and they'd pleasantly softened her compact, athletic build in a way that made Skye want to hug her every chance she got—not that her mother appreciated any random display of affection.

"Hey, Mom," Skye said. "What are you doing here? What good is it being in charge if you keep working Saturday nights?"

Her mom flashed the key fob at room 524's door, then shouldered it open and held it for Remedy and the luggage trolley. "Your father was driving me crazy. You know how grouchy he gets when his back's hurting him. I made him a poultice of herbs, brewed up my abuela's tea, and sent him to bed." She frowned sympathetically at Kimberly as Remedy and Tabby wheeled her in. "Poor thing."

"Kimberly made some bad choices tonight," Tabby said as she pushed.

Her mom shifted her focus to Remedy, a brow raised in a bid for more details, but Remedy just shook her head. "It involves the best man's belt buckle. You don't want to know."

"You're right," Skye's mom said, following them farther into the room. "Where are her friends? Why aren't they taking care of her?"

"The DJ had them busy running through the gamut of eighties dance styles at the reception," Remedy said. "Kimberly was attempting the Running Man on top of a table while a couple of groomsman were filming up her skirt when I found her."

"Bastards," her mom muttered. "Speaking of which . . . Skye, I thought you were on a date tonight."

The trolley wheels snagged on something, giving Skye a chance to look around. The room was a wreck. Every horizontal surface was covered with discarded champagne flutes, makeup, plastic dry cleaning bags, and glitter. So much glitter.

Skye reached down to see what the wheels had snagged on and pulled up a blonde weave. With a shudder, she tossed it onto the nightstand. "I ditched him to hang out with Remedy."

Remedy, Tabby, and Skye made careful work positioning the trolley next to the nearest queen-sized bed. Maybe Kimberly could be roused enough to crawl up into it.

Her mom cringed. "That bad?"

Skye was spared from answering by a sudden retching sound. The next thing she knew, Kimberly had hurled tequila and God-knows-what-else all over her dress, the floor, and the duvet.

Remedy and Tabby sprinted for the hall, squealing and gagging in disgust, but Skye and her mom merely groaned at the idea of what a pain in the ass it would be to clean it all up. Decades working hotel housekeeping did wonders for a woman's tolerance for coping with every manner of bodily fluid.

Gesturing to the mess, Skye shot her mom a wry look. "Still more fun than my blind date tonight."

With a roll of her eyes, her mom got on her phone. "Hey, Annika? It's Yessica. Would you bring your cleaning trolley and a new duvet to room 524 please?" To Remedy and Tabby, who stood in the hallway, eyes averted from the room, she called, "You two can get back to the wedding. We'll take it from here."

Some might not like working with their mothers, but Skye didn't mind. Except for a brief stint as a waitress during high school, she'd worked for her mom all her life. And she was proud of it. She and her family were the backbone of Briscoe Ranch Resort for nearly four decades. Her father had run the maintenance department until his back forced him onto disability, while her mom was the head of housekeeping—a mantle she hinted at passing to Skye someday soon.

Skye made short work of helping Kimberly off the trolley and out of her dress, leaving her in Spanx and a bra, while her mom fetched wet wash cloths and towels.

"You're too picky," her mom told Skye as she toweled off Kimberly's hair.

Yes, Skye was picky. She had to be. The next man she fell in love with had to be forever, no mistakes. "This is rural Texas. There are only so many men. All of the eligible bachelors who work at the resort or go to our church or live in town, I've either dated them or they're not interested in me. There's no one left, mama."

She swabbed Kimberly's face and arms with a wet washcloth, cooing to her as she worked. Skye had endured her fair share of drunken regret back in her early twenties, so she knew how awful the poor girl must be feeling.

Annika arrived pushing a housekeeping trolley. She assessed the situation with a frown and a shake of her head.

"Every weekend, every wedding," she grumbled as she walked to the bed.

Skye's mom left Skye to attend to Kimberly while she and Annika stripped the soiled duvet from the bed and stuffed it into a laundry bag.

"I can help you with your man problem, mija," her mom said as she pushed the voluminous skirt of Kimberly's bridesmaid dress into a second laundry bag.

It was an offer her mom had made before. There was just one problem. "I don't believe in old world magic, Mom."

With Annika busy mopping, Skye's mom watched with pursed, disapproving lips as Skye helped Kimberly crawl between the bed sheets. "It's your generation. You don't appreciate tradition. If there isn't an app for it, it doesn't exist."

Skye had heard that argument before, but she knew better. If her mom's old world magic actually worked, then her dad would be pain-free and back at work. If the old magic worked, then maybe Skye's marriage would have, too, along with everything else that went wrong during those fleeting months. Her arms, working of their own accord, wrapped around her belly. "Mom, there's no one."

Her mom grabbed a water bottle from the trolley and set it on Kimberly's nightstand. Then she squared up to Skye and took her hands. "Let me help you find someone to love."

Annika mopped around their shoes. "Yessica helped me last year when Mitch wouldn't commit. She gave me this magic coin that I stuffed in my bra and—*bam*—he proposed."

Skye's resolve started to crack. She took a long, hard look at Kimberly, slack-jawed and drooling, and going to bed alone—the perfect embodiment of Skye's wild, rebellious, drama-addicted, terminally single past. Not a very pretty picture. Not at all. "Okay, Mom. I give up. Let's do this your way."

Even if it didn't work—which it wouldn't, she was certain—then at least her mom would stop needling her about trying such ridiculous, old-fashioned methods. Then she could get back to her equally ineffective, often ridiculous modern day methods of online dating and ill-advised blind dates arranged by eighty-year-old Bingo players. The thought nearly made her wince.

Annika gave a quiet golf clap at Skye's agreement, while Skye's mom straightened up, an impish gleam in her eyes that reminded Skye of her fondest memories of her abuela, the two of them sneaking cookies in the kitchen for breakfast while her mother was in the bedroom ironing.

Without warning, she plucked a hair from Skye's head. "Ow!"

Impervious to Skye's shock, her mom dropped the hair into a mug lifted from the coffee caddy near the television. "This is going to be great, mija. You'll see."

Skye rubbed the tender spot on her scalp and gathered around the coffee maker along with Annika to watch. With Kimberly's snores as their soundtrack, Skye's mom brewed a cup of coffee right into the same mug that contained Skye's hair. Then, from the housekeeping trolley's mini bar replenishment kit, she pulled a bottle of bourbon and poured it in while chanting under her breath in Spanish, the words said too low and quick for Skye to understand them. Then she pinched silver glitter from the bathroom counter and sprinkled it over the magic brew.

"Glitter?" Skye hissed, because *Really?* The bourbon and hair, she could see, but glitter? *Oh, please.*

With eyes closed, her mom waved the cross pendant on her necklace over the mug. "No questions."

Skye darted a look at Annika, who only shrugged.

After another minute more of chanting, her mom's eyes flew open. "The rest of the ingredients, we need from the day spa."

All right. That sounded totally legit—*not*. Because what old world magic didn't require volumizing shampoos and nail polish?

Still, she and Annika followed her mom from the room like eager students. After stowing the housekeeping trolley in a housekeeping closet near the ice machine, they descended in the elevator to the ground level. They'd only taken a few steps into the lobby when they were stopped in their tracks by none other than Granny June, five foot nothing and sitting astride her hot pink riding scooter, dressed in an emerald jogging suit and with a lowball glass of liquor in her hand.

Skye's mom put her hand on her hip. "Aren't you up a little late for an old woman?" The teasing line was said with a heavy dose of affection borne from forty years of familiarity.

Granny June hoisted her drink, the ice clinking merrily. "I can sleep when I'm dead. What are you kids up to? Skye, shouldn't you be out with Pearl's son right now?"

"Vince Biaggi is a dud. No more dating advice from you," Skye said with a wag of her finger.

Granny June replied, "But his Facebook picture is so handsome!"

"She's listening to me now, June. We're doing this my way, and I have just the spell to help her find the perfect man. All we need a few final ingredients and we're off to get those now."

Granny June stood from her riding scooter with a spryness that belied her age and extricated a knobby wooden walking cane with a bejeweled handle from behind the scooter's seat. "I'm in. Let's go."

What a motley crew they made, marching through the lobby, past wedding revelers and clusters of hotel guests, then down a flight of stairs to the basement level where the resort's day spa was located. Skye's mom waved her master key fob at the spa's main door, then led the way into the darkened spa, flipping on lights as she blazed a trail through the hair salon room and into the corridor of private massage rooms.

In the first massage room, her mom went straight for the row of aromatherapy vials on the counter. "A drop of lavender. Two drops of cedar. And, finally, the secret ingredient . . ." She hunched away from the group, but Skye swore she saw her spit into the mug.

Gross. But Skye couldn't find it in her heart to mind. She was having a blast connecting with this side of her mom that seldom made its appearance anymore.

Then her mom was facing them again. "Skye, get a coin from your purse."

Skye dug through her purse and found a quarter loose in the bottom of it. She held the coin out, but her mom shook her head. "Kiss it first."

Her mom held out the mug. "Drop it in."

Skye said a quick prayer as she released the quarter from her fingers. *Bring my true love to me.*

"Hold the mug and tell the spell what you're looking for."

Skye knew the answer without thinking. She cradled the mug in her hands and stared down at the brown, oily liquid. "A man with a kind heart and a career. And I'm not going to move away from my family in Dulcet, so he has to be local."

"And Mexican," her mom added in a sage voice.

Skye gave her a side-eye. It would be nice to meet a man who shared her culture, but that wasn't mandatory. "And Catholic."

Now *that* was mandatory.

Granny June nudged her. "Think bigger. Sexier. You deserve it."

She did. Funny how low Skye's expectations had sank over the years. "Someone handsome and daring, with dark, soulful eyes, and who makes my toes curl every time he kisses me. Someone who will be all the adventure and thrill I need for the rest of my life and who loves me more than anything else in the world."

Granny June gave a sage nod. "That's more like it."

Skye's mom smiled. "Good. That sounds like a man I'd want for you. Now find the coin. Don't dry it. Just stick it in your bra, left cup, as near to your heart as you can."

Skye dipped her hands into the now-cooled liquid and did as she was told, though the coffee was sure to leave a permanent stain on her white lace bra. The wet coin was cold against her breast, but other than that, she felt nothing new. No magic zings ripple through her. No swirls of glittery magic surrounded her like Cinderella's fairy godmother had accomplished with her wand before the ball. Instead, she felt like the same old Skye.

"What's supposed to happen next?" Granny June said.

"We wait," Skye's mom said. "Your perfect man will come. You'll see."

Another silent moment passed, waiting . . . waiting. And then the door knob turned. The door opened wide.

Skye and her mom whirled towards it, using their bodies to block the view of the spell ingredients scattered on the counter, while Annika pretended to fluff the donut-shaped pillow at the head of the massage table.

"We're with housekeeping!" Skye called with a manic tone. "Just finishing up." The last word died on her tongue as she took in the interloper.

A tall, broad-shouldered man filled the doorway, all muscle and tawny skin and smoldering hotness.

"Oh! Didn't expect to see anyone. I, uh . . ." He scratched his head, tousling his inky-black hair in the most adorably sexy way. "I'm Enrique. I'm new at the resort and I have my first massage client scheduled for the morning, so I wanted to get set up." His attention slid to Skye. There was no mistaking the heat in his eyes as his gaze swept over her. Then his lips curved into a hint of a lop-sided smile, just enough to reveal a dimple on his right cheek. "I think I'm going to like this place."

Skye's mom nudged her in the ribs with a whispered, "It's working."

That was fast.

Like the addict she was, Skye's body lit up with the all-consuming thrum of adventure and drama—her own personal call of the wild. Except this time, there wouldn't be any negative consequences or shame brought onto her and her family, no repentance needed. This thrill was mother-approved. Skye was going to find a sweet, sexy local man to settle down with and then she wouldn't ever be tempted again to run off in search of trouble. She'd have everything she needed right there in Dulcet—in her home and in her bed, forever.

She reached out her hand to Enrique, dizzy and breathless with the realization that tonight's little spell was the first step in making all her dreams come true.

Catch up on Melissa Cutler's
One and Only Texas series!

The Mistletoe Effect
(E-novella)

One Hot Summer

Available now!